The Missing Years – Part II

The Missing Years
Part II

A Tyrell Sloan Western Adventure.

By: Brian T. Seifrit

The Missing Years – Part II

Published by

William Jenkins
2503-4288 Grange Street
Burnaby BC V5H 1P2 Canada

williamhenryjenkins@gmail.com
http://www.williamjenkins.ca
Telephone: 604-685-4136

Edition 1
ISBN: 978-1-928164-14-2 and 1928164145
Copyright Brian T. Seifrit © 2016

All rights reserved.

Without limiting the rights under copyright, no part of this publication may be reproduced, stored in or introduced into a retrieval system, or transmitted, in any form, or by any means (electronic, mechanical, photocopying, recording, or otherwise) without the prior written permission of both the copyright owner and the above publisher of this book.

Thank you for respecting the author's work. An ebook is licensed for your personal use only whereas a paperback edition can be given away or re-sold. The ebook may not be re-sold or given away to other people. If you would like to share the ebook with another person, please download an additional copy for each person with whom you share it. If you are reading this as an ebook and did not purchase it, or it was not obtained for your use only, then you should obtain your own copy.

The Missing Years – Part II

Dedicated to:

All my past and present readers.

The Missing Years – Part II

Special Acknowledgements:

To my wife for putting up with me while I wrote this book.

To William (Bill) Jenkins for his brilliant editing and his patience. Thank you.

To Brett Park – Maker of the A1 Quickdraw ECHO Double Holsters and gunbelt,

Circle KB Company
179 Lemhi Road,
Salmon, Idaho 83467
USA

Telephone: 1-208-756-1873

for permitting us to use the photo on the cover. This Quickdraw holster and gunbelt is available for sale at:

http://www.circlekb.com

The Missing Years – Part II

The Missing Years – Part II

"Chapter 1"

It was June 2nd, 1891. For two days Tyrell, with Black Dog at his side, travelled north at his leisure, making the distance to the town of Chase, where he stocked up on gear and odds and ends. He spent one night in the Chase Hotel. It was not a big hotel; it had only five rentable rooms, but the food was good and the hot bath he was able to have, made the short stop over worth the $12 it all cost. Clean, shaved and fed, he and Black Dog once more headed north.

There was no rush to get anywhere. In fact, he didn't even know where it was that he was going, except that he was going. In one little town whose name he never did know, he came across a wanted poster. The caption read: *'Tyrell- last name unknown. Wanted for killing Heath Roy, Ollie Johnson, Eli Ferguson and one Noble Bathgate. A $2500 reward is offered by the Mounted Police for his capture or information leading to his arrest.'*

The drawing on the poster did not look at all like the man he saw when he looked into a mirror and he half chuckled. He was also grateful that there was no mention of a dog, but then again, why would there be? Many folks likely had dogs.

Thank you, Emma, he thought as he carried on. For seven days and nights, he travelled the Chase Wagon Road in a northerly direction, chatting with those he met along the way and sharing coffee with a few.

He even shared a meal with an old fellow who only introduced himself as Nick. He didn't have much gear with him and was heading to Chase. Tyrell guessed his age to be in his late fifties. He wasn't a very big man, but he did look fit. His greying hair was short and the whiskers on his sunburnt weathered face told Tyrell that Nick had been on the trail for some time.

Knowing from his own experience what it was like to be out-and-about with such meagre supplies, made him think back to when he met up with Ed McCoy. He hadn't eaten in two or three days and Ed was kind enough to feed him, and so he passed the same gesture on to the old fellow. Nick was grateful; there was no doubt about it and thanked Tyrell repeatedly as they ate.

"You ain't got to keep thanking me, Nick. I heard you the first time," Tyrell said on a few occasions.

"I realise that, but you've been mighty kind in sharing this with an old folk who you have never laid eyes upon before now."

"I'm sure you would have done the same for me, Nick."

Nick nodded his head gesturing that indeed he would, as he took a long swallow from his canteen. They conversed for a few minutes afterwards, then Nick swung onto his horse, thanked Tyrell again and headed south in the direction of Chase. That was about the extent of their encounter. Tyrell felt good regardless, knowing that he was able to offer the old fellow some food and friendly conversation. Early as it was, with at least three hours of daylight left, Tyrell poured water over the fire he had lit to cook the meal he shared, making sure it was out. He swung onto Pony's back, whistled for Black Dog and once more headed north.

A small township called Valemount was not far from where he last stopped. It was a few days ride west of the Rocky Mountains. Turning east at that point, he headed toward the prairies. His destination, he finally decided, would be Fort Macleod and McCoy's Bounty Hunting office. After all, he decided, he could use a second horse, and if Ed was true to his word, he'd be able to retrieve the horse he had lent him when Ed's horse broke its leg. As he approached the dark and

The Missing Years – Part II

winding trail that would lead him over the Rockies, he had to keep reminding himself that bears would be out, and to be prepared for that time when one crossed their path. Black Dog, he knew, would do his best in keeping them clear of Pony. That was his hope at least.

The first night he spent on the trail was uneventful. He sat near the low, glowing fire as his mind filled with memories of Mac and Rose, Tanner and Buck, and those friends of his that he had left behind in Red Rock and Hells Bottom. Most importantly, he remembered Marissa, who by now was a mother of a three-month-old, bouncing baby boy. Tyrell couldn't know that, and he was beginning to get used to the fact that he would likely never see her again. There would always be those occasions where his mind would fill with visions of her alone. Tonight, though, he thought about all his friends, new and old, dead and living.

That evening of June 8th, 1891 for whatever reason, he decided he would take Ed up on the job he offered, if the offer still stood. *Travis Sweet, bounty hunter,* he thought as he smiled at the idea. What was to come would come. Perhaps it would be a way for him to stay close enough to the land he knew, yet far enough away to live in anonymity. The more he thought about the idea, the more he wanted to see it through. Maybe it would be something that would work out for him, and if not, then he would know that at least he tried. It was a challenge, and now he challenged himself. *Nothing like a personal challenge to change a man's direction in life.* He looked into the flames of his evening fire as he contemplated.

The howl from a nearby wolf pack echoed in the stillness of night and he sat up, alerted by their symphony of wildness. He remembered what Half Moon mentioned regarding the Blackfoot belief that the sound of distant wolves brought luck to travellers. He smiled as he reminisced about that time. Over the last eight months since he left Willow Gate, he had certainly met some interesting people. Adding another stick to his fire, he laid out his bedroll and, with Pony's saddle behind his head and Black Dog at his feet, he closed his eyes letting the symphony of wildness lull him to sleep.

Waking the next morning to the sounds of birds, refreshed and revived, Tyrell cleaned up his camp, loaded his gear and set off. Five miles later, Pony halted, snorted and neighed. He knew what that meant and he jumped off the saddle, grabbing his .45-70 rifle as the horse reared up and darted into some undergrowth. Tyrell could hear him as he crashed through the bush, Black Dog in the lead. The barking and snarling that followed told Tyrell that it was a bear. Not more than fifty feet from where he stood, a grizzly darted out and crossed the trail. Hightailing it down an embankment, the bear didn't even look in Tyrell's direction. Heavy as the bear was, he could feel the ground shake as saplings and deadfall snapped and broke while it made its way to safety. Pony and Black Dog stopped there and made their way back to him.

"That was an interesting start to an otherwise peaceful day. Sure happy the two of you aren't any worse for wear. That was a big bear; scared the hell out of me as it crossed the trail. I reckon it is on the other side of that draw by now. You two settle down, we need to get back to what this journey is all about."

He swung onto Pony's back and the three of them continued onward.

Stopping at a creek that cut across the trail, he rested in some shade as Pony drank and Black Dog frolicked. He filled his canteens with the cool, clear, glacial-fed creek, took a long swallow and wiped his mouth. In the distance he could hear an oncoming traveller. He gave the command to Black Dog to hide and be ready, and then he waited for the traveller to approach. It was a young fellow, maybe in his mid to late twenties. He pulled his horse to a halt as he saw Tyrell.

"Afternoon, mister. Beautiful day, ain't it?"

The young man removed his hat and wiped his brow.

"It is, yep. Going to get hotter, I think," Tyrell responded. "The water is cold, though."

"I suppose the horse and I could use a break. I've been travelling since the Fort."

The young man swung off his dun horse and led it to the creek. He splashed water onto his face while the horse drank.

"By the way, my name is Brady McCoy."

"McCoy? You Ed's boy?" Tyrell questioned.

"As a matter of fact I am; and you are?"

"I'm Travis Sweet. I met Ed a few months back, lent him a horse when his broke its leg. I am actually heading that way to see if I can gather it."

"The old man told me about that. It was when he turned in Ray Jackson. I'll be. It's a small world, ain't it? Nice to meet you, Travis."

Brady reached out his hand and they shook.

"The horse is in the corral behind the office waiting for you, and let me thank you personally for that. It helped out the old man. He said you might come around looking for it."

"How is Ed?" Tyrell asked out of curiosity.

"Took a couple of slugs a few weeks back. He's alive, but ain't too happy about being stuck in the office. He can't travel for a bit 'til he heals completely."

"I'm sorry to hear that. He's okay, though, at least, eh?"

"It'll take a few more than two slugs to knock him down," Brady chuckled. "The old man has taken a lot of bullets over the course of my younger days, more than I have in my pistol right now, and it is fully loaded. I reckon he's taken hot lead at least six; maybe even seven or eight times that I am aware of. Lucky Ed he is. He'll bounce back; always does."

"What brings a McCoy to these parts? Are you working, Brady?"

"I am. I've been following Nicolai Baurduer."

"Who is he?"

Tyrell was wondering if he might have been the old fellow he met along the trail a little more than a day ago. He went by the name of Nick.

"Ten years ago Nicolai was running with the Miner Gang that you may or may not have heard about. They was mostly down south. They came up this way a few different times, and did some robbing. Somehow they always seemed to get away. Finally, they did get caught ten years ago in California after they robbed a Sonora train and got away with three thousand, eight hundred dollars. The entire gang, except for old Nicolai who escaped, are in prison now. Nicolai headed back here to Canada. He has been in these parts ever since. The old man got a tip on where he was holed up, working a farm further east of the Fort. He was going by the shortened version of his name, Nick Baurer; sly bastard, eh? Anyway, one of the bounty hunters we have working for us, a fellow who started only a while ago, and the old man went to collect the bounty on him, but Nicolai slipped out of their fingers. That is when they both took lead from him. He killed the fellow working for us and shot up the old man. I picked up the hunt after that; been following him this way since. Now, that you know that, I might be inclined to ask if you have seen anyone on this trail. They'd be travelling light," Brady said as he filled him in.

"I've met a few folks. What does this fellow look like?"

Tyrell already likely knew, except he was not so inclined to mention it yet. He liked Nick. He seemed harmless to him, although he did kill a bounty hunter and shot up Ed. Tyrell imagined himself in the same situation and he, too, would likely try to escape by any means. Then again, he had to take into consideration that his situation was a little different. He was running because of his innocence. Nick, on the other hand, was wanted for a few robberies or so that is how it all sounded.

"He's an older fellow, mid to late fifties. Was told by the old man that he's riding a black horse branded with a P, a bar and a backward C. Stands for Pincher Creek Black Angus Ranch where he worked."

He dug into his saddlebags, withdrew a wanted poster and handed it to Tyrell.

"That's what he looked like ten years ago. It's an old mug shot, but according to the lead cowhand, his look ain't changed much, only his hair ain't as long."

Tyrell studied the black and white picture, grateful that there were no mug shots of himself other than a simple drawing on the wanted poster he had seen. He was torn between what was right and the sympathy he had for a man who for a decade worked his fingers to the bone and who stayed, as far as anyone knew, out of trouble for that long. He inhaled deeply.

"I ain't sure I saw anyone that looked like that," he lied as he handed the poster back. "Sorry I couldn't have been more help, Brady."

"No worries. That is okay. I know I'm getting close. Somebody will have seen him. I'll carry on to

Chase leastwise, maybe head into the Keremeos and Columbia regions. I hate tracking a man for that kind of distance. It don't take long to get weary, and when I'm weary I get slow. In this business that can be deadly."

Tyrell nodded as he thought about what Brady had said. He knew then that he should let Brady know he actually did see Nick and only a day's ride west of Valemount. After all, he knew the kid's old man, although not on a personal basis. Nonetheless, he knew him, and he really didn't want to hear later on that Brady had been killed by the man he was tracking because Brady let his guard down due to weariness.

"Hang on a minute there, Brady. Let me take another peek at that wanted poster."

Tyrell gestured for Brady to get it.

"Sure, something jar your memory?"

"Could be, yep. I may have seen this fellow west of Valemount, a day or two ride west of here."

He waited for Brady to hand him the poster, then taking it he looked at it again.

"As a matter of fact, I did see him. He even introduced himself to me as Nick. I thought nothing of it when you showed me the poster that first time. I even fed the fellow."

"Let me get this straight. The name Nick didn't come to you until now? I mentioned he went by the name of Nick Baurer."

Tyrell was nodding his head, as though he were somewhat embarrassed that he hadn't clued in to that. Brady, though, was no dummy.

"I guess you did mention that. Sorry, Brady. Slipped my mind is all."

Tyrell handed the poster back.

"A day or two ride west, you said?" Brady asked as he put the poster away.

The Missing Years – Part II

"Yeah, I ran across him a day or so west of Valemount. He did say he was heading to Chase. A man being on the run, though, ain't going to head to Chase, but that is what they'd say. It's the largest township in these parts until you get further to the south and west. He was in a good hurry, I can tell you that also. Could be, he knows he's being trailed or that he was in a rush to meet up with the riverboat. It would be making regular trips into Hells Bottom this time of year, twice a week, right through until late September. He probably knows that and I bet that is where he is heading. Once he gets on that boat, he'll be down into Fauquire, or Waldy Island in only a couple of weeks. He won't even go to Chase. He'll cut southeast at that one horse town called Barrie and likely head straight for the Arrow Lakes. And a man like him, I reckon, ain't going to stop until he gets there."

"I already figured that out, Travis. Still wondering why you needed a second look at that poster. I think, maybe you didn't want to tell me, and that is fine because you finally did. My old man is a pretty good judge of character and one thing I remember him saying about you, even though the two of you didn't know one another from dirt, was that he trusted you. Naturally, when I ran across you, I trusted you. I knew you probably saw Nick. Hell, I'm right on his ass. If he's ahead of me, then he must have passed you. When you told me you hadn't seen him, I had to ask myself why you would have said something like that. I wasn't going to pry, mind you. It is none of my business. I knew you were going to have second thoughts. I thank you now for telling me."

"I didn't see much point in saying anything, to be honest. Here's a man that's been clean and hard working for a decade or so, and there is still a bounty on his head. Doesn't make much sense to me. Besides, I will say it again, he seemed harmless to me, other than he was in a bit of a rush. I reckon he's a simple man trying to make a new life," Tyrell replied as truth.

"No one can deny that fact. That is exactly what he was doing. The difference between you and me is that to you it doesn't matter. To me, men like him are my bread and butter. It's two different worlds, that is all. I know you meant no harm by it and most folks would have said the same thing. Bounty hunters are keen to this human trait, so what you told me, I already knew."

"I'm glad that is cleared up and I do offer you an apology for not giving you the answers in the beginning."

Tyrell nodded his respect and acknowledgement to Brady who returned the same gesture. This meant by both their standards, that part of the conversation had finished.

"I guess I best get a move on. Nicolai might be near Barrie by now. That's a long haul."

"I may be able to help you out in that regard. That don't mean I'm turning around here and heading back with you, but there is a fellow I know lives in Willow Gate. His name is Tanner McBride. He's in the same business. We passed a telegraph office in Valemount. If you can get a telegram to him, let him know I gave you his name. He'll do what he can to help bring this Nicolai in. With Tanner's help coming from the west, travelling east you could box him in probably near Hells Bottom," Tyrell shrugged. "That might be something to consider, Brady. Makes your job easier and less dangerous."

"That is a good idea. He and I could split the bounty, I suppose. Nicolai ain't no small potato. There is a five thousand dollar bounty a man can collect on him, and that is breathing or not."

"Dead or alive, eh?"

Tyrell felt badly about that. Undoubtedly, if Nicolai didn't make it to the southern states he was going to die or be taken in as a bounty. It was a true and hard fact. That was the way the system worked and Tyrell knew that he, himself, was faced with a similar situation, only different circumstantially.

"Keep your eyes peeled for a grizzly. It crossed the trail down a mile or two. I'm sure by now it's long gone, but be aware. If it is you that catches up to Nicolai, you going to take him alive, Brady?"

"That all depends on him, I suppose. He's a tough son-of-a-bitch from what we know, and not too weak on the shooting either. My desire would be to get as close to him as I can without being noticed, then simply stab him in the ribs with the pistol. I'll identify myself, then haul him in, no gunfire at all. Most times that is how it works out. Gun play ain't desirous. Best to avoid."

Brady swung on to his horse's back and asked Tyrell to tell his old man where he was heading.

"You bet I will. No worries there, Brady. Anything else you want me to tell him?"

"Nothing that comes to mind. I'll telegraph the Fort in a few days, week tops. Should have a good idea on where we're going to catch up with Nicolai by then. Until then, and if we never meet again, it was nice to have met you, Travis."

"Same with you Brady, keep safe, and do telegraph Tanner McBride in Willow Gate."

Brady slowed his horse so he could look back and respond.

"I likely will. Thanks for that and the bear warning."

Turning now, he continued onward at a gallop.

Tyrell watched as Brady and the horse slipped around the corner. Pulling out his pocket watch, he looked at the time. It was 2:00 p.m. with plenty of daylight hours left. He climbed into his own saddle and continued southeasterly. In a way, he felt badly that he had given a few tidbits away regarding Nicolai's travel, but he also felt relieved that he had. Ed's kid Brady wasn't that old and was probably a bit green behind the ears, but he did certainly have a good head on his shoulders. If the information he shared with the kid could save the kid from being fooled by an old outlaw like Nicolai, then he would live with it.

"Figure the kid is going to be okay, Black Dog?" Tyrell questioned already knowing the answer. "I reckon he will be, especially if he follows through and gets Tanner involved. I feel sorry for that old Nicolai fellow, though. In a few more years he'll have likely died of old age. To spend the last years of one's life behind bars don't sound too appealing to me."

Tyrell shook his head as he contemplated the rest of his own life with the same burden of having a bounty on his head.

One slip of a lip is all it would take for folks to know who he truly was. How he hoped that day would never come. He would then be running further, faster, and no different than what Nicolai was doing. Not much of a life at all. With at least thirty years or more of life left in him, it was a long time to live under a name that wasn't your own. Anything, though, was better than subjecting himself to such circumstances or hanging from a rope, which, if caught, would likely be his fate. The only law he really needed to fear was the corrupt law of Willow Gate. Mounted Police, however, could go anywhere in Canada and how many of them had connections with the constables in Willow Gate, he didn't know. It was for that reason he hadn't talked to any of them regarding the Willow Gate incident and chances were he never would.

The more he thought about that, the more he wanted to delve into bounty hunting. It was a way not only to make a living, but also a fool-proof way to hide his true identity right under the noses of those looking for the man named Tyrell, accused of four murders. Travis Sweet had no record, wasn't wanted by any law. Only gunslingers would be in his way, which in all honesty wasn't much different from his younger days. He lived through that, and he'd live through this also and make an honest living at it too, for now at least. Granted it did get lonely, but a man could live through loneliness. It was only a matter of doing it, plus avoiding places where people who knew his true identity always helped. It sounded easy, but men like Nicolai were eventually found. Wanted posters never went away. They were as permanent as some of the trees that they were often nailed to. Only when a man was caught did they fade into history. Getting caught, for Tyrell, was no more of an option than turning himself in.

"Chapter 2"

On Saturday June 13th, 1891, he arrived at Fort Macleod. He pulled Pony up to a dirty yellow building with white lettering on the window which read McCoy's Bounty Hunting Service. Finding the place, he traipsed around back and looked at the few horses which were inside the corral. There he was, the horse he had lent Ed. He smiled as he picked him out.

Looking around, he noted a water tower in the distance. He knew it meant that the town had running water. A back staircase caught his eye next. It led up to a small office or room. Below that and on the bottom floor, there was a back door and beside that a stack of wood.

He swung off Pony and tethered him to one of the horse posts near the corral gate entrance. Looking down at Black Dog who was wagging his tail, he rummaged through his saddlebags and pulled out a stick of jerky.

"You can have this if you promise to lie here or in the shade somewhere near and behave. Are you going to do that for me, Black Dog?"

Tyrell knew the answer; Black Dog always stayed near.

Tyrell made his way to the front of the building and walked in. Ed almost fell off his chair.

"Hey, Travis. Jesus Christ, sure nice to see you," Ed said as he grabbed his crutch and met Tyrell at the front counter. "How have you been?"

"Surviving Ed, surviving. I'm here for my horse and to let you know your son Brady is heading west into Hells Bottom, still on the trail of the old codger who put lead in you and killed one of your men. It is a shame to hear about that. Brady mentioned he wasn't with you guys long."

"Nope. Four months, I think. Damn shame it was. The boy is headed west, eh. Sure hope he catches up with Nicolai. He gets on a riverboat, he'll be long gone. Washington, I reckon."

"Funny you should say that. Brady and I had the same conversation. I gave him the name of a friend of mine who is in the same business, Tanner McBride, lives in the Willow Gate area. I figured he could telegraph him and maybe the two of them can bring Nicolai in together. Tanner is a good man. If he helps, Brady ain't got no worries."

"That was a nice gesture. The kid is pretty bullheaded. It's not like him to take on help."

"I don't know, Ed. He seemed as though he were interested."

Tyrell looked around the office at the few desks and chairs that crowded the place. Ed's office was the only private one. He also noticed a holding cell with two bunk beds, and a bathroom next to them with a sink and toilet.

"You keep your bounties right here in your office?" Tyrell asked with curiosity.

"It's perfectly legal. Once in a while we've had to use the Mounted Police cells down the way some for the unruly. That don't happen often, but it has. Excuse the mess of the place. We have four men working for us, well, three now with the death of Smitty, and most ain't here often except for Brady. He kind of takes care of the things around here. I like the adventure of tracking down the bounties. Brady has done a few dozen. He's good at that part of the job as well, but I really like it better when he's here. One man short now, though. So you made it through the winter?"

"I did so. Worked at some horse logging and lived in a tepee. That's a true story, Ed," Tyrell smiled.

Ed nodded his head with interest.

"Excuse my manners; want a coffee, Travis?"

He gestured for Tyrell to join him at a small table behind the wall where a wood stove sat gently burning, keeping the pot of coffee warm. He poured one for each of them and sat down opposite Tyrell.

"This is the staff room and where we make quick meals for the prisoners, or bounties, whatever you want to call them when we have them."

He paused for a moment as he took a drink from his coffee.

"You said you were doing horse logging and living in a tepee. Sounds like it may have been interesting. How did you like it?"

"It kept me alive and sheltered plus I made a couple of good friends, Mac and Rose. Earned some money and was left alone for the most part. I'd do it again, Ed, if that is what you mean. The pay weren't that great, but it cost me nothing to be sheltered and to keep myself and horse fed. Add that to the wage and it ain't so bad."

Tyrell took a swig from his coffee.

"Geez, you feed this to your bounties?" Tyrell joked.

The coffee wasn't fresh, but who was he to complain.

"What? What's wrong with the coffee? It ain't but three or four hours old."

Ed winked at him.

"But, yeah, it ain't so good is it?"

"Ah, it'll do, not much point in wasting it."

He took another drink.

"Other than getting shot which looks like in the leg, what's new with you, Ed, and how have you been?"

"Things have been good. A lot has changed in eight or so months. When I ran into you, back then we were only a two-man operation. Today, we have the

The Missing Years – Part II

means to employ two other registered bounty hunters on top of Brady and I. We managed a few decent bounties. This Nicolai fellow Brady is chasing down will be the twelfth bounty over and above the usual twenty-five hundred dollars that most folks is worth that we've had the good fortune and opportunity to try and get the bounty reward on. Add that to the few others we've gathered here or there makes for a pretty good pay day when it's all over."

Ed brought his coffee to his lips and took a drink.

"Wouldn't have thought that there was enough work in this area to employ that many bounty hunters from one office. You must be doing something right."

Tyrell paused as he looked around.

"Are there really that many outlaws about?"

"Not until you get into this business, or should I say the law business, do you realise how many hoodwinks are running around. Lately, seems like all the old timers who have been around for a while are the ones we are catching up to now. Nicolai for instance has been in this area for ten or so years with no one the wiser on who he really was. That is a part of this business I could do without, you know, knocking down people that for the past ten or twenty years ain't so much as hurt a fly. Sometimes that gets bothersome. However, the law is the law and although bounty hunters ain't really bound by police law, we still follow ethics; or at least the ones that work from this office do. All it really means is that we can cut corners. That is the only difference between bounty hunters and the Mounted Police or, for that matter, the Pinkertons down south."

"I reckon some bounty hunters can be pretty reckless at times. Leastwise those are stories I've heard," Tyrell mentioned.

"There are those that are, and as long as they're within the morality of law, they're in the right. When they step beyond that boundary, that is when the full extent of the law breathes down on them."

"How is your coffee, Travis? Have another, then I'll take you out to your horse," Ed said as he stood up to pour another for himself.

"Sure, fill it up, Ed."

Tyrell handed him his half-empty cup.

"If you don't mind me asking, Ed, how does an office such as this pay their employees? Do you folks divvy up the proceeds once a bounty has been located and taken in? I hope that don't sound like I'm being snoopy. I'm more curious than anything."

"No, that's fine, Travis. It works kind of like what you said, but the less a bounty hunter spends when he's tracking determines his cut, even if he is the one that brings the fugitive in. Whatever is spent has to be paid back into the company. That includes gear, food, and drink, and anything else that equals an expenditure. Basically, I send my guys off with two hundred and fifty to five hundred dollars each, depending on distance and time of year, the worth of the bounty, that type of thing. Winter months, we don't make much money 'cause we end up staying in hotels. That costs money.

Here is an example. Brady headed off after Nicolai with only one hundred and fifty dollars. That amount was given to him from the office expense account and it comes right off the top of the turned-in bounty. Whether he's spent any of it or not, he keeps whatever is in his pocket at that time, so that is a gain for him. Bringing Nicolai in is worth five thousand dollars. The company gets a quarter of that right off the bat. That leaves three thousand plus left. Brady will get sixty percent of that and the other forty percent goes into the company account as well. There is money to be made as long as a man is careful and doesn't spend too much as he does it. Sounds as though you may be contemplating what we discussed on the mountain last fall."

Ed smiled with intent.

"I bet you thought I forgot. I didn't. If you are looking for work, we're short one man."

Ed sat down. He could tell Tyrell's mind was swirling and that he was as a matter-of-fact seriously considering the offer.

Tyrell looked across table at Ed.

"I have to admit, it has crossed my mind over the last week or so. Wasn't going to bring it up unless you did, and you did. Does the offer still stand? Otherwise I'll gather the horse I lent you, Ed and I'll be off," Tyrell said, man to man and with sincerity and commitment.

"Of course it stands. My word is my promise, Travis. There are a few legalities which ain't too intrusive. I'll need you to give me a thumb and trigger fingerprint. You'll have to hold a Bible and repeat or read aloud an oath in front of one of the Mounted Police constables. Most here in the Fort are friends of mine. You ain't got any worries with them. I'll need your full name, which includes a middle initial if you got one, and your date of birth and next of kin, if you got any. That is all we need. You could be employed by McCoy's Bounty Hunting Service by dusk if you want."

"That quick? Seems a little abrupt, but if it can be done," Tyrell reached out his hand to shake Ed's, "then let's get it done," he said as they shook hands.

"Excellent. We'll start with the paperwork."

Ed stood up, and retrieved some official-looking documents and set them in front of Tyrell.

"You look those over and I'll get a fresh pot of coffee going."

He turned and walked away as Tyrell pulled the papers closer to look at them.

"That's the legal stuff, name and such. You'll have a separate company contract to read and sign so you can work for us. It's pretty basic. Anyway, take your time reading that part and fill it in. There is a pen on the shelf behind you."

Tyrell turned and grabbed the pen. He took a couple of minutes to read it, then filled it out. This is what he wrote: *Name:* Travis B. Sweet- *Live Birth Date*: February 15th-16th 1853. He put it that way because he had been born only minutes before midnight or a little after. His old man couldn't remember either way. Usually he would have put the 16th. Today, though, he wrote it like that. Under *Place of Live Birth*: Unknown - Hells Bottom area. He signed the bottom *Travis B. Sweet:* Date: June 13th, 1891. He looked at it for a moment.

"It is the thirteenth, ain't it, Ed?"

"Yep, is too."

"Good, because that's the date I put down. Here you go."

He slid the paper over to where Ed sat earlier.

"How's the coffee coming?" he asked as to not show the anxiety he was actually feeling for signing off on the personal information. Although made up, it would be what identified him as Travis B. Sweet. It was a pretty smart move actually, that is of course, if the law and Ed both bought it. He wasn't trying to deceive Ed; he would do honest work for him and would never bite the hand that fed him. He would be Tyrell Sloan the man, under the persona and name of Travis Sweet. *Simple.*

"The coffee won't be much longer," Ed said as he picked up the document and looked it over.

"What does the 'B' stand for, Travis? You don't have to answer if you don't want to."

"That's okay. My middle name is Bentley. I'm named after a great uncle actually," Tyrell said with genuine honour.

"Travis Bentley, eh?"

"That's right, Travis Bentley Sweet."

"Born in 1853, near Hells Bottom on February 15th or 16th. Ain't sure which?" Ed chuckled.

"Nope, never knew my mother. She died birthing me. The old man raised me, and he wasn't a mother, if you know what I mean," Tyrell smiled.

"I do. All right then, this all looks good. Everything is filled out accordingly. I don't reckon you have a piece of paper with your birth date on it or some other type of legal ID?"

"I never had a need to carry any, Ed."

"That is fine; a lot of folks don't. You'll get a piece of ID that will look like this."

He pulled out and showed Travis the card that identified him as a registered Bounty Hunter. It had a tawny star, a number and name, plus a thumbprint on the face of it.

"Why only the thumbprint?" Tyrell asked.

"They keep the index, trigger fingerprint in their own files. That is the one which pulls the trigger." He half chuckled. "It's only ever dug out if there is an altercation with a bounty turn in where death is involved and it is unexplainable or witnessed differently. Anyway, enough said about that for now, are you ready to take the oath or do you want a coffee firstly."

"Yeah, I reckon that be best, a fresh cup of coffee to clear my head. I have to admit, Ed, I'm feeling a little jittery with all this legal stuff. Quite an opportunity and I thank you for it. I hope I don't disappoint."

"To be frank, Travis, it is hard to disappoint in a job like this, unless of course you break the sworn oath or break the law. Follow some simple ethics, be forceful when necessary, think like a man who is running. Being aware of his committed crimes and habitual behaviour are always good to keep in mind. Approach with caution and preparedness. That about sums up the entire oath. More than anything, that is the way you have to look at each individual case or bounty, whichever you prefer."

"Bounty it'll be. Case sounds too official," Tyrell teased. "I don't care either way. How do you fellows say it, case or bounty?"

"I use it both ways, but it doesn't matter. We all know what it is we're talking about."

He stood from the table and poured them a fresh cup of coffee. He handed the first one to Travis.

"Thank you, Ed."

He took the cup and brought it to his mouth and blew on it, then took a swallow.

"That is way better than that last stuff. How do you suppose Brady is going to react when he finds out I'm working for the two of you?"

"He'll be fine with it. You take the oath, get the proper ID, etc., and you're one of us then. No worries there either. Brady is levelheaded and knows how this business runs."

"Good to know. I wouldn't want to make him feel ousted."

"Brady would never feel that way, Travis. I can assure you of that. This will all be his one day. It might not amount to much when it is all said and done, but it'll keep his feet planted. That is all that matters and he knows it."

Ed now took his seat across from Tyrell. Pulling out his pocket watch, he looked at the time.

"By the time we finish the coffees, it'll be shift change down at the Mounted Police station. Today it'll be desk sergeant Willard Camrose. He's a good fellow, been here at the Fort for a while, since '87 I think."

They sat in silence as they enjoyed their fresh afternoon coffee.

"Actually, I think Willard came here in 1885," Ed mentioned to break the monotony of the moment.

"How far away is the station? I don't recall seeing one when I came in."

"That is because you came in from the west. It is east of town a bit further. Are you ready then?"

Tyrell sighed.

"As ready as I'll ever be. Let's get to it," he said as he finished his cup of coffee and they exited.

Ed locked the door to his office and instead of riding, they walked. Ed, of course, had to use his crutch. He pointed a few things out about the town, which saloon was best, which one had better food, the name of this fellow, the name of that, things like that as they made their way down main street. Finally the Mounted Police station came into view.

"There is the station," Ed pointed out.

"Ain't that big, is it?"

"Nope." Ed opened the door and they entered.

"Afternoon, Ed. Is this fellow a bounty?" Willard asked as he looked Tyrell up and down, as if sizing him up.

"Not at all. He's here to take the oath."

Ed handed Willard the paper that Travis had filled out.

His eyes got big and he smiled.

"You're that fellow who took down Earl Brubaker! It is a pleasure to meet you, Travis."

Tyrell grew flush with embarrassment as Willard cooed him.

"What?" asked Ed with surprise. "Earl Brubaker? You have to be kidding! I had no idea that was you. Hurry up and sign him off, Will," Ed joked.

Willard reached for the oath and Bible that was under the counter.

"Put your left hand on the Bible and raise your right. Read out the oath and add your name and the date where it says so."

Tyrell nodded then proceeded.

"I, 'Travis B. Sweet' on this date of June 13th, 1891, solemnly and honestly swear that I have not been involved in criminality of any sort, now or ever. I am of sound mind, and I hereby accept the responsibility and will be accountable for upholding the laws of Canada, as recognised by Canada's Privy Council, Provincial Judges, and Royal Canadian Mounted Police. I, 'Travis B. Sweet', will promote safety and integrity. I will work with honesty, compassion and professionalism to the best of my abilities. I will show respect and morality to those I may apprehend. I, 'Travis B. Sweet' will be ethical and use force only when force is necessary. I am bound by this oath and therefore it shall be."

Tyrell looked across to Willard as he finished.

"Is that it?"

"That is it, Travis. You can put your hand down now. Next, I'll need two prints from you: your right thumb and index finger."

Willard set an inkpad on the counter and gestured for Tyrell put his finger on it. He rolled it back and forth, then put it on a pad of paper, again rolling it back and forth. He went through the same process for his thumb. His thumbprint however went onto the pad of paper as well as an ID card that Willard needed to fill out. Because Tyrell used both hands and had two pistols, they repeated the process with his left hand. Willard handed him a piece of dampened cloth and Tyrell removed the black stains on his fingers and thumbs. Willard half sat down and started to fill out the card.

"You have any questions, Travis?"

"Not off hand." Tyrell leaned against the counter, as he waited for his official Bounty Hunter ID card. Finally, Willard returned and set it down in front of him.

"Sign right here."

Willard pointed to where Tyrell's signature needed to go and handed him a pen. He signed it, *'Travis B. Sweet'*.

"There you go, Travis. You are now an official Bounty Hunter."

Willard handed him a little booklet that highlighted a bounty hunter's procedures.

Tyrell took it from him and thumbed through it.

"Thanks, I'll keep this handy," he said with sincerity as he stuck it in his back pocket.

"Remember you are bound by the oath that you read out loud."

Willard pointed at the number on the card.

"That number there must be present on all legal forms that you may be required to fill out, and if requested you must show it to the law when you apprehend and turn a fugitive in for the bounty."

"Is that it?"

Tyrell looked at the card.

"I understand that I'm bound by the oath, and I will abide by it. I ain't sure, though, if I'm clear on the last part, using force. When is force acceptable and when ain't it?"

"If someone shoots at you, shoot back. If someone aims to cause you harm, protect yourself and innocents around you by all and any means. Don't apprehend those that you may with hostility or hatred.

Your job is to apprehend with dignity and professionalism. That is basically, what the entire oath states. You are expected to do your job lawfully. In other words you will be treated no differently than any other criminal if you overstep your bounds. Ethicalness and morality are two words that you will be expected to live by as you pursue wanted felons."

Tyrell nodded his head as Willard explained the oath to him.

"All right, I understand now. Thanks for clearing that all up for me."

Tyrell reached across the counter and shook Willard's hand. By now, Ed was standing beside him and grinning.

"Now that all the awkwardness is over and the preliminaries are out of the way, welcome to the elite law abiding bounty hunters of Canada," Ed joked as he looked at Willard and smiled. "Thanks, Willard. We don't want to keep you from your duties. Thank you for this undertaking."

"You bet, Ed. Always a pleasure seeing to it that men like Travis here get their credentials to help make this world a safer place."

He looked over to Travis.

"On behalf of the Mounted Police, we thank you for your contribution in helping to keep today's society as safe as you are able to, Travis."

"Thanks, Willard. I appreciate it. All right, Ed, I think we're done here. Let's head back to your office."

"You bet. See you later, Willard," Ed said as they exited the building.

"That wasn't so bad was it?"

"Nope, didn't hurt one bit. I'm still trying to piece together the entire idea, the 'why not' and the 'what for'. Anyone can turn in a bounty if they happen across some hoodwink and are able to get the upper hand. That being the case, I ain't sure what point the credentials make, you know, the oath, the card, that type of thing."

"Professionalism is what it adds up to. Means you could as long as you remain in good standings with the law and hold that card, that you could turn around tomorrow and legally start your own practise. You can be hired by private citizens, work for private law enforcement, plus you have the right to now pursue any bounty anywhere in Canada. You can present and execute warrants for the law courts. That card and taking that oath gives you more rights than civilians have when apprehending felons wanted by the law. You can enter dwellings forcefully if there is reasonable belief a fugitive is inside or resides there. No civilian can do that legally. You'll be able to access law enforcement resources. We get the first look and copies of those wanted posters that you sometimes see that the Mounted Police put out. Plus you can be hired by private Bounty Hunting Services, such as McCoy's."

By now, they had made their way back to Ed's office. Ed unlocked the door and held it open for Tyrell.

"Thanks, Ed," Tyrell said as he stepped inside.

"Next thing I reckon is to let you have a look at our contract. Let's head to the table and have a sit down. I'll get the contract for you. Help yourself to more coffee, Travis. I won't be but a minute."

Tyrell made his way over to the coffee pot and poured himself a cup.

Sitting down, he waited for Ed as he contemplated. This was it. This was a turning point in his life and he felt that satisfying feeling of self-worth that one gets when about to embark on something that is life changing. He wasn't sure how it would all pan out, but whatever was to come, he was ready. It was hard to believe how much could change in a day. *This morning I was Travis Sweet. This afternoon, I am Travis Sweet, certified Bounty Hunter,* he thought as he looked at the official ID card he held in his hand.

Meanwhile, Ed was thumbing through a stack of papers looking for a copy of the contract he offered all new employees. Finding it finally, he made his way over to the table and set the contract down in front of Travis, then poured his own coffee. Tyrell read it over, agreed to it and signed it. Then he went through the process of inking up his left and right thumbs and index fingers. On the back of the contract where it read thumbs and index fingers, he added his prints.

"There, that takes care of that. The contract is signed and sealed, Ed."

He slid the contract over to Ed who added his signature.

"Welcome on board, Travis. You are officially an employee of McCoy's Bounty Hunting Service. How do you feel about that?" Ed was curious to know.

"Feels good I reckon. What is next?"

"To start, you can grab Smitty's desk and make it your own. Anything he has there that you can use, feel free. His personals you can stuff in a box. It's getting on to 5:00 p.m. and I'm a might hungry. Come on, I'll buy you dinner."

Ed stood up with the help from his crutch and Tyrell followed suit.

"Where are we going to eat?" Tyrell asked as they once again exited the office.

"The Snakebite. Don't let the name fool you. They have some of the best steak and potatoes this side of the Rockies."

They conversed back and forth as they walked to the Snakebite. Ed led Tyrell over to his favourite table and gestured for him to sit. They ordered two coffees and two steak dinners.

"So, it was you who disposed of Earl Brubaker? I honestly had no idea that it was you until Willard mentioned it. How did that come about, anyway?" Ed asked, wanting to know.

"He came by my work place and beat up my friend Rose whilst her husband Mac was out. Then traipsed on up to where I was staying on Mac's property, claiming I was that Tyrell fellow, wanted for murder. Of course, his only reason for believing that was simply because I have a dog. I guess Tyrell has one too." Tyrell shrugged. "It carried on from there. He drew on me and I slapped leather with him and came up shooting before he did. It is as simple as that. I had no idea who he was until I heard it from Mac," Tyrell fibbed.

"You made yourself a name for beating him at the draw. Only thing I heard was he had been shot and that it was self-defence on the shooter's part. I don't recall hearing any name associated with who the shooter was. I feel good knowing he works for me," Ed chuckled, as their food arrived.

"Eat up, Travis. You are about to eat one of the best steaks you ever will."

"It certainly looks and smells good."

Tyrell took a swig from his coffee then went at the steak. Ed was correct. It was the best steak and spuds he had eaten. Putting the last piece into his mouth, he wiped his face with a napkin.

"That, my friend, was as good as you said it would be."

"I told you so," Ed nodded as he finished the rest of his.

They spent a few more minutes having another coffee and then Ed paid the bill and they exited.

"I don't reckon you've found a place to stay yet, so you can stay in the room above the office. Having a fellow living up there fulltime that works for us would

The Missing Years – Part II

be useful. Usually we pick who is going to be staying there when we have bounties. It ain't much, but it does have a bed and a dresser, as well as a sitting table, a cold running water sink and toilet. You have to keep the cistern full for the toilet, but that don't take much effort. Use the bucket to fill it. There is plumbing in for hot water, but the owners of the building before we bought it didn't bother putting in a boiler and neither have we. There is a pint-sized woodstove as well. Seems to keep the place warm in winter. You can even cook on it. There is always wood piled out back."

"Cold running water and a toilet won't hurt my feelings one bit. I'll live without the hot," Tyrell said.

He hadn't used a real toilet in a long time.

"Old man Donale did all the plumbing to the few places around here that have it before he died. We got lucky when we picked up this building because it was plumbed. The water comes from the tower you likely saw when you tethered your horse around back. I won't even mind if you let your dog in, which I ain't saw yet. You can live there if you like, as long as you don't mind checking up on the bounties downstairs every now and again when we have them."

"I'd do that, Ed, sure. As for the dog, I reckon he is out back likely sleeping in the corral, leastwise that is where I sent him. He won't be far. I'll introduce him to you once we get back to the office. Can I set my horse loose in the corral?" Tyrell asked.

"Of course. It is for employee and company horses and any man who owns a horse when he is brought in. If he gets sent to prison, his horse gets auctioned off or returned to the original brander, if it has been stolen."

"Good to know, thank you, Ed."

Tyrell looked around at the little town as the sun crested the western horizon.

"The Fort ain't that big is it?"

"Seventy-five strong," Ed chuckled. "It seems to grow every year as the ranchers further east buy up more land this way. It is in a good location, with being so close to British Columbia Rockies. A lot of ore mining going on up that way. We're close to the southern border going into the States, which is good for our business. A lot of our work comes from down that way."

They walked around to the back of the building and Tyrell introduced Ed to Black Dog as they made their way to the upstairs rental. Finding the key, Ed unlocked and opened the door, then stepped in as Tyrell followed behind.

"This is it. Like I said, it ain't much. You have a good view of the street below and views east and west."

Tyrell looked around. He had lived in worse.

"Ain't anything wrong with this set up. It'll work fine, I reckon. Is there a bathhouse in town?"

"Yep."

Ed walked over to the eastern window.

"Come here I'll show you."

Tyrell made his way over to where Ed stood and looked out.

"That building right there with all the laundry hanging on the line is the Fort's bath and laundry house. It is run by the widow Donale. She's probably eighty or ninety. She'll do up your laundry and scrub your back for two dollars. Even folds and irons what needs to be ironed. She gets a lot of business with all the coal mines near. How she puts up with some of them fellows, they stink so bad, I'll never know."

"I think I'll be visiting her tomorrow. I could use a hot bath and some clean clothes. For now, I'd like to get my horse settled and gear unloaded," Tyrell mentioned as a hint to Ed to let him go ahead and do that.

"Yeah. Okay, Tyrell."

He looked at his watch. "Business hours are over and I'm sure you are tired. I'll let you get settled."

He handed Tyrell the key to the door. "I live about two miles south of town in a grey house off the main wagon trail. The brown one is Brady's. If you run into any problems you know where to find me."

He nodded. "I'll see you in the morning, Travis. I'm usually here somewhere between 6:00 and 8:00 a.m., so I'll see you then."

"You bet, Ed. I look forward to my first day working for you. I'll see you tomorrow."

He watched as Ed headed down the stairs, saddled up his horse, and headed for home. Closing the door, he pulled up a chair to the table and sat down. He liked it there already. From where he sat he could see out both the east and west side windows. To look at the street he had to be standing and looking down. Sitting, all he could see were the roof tops of a couple other buildings, the open prairie to the east and the Rocky Mountains to the west. It was a spectacular view. The apartment was a single room. The only door inside, other than the door that led down the stairs, was for the bathroom, which had a sink and toilet and likely plumbed into the same system as the one downstairs in Ed's office.

The double bed, although old and shabby, sat against the north wall and beside that was a dresser and nightstand with a coal oil lantern and a box of wax candles accompanied by wooden matches. The table where he sat was in the center of the room and it, too, had a coal oil lantern that sat in the middle of the table.

On the wall nearest the door were a rifle rack and a hat hanger. Against the east wall, an arm's length from the table, was a counter that had a couple of shelves, and a cupboard. Sitting upside down on the cupboard was a washbasin. The woodstove, as Ed mentioned, wasn't big, but it was big enough to heat water and cook. The room wasn't fancy, but it would certainly do. *More conveniences than a tepee,* he thought as he continued to look around.

The sound of scratching at the door caught his attention. He stood up and opened it.

"Hello there, Black Dog, come on in."

Black Dog immediately jumped on the bed.

"What, you think that is for you? Your place will be here near the door."

Tyrell pointed at a rustic old mat.

"That'll be your lay down spot when I crawl into bed. I'm going to gather my gear and set Pony loose with the other horses. Hope he don't get too overbearing."

He left the door wide open as he made his way to the bottom of the staircase and over to where Pony was tethered

"Hey, Pony, thanks for being patient."

He untied him, removed the saddle and gear that was strapped to his back, then opened the corral gate and set him loose.

"Go make some friends and be nice, Pony," Tyrell said as he watched the other horses prancing about, showing off to their new visitor. The black horse he had lent Ed remembered Pony, or so it seemed, as it greeted him with a neigh and bit his rear. Tyrell chuckled as Pony farted and pranced around with the others.

Gathering up his gear and bedroll, he went back upstairs to his room. Black Dog was still lying where he had left him. Tossing the gear on the floor, he sorted through it as he put things away in the cupboard and on the shelves. He put both his rifles on the rifle rack and hung his pistol belt from the hat hanger. His hat he tossed on the table. His stuff put away now, it looked more like home.

"What do you think, Black Dog? Looks cosy now, don't it?"

Black Dog looked over to him and wagged his tail, then curled up on the mattress and went back to sleep.

"Chapter 3"

Sunday, June 14th, 1891. It was 7:00 a.m. when he awoke and, stuffing a duffle bag that he happened to find underneath the bed, he filled it with all his dirty clothes. Strapping on his holster and donning his hat, he grabbed the cleanest pair of clothes he could find and headed over to the bath and laundry house. He knocked on the door and an old, greying woman answered.

"Good morning, sir. Here to have some laundry done, are you?" she asked as she gestured for him to come in.

"Yes, ma'am, that and was hoping I could get a bath as well," Tyrell said as he set the duffle bag down on the floor and removed his hat.

"You're lucky; today I have heated up fresh water getting ready for the Sunday rush. Please, come in. I'll show you to your bath."

The woman closed the door and walked into a room that had two hot steaming baths. Tyrell followed close behind.

"You can use either tub. There is soap on the counter and a few cloths as well as a towel. I'll get your laundry started. Umm, your name is?" she questioned as she stopped and looked at him, while he was removing his trousers.

"Sorry about that, ma'am. My name is Travis Sweet. I started working for Ed McCoy yesterday. I live in the room above his office."

"You are a bounty hunter, then?"

"Yes ma'am, I am."

"Humph, all right then. I'll get your laundry started, Travis. Enjoy your bath."

The woman closed the door and made her way to the clothes-washing tub. Dumping the duffle bag, she

sorted through Tyrell's clothes and started washing them.
Tyrell slid into one of the tubs of hot water and washed his face and hair, his armpits and crotch. Using his small shaving mirror, he lathered up his face and shaved; then laid back and soaked in the cooling water. Clean and refreshed, he finally stepped out and dried off. Fetching the cleaner set of clothes, he dressed, holstered up and exited.

"Hello, ma'am," he said loud enough he hoped for her to hear.

"Yes, down the hall and to the right," the woman replied,

Tyrell followed her voice and finally found her.

"I'm done with the bath, ma'am. Could you also wash these for me, please?"

He handed her the clothes he had worn earlier.

"Yes, of course. Did you enjoy your bath?" she asked as she took the clothes from his hand.

"Indeed. It was quite nice, thank you. How much do I owe you for the bath and clothes cleaning? I hope the clothes are not too dirty for you. I haven't had them washed in a while, as you can probably tell."

"The first bath is free. The cleaning for the clothes will cost two dollars. They are quite filthy, but I have washed dirtier ones. You can pay me when you come back for them. I should have them washed, dried and folded in a few hours. With the sun as hot as it is going to be today, I would assume your clothes will be dry by noon. Come back then, Travis," the woman said as she continued washing his clothes.

"I will, ma'am. Thank you again," Tyrell said as he turned and walked back down the hall and exited.

He made his way back to his room, surprised not to see Ed's horse. Looking at his watch, he noted the time to be 9:00 a.m. *Ed is late today I guess,* he thought as he tossed some hay into the corral for the horses. He leaned on the railing and watched as they ate and frolicked. He was surprised at how well Pony was behaving. Usually he bullied most other horses. These ones, though, he seemed to have made friends with. Tyrell heard another horse approach. Turning, he watched as Ed came near.

"Morning, Ed."

"Morning, Travis; running a bit late today. Forgot it was Sunday; had to take the misses to church."

Ed swung off his horse and led him into the corral.

"I see you gave them hay already, thanks. How was your first night in the room?" he asked as he approached and closed the corral gate.

"I slept like a baby. It was nice not having to find a tree to pee behind this morning," Tyrell chuckled. "Had my bath already and the widow Donale is doing up my clothes. Nice woman, she is."

"Yes, she is. Get on her good side and she'll bake for you too. She makes the best pie in these parts, sells them to the Snakebite. She's always busy doing one thing or the other."

Tyrell followed Ed to the back door beneath the staircase that led to his room. Ed unlocked it and the two of them stepped inside.

"I'll get the fire going so we can have coffee," Ed said as he closed the door and locked it from the inside. "We keep the back door locked. Keeps folks from slipping in without our knowledge."

"Yeah, makes sense, Ed."

Tyrell looked around again at the desks.

"Which one of these desks was Smitty's?" he asked.

Ed pointed to the one closest the counter.

"All right then, I'll clear it out. Is there a box handy?"

"I'll get you one," Ed said cheerfully.

He made his way into his office and returned with a cardboard box.

"Put old Smitty's personals in here. Like I said yesterday, if there are things you can use, feel free to use them. I'll get the coffee going."

Ed turned and made his way into the staff room where the woodstove was and lit a fire; then set the coffee pot on it to make a fresh pot.

Tyrell went through Smitty's stuff, keeping a few pens and pieces of paper for himself. Setting the full box on the counter, he sat down at his desk and put his hands behind his head while he stared out the big window that looked onto the main street of the Fort. Even his desk felt comfortable. He smiled as he looked around the office. He liked this job already.

"Hey, Travis, come on, the coffee is done," he heard Ed holler from the staff room.

Standing, he pushed his chair in and made his way to where Ed was sitting at the table.

"Fresh and hot, Travis Help yourself before it gets old. We don't do much on the Sabbath. Go through reports and that is about it. Usually we close the office by noon. We will today, too."

Tyrell poured a coffee and sat at the table.

"Got all Smitty's stuff packed away," he said as he took a drink from his first coffee that day. "We don't do anything special on Sundays, eh?"

"Nah, only if there is something pressing."

He reached into his vest pocket and pulled out a key.

"This is for the back door. Use it whenever you want."

He slid it across the table to Tyrell.

"Thanks, Ed. If I get bored, I guess I could make my way down here and maybe look through some of the wanted posters and files. Maybe I'll recognise someone," he shrugged.

"You are welcome to do that whenever you want. You can use the cook stove down here as well to cook yourself a meal. You have a key."

"That I do, Ed, and thank you very much."

"Just don't forget to lock the back door behind you when you come in or leave."

"I will, Ed, no worries. You said you dropped off your misses at church. You don't go, Ed?"

"Nope, I ain't that religious. The misses is and always has been. We'll probably have you over for dinner sometime and you can meet her then. Mind you, she comes around here every now and again too. You might see her here first. Her name is Beth Ann. She is a good woman. Cooks up a mean pot roast and pretty decent pie too, not as good as the widow Donale, but close," Ed smiled.

"Sounds like she is quite the lady."

"Yep, she has a younger sister named Adele, single, pretty woman. You'll probably meet her too. Her and Beth stick pretty close together."

"Hmm. If I meet her, I meet her I guess."

He had an inclination on what Ed was trying to do, but he was less than interested. Maybe as time went by, but right now, although it had been a long time since he had been with a woman, his heart belonged to Marissa. He didn't know why he felt like that, but he did. He was more likely to spend a night with a whore. A relationship really did not interest him much, not at that time at least.

"I suppose you are right," Ed agreed.

"What are we going to do for the next couple of hours, Ed?"

The Missing Years – Part II

"Sit and talk I reckon, drink some coffee and get acquainted. There ain't much else to do today. It is Sunday, after all."

At 12:00 p.m., they locked up the office and Ed headed to the church to gather his wife. Tyrell went over to the widow Donale's place to pick up his laundry.

"Afternoon, ma'am," he said as he approached her sitting on her porch. "I'm here to gather up my laundry."

"It'll be ready soon. Would you like a drink of lemonade and a piece of pie as you wait?" she asked.

"Sure, Ed tells me you make the best pie around," Tyrell said as he sat next to her and looked around.

"Oh, that Ed, he's always saying that. His wife Beth makes it exactly the same way. We both use the same recipe. I don't know how he can say mine is any better."

She smiled at Tyrell as she stood.

"I'll get you a piece and a glass of lemonade."

She entered the house and few moments later came out with pie and a pitcher of lemonade. She handed him the pie.

"There you go, Travis; and here is the lemonade and a glass. Help yourself. I'll check on the rest of your laundry."

"Thank you, ma'am. The pie made his taste buds dance. He savoured every bite. Even the lemonade was good. He sat on the porch looking at the scenery and listening to birds chirp. The breeze bent the flowers growing in her garden, bees and humming birds buzzed around, and the warm noon sun caressed his cheek like a mother's warm kiss. He smiled at the serenity and peace he was feeling as he waited for his laundry. Hearing the screen door open, he watched as the widow brought him his clothes.

"They are all done, fresh and clean."

She set the duffle bag on the porch next to where he sat.

"How was your pie, Travis? I hope you liked it."

"Indeed I did, ma'am. It was very good, and I thank you for your hospitality."

He reached into his pocket and pulled out some coins that added up to $2 and handed the money to her.

"Here is the money I owe. Thank you very kindly for washing up my laundry, ma'am."

She took the money and smiled at him.

"You are very welcome, Travis. The baths are always ready by 8:00 a.m. and I do laundry from 9:00 a.m. until 5:00 p.m. every day as well."

Tyrell rose from where he was sitting and grabbed his bag of clothes.

"Thank you for letting me know about the baths and laundry times. I'll be seeing you again soon. Goodbye, ma'am, and have a wonderful rest of the day."

He had been on the trail for a long time and had never really rested. Today he would. On his return to his room, he noticed the influx of patrons and wagons that were now scattering the street. People were dressed in their Sunday's best. It was obvious that church was out.

Continuing on, he nodded friendly gestures to the ones who noticed him, and in return got the same nod back. Ed had told him that the population was a mere seventy-five. It sure looked like more than that, with all the horse carts and wagons that were passing him by. Of course, he had to take into account that some of the folks he was seeing likely came from further away. The prairies, he knew, were a sea of farms and ranches scattered near and far. Chances were the church at the Fort was the only one in close proximity to some of those places.

The Missing Years – Part II

Noticing as he crossed the last street that dust clouds were raising in the distance from the horses and wagons that were leaving the Fort behind, he smiled. *Glad to see, not everyone lives here,* he thought as he turned the corner and made his way towards the stairs to his room.

Black Dog was lying in the shade under the stairs near the woodpile and back door. It was good to know that he wasn't running amuck; not that he ever would; he always stuck close. As long as he could see Pony, he knew Tyrell was near and that kept him grounded. Tyrell trod over to him and knelt next to him as he scratched the dog behind the ear.

"Looks like you found a cool spot to lie. Good place for you to be too, I reckon, guarding the stairs and back door, all at once."

Tyrell stood up.

"I think I'm going to take a walk maybe have a look around town. You can join me if you like or lie there and keep an eye on things."

Black Dog wagged his tail with contentment.

"All right then, you stay here and I'll see you in a bit."

It was close to 3:00 p.m. when he returned. He enjoyed the walk, did a bit of window shopping, had a coffee at a little three-table smoke shop that served coffee, and even bought his first package of cheroot cigars. He hadn't opened the pack and he probably never would. They were more of a novelty for him than a need to have. Black Dog perked up his ears when he heard Tyrell approach.

"It is only me, Black Dog; glad to see you stayed put. I have some jerky upstairs," he began.

Of course that snapped Black Dog out of his lulled state and he stood up and came to Tyrell's side.

"I reckon that got your interest. Come on, let's get inside."

Black Dog raced ahead of him and met him at the top of the stairs. Tyrell unlocked the door and opened it. Black Dog ran straight for the bed and hopped up onto it as he waited for his treat. Tyrell shook his head and snickered.

"Let me see if I understand this. During the day that's your spot and I only get it at night. Is that how you think this is supposed to work?"

Black Dog tilted his head and wagged his tail as if telling Tyrell that is exactly how it was.

"I guess I can live with that. Know this, though, if I decide to take a noonday nap, you get the floor."

Tyrell reached into one of the cupboards and pulled out his leather bag where he kept jerky. Grabbing a couple of pieces, he handed one to Black Dog, then sat down at the table to enjoy his own piece. He pulled out the package of cheroots that he had bought and opened them. Taking a whiff, he set them on the table. *They smell good, actually. Maybe I will have one, just not right now,* he thought as he finished his jerky. Sliding his chair away from the table some, he swung his feet up onto it, tossed his hat to the floor and put his hands behind his head as he leaned back.

It had been a lazy Sunday, but he was clean, shaved and his laundry was done. There was nothing else to do, but ponder; and ponder he did. Never in his life did he ever think that he would be a bounty hunter, but here he was exactly that, a *'bounty hunter'*. He wondered then what his old man would have thought had he still been alive. Would he have accepted his decision? In all honesty, it mattered little. He was his own person. He made his own decisions both good and bad, and he would live with whatever the fate that followed might be.

His eyes got drowsy and in only a few minutes, he was snoring. He woke up a few hours later as dusk crept in. His legs were numb from being stretched out on the table. He hated that feeling and sat with his feet flat on the floor until the pins and needles went away. Black Dog was lying on the bed sprawled out like a drunk. Tyrell stood up and used the toilet. He splashed some cold water on his face and took a long swallow. Tomorrow would be his first full official day working for McCoy's Bounty Hunting Service. He was excited about that in a way, also a bit leery and unsure, but as with all new jobs that one takes in life, those feelings were to be expected. It was a new leaf, a new chapter to add to his book of memories.

"Hey, Black Dog, I'm going to check on the horses. You might as well follow. Come on, get up; let's get."

Black Dog rolled over and looked at him as he put on his hat and strapped on his holster.

"Are you coming or what?"

Black Dog casually jumped off the bed and followed him outside. It was a warm evening and a warm wind blew across the prairie causing tumbleweeds to roll across the plain. Tyrell checked up on the horses and added another few leafs of hay. He leaned against the railing, his back to the horses and looked out across the open flat fields, then averted his eyes westerly to the Rockies. One day he hoped to return to them and Red Rock. Until then, though, he was content to be where he was. There was nothing more he wanted or needed. It was what it was. What would be, would be. All he had to do was stay alive long enough to make his return to Red Rock. That was his ultimate goal. No matter how long it took, one day he would return.

"Chapter 4"

That Monday a telegram came in from Brady. He had contacted Tanner McBride and Tanner agreed to split the bounty. They were closing the gap between them, Tanner travelling east and Brady continuing to travel west. So far, there had been no signs of Nicolai. It was possible that he had backtracked and could very well be heading east. They would know more once he and Tanner met in Hells Bottom, their agreed upon meeting point. The telegram was sent on Friday. If neither one saw Nicolai, then they would back track easterly as well. Not all was lost, but nothing gained. There was a PS at the bottom: *Will contact again, next chance I have. Brady.* That was the gist of the message.

"I guess we may lose this one," Ed stated. "Nicolai knows how to stay clear of law and bounty hunters, and is good at it. Has to be, otherwise he would have been caught years ago. What concerns me the most is that he is also willing to shoot and kill to make a getaway and that puts me on edge some."

It was true that Nicolai knew what he was doing. He lost the bounty hunter he knew was following him, and had indeed turned back east through the bush, staying not more than sixty or seventy feet from the trail at any given time. The bush, though, was thick and visibility from the trail was minute. He had stopped two days earlier when he heard and saw the man following him. It was easy for Nicolai to tell that the man was a bounty hunter dressed as he was and by the way he paid close attention to the trail and tracks that came and went. That is what gave his identity away. Once the man passed his view, Nicolai proceeded easterly. He would head south and into Montana once he bypassed the Fort in a few more days. That was on the 10th of June.

"Could always head west myself, Ed. If Nicolai has turned back, chances are he isn't going to come back the exact way that he left. He'll head southeast right along this side of the Rockies. That'll keep him in cover with less chance to be spotted," Tyrell suggested.

"Yeah, I reckon that'd be his route, too. Might be best if we both head south toward Montana. That will be where he is heading. There are a few places where we could cut him off. If this was sent on Friday," Ed stated, referring to the telegram, "then he's already three days ahead of us. Where he headed south, if indeed that is where he is heading, we can't know. We can assume he'd head that way before making the distance back to the Fort. I would say he'd stick close to the Crow Pass."

"Can you even ride that far, Ed? You're still using a crutch to walk."

"I can ride, Travis. It's the walking that is slow. We stay close to this side of the Rockies as we head south, all we'll be travelling over will be the plains, so there won't be much to deter us as we go. It ain't nothing like cutting trail through the mountains. The plains are easy to traverse. Only need to keep our eyes peeled for Blackfoot and Blood Indians and the odd rattlesnake."

"What do you have to fear from the Blackfoot and Blood Indians?" Tyrell asked.

"Nothing, really. Sometimes they can be petulant. Should keep in mind also, that chances are we ain't going to be the only ones travelling at this time of year. We could run into a renegade or two. Regardless, I'm up for some action. It gets tiresome sitting here twiddling my thumbs whilst I wait for my leg to return."

"If you're up for the task, so am I. We'll need to gear up. Probably best to leave in the early morning."

The Missing Years – Part II

"Yeah, it's 1:00 p.m. already. It'll take an hour or so to gear up. Might as well get that done now. We'll leave at first light tomorrow."

"I reckon that be best. How far to the Montana border from here?"

"Two or three days of hard riding. Should be close by this Thursday if we leave tomorrow."

They discussed their plans as they packed up the necessities. The rest of the day Tyrell spent sitting at his desk reading the history of Nicolai and the Miner Gang. Then at 5:00 p.m., Ed headed for home. Their gear was packed and ready. All they would need to do in the morning would be to saddle up their horses and head out.

Tyrell remained at the office for another couple of hours reading and looking through case files and wanted posters. As he familiarized himself with Canada's most wanted, he found as Ed had told him, 'not until you were in the business' did you know how many felons there actually were that had eluded the law. Some posters were dating back twenty years.

The job obviously relied on luck, coincidences and tips from civilians. There was no way to decide on where the felons were. That is why there were wanted posters and why the business depended on tips and luck. The four wanted posters he looked at had a total in cash bounties upwards of $10,000.00 dollars and that was only four out of the thirty or so that were in the folder. Indeed, it could be a lucrative business. *If a man could track down only four felons a month, he'd be swimming in dough*, he thought as he put the posters away. Easy as it sounded, though, he knew that it wasn't by any means as easy as that. If it were, there wouldn't be so many felons running around. They'd all be dead or in prison.

The criminals weren't stupid; they knew how to fool the law. A simple name change and a different location, and all of a sudden, you were as hidden as wolves at night. The felons who had an advantage were the ones with no black and white mug shots. Those whose names were on wanted posters with only a sketch of their description would be the hardest ones to find. He was able to draw that conclusion without even looking through the wanted posters, due to his own experience so far.

Making his way into the staff room, he poured the last of the coffee into his cup and sat down at the table. Tomorrow and for the next few days until either he and Ed found Nicolai or Brady and Tanner did, he would undoubtedly be put to the test. After all, Ed wasn't quite up to par and probably shouldn't be travelling at all. As well, Tyrell knew Ed had a personal vendetta with Nicolai. That, in itself, could cause more harm than good.

Ed, though, was the boss and if he said he was up for the task, then who was Tyrell to say otherwise. Besides, this would be his first bounty. If he and Ed did find Nicolai, then who better to have at his side than a man with experience such as Ed. He could learn procedures and gain wisdom. He'd keep an eye on Ed and at the first sign of fatigue due to his wounded leg or hubris due to the vengeance he likely wanted, Tyrell would remind him of the oath or make him stop and rest.

Pulling out the *'Bounty Hunter Handbook'* that Willard gave him, he read a few pages. The correct procedures were common sense mostly. Most of what he read were things he already knew from explanations he got from both Willard and Ed; still, it was a good book to hold onto. He noted that the one Ed carried in his vest pocket was all torn and creased, which told him that even an old time bounty hunter like Ed used the booklet and so he would too. Putting it back in his pocket, he took the last swallow of his coffee and exited the office through the back entrance, making sure to lock it. He turned and walked over to the corral and checked up on Pony and the others.

Pony approached him along with two other horses and he scratched each of them behind the ear. He paid more attention to Pony and the other horses left. Tyrell ran his knuckles up and down Pony's forehead while Pony swatted black flies with his tail.

"Might have to look into some spray for them damn flies, eh? I reckon Ed might even have some. I'll ask about that tomorrow. You'll be okay until then, won't you?"

Pony neighed and bobbed his head up and down, then darted off farting and kicking. Tyrell chuckled as the other horses joined in. *Pony must have converted them from the docile horses they were to the boisterous ones they are now*, he thought as he looked on. He couldn't remember the horses being quite that rambunctious when he first set Pony loose in the corral a few days earlier, but they were now.

Black Dog came over and was sitting at Tyrell's feet, watching the same entertainment as the horses ran to-and-fro, darting this way and that. Tyrell looked down at him.

"Crazy, ain't they?" he stated as he continued to watch.

It lasted a few minutes; then the horses went back to their usual selves.

"I reckon it is time to head inside. The fun out here is over," Tyrell said as he turned and walked toward the stairs.

Climbing the first couple of steps, he leaned against the building and looked to the western sky. It was as orange and red as smouldering coals on a cold winter night.

The Missing Years – Part II

"You know what that means, Black Dog? It means tomorrow is going to be hot and a good day to travel."

At 5:00 a.m. on Tuesday morning, Tyrell was downstairs in the office prepping a pot of coffee. It wasn't quite light out, but it wasn't dark either. It was that misty blue of early dawn, that time between night and day where everything seems at peace. Black Dog had ventured in with him and by scent, he found Tyrell's desk. He lay on the floor next to it, unsure if he liked being in there or not. Thirty minutes later while Tyrell finished his first coffee of the day, Ed showed up.

"Morning, Travis. I see the dog has found his place," Ed commented as he hopped over to him and handed the steak bone that he had brought specifically for the dog. In his left hand he carried a small metal box about the size of a wanted poster.

"Yep, he found my desk right off the bat; ain't moved since," Tyrell said as he stood behind the counter and looked on. "What is in the box?"

"A medical box, bandages and such. I always carry one when I'm heading out. It has saved a few lives, including mine on different occasions."

"What, are you a doctor too?" Tyrell teased.

"Not by any means, but you learn as you go."

"Where did you get it?"

"Ordered it in through one of those magazine things you get every now and again from the Hudson Company."

"A catalogue you mean?"

"Yeah, that's it. Here have a look inside."

He set the box on the counter and opened it.

"Almost everything you see in a doctor's office. How much did that run you?"

"Six dollars, I think. You have to replenish it as you go. Most stuff I buy from the store here in town,"

Ed replied as he turned his attention once more to Black Dog.

"How you doing, boy? You enjoy that bone and welcome to McCoy's Bounty Hunting office," Ed snickered as he now made his way to the staff room and poured a coffee.

Tyrell followed behind and sat down.

"By giving that dog a bone, you've made a friend for life, I reckon."

"Good. I like dogs, especially ones like him. Are you ready for what lies ahead, Travis? It's going to be a hot one today out on the flatlands. I hope the dog is going to tag along."

"I'm ready and you can bet Black Dog is going to tag along; I wouldn't leave him behind. He'll keep the prairie grizzly away and will let us know of any approaching danger."

"Think we should bring a packing horse for the gear? I know old Sampson can pack a good amount. He is the company's best packing horse and is available. However, we ain't got much, do we?"

"Not really. A packing horse might only slow us down. Pony can pack all my gear easily enough. You figure your horse can pack yours?"

Ed nodded. "I think so."

"No need for a packing horse then. That is my opinion."

"I agree. We can make better distance without having to lead one."

They finished the pot of coffee as they conversed. Then Ed handed Tyrell $250 dollars and pocketed the same amount for himself.

"That is in case we get split up or need to split up."

Writing his name down and adding the amount of money beside it, he had Tyrell do the same.

"Every time we head out on a bounty hunt we need to write down the amount of company cash we have. Like I told you, that amount comes right off the amount for any felon we turn in. If we don't turn anyone in, then whatever we have left has to be put back and the amount spent comes off the next bounty. It is always good to keep that in mind."

"No worries, Ed. I get it. It is simple actually and makes sense too. Are we ready then?"

"I am if you are."

"All right then, I'll get Pony saddled and my gear loaded. Before I forget, I was going to ask you if you had any black fly spray for the horses?"

"I'll round some up when we get back. They do need it I agree," Ed responded.

A few minutes later, after double checking that they had all they would need, the two men and Black Dog headed west. Once they reached Crow Pass, they would turn south and stay in the shadows of the Rocky Mountains as they coursed their way to the southern border, all the while remaining alert for any signs of Nicolai or Nicolai himself. They travelled for a few hours until they came across another traveller who was heading east. They stopped and had friendly chatter for a few moments and passed a canteen of water around.

"Did you happen to see any other travellers today near Crow Pass?" Tyrell asked as he took the canteen and had his turn at a drink.

"Nope, mind you, I was already this side of the Pass when I packed up this morning. I was in the Pass the day before yesterday. I didn't see anyone then either; been quite a lonely ride actually. I did meet a couple with a wagon heading to the Pacific; they were a bit west of the Pass on the other side, three or four days ago. Like I said, it has been a pretty quiet ride so far."

The Missing Years – Part II

"How long have you been travelling?" Ed questioned in a friendly manner.

"I'm coming from the Elk Valley. Been on the trail for a week at least. I hate to pry, but it sounds like you folks are looking for somebody. Should a single traveller like myself be aware of something?"

"Not really. We are looking for someone, though. I'm Ed McCoy from McCoy's Bounty Hunting Service. This is Travis Sweet."

"Wait a minute, you're Travis Sweet?" the man asked with exuberance.

"Yes sir, and who might you be?"

"You're not the Travis Sweet who brought down Earl Brubaker are you?"

"Maybe. Who wants to know?"

"Sorry about that. It is an honour to meet you, Travis and you too, Ed. My name is Alex Brubaker. Earl was my brother and I've been looking for you, Mr. Sweet."

Tyrell knew what was going to happen next and so did Ed, but they were ready. Tyrell thought maybe he could try and reason with Alex.

"Hold on a second. Before you make a bad decision, your brother drew on me first. It was self-defence."

Tyrell slowed down his breathing making himself as calm as possible in the two or three seconds he figured he had. Tyrell and Alex locked eyes. Sweat formed on Alex's upper lip. It was a sure sign that he was nervous and not too sure of himself. In the instant it took him to draw his pistol and fire, Tyrell already sent lead his way, the bullet smashing into Alex's hand and knocking the pistol from his now feeble grip. He screamed in agonising pain as his pistol fell to the ground. Tyrell swung off Pony and pulled Alex off his horse, wrapping his own kerchief around the wounded hand.

"You'll live, you stupid bastard. What the hell is a matter with you. I could have put one in your heart. Now, stand up."

Tyrell reefed him up to a standing position.

"What do we do with him, Ed?"

All Alex could do was stand there in shock, pain, and fear. The little he saw of the wound before everything went hazy and he slipped into shock, was a jagged slash that looked as though a few of his knuckles were missing, or at least that is how he thought it looked.

"Holy, let me catch my breath for a second. Goddamn it, that was quick."

"You learn as you go," Tyrell quoted Ed's retort from earlier that day.

"What are we going to do with him is the question at hand, Ed. He's wounded."

"I guess we'll get him fixed up and send him on his way. He ain't going to be much of a threat."

Ed slowly slid off his horse and grabbed his medical box as he walked over to the young man.

"Are you aware that pulling a weapon on a bounty hunter is frowned upon by the Mounted Police and that Travis here had every right to protect himself. He could have killed you and we would have buried you where you fell. I suggest you let me look at that wound and patch you up some. You have a half-day's ride to make the Fort. Go there and see the doctor. His office is on Main street. Or, you can do whatever you want once I'm finished."

Ed undid the kerchief and looked at the wound. Alex's hand would never be the same. He'd never shoot a pistol with it again.

Tyrell made Alex turn his head as Ed did his best in staunching the blood and wrapping the disfigured hand with a splint.

"There, that should keep you alive until you can get to a doctor. The Fort is the closest one."

By the time Ed finished his work, Alex had passed out from the pain.

"Damn it. He's passed out, Ed."

"I don't blame him for that. Let's get him to that tree."

Ed gestured toward a tree that was a short distance away.

"We'll sit him up over there. We're going to have to stay with him or at least one of us has to."

Ed helped Tyrell get Alex propped up as best he could and Tyrell took him from there.

"I'll get him over there, Ed. Don't need you hurting that leg of yours. One wounded is enough. You grab the horses and your medical box."

"Will do, Travis. You got him?" Ed asked as he watched Tyrell walk away.

"Yeah, yeah," Tyrell responded as he made the distance and set Alex up at the base of the tree.

Ed followed close behind and the two of them rested hoping Alex would come to so that they could get on with their business.

"I wish we would have never run across him, Ed. I've crippled his hand for life. Didn't want to kill him, though. He's too frigging young; I reckon mid-twenties. What a shame."

Tyrell removed his hat and wiped his brow.

"You did the right thing, Travis. I witnessed it. You are quick with a pistol. You must have practised a lot as you grew up."

"I did. My old man used to take me out shooting as often as he could. I used to stand in our shed for hours on end, slapping leather with imaginary foes. Of course, the pistol the old man let me carry at age ten or so was never loaded unless he was there. The pistol was heavy at first, but I soon grew used to it. Eventually, I was beating his draw and he was no slouch at slapping leather. I guess it is one of those things as you go along in life and you find yourself having to use it, that it improves."

Tyrell shrugged, it was simply something he had always been good at. The truth was, it was more of a curse than a Godsend.

"The problem is, this happens," he said referring to the incident with Alex, "and after a while, you start to wish you never practised at all."

Around this time, Alex began to come to.

"He's waking up, Ed. You sure we should simply send him on his way to the Fort. You don't think one of us should help him get there?"

"I see no point in that, Travis. His wound isn't fatal. If nothing else, it'll give him some time to realise how lucky he is to be alive. You had every right to kill him. You do know that, don't you?"

"I'm quite aware of that. I saw no reason to cut him down. He's young and stupid, but he is still a man."

"He's a man who was going to kill you," Ed responded with authority.

Tyrell nodded. He knew Ed was right and chances were somewhere down the road of life Alex may try again with his left hand. A few years' practice and a man could learn to use it too.

"Maybe so, but I didn't want to kill him, Ed. I took away his pistol hand and that alone makes me feel not very good."

"Forget about it, Travis. Like you said, you took away his pistol hand, but remember this, you didn't kill him and you could have."

"I suppose you are right, Ed. Thanks for that."

Tyrell stood up and leaned on Pony as he looked over his saddle to the west.

Alex looked over to where Ed was.

"What has happened?" he asked in an unclear state.

When the pangs of agony shot up his arm, his mind became clear as he looked at his wounded hand.

"Damn! Why didn't you kill me? You sons of bitches, I can't move any of my fingers. What have you done?"

Ed looked at him.

"We spared your life. Be appreciative that you'll live to see another day."

Alex tried to stand and Ed helped him.

"I suggest you head east of here, go to the Fort and see a doctor. He'll fix you up better than I can."

"This isn't finished yet, Travis," Alex said as a matter-of-fact, as he winced in pain and made his way over to his horse.

"Do yourself a favour and let it go, Alex."

"Eat scat! You should have finished me off."

Alex swung up onto his saddle, turned his horse easterly and headed toward the Fort.

"I guess he and I have a destiny, Ed. It is a damn shame he feels that way."

"He ain't going to ever use his hand for a pistol, Travis and it'll take him years to be able to slap leather with his left."

"True as that might be, I see a bad ending for one of us. Anyway," Tyrell sighed, "enough of this lollygagging. Are you ready to continue, Ed? We have a bounty to apprehend," Tyrell said as he looked east and watched as Alex disappeared from view.

"I reckon you are right. No use in sitting here; what is done is done."

Ed made his way to his horse and climbed onto its back. Tyrell followed suit and once more, the two men headed west toward the Crow Pass.

"One thing is for certain, Ed. This day didn't turn out as I was hoping. Don't want any more incidents like that."

"To be honest, Travis, you do know that every fellow who thinks he is a gunslinger is going to be slinging for you, don't you? You beat Earl Brubaker and the word is out. You're going to have to live with it and all the crap that comes along with it. That is just life circumstances."

"I know. I only wish it didn't have to be. It is what it is, though, and you are right. There isn't a damn thing I can do about it."

"Nope," Ed replied as they carried on in silence.

Travelling into the sunset that day, they set up their evening camp near the place where the Crow Pass entered the prairie. In the morning, they would travel south following the Rocky Mountain valleys that would eventually lead them to the southern border. If there was no sign of Nicolai's presence by then, they would turn back and head deeper into the northwest Rockies, circling around on the other side of the Pass. Somewhere along their planned route they were bound to run into him. There was no other route through the Pass unless a fellow went cross-country. Chances were, though, a man packing as light as Nicolai, wouldn't risk an escape via cross-country. That was their hope.

Tyrell stood from the low burning flames of their fire. It wasn't for heat and so it was small. The fire was to cook some beans and salt pork and to make coffee. He looked out across the plains the sun behind him. It seemed as though he could see forever.

"It just goes on and on, don't it, Ed?"

"If you mean the prairies, they do. You can see further than you can travel in a day. At one time you could even see herds of bison; not any more, though. There might be some herds, but most been hunted. The prairies never change, only its inhabitants do, and most times not for the better."

The only sound was that of sizzling salt pork as they continued their gaze. It was a vast and open land. The first dwellers were the Blackfoot and Blood Indians. How unfair life must have been for them when the white man appeared. Tyrell thought about that as he looked around. A gentle evening breeze blew making the flames of their fire dance as the scents of beans and salt pork wafted in the air.

"The food is done," Ed said as he scooped some onto his plate.

Tyrell gathered his own plate and filled it. They sat close as they ate, talking every now and again. Black Dog was alerted by something. He looked into the distance.

Tyrell nudged Ed's elbow.

"I think Black Dog sees something. You see anything, Ed?" Tyrell asked as he set his plate down and rose.

Standing with his back to the fire so the flames wouldn't affect his vision, he looked in the direction that Black Dog stared. He saw nothing. The only sounds were the crickets and that odd snap from the fire.

"I don't see a damn thing, Black Dog. What are you looking at?" Tyrell asked as though the dog would answer.

Black Dog stood stock still, his ears half perked. Continuing to look on, Tyrell thought he saw something move and he tried to focus in that direction. By now, Ed was standing next to him.

"You see something, Travis?" Ed asked in a whisper.

"I ain't sure."

He pointed to where he was staring.

"Do you see something over there?"

Ed squinted as he looked in the direction Tyrell had pointed.

"Looks like there might be something there. It ain't moving fast; it's kind of just standing there. The dog ain't reacting, but he is looking that way, ain't he."

"Uhuh, he is. If it were a threat, he'd let us know. Wait, did you see that? It moved. There is something over there for sure. Should we grab our rifles and see if we can get closer or shoot in the air from here. Might scare it away or make someone talk if it is a person. It's kind of spooky the way it stands there."

"Keep your eye on it. I'll grab our rifles," Ed said as he trod over to where their rifles were.

He handed Tyrell's to him and they cocked them, making them ready to fire. Whatever it was didn't seem to be doing much more than simply standing there. Tyrell and Ed were baffled.

"Are we going to try and get closer?"

"Might be an idea. It has to have seen the fire and likely us too. Why the hell would it stand there like that. Maybe we should call out?" Tyrell questioned.

"Sure go ahead. I'll train my sights on it."

Ed brought his rifle up to his shoulder.

"Psst, Travis, call out would you."

"Hang on, I seem to have lost view of it. Are you still seeing it, Ed?"

"Actually, I can't. Damn it. I didn't see it move."

Tyrell hollered out: "Hello, anyone over there!"

His echo was all that answered back. He hollered again and this time they saw movement, but whatever or whoever it was disappeared in the darkness out of their view.

"Did you see that, Ed. It took off like a bullet. Wonder what the hell or who the hell it might have been. You don't suppose it was Nicolai, do you?"

"I ain't sure what it was. There was something there. I saw it. The dog didn't seem to be too threatened. Maybe it was a bear something."

"Nope, it weren't no bear. Black Dog would have been on it like flies on scat. Pony would have acted up too. I don't know." Tyrell shrugged as he made his way back to the fire.

"I ain't putting the old .45-70 down tonight, Ed. I'm a bit stirred at what that might have been. We'll have to take a gander over there in the morning. Might see a track or something."

"Nothing is going to look the same in the morning, Travis. This is the prairie. In daylight we ain't going to be able to judge where it was, unless we do stumble on tracks; otherwise, forget about it," Ed assured.

"The grass will be trampled down, won't it, Ed?" Tyrell asked with some confusion.

"Nope, it'll be standing straight up by morn. We'll stay alert this evening, but I don't reckon whatever it was will be coming back."

Tyrell tilted his head.

"I hope not. It was awful strange. Most things would have taken off at the sight of a fire, you would think."

"The flames are pretty low, Travis. It might not have even seen it. Would have smelled the food and smoke. That could have been what made it stand there, trying to scent where the smells were coming from."

"A possibility, I suppose. Black Dog is lying there contently. I reckon it is gone now. That is all that matters," Tyrell responded as he poured another coffee. "Maybe it was a mirage we was seeing?" he joked as he took a drink from the cup in his hand.

Immediately as he moved his cup from his lips, a rifle sounded and the coals in the fire burst into smaller shards of orange coals. Whoever was shooting at them had missed, but their bullet had slammed into the fire only a few feet in front of them. They knew that they had only a few seconds before the shooter tried again. They both dove for cover in opposite directions.

"Jesus Christ, Ed, did you see where that came from?" Tyrell asked as he raised his head above the tall grass and looked into the darkness.

Black Dog was at his side waiting for a command. Tyrell sent him to cover telling him to stay low and approach. Black Dog darted to some undergrowth, raising his nose to the air as he scented for the intruder. Pinpointing the location, he crawled through the tall grass ever slowly getting closer. Again, a second shot echoed in the dark and silent night and this time it hit the ground only inches from where Tyrell was lying. He quickly rolled in the opposite direction.

"That one came close, Ed. Be careful and get into the shadows."

"I have no idea where the shots are coming from!" Ed hollered back as he dove behind a boulder.

"That's okay. We have an advantage. Hang tight."

They waited for a few minutes and again another shot was fired, this time in Ed's direction, the bullet hitting the dirt in front of the boulder he was hiding behind.

"What is the advantage?" Ed asked with concern.

Then he heard the growls and snarls of Black Dog and the screaming agony of the shooter as Black

Dog clamped down on the man's arm and tore at it shaking it like it was chew toy.

"Call your dog off! Call him off! He's going to kill me!" the man hollered in pain as Black Dog continued tearing at him, his jaws snapping as he jumped this way and that with savage intent.

"Black Dog, hold!" Tyrell commanded as he stood up knowing that the shooter was now incapacitated.

"That is our advantage, Ed, the dog."

Unable to see in the dark, Tyrell called out for the shooter to yell out so that he knew where he was.

"I'm over here, hurry."

Following the voice, he finally stumbled upon the dog and the shooter. Black Dog had his jaw clamped down on the man's bicep. His clothes were tattered and ragged. He had six or seven wounds from where Black Dog had bitten, none life threatening, but had Tyrell not told him to 'hold' he would have killed the man. Tyrell knelt down and removed the man's pistol from its gun belt and kicked the rifle out of reach.

"Good boy, Black Dog. Release, let him go, I got him now."

Black Dog released his grip and sat.

"Who are you?" Tyrell asked as he pointed the barrel of his rifle at the man. The man, though, didn't speak, only lay there.

"Hey, Ed, bring a torch down this way. I think we have ourselves Nicolai."

It took Ed only a few minutes to make the distance. In his hand he held a burning piece of wood. Bringing it close to the man on the ground, he made the man roll over.

"Goddamn right, that is Nicolai. Get him standing, Travis," Ed said as he stood back holding the torch so that Tyrell could see.

Tyrell set his rifle down and went to help him up. Nicolai came up swinging a hunting knife in his hand and made a brazen attempt at plunging it into Tyrell's gut. It was a bad move on his part. Black Dog pounced forward knocking Nicolai onto the ground his jaws in a death grip around his throat. Tyrell fell back almost stumbling, but he kept his balance.

"You stupid bastard! I should let the dog have you!"

He reached down and pulled Nicolai to his feet as he twisted his arm behind his back, his left arm around his throat.

"Are you going to settle down some?" Tyrell asked.

Nicolai only nodded his head as Tyrell removed his arm from around his neck. Keeping Nicolai's arm behind his back, Tyrell pushed it up toward his shoulder.

"Now, you're going to walk gently-like up to our camp. You try anything stupid, Ed here will put an ounce of lead in you. Do you understand?"

Nicolai nodded.

"Good. Let's get."

It took a few moments to make the distance to where their fire once burned. Tyrell had Ed grab him some rope and they secured Nicolai by tying his hands and feet. Then Tyrell kicked his feet out from under him and he fell to the ground.

"Hello, Nic," Tyrell said as he looked at him and Nicolai was able to see his face.

"You... you're that Travis fellow who fed me along the trail a while back."

"I am. Now I work for McCoy's Bounty Hunting Service out of the Fort. You already know Ed. You shot him once already and you killed the man whose place I've took. You should never have shot at us, Nick. You might have made Montana if you had kept going. Why did you shoot at us anyway?"

"Lost my horse to a rattlesnake a few days back. I wasn't going to kill you, only wanted to scare you so I could take one of your horses."

There was a short pause.

"I won't be saying anything else."

Nicolai shut up then.

"That is fine. You don't have to say anything else," Ed said as he brought over his medical kit and looked at the few dog bites and tears. He cleaned them and added a salve, then gauzed and bandaged him up.

"There, you'll live."

Ed put his box away and gave Nicolai a drink of water from the prisoner canteen.

"Nicolai Baurduer, you have been apprehended for crimes of the past and one recent murder, not by the law, but by registered Bounty Hunters of Canada. You will be brought back to Fort Macleod, Alberta to face these charges by the law courts of Canada. Since you have already stated you ain't going to say no more, you obviously know your rights," Ed said as he turned and looked over to Tyrell, who was adding sticks to the few remaining coals of their fire.

"There, this bounty has been told why we've apprehended him. It is always good to let them know."

"Is it even necessary to say any of that, Ed?"

"Nope, but if you don't, then anything he might say to you won't be admissible. For example, if he told you something about his crime or crimes that no one knew and it made his crime greater or lesser, it won't mean a thing."

Tyrell gently blew the coals to get them to take a flame.

"I see. I guess that makes sense."

The Missing Years – Part II

Finally, flames began to flicker and Tyrell filled the coffee pot with fresh water from his canteen and coffee grounds.

"I figure another pot of coffee is a good idea. I know it's getting late, but we have what we came for. That makes my day, after being shot at three times and forced into a draw all in one day. I'll tell you, Ed, I wasn't expecting all that on my first day out."

"Nor was I. We can turn around at first light now that Nicolai is in our custody. I'll have to get word to Brady. Hard to decipher where he is, unless he sends another telegram soon."

"I guess that could pose a bit of a dilemma. There are telegraph offices right through to Hells Bottom and I reckon Willow Gate too. Send one to each. He'll get it when he sends one from either of those places."

"Yeah, that would be best."

Ed looked over to Nicolai.

"Are you settled enough to be civil?"

Nicolai shrugged his shoulders.

"I was asking to see if you wanted a coffee. I would untie your hands for that, but only if you are civil. If you try anything, I'll shoot you."

"I'll take a coffee," Nicolai replied as Ed made his way over to him. Ed untied his left hand and tied his right behind his back using Nicolai's gun belt to anchor the rope. Tyrell poured him a cup and handed it to Ed who then handed it off to Nicolai.

"Thanks," Nicolai replied as he took the cup.

Tyrell poured another and handed that one to Ed, who sat close to Nicolai, keeping an eye on him. Noticing that, Tyrell smirked.

He called for Black Dog and told him to 'go watch' gesturing with his chin toward Nicolai. Black Dog wagged his tail and pranced a few paces away where he was close enough to pounce and far enough away to avoid any attempt by Nicolai to cause him harm. Black Dog wasn't stupid.

"Ed, the dog has him now, no worries. Relax."

"Yeah, I suppose you are right. Still, I ain't going to let my guard down. I kind of hope he does try something so I can kill him."

"Ah, you don't mean that, Ed. Let it go. He'll get what is coming to him. Murder, of course, will be added and likely that fancy assault legality, bodily harm and whatnot."

"I know. It's hard to look into a man's eyes knowing he killed someone you knew and tried killing you as well," Ed replied as he began to relax.

"I ain't hurt no one in years. Was trying to make an honest life for myself, what little bit I have left. The Miner Gang don't even roam no more. Think about that. Think about how I felt knowing that I would likely be put behind bars once you and that other fellow came snooping around asking about me. I think you would have done the same thing."

Nicolai took a swig of his coffee as he looked into Ed's eyes.

"Ten years might change a man, but any crime he may have committed and was proven to have committed never changes. You are wanted for a reason, Nicolai."

"I reckon it is going to be a long night. Especially if the two of you keep going back and forth. The best thing for you to do, Nick or Nicolai, whichever, is to shut up. That be best I think."

Nicolai looked at him and nodded.

"You're probably right, I've said enough already."

Before dusk the following day, they had returned to the Fort and Nicolai was comfortably in one of the holding cells at Ed's office. Ed showed Tyrell how to fill out the paperwork and had Tyrell sign off on it.

"Now you have to take this to the Mounted Police. They'll go over it, stamp it, and in a day or two they'll send one of their Mounted Police Lieutenants to collect him and pay out the bounty. Whilst you do that, I'll wait here. When you get back, I'll send off telegrams to Brady."

"Should I ask for anyone in particular?"

"Whoever is on duty will do," Ed said as Tyrell exited and headed over to the Mounted Police station, a couple of blocks away.

Ed made his way over to the holding cell where Nicolai sat on the bunk his back against the wall. Ed pulled up a chair.

"How are you doing, Nicolai? Is there anything you need? Are you hungry?"

"I could use some food. Ain't eaten in a while," Nicolai answered not saying anything more.

"I'll get you a plate of beans in a bit. Hope you don't mind beans."

"Beans are fine."

"How did you ever manage to stay clear of the law for this long, Nicolai?" Ed asked with interest and curiosity.

He wasn't trying to pry the man, only making simple conversation.

"It doesn't matter now anyway. I'll say this, the law is lacking."

"Don't feel much like talking, eh?"

"Not really."

"All right then."

Ed stood up and put the chair back at the desk he took it from.

"I'll get your beans cooking."

The Missing Years – Part II

Making his way into the staff room, he grabbed a can of beans from the cupboard and lit the wood stove. It took a few minutes for it to warm up and a couple more minutes for the beans to cook. He brought them to his prisoner.

"Here you go, Nicolai. There is some bread there too."

Ed handed him the plate and a wooden spoon as Nicolai nodded his thanks. Ed watched him for a few minutes, then turned and made his way back to the staff room. He set the coffee up to brew and slumped into a chair at the table. By now, Tyrell was talking with the staff sergeant at the Mounted Police station, going through the apprehension papers.

"So, he's wounded? But not in any harm of death; is that correct?"

"Yep, my dog took him down," Tyrell smiled.

"Maybe he should get the bounty," the staff Sgt. teased as he signed it and stamped it.

"He'll get something, you can bet on that. A big soup bone from the Snakebite, I reckon. Is that it, Sergeant.?"

"Yes it is. The paperwork is filled out correctly and we'll make a positive identification of him tomorrow. The lieutenant will be by sometime after that, depending when he gets in from the east. A couple of days most likely. Is Nicolai secured? You folks don't need the use of our cells, do you?"

"I don't believe so. I live right upstairs of the office. I'll be checking on him."

"Good enough. Thanks for bringing this to our attention so quickly, Travis."

"No problem. I guess we'll see one of you tomorrow, eh?"

"Yep. An identifications officer will be there sometime in the morning. Good night."

"Good night to you too," Tyrell said as he made his way to the door and exited. A few minutes later, he was sitting with Ed, drinking a coffee.

"The ID officer is going to be by in the morning to make sure we have Nicolai. It'll be a day or two before they come for him," Tyrell mentioned as he took a drink from his coffee.

"Good, we got lucky on this bounty. It usually ain't so easy. Most times we end up having to be on the trail for a few days at least."

Ed paused as he poured another coffee.

"I'll finish this," he said referring to his fresh cup of coffee, "then send off a telegram so that Brady knows Nicolai is here. He might as well head back to the office."

"Chapter 5"

On June 18th, 1891, the identification officer showed up at 8:00 a.m. and identified Nicolai.

"You have the right man, gentlemen. Ten years of running for him has ended. Our friends to the south will be happy to know he's been apprehended."

He signed his name to an identifications document and handed it to Ed.

"That'll let the lieutenant know he has been identified. I guess that is all. Have a good day, gentlemen," the officer said as he made his way to the door.

"You too," they said in unison as the officer stepped out into the street.

"There you have it. Your first bounty signed and sealed," Ed said as he looked at the document.

He handed it to Tyrell, who read it word for word as he made himself familiar with the legal identifying process.

"I guess I need to give you back two hundred-fifty dollars, eh?"

Ed chuckled.

"You thought I forgot did you?"

"Nope, I was only making sure that you didn't."

He reached into his pocket, and pulled the money out and handed it to Ed.

"I guess I have to sign that book too, eh?"

"You sure do."

Ed grabbed the book and scrolled down to his and Tyrell's names and crossed out the amount owed and then had him sign his name where it read 'Paid in Full'.

"There. Do you want a quick calculation on what your cut of the bounty is?"

"I think I have it figured. The company gets twenty-five-percent. The balance, is divvied up fifty-fifty, I reckon. Makes my cut, one thousand eight hundred and seventy five dollars or thereabout. Am I correct?"

"That is right. Feels pretty good, doesn't it?"

"It is definitely a nice pay day, indeed. Some things could have been a lot worse, I suppose. Either way, I am happy with the outcome; we are both still breathing and a wanted man is behind bars. To be honest, he was quiet last night. Didn't say two words to me about anything when I checked on him. They always say the quiet ones are the most dangerous," Tyrell smirked. "I reckon, though, Nicolai is going through every step of his life, wondering why and what it was all for. Sad in a sense, I think. But we ain't here to be self-involved with those we apprehend."

He surprised himself when he said that. It was right out of the handbook.

"That is true. Sometimes it is hard not to be a bit sorrowful. You bring in a young kid, for instance you know, a nineteen or twenty-year-old and you know he is going to hang. Sometimes you want to turn your back on that bounty or let them slip through your fingers."

"I don't know, Ed. If one is going to hang, the crime must warrant it. Young or old, an eye for an eye. Ain't that what the Bible says somewhere?"

Ed chuckled knowing Tyrell knew that he wasn't religious.

"I'll ask the wife," he smiled. "I do know what you mean, Travis and you are right. You can't go soft in this business and you have to stay levelheaded at all times. I wanted to put lead in Nicolai for killing Smitty, but I knew that was plain vengeance talking. So help me God, if he had tried anything after we secured him, I would have killed him, simple as that. The courts will decide his fate now. Lucky him."

That was when the front door opened. They rose from the table and stepped out to the counter. It was Alex.

"What do you want, Alex?" Ed asked calmly.

"Was only seeing where the two of you work from."

"You could have read that from the sign outside," Tyrell said with conviction.

"I did read it outside. You have something against the public coming into this establishment?"

"Not at all. We get a little concerned when a man that tries to kill one of us, shows up a day or so later," Ed made clear.

"Like I'm a real threat."

He lifted up his hand.

"The doctor says I'll never use it again. You crippled me for life, Travis. You took away the only thing I had to make a living."

"You make a living with your pistol?"

"You do, why can't I?"

"If that is the case, what are you doing pulling it on one of your own kind? We're both bounty hunters, I assume."

"You're little bit right. I don't have the fancy piece of paper which says so, but I did work with Earl. Private folks hire us. I'm thinking you might know something about that Tyrell fellow Earl was tracking. He wouldn't have come to you otherwise. In fact, maybe you are that Tyrell fellow."

Tyrell laughed. "You're making the same mistake your brother did, Alex. I never knew anyone named Tyrell. First time I heard the name was when Earl came a knocking."

"I guess time will tell, won't it? If that fellow is caught, I guess you'll be in the clear. Anyway, I ain't going to take away any more of your time for now. Thanks for patching me up, Ed. I'll be seeing you two again."

"Hold on a second," Ed started. "Are you threatening us?"

"Not at all, come on. We're all men here. I was simply letting you know that I'd be seeing you two again. We kind of work in the same circles. I'm sure our paths will cross again."

"Until that time, Alex, good luck in all your future endeavours. Now we're about to close up shop for the day, so you might as well let yourself out."

Tyrell lied to get him to vacate.

"Was already once on my way out when Ed asked me a question. I answered. I'll see you," Alex said as he stepped out onto the street and walked away.

Tyrell leaned on the counter and watched as he disappeared.

"I don't think we have much to worry about. He seems more interested in hunting down that Tyrell fellow. What do you know about that, Ed? Anything?"

"Only what I heard second hand from Riley Scott as I mentioned before. His wanted poster hasn't made its way to us yet. It will in time. The hand sketches being as they ain't definitive of the felons likeness usually stay in the hands of the Mounted Police, which makes sense, otherwise innocent folks could get shot. They put the odd one out here or there. That's about it. Eventually someone will drop one off here and it'll go in the pile with the others that are hand sketches. Those are the toughest bounties to track down. Private folk and people like Alex and Earl have a history of turning them fellows in. I don't know why that is, but it sure seems that way."

Again the front door opened. This time it was the town's telegrapher, Bud Donale.

"Got this in today from Brady, Mr. McCoy. He retrieved the one you sent yesterday to the Crow Pass township of Coalman."

He handed it to Ed.

"He's close, good to know. Thanks, Bud," Ed said as the telegrapher turned and exited.

"That's the widow Donale's boy Bud. He's one of the telegraphers here at the Fort," Ed mentioned as he unfolded the piece of paper and read it.

"Says he and Tanner are going to head back. Says he wants Tanner and me to meet and maybe offer him a job. You said Tanner is a friend of yours?"

"That he is. Wonder why he'd want to work in an office. He and Buck Ainsworth, another bounty hunter I only recently met, work together. I hope nothing has happened to Buck."

"I guess we won't know for a day or three. Won't see them until then. Is Tanner a lone wolf?"

"Hah. I'd say he's pretty levelheaded. He's good with a pistol and can fight some. I wouldn't say he's a lone wolf, but he does have a few quirks. He can't handle booze and is a good card player. Geez, what else? He is a bit of a ladies man or likes to think he is. Most times, he makes a fool of himself in front of them. Says things that ain't always appropriate, but it is all harmless. I don't know. I ain't trying to sell you a product from the Hudson Company," Tyrell chortled.

"I know. Figured you know him and I wanted to know a little about him. If he and Brady worked together and Brady didn't shoot him, then he must be a good fellow."

"That he is, Ed. Are you saying that Brady doesn't get along with folks?"

"He ain't worked with anybody. He does it on his own or he doesn't do it. If Tanner is likeable by him, might be an idea for the two of them to work together."

"Sounds like you are looking for a guardian for Brady."

"I suppose in a sense I am."

"Trust me, Ed, Tanner won't be that guy. Hire him if you like and send them off on a few bounties, but don't tie Brady to Tanner's apron string or mine for that matter. I'm sure Brady wouldn't even appreciate that. He is a man, Ed, and he is a bounty hunter. He's following your example. However, let him walk alone. You start babysitting him and you'll only be looking for trouble. You said yourself he is good at what he does, both here and out there."

"He is, but being good only makes enemies. I don't want him to die at the cost of a damn bounty."

"That can never be promised to anyone in this business."

The air grew still with an awkward silence.

It was hard for Ed to look at it that way and how could he expect anyone but a father to understand. He nodded his head as he reminisced.

"Anyway, we'll see what Tanner is all about when he and Brady make it back."

"Yep, that you will. I'm going to go check on Nicolai, maybe give him a coffee," Tyrell said as he turned and walked around the corner to the holding cells.

"Afternoon, Nicolai, how was your lunch?" Tyrell questioned as he picked up the plate and set it in the bucket.

"What could be disappointing about beans and bread," he said with little enthusiasm as he shrugged.

"I know; likely getting tired of beans. I'll make something different for supper. Want a coffee?"

"I would, thanks."

"No problem. I'll get it for you. Be back in a bit."

Tyrell grabbed the bucket that held Nicolai's dirty dishes and went to the staff room. Setting the bucket on the floor next to the cold water sink, he filled a cast iron pot with water then set it next to the coffee pot on the woodstove so it could heat up and he could do up the staff room dishes. He poured Nicolai a coffee, added cream and sugar and brought it to him.

"Here you go, Nicolai."

Standing, Nicolai took it from him.

"Thank you," he said as he sat back down on his bunk.

"I'll only be around the corner if you need anything."

"Yeah, I know."

Tyrell nodded and headed back to the staff room and waited for the water to get hot. Ed was in his office quiet as a mouse. He called out asking if Ed wanted fresh coffee and that he would make some.

"Sure, Travis, we have a few hours left before we close up. Go ahead, make a fresh pot. I'm reading next Tuesday's court dossier. There are going to be some men being sentenced that ain't the friendly sort. Means a possible outlaw reunion, if you know what I mean."

"Who are these men?" Tyrell questioned as he called back.

"Two men. One fellow who goes by the name of Ben Blackwell, is accused of three counts of cattle rustling, one of rape, two murders and four counts of attempted escape. Next fellow, Talbot Hunter of the Kingsley Gang, is accused of two counts of robbery, five assault with deadly weapon, four intent to kill, and six murders. Says here that he was once a regulator for a large cattle ranch southeast of Calgary. What do you figure? Those are a couple of guys you wouldn't want on the street, eh?"

Tyrell shook his head.

"You got that right, Ed."

"They're only being accused. It don't mean they are guilty yet."

"How can one be accused with so much if they haven't done it."

Tyrell was fishing for answers, legal answers that he knew Ed could answer.

"They get arrested for it, likely caught in the act. The Mounted Police are quite thorough when they investigate and if they can compare other crimes to the felons, they go ahead and charge them with those too. The judge, prosecutors, and lawyers decide after that. The law ain't perfect, I can tell you that. How is that fresh coffee coming?"

"It won't be long," Tyrell replied as he washed the bucket of dishes.

That done, he checked up on Nicolai. They didn't share any words. Nicolai was snoring and so Tyrell returned to the staff room. Sitting at the table with Ed, he drank a coffee.

"What else do we have to feed our friend in the cell? Can't only feed him beans, can we?"

"Can so, he's being fed, ain't starving," Ed chuckled. "I'll bring in some stuff tomorrow. We ain't had a bounty in a bit so we haven't stocked up. I'll get him something from the Snakebite tonight."

He lifted his cup to his lips and took a swallow.

"Things might get a little exciting here next Tuesday, being as we are the only registered bounty service in the Fort. We might get a judicial contract for the day."

"I guess that entails safeguarding the court proceedings and those in attendance. Why don't the Mounted Police do that?"

"They do, but they ain't as mobile as us. They have legalities and procedure to follow if something goes awry while we can act on our own accord."

He paused for a minute.

"For a business such as this, it is good quick money. There ain't any cost to us whatsoever. The court even pays for any bullets we can account for that we might have to use. It is a little thing, but it all adds up. It is good for the reputation of the business too."

"I imagine you already know what my next question would be, since I'm a greenhorn," Tyrell smiled. "Hold on a second, I think the dog is scratching at the back door. Hang on, Ed, we'll get back to that."

Tyrell walked to the back door and opened it for Black Dog, who made his way to his desk and took up his usual spot.

"Thought I heard you out there scratching. Got bored staring at the horses, eh?"

Tyrell knelt next to him and scratched him behind the ear.

"See you in a bit," he said as he returned to the conversation with Ed.

"Yep, it was the dog. He's in now. Since I'm a greenhorn, how does the pay work for a judicial contract?"

"It depends on how many fellows they ask for. Most times they take all or none. Anyway, they pay the company a flat fee of say two thousand dollars. For each man they pay two hundred to three hundred dollars a day. Until the trial or preliminary trial is over, each man earns that amount. The two thousand dollar flat rate, of course, is distributed to the men equally. That is how I work it anyway."

The Missing Years – Part II

"The company doesn't take twenty-five percent?"

"No need, because it cost the company nothing. Even lunch is paid by the court. Same as when there is a need to track someone down. If someone manages to escape, the judicial contract has an amendment that states they are responsible for all expenses for travel, shelter, etc., to the bounty hunting office of which the judicial contract was offered to and accepted by. That would be us."

"I guess that is a pretty good contract. A trial alone could last weeks. You're right that is a pretty good pay."

"It is. It doesn't happen often, but I bet it will next Tuesday. The entire Kingsley Gang outfit is well known in these parts, Calgary and beyond. I have some literature on them at home if you'd like to have a look. I'll bring it in with me tomorrow."

"Sure, always interested in reading literature."

Ed nodded.

"All right, I'll bring it with me tomorrow. You can have a read through."

The hours of the workday slowly dissipated into dusk and at 5:00 p.m., Ed headed over to the Snakebite to grab food for Travis, himself, and Nicolai. A round of steaks and all the fixings is what he ordered. On top of that, at Travis' request he bought a twenty-five cent soup bone that hadn't been scrapped of meat for Black Dog. The bone was the size of Ed's forearm in length and nearly as thick.

"I think the dog will like that one, Camille," Ed said to her as she wrapped it up.

"We could make a good soup from this one, Ed. You sure you want it for a dog?"

"The dog I'm talking about deserves it. It is the one I want, Camille."

The Missing Years – Part II

She finished wrapping it and handed it to him.

"The steaks will be ready in a few minutes. Anything else you want?"

Ed scratched his chin as he contemplated.

"How about one of those huckleberry pies the widow Donale has made."

"A whole huckleberry pie, Ed?" she asked as she grabbed one from the pie shelf.

"Yep," Ed replied.

He could almost taste it as Camille put parchment paper over it and slid it into a pie box.

"What is the total, Camille?"

Camille did a quick calculation.

"All together the steak dinners, the pie and the soup bone comes to eight dollars and fifty cents. You have that kind of money to throw around, Ed?" she joked as Ed reached into his pocket and paid her.

"For steak and pie, I better have," he replied as he counted out the coins and a few dollar bills he had. "There you go, Camille, nine dollars even. The extra fifty cents is your tip."

He smiled at her as she poured him a coffee to have while he waited.

"The coffee is on the house, Ed. I'll go check on the steaks."

Camille turned and made her way into the kitchen, while Ed sat at his favourite table and waited. The smell of cooking food made his mouth water. The Snakebite eatery always smelled good. His coffee was half-finished when Camille packed his to-go meal.

"Here you go, Ed. Steak, potatoes and corn on the cob, one widow Donale's pie and you already have the soup bone."

She slid his order across the counter to him.

"Enjoy, Ed," she said with a smile as he picked it up.

"You can bet we will, Camille. Thanks. We'll see you again," Ed said as he exited and headed back to his office.

It took a few minutes to make the distance. Setting the steaks on the counter, he pulled one out and took it to Nicolai.

"You get steak tonight, Nicolai. Travis told me you were getting tired of beans and bread."

"I am," Nicolai replied as he stood up and took the paper plate. "How am I supposed to cut the steak. You only gave me a spoon."

"Sorry, Nicolai. You'll have to eat it with your fingers. I can't allow you to have a knife and you know that."

"Yeah, yeah. Thanks. It sure smells good. I haven't had any meal like this in a long while. I'll make do without a knife."

Nicolai sat back down on his bunk.

"You have any inclination on when the fellows will be coming by to pick me up?" he asked Ed, who was still standing outside his cell.

"Best we know is a couple of days. You might be here until Monday, Nicolai. No worries, though. I'll be stocking up with grub tomorrow. You won't just get beans and bread."

"It wouldn't matter. I'll only get bread and water at the Mounted Police cells. This here is good steak, Ed. Thank you for that," Nicolai said as he continued to eat.

Ed turned and made his way to the counter where he set his and Travis's meal down and pulled out the soup bone for Black Dog. He brought it over to him.

It was almost too big for Black Dog's mouth, but he would manage. Ed chuckled as he brought Travis his meal into the staff room and set it on the table.

"Here you go, Travis. Steak and potatoes and corn on the cob. Plus, we have a huckleberry pie to eat for dessert and the dog has his soup bone," Ed said as the two of them dug in.

"Thanks, Ed. Are you going to let Nicolai enjoy a piece of pie, too?" Tyrell asked as he shovelled some food into his mouth.

"Of course, why wouldn't I? I might be a bounty hunter, but I like to think I ain't an asshole," Ed chuckled. "It would be cruel not to let him enjoy a piece of the widow Donale's pie. He'll be served bread and water soon enough, the poor bastard."

An hour later, they shut down shop and Ed headed for home.

"I won't forget to bring that literature on the Kingsley Gang tomorrow, Travis."

"I look forward to reading it."

Tyrell walked Ed to the back door and exited with him to the corral.

"We have any plans for tomorrow?"

"Nope, not that I know of," Ed said as he saddled his horse.

"How about bringing some black fly spray for the horses? We can spray them down at least. I reckon the flies are a bother for them."

"Alright, thanks for reminding me. I will, Travis."

Ed swung onto his horse.

"I'll see you tomorrow, Travis. Have a good night."

"I will. I still have some pie to eat," Tyrell remarked as Ed headed in the direction of home.

"Save me a piece?" Ed hollered back.

"Maybe," Tyrell teased.

He watched as Ed turned the corner then made his way back inside. He talked a few minutes with Nicolai and offered him a coffee.

"There are only a couple cups left. You might as well have one."

"Thanks. I would. That was quite a nice meal Ed brought me. I ain't ever had pie as good," Nicolai mentioned as Tyrell handed him a cup of coffee.

"The steak, I think, was better."

Tyrell pulled up a chair and sat outside the cell as the two of them conversed in friendly chatter.

"What do you suppose is going to happen to me?"

"I can't say, Nicolai. It is up to the judge, I reckon. You are being accused of a few train robberies, murder, and from what I've read, a fleeing charge from the Marshals down south. It was a long time ago, and you have been law abiding for the past ten or so years, but that ain't going to matter much since you killed one of Ed's men."

Tyrell took a drink from his coffee.

"Whatever made you come back to Canada after the Miner Gang was apprehended?"

"I was never really with them. I helped in a couple of train robberies, but I was never really one of them. They were a good bunch of fellows, if you put the law breaking to the side. I saw old Bill Miner give half of his loot away to a young family that was starting out. Another time he gave it all away to a young widow, whose husband he had killed that had pulled a pistol on him. He felt bad about what he had to do to eat, but he wasn't the type of fellow who could be tied down to a job. Didn't like being told what to do. The stealing became more of a game for him. He liked being able to fool the law. He took no greater pleasure than in that and for years he evaded them, until down in Sonora. I got lucky, I guess. When I made a break from the law and was able to get away, I said to myself I was done with those type of shenanigans. Wanted to turn my life around and so I took steps to do that, even though I knew there was a bounty on my head and that the law was doing all it could to track me down.

    I changed my name and took that job on the farm. Was there for ten years. No one knew who I was. Hell, I think even I forgot. When Ed started snooping around, I must have been a little bit turned around and jumped the gun I suppose. He might not have ever known who I really was if I had simply stayed calm. The fear of being turned in to the law took over and what happened is what happened. I don't feel any better for killing that man and for putting lead into Ed, but I'd rather die, in all honesty, than spend the rest of my meagre life behind bars."

    Nicolai paused as he took a drink from the coffee in his hand. He was already planning what he was going to do. At the first chance he got, he would take his own life, tonight in fact. He had eaten a good meal, spilled a little bit of information on how he was feeling. There was nothing left. No judge or prison was going to see him alive.

    Tyrell listened and although he felt sorry, he knew there was nothing he could do for Nicolai.

    "I don't know what to tell you, Nicolai. You broke the law. I can't say what will ever come from the train robberies, but killing a man for doing his job, I don't think will be tolerated. The courts will decide."

    "It has already been decided, I think."

    Nicolai grew silent for a moment and sighed.

    "The last of the outside I will ever see was out there near the Crow Pass where you and Ed caught me. I probably should have waited for the two of you to fall asleep, but at my age the mind doesn't always work. I could have stolen one of your horses if I had only waited."

The Missing Years – Part II

"I don't think so. Once we saw that someone or something was skulking around, we weren't going let our guard down. You might have been killed."

"Still, that is better than what is in store now."

"Maybe, anyway Nicolai, I have some things to finish up."

Tyrell stood from the chair and slid it back under the desk.

"I'll check up on you again."

"Yeah, sure. Thanks for talking with me," Nicolai said with sincerity.

Tyrell nodded as he turned and walked away.

He felt badly for Nicolai and wondered how his own life was going to play out. There were bounty hunters, hired gunmen and the law looking for him as well. He could relate to how Nicolai was feeling. Nicolai's past had caught up with him and chances were Tyrell's would too. Although their crimes differed and Tyrell had acted in self-defence, Nicolai did kill a man in cold blood and was wanted for robbery. If he hadn't killed Smitty, he wouldn't necessarily be hanged. That changed, though, the minute he pulled the trigger and Smitty died. Tyrell wondered as he sat down if the tired, old eyes of Nicolai would one day be his own.

Alone now with his cell slowly darkening as night came, Nicolai quietly ripped the blanket into a few skinny lengths. He tied them together until he figured he had enough length to tie around the barred window that sat high on the wall. Satisfied, he tucked it away under his pillow and waited. Once Tyrell left, Nicolai knew he wouldn't be back to check on him for about an hour and that was plenty of time to make redemption with the Lord before taking his last few breaths. He sat in self-contemplation, thinking about his past, his good deeds and his bad, and although he remembered more good than bad, he knew he was getting old. His mind had been failing him for a few years already, what with him forgetting things and doing things twice before realising he had already done it once. Nope, he was done with it. He'd much rather die from a bullet or take his own life than to spend it in prison.

At 8:00 p.m. that night, Tyrell offered a few more words to Nicolai as he bid him good night.

"I'll be back down and check up on you in a bit, Nicolai. If you need anything, then let me know."

"I will. Good night, Travis."

"Same to you, Nicolai. I'll see you in a bit," Tyrell said as he and Black Dog exited and headed upstairs.

"Time for a couple of minutes of shuteye, Black Dog."

Tyrell unlocked the door and the two of them entered. He sat down at the table and lit the lantern. The package of cheroots was sitting where he had tossed them a few days back and he picked the package up. *I'll see if Nicolai would like one, when I go back down,* he thought as he set them down.

Meanwhile downstairs, Nicolai was tying the shredded length of blanket around the barred window to the right of the top bunk bed that he now sat on. Making sure it could hold his weight, he yanked on it a few times as he wept. He knew what he was about to do was forever, that he would never see another sunrise or sunset or breathe in the fresh air that followed after rain. This was it. This was the end. He wiped away his tears, said a prayer asking for forgiveness, then slid the slipknot over his head, cinching it down until it was almost tight. He threw himself off the top bunk and died in only a few short minutes.

Tyrell found him hanging there at 9:30 p.m. The first thing he did was open the cell and check on

Nicolai's vitals, although he knew by Nicolai's urine-stained pants that not a breath of air was left in him.

"Jesus Christ, Nicolai! You stupid old man."

Tyrell fell back on the bottom bunk and stared. There was nothing he could do for him. The man was stone-cold dead. The protocol, he knew, was to leave him hanging there and to get one of the Mounted Police. After a few minutes of staring and shaking his head in both disbelief and horror, he stood up and reported the incident to the Constable on duty.

By 11:00 p.m., Tyrell and the constable hauled Nicolai's body by horse to the doctor's office where the doctor pronounced him dead and signed the death certificate. Tyrell didn't see the body after that. All he knew was that Nicolai would be buried in the prison graveyard near the courtyard of the Mounted Police station. Ed received the information an hour later and he came to the office immediately where he found Tyrell cleaning up Nicolai's cell.

"A damn shame what took place here, Travis. I've been in this business a long time and have only had this happen a time or two before," Ed said as he helped with the cleanup.

"He was bluer than a jay and as cold as ice, Ed. He crapped himself and pissed himself. I wish it would have never taken place on my watch."

"Sometimes these things are going to happen, Travis. It wasn't your fault. Nicolai took his own life. Any man wanting to take his own life is going to do it. You can't stop that."

"It eats at me, though, like worms in an apple."

Tyrell leaned on the mop as he contemplated.

"I should have stayed here a while longer. Maybe I would have learned what he was up to and could have prevented it. I would have taken his damn blanket away."

"Answer me this. Would you have killed him if he tried to escape or harm us when we apprehended him?"

"I know where you are going with that, Ed, and yes, I likely would have. There is a difference between being killed by another man in a struggle or fight and wrapping a few pieces of wool blanket together and killing yourself. A man has to be desperate to escape life to do that, so imagine how desperate Nicolai must have been not to want to spend a day in prison. Pretty desperate I would think."

"Sad as it is, Travis, remember what we talked about. We can't involve ourselves with felons or feel any guilt for doing our job. We apprehended him and we took care not to kill him. He did that all on his own. I am saddened, but I also know this is my job. It is what I do, and last I checked, it was your job too."

"Maybe you're right, Ed. I'll always remember the first bounty hunt I was ever on. I wounded one man for life, made a lifelong enemy, and the bounty killed himself. Not a very good track record to start with."

"I think you are looking at this all cockeyed, Travis. The man you wounded could have killed us both. The man we brought in, shot at us three or four times and even tried to stick you with his knife. I'd say your track record is perfect because you are alive to remember."

Ed grabbed the bucket of dirty water and dumped it outside, leaving Tyrell in his own realisation that indeed he '*was*' looking at it all cockeyed. Ed, was right. They were both alive.

He inhaled deeply. He made himself a promise then and there that he would never befriend any bounty he or anyone else brought in. This was his job and in a sense he liked it for a number of reasons. The pay was good, it kept him sharp and hid his identity. Not only

The Missing Years – Part II

that, he felt as though he was doing a service for the society he lived in. There were worse men running from the law than he could ever be and if he could help bring them in, the safer society was. The work wasn't so law-abiding that he was strapped down with bureaucracy and red tape. Bounty Hunters played by their own rules with very little red tape. There was an oath and that was virtually it.

The back door opened and Ed stepped in.

"The bucket is clean and the mop is leaning outside. It's getting on to 2:00 a.m. A few more hours and we'll be back here again. I'm heading to home."

"Yeah, okay Ed, thanks for helping me."

Tyrell looked at the floor and up the wall to where he had found Nicolai hanging. Pulling out his package of cheroots, he stuck one in his mouth and lit it. He coughed a couple of times at first, but soon grew used to the acrid smoke as he filled his lungs for the third and fourth time.

Ed still standing at the back door smelled the smoke and peeked around the corner.

"When did you take up that habit?"

"Just now. Care to join me?"

"Sure. I ain't smoked a cigar in a long time," Ed replied. "How about we smoke it out here," he suggested as Tyrell handed him the pack and he took one.

"Yeah, I'm done in here," Tyrell said solemnly as he met Ed at the counter. "Brought these down. Was going to see if Nicolai wanted one. I got my answer, though, without even asking. I ain't ever smoked one before. Bought them at that smoke shop down the way a few days back. I kind of like them better than the chew, I reckon," he said as he inhaled another lung full.

"They'll kill you, too. They are good for a treat. What makes the treat even better is a good shot of whiskey."

Ed went into his office and brought out a half bottle of whiskey. He poured a shot into a coffee cup and handed it to Tyrell, then poured one for himself. He was glad he hadn't left. There were things eating at Tyrell and Ed knew it would be best if he listened a while longer.

"Ah, thank you very much, Ed."

Tyrell kicked it back and Ed poured him another.

"Not in the need for anymore after this one, Ed. These two will take the edge off. Thanks."

"Are you going to be okay, then?"

"Am too. Going to be fine, Ed. What is done is done. You made me think there when you went and dumped that bucket of mop water. It made me realise that I was, as you said, looking at the whole thing cockeyed. I get it now and nothing more needs to be said."

Tyrell downed the second shot of whiskey and Ed filled it again.

"Hey, Ed, stop that," Tyrell replied as he downed that one too. Taking a breath, he shook his head. "Okay now, that has to be the last one, Ed. We got work coming soon."

"One more for the road, Travis and then I'll get."

Ed poured them each a fourth shot and they downed it in unison.

"All right, I guess that'll be it."

Ed left the bottle on the counter as he walked toward the back door humming as he went. He was feeling the whiskey, not so intense that he was drunk, but he did have a glow on and he hoped Travis felt the same. It would help him sleep if nothing else. Ed remembered back to one of the incidents he had mentioned, where a fellow by the name of Joe Hanover grabbed a pistol from one of Ed's men and right there

The Missing Years – Part II

blew his own skull apart. The only thing that helped Ed sleep for two days afterwards was whiskey. The visual horror of seeing a man do that at such a close proximity shattered his mind even now as he thought about it. He shook his head as he opened the back door. Tyrell was leaning against the counter as he looked on.

"Okay, Travis, I'm off. I'll see you in a couple, three or four hours."

Tyrell noticed the bottle sitting there.

"Hang on, Ed. You left your whiskey out," he began as he heard the door close. *Well, maybe I'll have another shot, then head upstairs,* he thought.

Finally, at 4:00 a.m., he made his way upstairs. The whiskey bottle had a couple of shots left and he carried it with him and finished it off as he sat at the table in his room and watched as the sunrise painted a brand new day for him.

The Missing Years – Part II

"Chapter 6"

Both he and Ed were late for work the next day. Only Ed was lucky enough to fall asleep. Tyrell stayed awake, drinking whiskey and thinking, a bad combination at the best of times. They were sitting at the staff table drinking black coffee, hoping it was going to make them feel better.

"Oh yeah. I brought some fly spray for the horses," Ed said with little enthusiasm and Tyrell listened with less.

"Uhuh, good, good. I'll ah, I'll get to that some time, I reckon."

"Ah, it can wait. Have another coffee, Travis and pour me one too, please."

Tyrell looked at him his eyes weary and bloodshot.

"I stand, Ed and I'll pass out. I didn't sleep a wink last night. Can barely keep myself focussed. I hate whiskey. You know that, Ed. I hate it. But, if you're getting yourself a coffee, I'll take one too," Tyrell smirked.

"Alright, I'll get it."

He brought the entire pot and set it on the table so that they wouldn't have to get up again unless necessary. Until the coffee grew cold, they sat in the silence. For the most part, as their bodies slowly came back to life and their heads stopped pounding. It was mid-day by then and only a few more hours until quitting time. They were feeling better and looking better when the Mounted Police Lieutenant showed up with their bounty check. Although Nicolai was dead, the bounty was due and he was there to pay it.

He also brought other news regarding a second death. Emery Nelson, a bounty hunter out of Ed's office who had been tailing Matt Crawford, had been found dead in his hotel bed. Six bullets riddled his body. All evidence gathered by the Mounted Police up in Hazelton, two hundred miles north of the Fort where Emery had tracked Matt to, pointed to Matt as the killer. It was bad news and the Lieutenant knew that, especially since Ed's latest employee Smitty Rogers, had also been killed only recently. The Mounted Police were beginning to think that Ed might be at fault by sending men with very little experience and lesser credentials to be tracking such unpredictable felons. The good news was that he also had with him a judicial contract.

"Afternoon gentlemen. Quite the event last night, I assume," he said leaning against the counter as Tyrell and Ed came out from the staff room.

"In more ways than one, Lieutenant," Ed said as he approached.

"Got your bounty check and some other news which isn't the best. Emery is dead."

Ed almost fell over backwards. His heart jumped into his throat and he felt as though he was going to be sick. He swallowed deeply and inhaled.

"What happened?" was the only thing he could muster as he put both hands on the counter to keep his footing.

"It is under investigation, but evidence gathered during the preliminary investigation points to Matt Crawford as the killer. He shot Emery six times. You do understand, Ed, that you cannot pursue Matt until the investigation is over. It has to be handled without prejudice and so some other office or the Mounted Police are the only ones who can pursue him."

"I know, Lieutenant. What a bloody shame. Emery was a good fellow. I'll get all the information we have on Matt for you, Lieutenant," Ed said as he turned away and went into his office.

"Thank you, Ed," the Lieutenant said as

he looked over to Tyrell.

"You must be Travis Sweet?"

He slid down the counter to where Tyrell stood.

"Yes sir, I am Travis."

"It is a great pleasure to meet you, Mr. Sweet."

He reached out his hand to shake Tyrell's.

"I'm Lieutenant Bob Cannon."

Tyrell reached across the counter and they shook hands.

"Nice to meet you, Lieutenant."

"You have quite the reputation due to that incident with Earl Brubaker."

"I reckon that is true. I wish things were different, but they ain't and I can't change it."

"Nope, you can't. Keep your presence of mind as you carry that Bounty Hunter license. As long as you have it you are bound by the oath not to provoke violence."

"You don't have to worry about that, Lieutenant. I know my place."

"Good, I'm glad to hear you say that."

Finally, Ed returned and the Lieutenant's attention turned to him.

"Here is everything we have on Matt Crawford."

Ed slid the folders over to the Lieutenant who briefly thumbed through the stack.

"There is something else, Ed. I have a judicial contract for you if you are interested. It is for four men. However, when it was sent we didn't know yet about Emery. I think as long as there are at least three of you, your company will be offered it."

"That puts a bit of brightness in my day. I think we can manage, Lieutenant. Thank you very much," Ed replied as the Lieutenant handed him the contract to sign.

The Missing Years – Part II

Ed opened, read and signed it, then handed it back so the Lieutenant could do the same.

"There is something else I need to bring up, Ed. What do you think is going on with these two deaths?" he asked as he signed the contract and handed it back to Ed.

Ed looked at him confused.

"What do you mean?"

"Doesn't it seem strange that two of the men you hired as bounty hunters are dead. Are you sure these men had the experience and training to head out after men such as Nicolai and Matt?"

"What training? There is no training," Ed blurted out.

"I meant, Ed, are you sure you were selective? You and Brady have been at it a long time without one casualty. Now there have been two. What I'm trying to say, Ed, is maybe you didn't send out the right men with the right experience. In a business such as this, it is best not to hire men who say they can do it. Hire men that *'you know can do it'*. That is all I'm trying to say."

"Both Smitty and Emery knew what they were doing. Emery worked for that outfit west of here and Smitty was one recommended by the Mounted Police out of a list of ten."

"I know. Let's just be a little bit more selective, you and us. We want professionals in this business."

Ed inhaled deeply he was getting a little hot under the collar.

"Selective? All right. I will be and maybe the Mounted Police ought to be too."

"Okay, Ed, I get it. I've wore out my welcome."

He picked up the folders regarding Matt Crawford, tilted his hat and began to exit. Turning, he confirmed that Ed and his crew would be on site at the Fort Macleod Courthouse that coming Tuesday.

"We'll be on site, Lieutenant. Have a good day," Ed responded as the Lieutenant nodded and exited.

"He was a bit of an ass, wasn't he, Ed?" Tyrell asked as the Lieutenant left.

"That is the way Cannon is. I understand his concern and it concerns me too. Maybe he is right. Good thing I've hired you," Ed said with sincerity. "How long has your friend Tanner been doing this stuff?"

"You'll have to get that information from him. I ain't sure," Tyrell said with some confusion.

Ed had just lost another one of his men. To ask such a question seemed odd at best.

"You ain't got anything to say regarding your man Emery being killed?"

"What is there to say?"

"Geez, I don't know. Maybe say something about how you feel about it."

"How I feel Travis isn't going to bring him back. He was killed; it is that simple. I am moved by it, but there is nothing that can be done. We can only hope whoever did it gets caught, even if it was Matt Crawford."

"You don't sound so sure that he's the killer."

"The fact is, I know that he isn't. Someone else did that to Emery."

"What do you mean?" Tyrell was curious.

"Matt Crawford doesn't use a pistol and would have never wasted six bullets."

"He's a rifleman then?"

"Long range shooter. His motto that he lives by is '*waste no lead on the living dead*'. Every man he has killed has been shot only once and from a good distance, nine hundred feet and further."

"That is some damn good shooting. How many men is it claimed that he has killed?"

"No one knows. We have information that says he's killed twenty-two men, but nobody knows for certain. Some claim he's shot more."

"Why was Emery tracking him?"

"He's got a bounty on his head worth ten thousand dollars. It is one of the biggest bounties ever offered. It wasn't only us tracking him; there are others. Riley Scott, the fellow you've heard me mention a couple of times, has been tracking him for a few years and although Riley is one of the best, he hasn't found him yet. Emery was getting close, but that has ended now."

"Ten thousand dollars! That is a tidy sum, ain't it?"

"It is, and we ain't going to be able to collect it until the Mounted Police find Emery's killer. Here is the thing. We can't track Matt Crawford. That is what the Lieutenant said, isn't it?"

"It is and I reckon you have found a loophole."

"Not really found. It was given to us by the Lieutenant. Since I know that Matt Crawford isn't the killer, I think we have every right to seek out Emery's true killer."

"True. So, what are we going to do?"

"We're going to wait for Brady and that Tanner friend of yours. If I think Tanner is a good fit for us, I'll hire him. Once we get him squared away and he signs the company contract, we'll decide on how to play our chips. The courthouse is expecting at least three of us and the Lieutenant knows that. If we have four men working here, I reckon I can send one up to Hazelton," Ed smiled.

"You're a genius, Ed. I reckon you are right. The Lieutenant didn't say you couldn't track Emery's killer.

Said only you had to stay away from Matt Crawford because the Mounted Police believe he's the killer. Uhuh, I get it now."

Tyrell nodded his agreement. It made sense.

"And that is exactly what we're going to do. Come on, I kept one folder about Matt."

"You sly fellow. Ain't that a bit illegal?"

"Not really. The folder must have fallen behind my desk," Ed shrugged with a grin from ear to ear.

"How is that going to help us find Emery's killer?"

Tyrell was curious. He understood that they could track down Emery's killer, but also knew they were supposed to stay away from Matt Crawford.

"This is the tricky part. You see, Travis, Matt Crawford goes by two names, Matt Crawford and Ronald Reginal. Both men are wanted, although Ron is wanted for some minor offences and his bounty is only worth five hundred dollars to a bounty hunter who doesn't know who he really is. If we can find Ron, then we have also found Matt."

"Don't the Mounted Police know that he goes by two names?"

"They do, but we bring in Ronald Reginal and to us he's just another bounty. Imagine our surprise when we learn that Ronald is Matt. Is it making sense yet?"

Tyrell was chuckling.

"It does now," he said with a smirk. "The Lieutenant never said you couldn't track down Ron Reginal. I take it we'll be tracking down two people then, Emery's real killer and Ron Reginal. Is that the gist of it, Ed?"

"That is the gist of it, Travis. Come on let's go have a talk in the staff room. I'll grab that folder on Matt Crawford."

Ed turned and walked into his office while Tyrell made his way into the staff room and made fresh coffee. It was going to be a long day of discussion and planning. From what Tyrell was getting out of the entire conversation so far was that they were going to try to find Emery's killer and at the same time track down a fellow named Ronald Reginal. If they found Emery's killer before the Mounted Police found Matt Crawford, they would be in the clear to track Matt. In the meantime, they would track his alias Ronald Reginal and investigate Emery's death, and his killer on their own accord. *Two birds with one stone,* Tyrell thought as he sat down. With all this new excitement and intrigue, Tyrell forgot he had a hangover. From the way Ed was incubating his devilish ploy, it was apparent that he had forgotten too. All was good.

Ed came from around the corner and tossed the folder on the table.

"There it is. There's that folder on Matt. Before we get started on that, I think I'll head over to the Trans Union Bank and cash this bounty check. You have a bank account, Travis?"

Tyrell looked up at him and shook his head.

"Nope. Don't you know that banks get robbed, Ed?"

"They do, but the money in them is insured. You want straight cash then?"

"I ain't sure. That is a lot of cash money to have on hand. Maybe I should tag along with you and open an account?"

"Yep, we can do that."

"All right then, we'll do it that way," Tyrell said as he stood and followed Ed.

The Trans Union Bank wasn't too far away and they got there in a few minutes.

"Here we are, Travis."

The Missing Years – Part II

Ed opened the door and Travis stepped inside. It had been years since he had been in a bank. They walked up to the counter and Ed set the check down.

"We're here to cash this."

The teller took it from him and looked at it, then had Ed sign it.

"Cash or are you depositing some?"

"I want one thousand, two hundred and fifty dollars put into McCoy's Bounty Hunting Service account. I'll take the rest in cash."

"Okay. Give me a minute to get it done," the teller said as he turned and walked over to a desk.

It took him a couple of minutes.

"All right, Ed, sign this deposit slip and let me stamp your book."

Ed signed the deposit slip for the amount he stated and the teller stamped his corporate account book. Then he counted out the balance and handed that amount back to Ed. Ed then counted out Tyrell's cut and handed it to him.

"Also, Travis here wants to open an account," Ed said as he stepped aside. The teller took down Travis' credentials, which consisted merely of his name and Bounty Hunter ID.

"There, all done, Mr. Sweet. Welcome to Trans Union Bank of Canada."

"Thank you. I'd like to deposit one thousand dollars."

Tyrell counted out a thousand bucks and held on to the rest. He handed it to the teller who deposited it into Travis' account and wrote it down in Travis' bankbook. He stamped it with the date.

"Okay. That's done. Is there anything else, gentlemen?"

"Nope, I'm done. Ed you have anything else?"

The Missing Years – Part II

"Nope, I'm done too. Thanks for the help, Clay."

"You're welcome, Ed," the teller said as they turned heel and headed back to the office.

"That wasn't so bad was it, Travis? You have a bank account now and a thousand dollars sitting in it."

"Yep, what am I ever going to do with a thousand dollars?" Tyrell questioned with humour.

"Save it and maybe buy me dinner sometime," Ed teased as they continued on to the office. "I guess we can go over that folder. Also, I forgot that I brought that literature on the Kingsley Gang for you."

"Good. I'll take a look at it once we finish up with the Matt Crawford folder," Tyrell said as he held open the office door for Ed.

They went back into the staff room and poured themselves yet more coffee and sat down.

"How many cups is this, Ed? A dozen or so?" Tyrell joked as he opened the folder while Ed sat.

"Probably something like that. Have a read through that and feel free to ask questions."

Ed brought his cup to his lips and took a slurp.

"Some interesting things in here. It says that Matt Crawford may have possibly killed up to thirty men, but there is evidence on only twenty-two. It says also that he is an ex-Ranger from the USA. What happened? Did he lose his marbles or something?" Tyrell asked as he looked over to Ed.

"Keep reading," Ed responded.

Tyrell took a swig from his coffee and continued to read.

"It says here that he was discharged from the Rangers for not following an order to kill. Lost all his honours, his pension and even his home. What the hell is that all about?"

Tyrell paused as he tried to make sense of that.

The Missing Years – Part II

"Apparently, he was ordered to kill someone but refused because the person that was supposed to die was a U.S. Government appointive, who was a woman by the name of Anne Greenwhich. Her husband was a cattle baron and a left wing official. Because he refused to kill a woman, they took away everything Matt had. That doesn't seem right."

Tyrell took a break from reading and looked over to Ed.

"Does that seem right to you, Ed?"

"I guess you haven't come to the part where it says those he has killed were all involved in the conspiracy to kill Anne Greenwhich. Everyone he has killed was a government appointive, attorney or right-wing official. That is another reason I don't think he killed Emery and why his bounty is worth so much. He killed folks that conspired against Anne to have her killed. It's still murder, though."

"Okay, so let me get this straight. He has killed twenty-two people who were involved in a conspiracy to kill Anne, who was running for some official office in the U.S. Government. The U.S. Marshals claim he may have killed thirty people. So who were the other eight?"

"That, Travis, is hearsay. They're trying to make Matt look like a mass murderer, which in a way he is. He has killed twenty-two people, all government employees at one level or another. What isn't told about Matt's rampage is that those he killed were as crooked as the jagged peaks of the Rocky Mountains and that the other eight were actually killed by someone other than Matt. I bet that was as clear as mud."

"Okay, I'm starting to understand where and how the missing eight were killed, but if that ain't written here, Ed, how do you know?"

"When all this started to happen three or four years ago, Brady and I were down in Washington. We were hired by Anne's husband, Neil Greenwhich, to keep our eye on Anne. We never met her personally. Her husband figured she wouldn't like that so much and we obliged to his wishes and kept our eyes on her from a distance.

When Matt was arrested for disobeying the order to kill Anne, he wrote a letter telling her about the attempt on her life and the conspirators who were involved. Anyway, she never got the letter.

As part of our contract with Anne's husband, we were supposed to monitor incoming and outgoing mail, that type of thing. Brady and I intercepted that letter. We never gave it to Neil or Anne, which I must say now wasn't probably the most professional thing to do. I figured this Matt Crawford fellow was a lunatic, just from skimming through the letter. I thought it would be best if we simply destroyed the letter, but we didn't and for one reason or another we kept it."

Ed paused there for a moment as he caught his breath and contemplated.

"When Matt escaped from prison and we started to hear about folks in all levels of U.S. Government being shot off their horses, through office building windows, hotel windows and the like, from distances over and beyond nine hundred feet, I knew then, from the letter, that it was Matt Crawford. As well, the fact that he was a sharpshooter from the U.S. Rangers, made it obvious to us. Brady and I figured that it would only be a matter of time before a bounty for him would be offered and that it would be worth more than any one bounty we have ever taken in. The rest is easy to figure out."

"That is quite the story, Ed. Have you ever been tempted to hand that letter over to the law?"

"Nope, I have no reason to do that. They have no idea that a letter to Anne from Matt even exists. No one does except you, Brady and me."

Tyrell scratched his face and swatted at a fly.

"How long was it before Matt made his way here into Canada? You said that it started three or four years ago. Is he wanted for anything up here in Canada?"

"As far as we know, he hasn't committed any crime here in Canada, but like the Lieutenant said, the Mounted Police believe he killed Emery," Ed shrugged. "Until that is proven otherwise, you could say he has committed a crime here in Canada, leastwise from the law's point of view, which ain't always the truth. We know he's been here in Canada on and off for a few years. He's a Ranger and isn't easily tracked. That is why most ain't got close enough to take him in."

"How does his alias Ronald Reginal fit into all this, and how do the Mounted Police know about that?"

"At hotels he's stayed in he often used that name when he registered. He's also been with a few cancan girls who knew him as Ron Reginal."

Ed stood up and dumped out his coffee. It was cold, black and bitter, not very good at all.

"I guess I ain't seeing the correlation, Ed. Ron Reginal could be anybody."

"I suppose so, but the description these woman have given of him, all claim he carries no pistol but has a long range rifle that never leaves his side. And then, of course, they described his physical appearance: brown hair, green eyes, about six foot, 210 pounds, left shoulder scar."

Ed rinsed his coffee cup and took a drink of water.

"There you have it, Travis. That is how the Mounted Police know Matt Crawford's alias, Ronald Reginal. I know it differently, other than those facts, because under his name Matt Crawford where he signed his name to the letter he wrote Anne, he added Ronald Reginal. I figure that was the name he wanted Anne to contact him by. It is the only thing that makes sense. My plan has always been to take Matt Crawford in, then offer the letter I have to his defence lawyer. It would release him from all wrongdoing, and he would get everything back that was taken from him. The other topside is that we'd make ten thousand dollars. Someone else turns him in, I'll still give up the letter to his defence, just the same. He dies or gets shot, I'll make the letter public and he'd be exonerated. I look at it as any other bounty because that is what it is."

There was a long silence as Tyrell digested all of what Ed told him. Some things weren't clear. However, he blamed that on lack of sleep. He understood Ed's reasons in keeping the letter away from the law. It was a simple equation of economics.

Capture him while he is presumed to be guilty of murder and you gain $10,000 dollars.

"I think I get it now, Ed. It makes sense in a round-about way. I ain't sure I like the way it feels, though. I mean you hold some kind of proof that Matt Crawford ain't what the U.S. Marshals and even the U.S. Government have made him out to be. You hold that one piece of information that can change the man's life from having to run to being able to maybe pick up where he left off," Tyrell shrugged. "I ain't saying it is one hundred percent wrong, but ain't it wrong by a little bit?"

Ed chuckled and shook his head.

"It might seem like a nasty way to collect ten thousand dollars, but consider this. Consider I didn't have a letter that would clear his name and we tracked him down, apprehended him, and turned him in for the bounty. He'd go to court and after that straight to the gallows for thirty murders. My way, we get ten thousand dollars and some corrupt people get put away and Matt Crawford walks free. That, Travis, is the big picture: justice for Matt and the right people put in prison."

Tyrell was smiling now and nodding his head. He saw the big picture. If Ed turned the letter in out of the kindness of his heart, it would be destroyed before it made it into the hands of the right people. It made sense that Matt Crawford's capture had to be the catalyst to bring attention to it.

"I don't know if it was the way you said what you said, but I see the big picture, Ed. It makes sense now and I feel better about what we've talked about."

"Good. I was beginning to think I was losing you. Anyway, I reckon we'll call it a day."

Ed stood up and made his way to the front entrance, closed the window shades and locked the door. From his office, he retrieved the literature on the Kingsley Gang and brought it to Tyrell.

"Here's this. The front is locked up. I guess I'm going to head home for some rest. I'm starting to lose my second wind."

"I hear you, Ed. I reckon I'll do the same. I'll take this Kingsley stuff upstairs with me. It'll give me something to do this evening."

Tyrell remained seated, looking around and contemplating if he even had the energy to make it up the stairs. Finally, with a bit of effort, he stood and exited.

Making his way to his room, he tossed the literature regarding the Kingsley Gang on his table, removed his boots and hat, hung up his holster and fell into bed.

"Chapter 7"

The sound of footsteps coming up the backstairs a few hours later as he slept made him sit up and listen. Black Dog was already standing at the door, wondering himself who might be coming up the stairs at that time. Tyrell made his way to the door and grabbed one of his .45s as he waited.

"Who do you think that might be, Black Dog?" Tyrell asked in a whisper.

The door flung open and he was face to face with Tanner McBride.

"Tanner?" he asked.

"Whoa, who the hell are you?"

Tanner almost fell backwards when he realised who he was looking at.

"Tyrell?"

"Yeah, it's me. What are you doing here?"

"We just rolled in, me and Brady. He said I could sleep here and gave me the key. He took off for home."

"Come on in."

Tyrell stepped to the side as Tanner made his way in.

"Ed and I weren't expected you guys until Saturday. Did your horses grow wings?"

"We travelled straight through. What are you doing here?"

"Come in and grab a seat. I'll fill you in," Tyrell said as they sat down at the table. "Brady didn't tell you?"

"Tell me what?"

"I'm working for the McCoy's," Tyrell said with a smile. "Can you believe that? I took the bounty hunter oath and the works, full-fledged Bounty Hunter I am."

"Ain't that something. Brady never said it was you. Glad it is, though. Said only his old man and another bounty hunter rounded up that fellow Nicolai we were tracking. Jesus, this is a nice set up." Tanner looked around. "You even have a flushing toilet," Tanner said as he stood and made his way into the bathroom, "and cold running water. This is the cat's meow, Tyrell."

"It is. Forget about it for now, though, unless you need to use it. Sit down and fill me in on what has been going on with you. How are you?"

"I'm doing okay. Scraping by. Lost a few bucks in Hells Bottom last February when Buck and I left you. And now you are a bounty hunter. How did that come about? Last time I talked to you, you said you weren't interested in bounty hunting."

"I wasn't then. Things change, Tanner. How is Buck?" Tyrell wanted to know.

"I couldn't tell you. Haven't seen him since March. We made our way back to Willow Gate and told Gabe Roy that you, or should I say Travis Sweet, wasn't interested in his offer. He wasn't happy about that, but it didn't matter. Anyway, we went to the saloon that night and Gabe and one of his hired jackasses showed up. He tried pulling the heavy on Buck and Buck shut him up."

"What do you mean shut him up? Did he kill the fellow?"

"The man probably wished he had. After Buck finished with him, the Mounted Police arrested him and hauled him off. They wouldn't even let me see the poor bastard. They revoked his bounty hunting license and told him he had two days to leave town. We were supposed to meet up before he left, but we never did. That would have been early March, I think. I ain't seen him since."

"It was likely Gabe Roy's doing that Buck was chased off. The more I hear of Gabe Roy, the less I want to hear. You have any idea where Buck is?"

"I figure he headed north. The Yukon, I reckon. He always did say he wanted to go back there. Are you working for the McCoy's under Tyrell or Travis? I best know now, so I don't call you by a name you ain't using."

"Good point. I'm using Travis Sweet. Ed knows nothing about my real name and I want to keep it that way."

Tanner smiled at him.

"I'll follow your wishes."

"Thanks, Tanner. Are folks still looking for Tyrell?"

"They are. A lot is looking for Travis Sweet, too. You're a legend, Travis. I bet that gets bothersome?"

"It does. Alex Brubaker, Earl's brother ran into me. He's one of the first so far."

"I ain't heard anything about Alex. Is he dead?"

"No. Won't be using his right hand ever again to slap leather."

Tyrell went on to explain all that had taken place since he left Mac and Rose's place.

"I'd say a lot has changed for both of us."

"It is what happens, I guess. Sometimes it can be for the better and other times for the worse."

"What would you categorize your present state of being, Travis, for better or for worse?"

Tyrell chuckled.

"To be honest, it's both. Good that I took this job and bad that I have to be on the alert for every man who wants a piece of Travis Sweet."

They continued to converse and reacquaint themselves with each other. They reminisced about their time down south when both of them were a little bit wild and stir crazy. They talked about how their lives had changed since then, and how odd it was that after all those years, they were in the presence of each other's company and on the right side of the law.

"Yep, things change, Travis. We had good times, I reckon."

"We did, Tanner. We had a good run."

Tyrell nodded and smiled as he thought about those times.

"Do you mind if I toss out my bedroll on the floor. It's almost daylight and I wouldn't mind a few hours of shuteye before I meet up with Brady and his old man."

"By all means, Tanner. You go right ahead. We'll catch up more tomorrow," Tyrell said as he stood from the table and made his way back to the bed, while Tanner rolled out his bedroll.

Tyrell was the first to rise that morning and he gently kicked Tanner.

"I smell coffee, Tanner. Ed and Brady must be downstairs. Get up," he said as he made his way to the bathroom and took care of business.

"Morning, Travis. Yeah, I heard some ruckus down there earlier; was too tired to care."

Tanner slid out of his bedroll and sat at the table as he put on his boots and jacket, then strapped his holster on.

"You almost finished in there, Travis?"

"Give me a minute."

Tyrell washed his hands and face.

"All right all yours, Tanner," he said as he stepped out and dressed himself while Tanner took his turn.

A few minutes later they were all together in the staff room and the introductions were over as they had their first morning coffee.

The Missing Years – Part II

"So, Tanner," Ed started. "Are you a registered bounty hunter?"

"Have been for the past five years, Ed. I took my oath and gave away my prints down on the west coast. I've been living in the Willow Gate area for the past couple years," Tanner said as he took a drink of his coffee.

"Brady tells me you might be interested in working for us?"

"I would be, if there was an opportunity to do so."

"There is. I'll need to see your license and you'll have to give away your thumb and index finger prints to me."

Tanner reached into his pocket and handed his Bounty Hunter ID card to Ed.

"There is the card and my fingers are ready," Tanner smiled.

Ed looked at the card and handed it back.

"The card looks good. If you are ready for the ink pad, let's get on with it," Ed said as he and Tanner rose from the table. "Follow me, Tanner and we'll get you squared away."

It took a few minutes and finally it was official. So it was that Tanner McBride, on June 19th, 1891, became an employee of McCoy's Bounty Hunting Service, together once more with his old friend Tyrell Sloan now going by the name Travis Sweet. Only time would tell when and how it all might end.

"It's nice to be working for such a reputed Bounty Hunting Service," Tanner said as he took another slurp from is coffee.

"You might feel that way now, but once the old man starts harping at you, you might have second thoughts," Brady joked as he looked over to Ed.

The Missing Years – Part II

"You're the only one I have ever heard harp, Brady," Ed replied with humour. "Don't be trying to scare off our help. We have two good men working for us now, son."

"Yeah, I reckon you are right. Tanner and Travis, I guess I'll officially welcome you both to this operation. Welcome to McCoy's Bounty Hunting Service, where our motto is: *'If you can't find them, we will'*."

Ed started to chuckle.

"When did that become our motto, Brady?"

"Today, June 19th." Brady smiled back. "I'm going to talk to Innis about doing it today. You don't mind, do you, old man?"

Brady always called Ed old man or Ed ever since he started working for him back when he was eighteen.

"Whatever, I don't care. Do what you want, Brady. It doesn't make no never mind to me either way."

"Good, because I would have had it done one day when you weren't here. Anyway, welcome on board Travis, Tanner. It will be nice having a few new faces around here that know what is going on. I don't want to say anything bad about Smitty or Emery, but I really didn't like either of them. They were hot heads in my opinion, but Ed liked them so I had too."

"How come you didn't like them, Brady? That is news to me," Ed responded.

Brady waved his hand through the air.

"It doesn't matter why. They aren't here to defend themselves, so I'll leave it at that."

Ed shrugged.

"All right then, but it is news to me. Now that we are back to full capacity, we have a judicial contract coming up on Tuesday here at the courthouse. A Kingsley Gang member by the name of Talbot Hunter and another fellow goes by the name of Ben Blackwell will be gracing our fine community on that day. I know it is a few days away, but I think each of us should prepare for it. However, I need one of you to head up to Hazelton and look into Emery's death. Any volunteers?" Ed asked as he took a swig from his coffee. "It is better that someone volunteers rather than me delegating someone."

"I'll do it, Ed," Tyrell responded. "I reckon Tanner and Brady are trail ridden."

"Are you sure?" Ed asked.

"Why not?" Tyrell shrugged. "I know what it is we're looking for."

Ed nodded his head.

"Alright, Travis. I'll get a map for you and a few pieces of information on the bounty. It is early enough that you could even get a good start today. Brady, Tanner, and I will take on the judicial contract."

"I'll meet you back here in a bit, once I get my gear loaded. I reckon Tanner can stay upstairs whilst I'm gone. When I get back, though, I'll want that place back."

He looked over to Tanner and smiled.

"Sure, Travis, you can have it back when you return. I'll see if I can't find a rental in the meantime."

Tyrell rose from the table and headed upstairs to pack his gear. Black Dog followed him and an hour later Pony was loaded up and eager to go. Tyrell gathered the few pieces of information that Ed had on both Matt Crawford and Ron Reginal.

"There are about five towns between here and Hazelton. Send us a telegram from one of them so we know you are close and alive," Ed smiled.

"I will," Tyrell said as he took the map and stuff from Ed and briefly looked at them. "Two hundred miles, eh? Depending on travel circumstances, I reckon Pony and I can travel thirty or so miles a day, so in six or seven days I should be getting close," Tyrell said as he waited for Ed to hand him some travel cash.

"Here's five hundred dollars. Sign here."

Ed handed Tyrell a pen and he signed off on it.

"Five hundred seems like a lot, Ed. You sure I'll need that much?"

"It is better to be safe than sorry."

Tyrell nodded.

"I guess I'll head out. Good luck to you folks with that judicial thing on Tuesday. Be careful as it proceeds. And Tanner, Ed dropped off some literature on the Kingsley Gang. It's upstairs on the table. If you don't know much about them, it might be worth your effort to have a read through. I started, but never did get finished," he shrugged, as he looked at Tanner.

"Yeah, I saw that this morning. I will have a read through. You be careful out there too, Travis."

Tanner shook Travis's hand for good luck.

"No worries, Tanner. I have the dog," Tyrell smiled. "See you all when I get back, in a couple weeks, I reckon."

Tyrell made his way to the back entrance and whistled for Black Dog, then swung on to Pony and the three of them left, heading north to Hazelton.

"Think he'll be okay, old man?" Brady asked as they watched him pass by the front window.

"I haven't got any concerns. Travis knows what he is doing and, like he said, he has that dog of his. He'll be fine."

"I'll vouch to that too, Ed. He ain't going to run into anything that he won't be able to pull himself out of," Tanner said.

He knew that without even second-guessing himself.

The Missing Years – Part II

"Well then, if you both think that, then I guess I ain't going to worry for him," Brady added as he walked over to his desk and sat down. "Hey, Tanner that desk nearest the cell was Emery's. It is yours now. Grab a seat and go through his stuff. Anything you need feel free to use. The rest you can give to Ed. He'll take care of it."

Brady pulled out some paperwork he had got behind on and started working through it as Tanner made his way to his new desk and started to make it his own.

"Good idea in getting caught up on your paperwork, Brady. I reckon I have some too," Ed responded as he made his way into his office and sat down at his desk.

It took Tanner only a few minutes to go through Emery's desk.

"I got the desk all cleaned out, Brady. Now what?" Tanner asked.

"You and I ain't going to be here long today, Tanner. We just rode in a few hours ago. I'm tired and need a long rest. I reckon if you have that desk to your liking, then you're good to go. Take some time and check out the Fort if you want or go have a rest yourself. I'll be heading home shortly. The old man can handle things here for a day. He might be old, but he ain't senile yet."

"I heard that, Brady," Ed hollered from his office.

"Good to know you ain't deaf," Brady replied with a smile. "There you have it, Tanner. Take today to rest up and do some sightseeing if you like. Be back here at 6:00 a.m. tomorrow."

"All right. I guess I could use a sleep. I'll see you fellows tomorrow," Tanner said as he made his way upstairs.

The Missing Years – Part II

Tossing his bedroll on the bed, he laid down. Although it was only 10:00 a.m., he fell asleep in only a few short minutes.

"Hey, old man, I have to get too. Tired as hell and could use a rest. I'm going to stop off at Innis' place and get him to paint that motto on the window first. You'll get some company at least. I'll pop over to the house after you get home today. Think you can manage without me here?" Tanner teased.

"Go on, get the hell out of here. Of course I can manage. Ain't got nothing on my plate other than some paperwork and I need you and Tanner rested and alert. You go on, go home and rest up, Brady. I'll be fine."

"Alright, I'll see you tonight," Brady said as he exited.

At 1:00 p.m., Innis showed up with his stencils and paint. He had painted most of the office buildings in the Fort and even a few of the private residences. Ed had been thinking about having the building painted inside and out and he would ask Innis if he could do it.

"Afternoon, Ed. Brady sent me over to paint that motto of his. How have you been doing?" Innis asked as he set his paints down.

"Surviving, Innis. How about you? Keeping busy?" Ed responded as he leaned on the counter and watched Innis at work.

"The print shop is doing okay, although we ain't had many painting jobs as of late. Nevertheless, we make do. Sorry to hear about Emery. What a tragedy that is," Innis said as he continued painting.

"Regrettably, in this business, it comes with the job. Any one of us could die tomorrow. I'm going to make fresh coffee, Innis. Care to join me?"

"Sure, I'll get the words outlined first. Printing backwards is always a bit tricky," Innis responded as he carried on and Ed went about brewing fresh coffee.

He watched Innis for a bit and even went outside to look at the work he was doing.

"Looks good, Innis. You have any more of the white paint you used for the company name?"

"I do. You want me to touch it up, Ed?"

"Sure, Brady is paying for it. Why not," Ed chuckled.

"Okay, I can do that for you. No problem."

"Good, I'd appreciate it, Innis. The coffee is probably done. Let's go have one," Ed said as he waited for Innis to clean up his brushes and put the lid back on his paint.

"I'll be right there, Ed. Just want to go have a look see at what I've done so far."

Innis walked outside and looked at the window. Everything looked fine.

"Yeah, that looks okay," he said to himself as he looked at it.

He met Ed in the staff room and the two of them drank a coffee as they conversed.

"You know what, Innis? The building is starting to fade. You have time to paint it?" Ed asked as he took a swallow from his coffee.

"I do. I could get started on Monday. You want the same tattered yellow?"

"I don't know. What color would you suggest?"

"I think the yellow does work for this building. Maybe go with a different yellow and blue or a grey trim. That would perk it up."

Ed shrugged.

"You would know better than me, Innis. Yellow and grey or blue trim sounds fine by me. What about the inside?"

"You want the outside and inside done?" Innis asked as he took a swig from his coffee.

"I think so. The inside ain't had fresh paint since the day I bought it. I was thinking some kind of light green or something. You know, office colours."

"How about white and green? That would smarten the dullness up."

"White and green it is," Ed said with a smile.

"I'll get the outside done first. That might take a week. It'll also give you some time to decide for sure what colour you want the inside. I'd stick with the flat grey for the holding cells. We can paint the bars flat black. I think that would improve the entire inside look."

"You are the painter."

Ed poured himself another coffee and offered another to Innis.

"Nah, I might join you for one once I get that window done up," Innis said as he stood and went back at it.

Three hours later Innis and Ed were standing on the street looking at the window dressing.

"Damn, that did smarten the window up," Ed said as he admired the new look and the motto.

"Thanks, Ed. It sometimes gets tough painting on glass, but this here turned out nicely. I guess that is it until Monday. I'll have that coffee now," Innis said as they made their way back inside.

Ed poured him a coffee and another for himself and they discussed the cost to paint the building's exterior and the interior.

"To do the building inside and out, including paint, I think you'd be looking at near three hundred or four hundred dollars. Does that seem fair, Ed?"

"Three hundred to four hundred dollars is fine by me, Innis. I'd pay that. You do good work and I know you are prompt. Yeah, for that amount, go ahead and paint her up."

"Okay then. I'll get the paint together and will start on the outside Monday morning. By the time I get that done the other colors will be here. I'll ask you again on Monday what colour you want for the inside. I'll order it then. I have enough yellow for the outside and likely enough for the trim too. The rest will have to be ordered. It won't take long to get here, though."

Innis took a drink from his coffee.

"What is Brady paying you for the window dressing?"

"I told him twenty dollars. That covers the paint and my time. Are you going to pay that or should I get it from Brady?"

"I'll cover it. Brady can pay me back," Ed smiled as he winked at Innis.

Reaching into his pocket, he handed Innis a few dollar bills, a ten and a five.

"There you go, Innis, twenty dollars. Worth every penny, too," he said as they continued to converse and drank another coffee.

"I guess I should head back to the shop, Ed. Thanks for the coffee and the contract to paint up the building. See you Monday," Innis said as he rose and Ed followed suit.

"Yeah, should probably lock up myself and head for home. It is early, but the smell of fresh paint gives me a headache. How do you work with that stuff anyway?" Ed asked as he walked Innis to the door.

"You get used to it after doing it for as long as I have," Innis said as Ed opened the door for him. "I'll see you Monday, Ed."

"Yep, I'll be here, Innis. Thanks again, eh," Ed said as he waved at him and looked once more at the window dressing. It did look good. Even the motto: *'If you can't find them, we will'* seemed to sum up what McCoy's Bounty Hunting Service was all about. Ed smiled as he read it a few times. Making his way back inside, he put the closed sign in place, closed the window blinds and locked the door. He sat at his desk for a few minutes as he contemplated until the smell of the paint overwhelmed him. Although not much work was done that day, he was pleased that Brady was back and that Tanner McBride now worked for them. The day hadn't been a total loss. Travis was heading north and Ed was happy about that as well. He knew Travis would get to the bottom of Emery's death and might even bring in Matt or Ron. Either one would be fine by him. *Yep, I have the right person looking into that,* he thought as he swung onto his horse and headed for home.

By early evening, Tyrell had managed to put some distance behind him and the Fort. He didn't quite make thirty miles, but he did put on more than ten. He was setting up his evening camp and would get an earlier start in the morning. He sat near the fire waiting for his canned stew and coffee to cook, Black Dog and Pony at his side. He was content he was doing something at least and not sitting back at the Fort trying to find something to do. He could understand now Ed's desire to be tracking down bounties. It was boring sitting behind a desk, hoping for some kind of break on a wanted poster. *Glad I volunteered for this trip,* he thought, as he now poured a coffee and scooped out his dinner. He ate what he could and fed the leftover stew to Black Dog.

The Missing Years – Part II

"Chapter 8"

Early Saturday morning, Tyrell, Black Dog and Pony continued north. They made the distance to one of the towns on the map that Ed had given him by noon that day. It wasn't a big town, but it was nestled nicely in the Rocky Mountains, which he would now follow. The town was named Hexton. It was smaller than the Fort and had only a mercantile, a hotel/saloon and a barbershop. Three roads now turned south, north, and west. He followed the one northerly that took him into the Rockies. He looked at the map as he rested on the outskirts near a creek. The next town was fifty miles north, a good full day's ride.

"Fifty miles to the next town, Black Dog. We should get there some time tomorrow, depending how far we get today," Tyrell said as he filled his canteens and shared some jerky with the dog.

Pony was enjoying a feeding of plush green grass that grew along the creek. Tyrell didn't even bother tethering him as they rested. He knew Pony would stay close. He looked around the trail; wagon wheel ruts scattered it and countless single horse tracks were obvious. The forested wood on either side of the trail was thick with spruce and cedar, thorn bushes and willow.

It was a nice area. The Rocky Mountains always were. He took a few more minutes to look at the beauty that surrounded him, then swinging into the saddle, the trio continued on their way. For three hours they sauntered on and for three hours all they heard as they travelled were the clip-clop of Pony's hooves and the pitter-patter of Black Dog as he trod alongside. Every now and again a bird chirped or a squirrel chattered, but other than that, it was quiet. There were a couple of homesteads along the way when the trail opened up to flat land. They were in the distance, but he could see them. Cattle walked about freely and grazed in the fields. He was surprised that there were no cowhands about, watching over the herd. Obviously, the ranchers or farmers had nothing to fear. A few miles later, a man approached.

"Afternoon," the man said as he grew close.

"Same to you. Quite the ranch you have there," Tyrell said referring to the one he passed a few miles back.

"Not mine. That belongs to Cruikshank. Mine is a couple miles north of here. You wouldn't have happened to see a few whiteface cows out and about, would you have?"

"Nope, saw some cattle grazing in a field. Ain't sure they were whiteface though."

"Was that down the trail some?"

"Yeah, near that last ranch."

"Those would have been Cruikshank's cattle. I guess I'll head back the way I came. Wouldn't have thought they got this far away. You don't mind if I ride alongside you?"

"Not at all. I ain't seen no one along this trail since I left Hexton. I thought by all the old tracks I would have ran into a passerby or two," Tyrell said as they continued north.

"I haven't seen anyone in a couple of days myself. I guess the mad rush to the Hexton gold fields is over."

"Hexton is a mining town, I gather?" Tyrell questioned out of curiosity.

"It is. The gold mining is about ten miles west of it. Over the past while a lot of folks have been heading that way."

"I had no idea they were mining gold there. It's a new strike I guess?"

"Fairly new, six or so months. The town ain't new. It's been there a while, at least five or six years. They mined silver there until it ran dry. Someone picked up on the gold. I reckon it is a pretty decent find, too, from all the wagons and such that have been going that way."

"You wouldn't know how far it is to Hazelton from here, would you?" Tyrell asked.

"Five days riding I would suspect. That is where you are heading?" the man asked.

"Yep. How about the next town. How far is that from here?"

"That would be Crab Apple. You could make the distance there by nightfall."

"Crab Apple?" Tyrell questioned. He didn't see that name on the map.

"Yes, sir. It is smaller than Hexton, but has a Mounted Police outpost which Hexton don't have yet. It has a hotel and a stable and an old mercantile. That is about all. Crab Apple was one of the first outposts this side of the Rockies coming from the northeast. It is an old town and at one time was likely bigger than it is now. A lot of old buildings and dilapidated homesteads, it is practically a ghost town now. That is the thing about gold and silver towns. The mining stops and folks move on. Well, here is where I turn off. Good luck on your travels," the man said as he slowed his horse and cut west on another trail which obviously led to the man's ranch.

That was the extent of their encounter. He never knew the man's name and the man didn't know his. Neither one had introduced himself and Tyrell was fine with that.

Crab Apple, what kind of name is that for an old gold town? he thought as he continued onward. At 5:00

The Missing Years – Part II

p.m., he made it to the outskirts of Crab Apple. Old crab apple trees grew on either side of the trail. Their apples at that time of year, though, looked like nothing more than little green nuts. He knew what a crab apple tree looked like and the trees he was looking at were definitely crab apple trees. Obviously that is where the town got its name. He sauntered on and even passed an old graveyard to the right of the trail. The old wrought iron fence and the graveyard gate were falling over.

He could make out the old headstones although hidden by the tall grass and weeds. He noticed an old, dilapidated building that was next to it and he swung off Pony. Tethering him to one of the old apple trees, he walked over to the building to have a gander. It looked like a church from the trail and as he approached he could tell that is exactly what it had been at one time. Black Dog trod along with him and they spent a few minutes looking at it and walking through it. Out of curiosity, he walked the short distance to the graveyard and walked around, looking at the headstones and reading names. Some of the dates dated back to 1810.

"Yep, this is an old graveyard, Black Dog. This here headstone has 1810 on it. Kind of interesting, I'd say."

They spent a few more minutes checking things out then headed back to Pony who was munching away at the small green apple buds. Tyrell had a bit of an argument with him to get him going. Finally, he relented and they continued into town. As he had been told, there wasn't much to the town of Crap Apple.

It was getting onto dusk so he decided to spend the night at the hotel. He would pick up his travels in the morning. He trod over to the stable to have Pony stabled for the night and after he pulled the bell rope for service a couple of times, a young woman approached.

The Missing Years – Part II

"Hello, mister. You here to stable your horse?" she asked.

She was a beautiful woman, dressed in denim pants and a long-sleeve shirt. Around her waist she wore a pistol that in itself was intriguing. Her hair was long and golden and her eyes were brown. She made Tyrell's heart skip a beat.

"Yes, ma'am," Tyrell said as he slid off Pony and led him closer to her. "I hope you don't mind if the dog sticks close."

"Not at all, as long as he doesn't bite."

She stooped down and scratched him behind the ear.

"He doesn't bite unless commanded," Tyrell smiled. "How much does it cost to board my horse overnight?"

"It is five dollars a night including feed and water. What brings you to Crab Apple?" she asked as she took Pony's reins and led him to an empty stall.

"Passing through. I'm heading to Hazelton," Tyrell said as she watched her remove Pony's saddle and set it on the saddle rail.

"You have a ways to go. You are getting close, though. You are going to be staying at the hotel, I suppose?" she asked, as she looked at him and smiled.

"Yes, ma'am. Are there any available rooms?"

"As far as I know, there is always a vacancy here. Not many folks pass through. Has your horse eaten anything today?"

"He helped himself to a hoard of apples down by the old graveyard."

"I'll get him some grain later then. By the way, my name is Serena Boalee."

She reached out her hand to shake his.

"Nice to meet you, Serena. I'm Travis Sweet," he replied as he shook her hand.

Her eyes got big.

"Are you Travis Sweet; the man who beat Earl Brubaker to the draw?" she asked with surprise and titillation.

"You heard about that way up here?" Tyrell asked.

"Of course. Everyone knows the name Travis Sweet. Are you him."

Tyrell nodded.

"I am he. I can't believe folks have heard about that this far north."

"It is my pleasure to meet you, Travis. You are a legend around here. Brubaker came through here a while ago and had his way with the town. We were all glad when he left. Not even the Mounted Police constable who was here at the time could get him to leave. Finally, he left on his own after taking advantage of our hospitality. He wasn't a very nice man. When the tale made its way here a few months ago that he had been killed, we all sighed in relief, glad to know that he was dead. I can't believe I'm talking to the man who ended his life. Brubaker beat up the owner of the hotel for no reason other than Mel asked for him to pay for the room he stayed in for three or four days. He never did pay."

"He wasn't a very nice fellow that is for sure. He beat up a woman friend of mine as well while her husband was out. He deserved the lead I put in him. Enough about that. I think I'll go grab a room at the hotel and be settled for the night. It was nice talking with you, Serena. Maybe I'll see you later."

"Maybe you will, Travis."

Tyrell nodded his respect and made his way to the front counter at the hotel. An old man in his late sixties approached the counter from a back room office.

"Good evening, sir. My name is Mel. Are you looking for a room for the night or a few days?"

"One night only. Is the hotel eatery open?"

"It is; so is the bar. The kitchen closes at 9:00 p.m., the bar at midnight," Mel said as he pulled out the registry for the hotel. "And your name is?" he asked as he looked at him.

"Travis," Tyrell responded not wanting to give up his fake last name, knowing it wasn't necessary. Mel wrote the name down and handed him a key.

"Here you go, Travis. It's room number 4 up the stairs and the second door on your left. I take it Serena has already taken care of your horse?"

"Yes, she has," Tyrell said as he grabbed his saddlebags and headed up the stairs.

The room wasn't big. It had a bed, a nightstand, a washbasin and a hand pump sink for water. The toilet was in the hall and shared by those staying there. Tyrell tossed his bags on the bed and looked around. It would do for the night. Looking out the window he could see the stable and across from that was the Mounted Police station. To the back of the stable was a small house. Obviously, it was where Serena lived. He could see her as she made her way to it and slipped inside. He closed the curtain. Making his way over to his bed, he lay down wanting to have a quick nap before he went and ate. He looked up to the ceiling rafters until his eyes got heavy and he gently dozed.

When he awoke, it was too late to eat; the eatery was closed, but he could hear that the saloon was starting to get busy. He thought for a moment that he might head downstairs and have a drink. Deciding instead to stay in his room, he ate beef jerky and sipped on water.

Serena stopped by an hour or so later. She had a bottle of whiskey and some sandwiches.

"Evening, Travis," she said as Tyrell opened the door for her. "I brought you some sandwiches, and if you like, a drink of whiskey too."

She smiled as she set the plate of sandwiches and the bottle down on his nightstand.

"I didn't see you in the eatery earlier and figured you might want something to eat."

She looked at him and sat down on the bed.

"Thanks, Serena. I am a bit hungry and the sandwiches look good."

He helped himself to one and sat down on the night chair by the window.

"Are you going to join me?" he asked as he took a bite.

"Only, if you'll join me in a shot of whiskey."

She stood up and poured them each a shot, then handed him one. He took it, not sure he wanted it, but he took it anyway.

"Down the hatch," she said as she brought the shot to her lips and kicked it back.

Tyrell smiled and did the same. By the time the sandwiches were finished, they both were a little bit on the tipsy side and the innocent visit turned into a night of lust. Serena fell onto his bed and gestured for him to join her and he did.

It was early morning when Serena rolled out of his bed, dressed, walked tippy-toed to the door and exited. Tyrell opened one eye as he watched her leave. Smiling to himself, he put his hands behind his head, months of aching desire now satisfied. She was a beautiful woman and the night he spent with her, he'd not soon forget, nor would she. She had made love to Travis Sweet, the legend. She left him that morning with a smile of satisfaction. It had been a long time since she had been with a man and she could tell it had been a long time since Travis had been with a woman. All was well.

Tyrell dug into the pocket in his pants that were lying on the floor and pulled out his watch. It was 6:00 a.m. *I guess I should head out, the morn is here,* he thought as he dressed. He stopped off at the eatery and had a morning coffee, then made his way to the stable. He didn't bother pulling the bell rope and instead put a five dollar bill in the pay can that was nailed to the stall. It was there for those who left before Serena was on duty. Each stall had its own can.

Saddling up Pony and loading his gear, he whistled for Black Dog who wasn't too far away, and the three of them continued with their journey heading north to Hazelton. On his return trip, if he happened to come back that way, he would spend the night again at the hotel and buy Serena dinner.

At 11:00 a.m. that Sunday morning after travelling for four hours, Tyrell pulled Pony to a halt and swung off his back.

"We're going to take a rest here for a bit, Pony. There is some nice green grass for you and some welcoming shade for me and the dog. Sure got hot today, whew," Tyrell said as he removed his hat and dumped water from his canteen over his head.

After he had a long swallow, he cupped his hand and poured some water for Black Dog who lapped up the cold drink.

"Hope we can find water soon, the canteens are getting low," Tyrell mentioned as he took another long swallow and offered another to Black Dog.

They sat in the shade, listened to the birds and watched as butterflies fluttered by.

The sound of an approaching wagon got his attention and he commanded Black Dog to stay alert as he sent him off to hide in the undergrowth. A man, a woman, and two kids were riding in the wagon he could see. As they approached, he stood up.

"Hello there," he said as the man got his horse team to slow down and then halt.

"Hello back. How are things this morning?" the man asked as his children scurried into the back of the wagon and looked on.

"Good so far. Nice and hot today," Tyrell said as he walked closer.

"July is going to be even hotter, I reckon. We're heading home to Crab Apple. Been on the trail for a few days already," the man mentioned as he squirmed on the wagon seat, trying to get comfortable.

"You live there then?" Tyrell asked in a friendly manner.

"Yep, we own the Boalee stable."

It was then he realised that he was likely talking to Serena's father. He felt a little bit embarrassed, but he and Serena were both consenting.

"Isn't that interesting. I boarded my horse there last night."

"In that case, I reckon you met our oldest daughter Serena, right?" the man asked.

"I did. She was very accommodating. I'll be boarding my horse there on my return too. I'm heading to Hazelton and have some business up there."

"The weather stays as it is, you'll make good timing. It will be a few more days 'til you get there. It is a nice ride. The trail is in good shape and we didn't run into even one renegade Blood Indian. Usually one does."

"Are they a friendly sort?" Tyrell asked.

"Most is, yep. Offer them some food and maybe tobacco and they let you be."

"That is good to know. I have never met any Blood Indians. I know the Blackfoot, though."

"You're coming up from the south then?"

"Am so. Been on the trail for a couple of days myself, slowly making the distance I need to make. I ain't in any rush." Tyrell looked around. "Too nice of territory to be in a rush. You see any bear along the way?"

"Saw some tracks, no visual on bear. It has been a pretty peaceful trip. Ran into a couple of folks heading north, but that is about it."

"Do you know if the next town has a telegraph office?"

"Not the next town, but Fairmount does. It is about thirty miles from here. You should get there some time tomorrow. The next town ain't that far from here, ten miles maybe. It ain't very big; in fact smaller then Crab Apple. It is more of a stagecoach outpost than a town. There is a mercantile with a coffee counter that has soup and stuff. That is about all there is."

"What is the name of the town?"

"Cresdale," the man said as he looked down the trail. "Anyway, we best get going. We have a few hours before we get home. It was nice talking to you," the man said as he tilted his hat and snapped the reins, to get his horse team to giddy-up.

"Nice talking with you, too," Tyrell said as he tilted his own hat to show respect.

He watched as the wagon creaked by and he waited a few moments for Black Dog to come out from hiding.

"Those were friendly folks eh, Black Dog?"

He swung up onto Pony's back.

"I figure we've had a long enough rest. Come on, let's see if we can't get to Cresdale before the stars are out. That way we will make the distance to Fairmount by tomorrow and I can send a telegram back to Ed... I wonder how they're getting on with Tanner?" he questioned in a low murmur to himself.

A few hours later, he was at the mercantile in Cresdale sitting at the counter and waiting for a coffee and water to fill his canteens. The stagecoach pulled up a few minutes later and it didn't take long for the coffee counter to fill up. He saw a rickety old man standing looking for a place to sit, and so Tyrell rose from his stool and offered it to the old fellow.

"Here, let me offer you my spot. Go ahead, you can sit there," Tyrell said as he gestured toward the stool.

"Thank you," the old man said as he made his way to the stool and sat.

Tyrell leaned on the counter next to him, still waiting for his coffee.

"What are you having, young fellow?" the old man asked.

"Waiting for a coffee to drink and water to fill my canteens," Tyrell replied as he smiled at the man.

"Yes, coffee and soup I think I will have. Can I buy you a bowl?"

Tyrell shook his head.

"No sir, that is all right. I can't be stopped for too long. Trying to get to Hazelton."

"You ain't going to make that distance today. Let me buy you a bowl of soup. You were kind enough to give up your sitting stool. It is the least I can do for you."

Tyrell chuckled.

"Sir, I appreciate your offer, but like I said, I really only want a coffee."

"Okay, I won't bother to press you anymore. At least let me pay for your coffee."

"All right, I'll let you do that," Tyrell relented, so the old man wouldn't feel offended.

He was finishing the last of his coffee when the old man's coffee and soup showed up.

"I guess I should be heading out. Thanks for the coffee, sir."

Tyrell nodded and tilted his hat as leaned away from the counter.

"You are welcome. Thank you for the stool," the man said with sincerity and appreciation.

Tyrell nodded and tilted his hat again, then made his way outside to Pony. They travelled for another two hours until finally finding a suitable spot to set up for the evening. As darkness settled in and his evening fire burned, he slurped coffee and enjoyed the serenity of the Rocky Mountains. The eerie sound of an owl as he looked into the flames caused goose bumps to crawl up his arms and he shivered as it sounded again.

The Missing Years – Part II

"Chapter 9"

As the morning dew glistened, Tyrell rose from his bedroll. Stretching, he added a stick to the slow burning embers of his past evening fire. It was June 22nd and even at that time of day, the sun was already warming things up.

Back at the Fort, it wasn't only the sun warming things up, but also all the hootenanny that was going on with the arrival of two prisoners due in court the next day. Ed, Brady and Tanner had already shown their presence by securing the courthouse holding cells where the two felons were being held. They meandered around outside and on the street, counting folks coming and leaving the town, paying close attention to the more unsavoury type. The Mounted Police all wore their 'on duty' garb. Dressed as they were in their reds, blues, and yellows, they stuck out like swollen blistered thumbs. That in itself caused more wonderment and curiosity from the town folk and visiting patrons. Tanner leaned up against the outside wall of the courthouse and tilted his hat over his eyes as he looked easterly.

In the distance, he could see dust rising. He guessed between four or five riders packing heavy were approaching and at a good speed too. He shook his head, *damn, that just might be trouble,* he thought as he braced himself and waited.

He wasn't the only one who had taken note of the approaching riders. The six or so Mounted Police split up and went in different directions as though they too were expecting an unwanted presence to envelope the town. Finally, the riders came into view and halted their horses as they approached the Snakebite Hotel. Dismounting, they tethered their rides and entered. Tanner slowly walked in that direction, appearing as though he was uncaring, keeping his eyes on the hotel

The Missing Years – Part II

entrance and the four horses tethered outside. He purposely bumped into one of the men as they exited the hotel.

"Whoa, sorry about that; you okay?" he asked as he turned to be apologetic.

"Maybe you should be a little bit more vigilant, but yes I'm fine," the man said as he continued onward and made his way to his horse. "By the way, mister, can you point me in the direction of Mounted Police station? I'm Arthur B. Talmore, with the U.S. Marshals office."

"Head down that way and take a left. You'll see it."

The man nodded his appreciation, tipped his hat and sped off. Tanner shook his head. He wondered if the Marshals were there due to the big court case the next day. The truth was that the Marshals were there because word had spread that Matt Crawford was responsible for another death, the death of Emery Nelson who worked for McCoy's. The Marshals were there to pick up all information that McCoy's Bounty Hunting Service had handed over to the Mounted Police. It was only coincidental and had nothing to do with the Kingsley Gang trial, nor were they there for the Blackwell case.

Marshal Talmore swung off his horse as he got him to stop and tethered him to the horse rail. Entering the Mounted Police station, he introduced himself and requested all the information the Mounted Police had on Matt Crawford and his recent victim, Emery Nelson. The constable handed him the requested material.

"This here is all we got. Hope it helps," the young constable said as he handed the documents over.

"What do the U.S. Marshals want with this information anyway?" he asked as he leaned up against the counter.

"Crawford's been charged with a few more crimes south of the border. This information here tells us where he was last. We assumed he'd made his way north. This here tells us our assumption is correct."

"Keep in mind, Marshal, this is Canada. You really have no jurisdiction here."

The marshal turned and looked at who was addressing him. It was Lieutenant Bob Cannon.

"No worries there, Lieutenant. We aren't here to track him down, only to get the latest information on his last whereabouts. We'll catch up with Crawford down south. Chances are that is where he'll end up next."

The marshal nodded, as he briefly looked through the documents.

"Looks like this is all in order. Thank you kindly," he said as he turned and began to walk out the door.

"Hold up a second there, marshal. I'm not so sure you get to keep those documents."

The marshal turned and looked over to Bob Cannon.

"Crawford is an American citizen, wanted by the U.S. Marshals. This information is U.S. property."

Lieutenant Bob Cannon shook his head.

"That is the property of the Canadian Mounted Police. You are welcome to look at it and copy it all you want, but you don't get to take it. Crawford is as much of a priority to us as he is to you marshals."

The marshal knew Cannon was right. Besides, the entire charade was a ploy. Walking back to the counter, he tossed the documents down.

"I'll send over one of my men to copy this," he said with a bit of anger as he turned and made his way outside and to his horse.

Cannon picked up the folder containing the documents.

The Missing Years – Part II

"If and when someone from the U.S. Marshal's office shows up here, send him to me. I'll be in my office," he said as he walked away.

"Will do, Lieutenant," the young constable replied as he returned to his own paperwork.

An hour later, a deputy marshal showed up to copy the documents that the Mounted Police had. He was directed to Bob Cannon's office. It took him four hours to complete the task of writing it all down. Finishing up, he rose from behind Bob's desk, thanked the Mounted Police and strode off. That was the last time the Marshals were seen. It left a bad taste in Cannon's mouth, but he knew he was required to share information with the U.S. Marshals even if he didn't like them that much. He watched as the deputy headed to the hotel.

"Goodbye and good riddance," Cannon said as he turned and made his way to the counter. "My shift is about done. Who's coming on tonight?" he asked of the young constable, who did a brief read through of the nightshift list.

"Looks like Camrose and Becker are on tonight," he responded as he too stood and got ready to leave.

"Good enough," Cannon replied as he jotted down a few notes about the U.S. Marshal's arrival in his shift book. "I guess you are heading out?" Cannon questioned the young constable as he finished up with the note.

"Yeah. I'll see you in the morning, Bob," the constable said as he exited the building.

"Yep, yep. See you then."

Cannon heard the back door close. He looked at the note again, then closed his book. It was his responsibility to wait for the nightshift and so he waited. Desk Sergeant Camrose was the first to arrive.

The Missing Years – Part II

"Evening, Bob. How was your day?" he asked as he made fresh coffee.

"The damn U.S. Marshals showed up and copied the files we have on Crawford. The Marshal himself thought he could leave with the documents. You know those U.S. Marshals really think they are the horse's oats. Anyway, tomorrow is the big day when the trials will get underway. It's going to be a long haul, I think."

"I sure hope it goes well. The last thing we need is the Kingsley Gang causing a ruckus. We got good back up with the McCoy's."

"Yeah, I suppose you are right. Anyway, I'm out the door," Cannon said as he put on his jacket. "You guys be safe tonight."

"No worries, Bob. Constable Becker and I will be fine. Have a good evening," Camrose responded as he sat down at his desk. The back door closed for the second time that evening and Bob Cannon headed for home.

It had been a good day for Tyrell and by late afternoon he was starting to get a bit saddle sore, so he halted Pony.

"I reckon we put on thirty or so miles today, Pony. It's been a good day, was warm most of it. Now, though, it seems a bit chilled. Damn ears are even cold," he said as he stacked wood for his evening fire. "I reckon by this time tomorrow we'll be in Hazelton or close to it."

Tyrell lit a match and watched as the flames came to life. Adding a few bigger pieces of wood, he stood back and looked in the direction they had come. *Tomorrow is going to be the big day back at the Fort. Sure hope all goes well,* he thought as he walked over to Pony and removed his saddle and gear. Black Dog lay near the fire and curled up as Tyrell made coffee and cooked a can of beans. Pony became a bit unsettled as he always did whenever he cooked beans.

"What is it about beans you don't like, Pony?" Tyrell asked as though the horse would answer. "That little quirk of yours has always made me wonder."

He shook his head as he stirred them and waited for them to cook. It didn't take long and soon he was scooping up the last spoonful. Fed now and somewhat full, he set the pot down and let Black Dog lick it clean.

Sitting on the big rock that was next to his fire, with a coffee in his hand, he looked at and admired the fading sun as it slowly crept behind the western horizon and the early evening approached. In the silence of the moment he could hear in the distance the sound of horse hooves. The clip-clop sound seemed to echo. He commanded Black Dog to stand watch as he sent him to the undergrowth. As always, the dog obeyed.

Tyrell tilted his head as he waited impatiently for the rider or riders to approach. He wasn't so far off the dirt road that he wouldn't be noticed so there was no point in trying to hide his presence. There were two riders in all.

"Evening, gentlemen," Tyrell said as he stood up and greeted them as they made their way to his small fire.

"Right back at you. mister," the one rider said as he dismounted his pinto mare and walked over to Tyrell.

"My name is Will Anderson, Special Constable of the Northwest Mounted Police. I work out of the Candora office, about fifty miles east of here."

He removed his credentials and handed them to Tyrell. It was only then Tyrell noticed the handcuffs and shackles the other man was wearing.

"I see," he said as he nodded and handed back Will his credentials. Reaching out his hand he offered a more honourable introduction.

The Missing Years – Part II

"I'm Travis Sweet," he said as the two shook hands. "How long have you been travelling alone with a prisoner?" Tyrell asked out of curiosity.

"Not long, because he's still alive," Will chuckled. He looked back at the man alone on his horse. "He's no danger, just some two-bit card cheater."

"Since when do card cheaters get shackled to their horse?"

"That is the way I keep him in line. A card cheater is still a law breaker," Will replied. "You don't mind if we join you for a while, do you?"

Tyrell stepped closer to the rider who remained mounted. There was a familiarity he saw in his face. It was Buck Ainsworth. Tyrell shook his head and began to chuckle.

"Looks like you have my old friend and associate Buck Ainsworth sitting on that horse."

"Hell, couldn't you have just kept quiet, Travis?" Buck said as he looked at him. He only knew Tyrell as Travis. He didn't know who he really was, not yet at least.

It was then that Will stepped forward.

"You know this man?" he asked as he pointed at Buck.

"I do. He's an old friend of mine. It sounds as though he doesn't want me to remember."

"It ain't that, Travis. I didn't want old Will there to know who I was."

Will scratched his chin.

"Your real name is Buck? You aren't Dan O'Malley?"

"Nope. Just a name I was using?" Buck replied solemnly.

"Why are you using a fake name?" Will now asked.

Buck sat silently and didn't answer.

"It doesn't matter to me either way. You are still going to be tried. You broke the damn law, you got caught, and we'll see what the judge has to say."

Will didn't care if Buck was his name or not. All he cared about was his job and transferring his prisoner.

"Can I even ask what he has been charged with?" Tyrell questioned as he looked at Will.

"Buck or Dan or whatever his name may be was caught cheating at cards, drunk and disorderly and assault. He'll certainly get a hefty fine, which to me looks like he can't afford, in which case he'll get ten days or so in jail. Of course, I'm sure the judge may want to know why he's going by a false name. You wouldn't know why, would you?" Will questioned with authority.

"Nope. I haven't seen him in a long while. I have no idea," Tyrell said as he looked over to Buck. "What do you suppose his fine would be?"

If there was any way at all that Tyrell could get Buck released, he'd do it. They could travel together up to Hazelton and track down Matt Crawford or his alias Ron Reginal together. He'd offer Buck a good payout. Although Buck's credentials had been taken away months earlier by the Willow Gate law, if there was anybody Tyrell would like to have along for the hunt, if it couldn't be Tanner then it would certainly be Buck. Convincing Buck to help would be a different story. Tyrell would cross that bridge if and when the time came. The first thing he needed to do was to get Buck set free.

"For what he's been charged with, close to one hundred and fifty dollars I would think, but it is entirely up to the circuit judge. It might be more," Special Constable Will replied.

"Could, say a fellow like myself, volunteer to pay his fine and have him released?"

"He needs to go before the judge first. However, there is no law that says friends or family can't pay his fine. Why are you so interested anyway? Didn't you say he was an old acquaintance of yours?"

"I did say that and he is. Was curious is all. Come on, let's go have a sit down at the fire. I can offer you and your prisoner some coffee," Tyrell said as he and Will turned and made their way to it.

"Now that we are out of earshot, Will, I'm a bounty hunter," Tyrell began as he now handed Will his license and credentials.

It wasn't until Will had the information in his hand did he realise who Tyrell was.

"You are that Travis Sweet fellow who took down Brubaker some months back, aren't you?" Will asked with admiration.

"I am, but I'm not that same man anymore," Tyrell wanted to make clear.

It was getting tiresome to hear comments and the praise he seemed to get for killing Brubaker.

"My friend Buck there is also a bounty hunter, or was until the law took away his credentials. There is more to the story than I would like to get into, but let me say it wasn't any fault of Buck's."

Tyrell poured Will a coffee and handed it to him, as he took back his credentials.

"I'd like to pay his fine directly to you. You can take down my information and hand it to the judge along with his fine fee. I need Buck to help me with a bounty.

I was actually on my way to meet up with him," Tyrell lied. "You can see the predicament I'm in."

Will took a long swig of coffee as he contemplated Tyrell's offer. Under normal circumstances, there would be no way he'd even consider the idea.

"What outfit was it that you said you worked for?" Will asked.

"I didn't say, but if it makes a difference, I work for McCoy's."

"Out of the Fort?"

"That's right. You know of them?" Tyrell questioned.

"We all do."

Will took another drink from his coffee.

"The Mounted Police don't often consider such requests, but I know Ed well enough to trust anyone that works for him."

Will inhaled deeply as he further contemplated turning his prisoner over.

There was a hidden Canadian law that did allow special constables to release felons into the custody of friends and family, as long as the felon had not been charged with a serious crime.

"I'll take the cash for your friend's release and turn it over to the judge, but you'll have to take full responsibility for him until I can get the fine paid. It is going to take me another three days to get where I need to get to, so if you are willing to take responsibility for any infractions he may commit between now and say, five days, I'll release him to your care."

Will reached into his vest pocket and pulled out a notepad, scribbling in it he handed it over to Tyrell.

"That there basically states you paid Dan O'Malley's fine of one hundred and fifty dollars and have agreed to take full responsibility for any infractions or laws he may break for a period of five days. Fill in your name and sign it."

Will handed his pen to Tyrell.

Tyrell briefly read the scribble and signed it. He handed the notepad back along with the one hundred and fifty dollar fine payment.

"There you go, Will."

Will walked the short distance back to Buck and told him what had transpired. Removing his handcuffs and shackles, he helped Buck off his horse.

"You are now the responsibility of your friend there, Buck or Dan or whatever your name is. Don't let me catch you cheating at cards or picking fights again in my jurisdiction," Will made clear as he put the handcuffs and shackles away.

"You have no worries there, Will. I aim to stay as far away from Candora as possible. It wasn't very hospitable," Buck commented as he turned his back, undid his fly, and urinated. "Ahh, that feels better," he said as he zipped himself back up and walked over to where Tyrell was standing.

It was early enough that Will decided he wasn't going to stick around and so he once more clarified what Tyrell's responsibility was. Satisfied that Tyrell understood, he swung back onto his horse.

"Good luck in your endeavours, Travis, and keep that friend of yours at an arm's length."

"You have my commitment, Will. Thanks again," Tyrell said as Will turned his horse and continued onward.

Tyrell and Buck watched as he disappeared into the shadows.

"Thanks for paying that fine, Travis," Buck said with sincerity. "How the hell have you been?" he asked, as he reached out his hand and shook Tyrell's. "You are looking well."

"You aren't looking any worse for wear either. I take it you got into some whiskey and raised a little hell, eh?"

"Something like that. Never did cheat at cards; that is all bullshit. I won't deny the other, though."

Buck grew silent as he looked around.

"I guess I owe you one hundred and fifty dollars, eh Travis?"

"I know you are good for it, Buck. I ain't in any rush to get paid. You'll pay me when you can."

"How did you ever convince old Will to release me?" Buck asked.

Tyrell reached into his pocket and handed Buck his Bounty Hunting credentials.

"That is how I did it. Told Will I was actually going to meet up with you and that I needed your expertise in helping track down a bounty."

"I ain't done any bounty hunting in a while. Don't even have my credentials anymore. The damn Willow Gate law and that prick Gabe Roy saw to it. I ever get my hands on him alone..." Buck trailed off there. "Ah, I ain't been doing so badly without that piece of paper. Tell me, Travis, how does a fellow like you decide upon becoming a bounty hunter? The last time I saw you, you weren't so sure that would be something you'd like to do. What changed?"

"Life, I reckon. I came to a conclusion that I haven't done much with mine. Thought if maybe I could change the world we live in a bit, I'd have accomplished something. Hell, could just be a whim, too."

Tyrell turned toward the fire.

"Want a coffee, Buck. I have a little bit left in the pot."

"Yeah, that'd be good. By the way where is that dog of yours. I ain't saw him. He is still running with you, ain't he?" Buck asked as Tyrell handed him a coffee.

"He ain't far, I reckon. Should be coming around anytime."

Tyrell poured himself a coffee and tossed another stick on the low burning embers.

"I see you ain't got no bedroll or gear, Buck. Since when do you travel without gear?"

"All the gear I had is still in Candora. Once they arrested me and tossed me in their holding cells, it was only a few hours later that Will decided he needed to transport me to face a circuit judge. I guess the Candora judge wasn't going to be around for a couple weeks. I'm kind of grateful that Will did decide to transport me. A couple days on the trail is better than a few weeks in the Candora holding cells. I can't even remember the place he was taking me to. He and I didn't talk much," Buck responded as he took a drink from the coffee in his hand.

"Will said Candora is about fifty miles east. We could head that way in the morning and gather your gear. I have an extra bedroll that you could use until then."

Tyrell took a drink from the cup in his hand, as he waited for Buck's response.

"I suppose so. We could slip in and slip out. I ain't sure I'd want to stick around there long. Do need my gear and my money satchel. Then I can head off. Ain't sure where to, but I hear the great Yukon calling my name."

"Just so you know, Buck, I have to keep you close for at least five days. That was all part of your release which I agreed to."

"That is to keep me from some infraction I presume. That's okay I guess. I ain't got a problem with tagging along with you for a few days. It'll likely take us a day or two to get to Candora. That takes care of two days. What are we going to do for the remaining three?"

"You said you wanted to head north to the Yukon. It just so happens I'm heading to Hazelton. That is where I need to pick up the trail of a bounty. I guess you'll have to tag along until then I reckon."

"Hazelton? If you don't mind me prying, who is it you are tracking?"

"I guess I could tell you. A fellow by the name of Ronald Reginal. He ain't a bigwig, just a petty criminal that has a five hundred dollar bounty."

Tyrell didn't want to tell Buck at that point who it was that he was really after. He wanted to stoke Buck's flames a while first; maybe find out if he'd be interested in helping him.

"That is a long way to travel for a petty criminal. You seem to forget I was once in this business. I don't think you are being completely honest there, Travis," Buck said with a smile. "Who is it you are really after?"

"Alright, you got me, Buck. I hope to bring in Matt Crawford who is also known as Ronald Reginal."

"Matt Crawford? Do you know how many folks are looking for him. Last, I heard he had a ten thousand dollar bounty on his head. Heard he's also a U.S. Ranger sharpshooter. He ain't no small potato," Buck commented.

"Nope, he ain't. The law has claimed that he's responsible for the killing of a bounty hunter who went by the name of Emery Nelson on top of a list of other killings from down south. He's a bigwig there. Ain't no doubt about it. There is more. Sit down and I'll explain it to you."

It took another twenty minutes to explain who, what, where, and when to Buck.

"I had no idea you were working for the McCoy's, even more intriguing that Tanner works there as well. I ain't saw him in a long while. Was supposed to meet up with him before I left Willow Gate. Things didn't come together and I was so disgruntled when they cut me loose that I up and left. That is quite the story you just told, Travis."

"I don't suppose you'd be interested in helping me hunt down this Crawford fellow, would you? I can offer you a cut of the bounty. Are you interested, Buck?"

"I don't have my credentials, Travis. I ain't sure how much help I'd be without them."

"I'll take care of all the legalities, Buck. As you know, anyone can take down a bounty. That little piece of paper we get as bounty hunters only allows us a bit more leeway."

"I know. Let me think about that for a minute. You are saying if I help you folks out, you'll cut me some cash from the bounty, correct?"

"Of course, you might even get back your credentials. McCoys can always use good men and from what I know they are short still one man. They are good people to work for," Tyrell added.

"I know. I've heard of them," Buck replied.

Tyrell could tell he was seriously considering the idea. It seemed odd how only by coincidence he ran into Buck again. He thought for sure that he would never see him again and it seemed Tanner also thought the same thing, yet there he was, Buck Ainsworth in the flesh. Tyrell's mind drifted back to the first time he ever met Buck and how even then it was only by coincidence that his old running partner Tanner McBride was with him. It seemed odd how things in life sometimes didn't make sense and how people who were once acquainted years later became acquaintances again. Tyrell looked over to Buck once more and then averted his eyes to the small flames of the fire. *Life is sure strange,* he thought as contemplated his past.

Buck's voice brought Tyrell back to the here and now.

"Okay, Travis, I'll help you. I could use some direction I reckon. Been running wild as of late. You

The Missing Years – Part II

got yourself a deal," Buck responded as he reached out his hand again.

"Glad to hear that, Buck. I truly am," Tyrell responded as they shook hands to seal the deal. "The first thing we need to do, I reckon, is to get your stuff. We'll head up north together after that and I guess whatever comes of it, comes of it. I can promise you a good payout, and I will do all that I can to help you get back your credentials once this is all said and done."

"That is fine, Travis, but I'm more inclined to take the cash and be gone. Wouldn't mind seeing Tanner again."

"Of course, Tanner will be elated to see you. He'll know you're with me long before then because I'm expected to send a telegram back to the office once I get to Hazelton and I will be obligated to tell Ed that I have hired on help."

"What is Ed going to say about you hiring on help?"

"I reckon Ed trusts my judgement. I don't think he'll have an issue with it. Crawford is a healthy payday and I know you and I can bring him in."

"What makes you so confident in that, Travis? Many bounty hunters have been tracking him for a while and not one of them has succeeded in bringing him in. There is that one fellow umm... what the hell is his name?"

Buck looked around as he tried to grasp the name.

"Damn, I can't remember his name. He's a bounty hunter and has been tracking Crawford from what I have heard for a few years."

"You mean Riley Scott?" Travis questioned.

"Yeah. Riley Scott. That's his name. He hasn't even spotted Crawford and from what I heard about Riley Scott is that he's a bounty hunter legend, an old timer, been in this business for thirty or more years. He ain't found Crawford yet, nor have any of the others, so what makes you so sure you and I can find him?" Buck asked as he referred back to his original question.

"Just a hunch I have, Buck. Remember we know one more thing about Crawford that some might not. That is our edge."

"It is indeed an edge, but I'm sure others have the same information."

"I don't think so, Buck. Not many bounty hunters care too much about Ron Reginal. He's a petty thief; that is all that he is. We aren't even going to be looking for Crawford. It is Ron Reginal that we want and, of course, the true killer of Emery."

Tyrell paused for a moment.

"The more I think about this, the more complicated it gets. That, though, just makes for an interesting bounty. Wouldn't you agree, Buck?"

Buck chuckled.

"It does make things interesting. Makes things a bit perilous, too."

The two men sat in self-contemplation as the sun finally winked out and the evening grew dark. Tyrell retrieved his bedroll and handed Buck his second.

"I say we should get some shuteye. We have fifty miles of ground to cover tomorrow."

Tyrell rolled out his bed near the fire and whistled for Black Dog, who to his surprise was only a few feet away.

"There you are, you old hound. I didn't even see you there. Come on over and meet Buck again," Tyrell coaxed as Black Dog traipsed over and gave Buck a sniff.

"Hello there, dog. Yeah, it is me, Buck."

He scratched Black Dog behind the ear as he stood up and rolled out his own bed.

"Well, Travis, I guess I'll see you in the morning," Buck said as he removed his boots and hat then climbed into his bed.

"Yep. See you in the morning, Buck," Tyrell responded as he did the same.

The Missing Years – Part II

"Chapter 10"

Tuesday, June 23 1891. It was 9:00 a.m. when the first trial back at the Fort began. By that time, Buck and Tyrell were a few miles west of where they spent the night. It was a warm day, much as it had been the day before. Tyrell seemed out of sorts and Buck noticed it.
"What is a matter, Travis? You seem somewhat blank."
"It ain't anything, Buck. Just thinking about Tanner and the others back at the Fort. There are a couple folks being tried today and they ain't that nice. Ed got a judicial contract from the Mounted Police some days back and today is when he and the others are on guard duty. I hope things go well for the three of them."
"Those judicial contracts are quite simple actually. All they are required to do is keep the judge and audience out of harm's way in case something goes awry. Most times these things go off without a hitch. I wouldn't worry about it, Travis. Tanner and the others will be fine," Buck commented as they continued onward.
"Yeah, I reckon you are right Buck. There ain't much we could do anyway, if something does go awry. I only hope it doesn't. Ed seemed to think there might be trouble."
"Do you know who it is that is facing the judge?"
"A fellow who goes by the name of Ben Blackwell, accused with three counts of cattle rustling, one of rape, two murders and four counts of attempted escape. And another fellow goes by the name of Talbot Hunter. Apparently he belongs to the Kingsley Gang. From what I remember, he's accused of two counts of robbery, five assault with deadly weapon, four intent to kill and six murders. He was once a regulator

for a large cattle ranch southeast of Calgary. You ever hear of those folks, Buck?"

"Never heard of that Ben fellow, but I have indeed heard about the Kingsley Gang. From what I recall, they were once involved with old Bill Miner. Bill couldn't handle their ignorance and if memory serves me right, he sent them on their way. That is about all what I know. Keep in mind it is all hearsay. I ain't ever met them and couldn't say if what I heard about them and the Miner Gang is true."

"Either way, they don't sound like very nice folk."

"Nope, but they are only as bad as their gang. Get one alone and most men can make them wet their pants. They ain't at all that brave and most ain't even that good with a pistol. That is why they run in gangs."

"I don't know about that, Buck. There are some exceptions I'm sure. Take old Bill Miner for instance. I heard he is or was quite quick on the draw; heard he also ain't afraid to fight."

"True, but we only know about Bill. We don't know much about the men that ran with him. Their reputation lies with Bill. And you are right, I would say Bill was an exception. Most ain't like that. They're bullies is all."

They continued onward in silence.

At 11:00 a.m., Ben Blackwell was sentenced to hang and the Mounted Police hauled him off, screaming and hollering, kicking and thrashing. Talbot Hunter's case was next, but the judge called a recess and lunch break. The audience in the courthouse exited and milled around outside. Tanner, Brady, and Ed met up with the prosecution, judge, and officers of the court. They were informed that there had been a bit of scuffle with Talbot. He was threatening to kill the judge and said that if he

The Missing Years – Part II

didn't do it, one of his men would. Judge William Frank, though, wasn't a coward. He had sent worse men to the gallows and not much ruffled his feathers.

"Regardless of what the man has said, he'll stand before me and be sentenced. Mr. McCoy and his men have the right to shoot any intruders that may wish to halt these proceedings. With their expertise and the Mounted Police presence, I see no reason to stop the sentencing of Mr. Hunter. That is all, gentlemen," Judge Frank said as the meeting ended and those in attendance left his chamber.

"I guess we better step outside for a bit and have a quick look around," Ed said as he and Brady along with Tanner exited into the warm afternoon. The three of them kept their eyes open as they scanned the street and rooftops looking for anything out of the ordinary. Brady noted two unsavoury types sitting alone and he pointed them out to Tanner.

"What do you think those two are up to?" he asked Tanner as he looked in their direction.

"Not sure. They do look like they're looking for trouble. We best keep our eyes on them until this is all over. I might even wander over that way and see if I can't get a conversation going with them," Tanner smiled as he looked at Brady. "I'll be back in a minute."

Brady watched as Tanner made his way over to the two men and he shook his head.

"Brass balls, I guess," he murmured to himself.

The two men, however, didn't stick around long enough for Tanner to make conversation with them. Instead, once they saw Tanner approaching, they simply mounted their horses and headed out of town. Tanner watched as the two men vanished from his view.

"There is definitely something going on," Tanner said as he made his way back to Brady. "They certainly didn't want me getting near. We better inform the

Mounted Police and fill Ed in. Something is going down, Brady."

"I reckon you are right. I'll let Ed know. You go ahead and inform the law," Brady said as he turned and looked around for Ed.

"There's Ed, I'll let him know."

Brady turned heel and made his way over to his dad.

"Hey, old man, Tanner and I just watched a couple of new faces mount up and head out of town. Tanner was going over to talk to them but they mounted up and headed out once they saw him coming. Ain't sure what it is all about, but it does seem a bit suspicious."

"Good eye. Alright then, we know what we have to do. You and Tanner get up on those rooftops. I'll stay near the judge. Is Tanner letting the law know?"

"He is. I'll get together with him and we'll get up there."

Brady pointed to the roof of the building that stood across from the courthouse.

"Keep your eyes peeled, old man. You took some lead a while ago. Ain't sure you could take more," Brady said as he turned and went looking for Tanner.

It didn't take long for them to make their way to the roof of the building. From there they had a good view of the courthouse and could see some distance out onto the prairie. If any riders were going to charge the town, Brady and Tanner would certainly see their approach. They watched as the Mounted Police swarmed the courthouse and surrounded it.

"Think we have enough men?" Tanner questioned as the two of them continued their gaze.

"Looks like six Mounted Police, us and Ed, nine men in all. I ain't sure. Depends I guess on how many of the Kingsley Gang are near, if any.

The Missing Years – Part II

It was only by coincidence that Tanner looked at a wagon that was near. He squinted his eyes to block the sun. He wasn't sure what he was seeing, but it looked like a man was dressing up in women's clothing. He even donned a wig.

"Jesus Christ, look at that, Brady."

Tanner pointed down at the wagon and the man that was now a woman.

"What, that woman?"

"That ain't a woman, Brady. That is a man dressed like a woman. You stay here and keep your eye on him. I'll get down there and see if I can't stop him from whatever it is he has planned."

Tanner slowly made his way to the ladder and slid down it. Remaining crouched, he looked up to Brady, who gave him the signal that the man was still near the wagon. Tanner darted to the edge of the building and peeked around the corner. He watched as the man stuffed a couple of pistols into his dress and then began to walk toward the courthouse entrance. At that moment, Tanner went in the same direction, catching up with the man only a few steps ahead.

"Hold up there, mister," Tanner said as he pointed his pistol at the man. "Drop those six-shooters you have tucked away in that ugly dress of yours."

The man spun around, his pistol already drawn. He fired point-blank at Tanner, who like many times before, managed to sidestep the .45 slug. The man fired a second time and his pistol was answered by two other loud claps as Brady fired at him from the roof and Tanner from the street. The two bullets slammed into the man's chest knocking him onto the courthouse stairs. The man landed with a solid thud in a pool of blood.

Tanner lay on the ground, his blood-soaked shirt telling the story. The second shot the man fired at him had hit home, but not before Tanner managed to squeeze his own trigger. Trying to stand, Tanner passed out from loss of blood and extreme agony. By now, the Mounted Police were at the scene and Brady was running towards Tanner.

"Jesus, Tanner are you okay, can you hear me?" Brady yelled as he cradled Tanner up in his arms. Brady could see that the bullet had pierced one of Tanner's lungs.

"I don't know..." Tanner began before he slipped into unconsciousness. Brady gently laid him down, relieved that he was still alive. The man they had shot, however, would never dress in women's clothing again.

It was then that twenty horses and riders stormed the courthouse. They came so fast it was hard to decipher in what direction they were coming from. Hot lead smashed into the side of buildings, smashed windows, and knocked down anyone in the way of the vicious onslaught. Still, Brady managed to pull Tanner out of harm's way as he fired nonstop at the riders who were shooting at him and anyone else that got in their way. The echoing sound of so many rifles and pistols enveloped the town of Fort Macleod like an unrelenting rainstorm, the gun smoke so thick that it hung in the air like a low laying fog. Bystanders took for cover as the wounded and dead fell around them. Yelling and screaming in horror, they darted this way and that. For what seemed like eternity, the unrelenting sound of gunfire and the ever-present scent of blood filled the warm summer day.

The law finally did get the upper hand, but not before Talbot Hunter and his unrelenting gang sped off. There were twelve dead men scattering the street when it was all over, three of whom were Mounted Police. Only some of the Kingsley Gang along with Talbot Hunter managed an escape. The others were dead or wounded. Brady darted over to the courthouse and bolted inside.

The Missing Years – Part II

He hollered for Ed, but got no reply. Bullet holes riddled every piece of furniture, and trails of blood stained the floor. He followed one trail to a back room and kicked open the door, with his pistol drawn; he looked around relieved to find his dad and the judge, both wounded but alive.

"Did they get away?" Ed asked nonchalantly as though nothing at all was wrong.

"They did. Now, let's get the two of you out of here. Come on," Brady said as he helped his dad stand. Standing now, Ed helped Brady with the judge who was in worse shape and the three of them exited through the back door to the safety of the Mounted Police station.

"Where is Tanner?" Ed asked as they made their way to safety caring little about his own wounds.

"He's been hit, but is alive for now. Let's get the two of you inside. I'll worry about Tanner," Brady said as he swung open the big doors of the Mounted Police station.

A constable greeted them inside and took both Ed and the judge to a back room where he laid them down.

"They'll be okay here, Brady, no worries," the constable said as Brady exited and made his way over to where he had left Tanner. To his surprise, Tanner was leaning up against the building his hand covering his wound.

"Dammit, Brady, I took one," he began to say as he once more faded into unconsciousness, a trail of blood painting the wall behind him as he slid to the ground.

Brady wasted no time in slinging Tanner over his shoulder and taking him to the safety of the nearby mercantile, where he laid him down on the counter.

"You're going to be okay, Tanner. Just hold on a bit longer. The doctor is on his way."

Brady exited the small store and for the first time noticed all the carnage that had taken place. There were bodies scattered here and there. Broken glass and shredded wood littered the street. It took another four hours for the wounded to be cared for and the dead removed. The death of three Mounted Police officers and two bystanders added up to five good men dead. The remaining seven were all members of the Kingsley Gang and their bodies were quickly put into the ground. The people of Fort Macleod had five dead men to mourn and would never be the same.

Brady sat alone in the office behind his dad's desk still shaken from what had taken place. He poured himself a shot of whiskey. The office was empty and silent as he sat there, the events of the day slowly taking their toll. Not even the whiskey seemed to flush out the anger and sorrow he was feeling. Short two men, and one only God knew where, Brady was in a bit of a fix.

The judicial contract required the McCoy's to pursue the prisoner if the prisoner escaped, which today he had.

As far as Brady could tell, there were thirteen men in all that escaped including Talbot Hunter. *Even the number of escapees is unlucky,* Brady thought as he poured himself another whiskey. He was about to pour a third when he heard the front door open. He stood up and exited his dad's office to meet whoever it was. A greying haired man dressed in leather and buckskin sporting two side arms approached the counter. Brady knew exactly who it was.

"Jesus Christ, if it ain't Riley Scott," he blurted out as he made his way from behind the counter and met up with him.

"Early evening, Brady. I guess I'm a bit late," Riley started.

"What do you mean late?" Brady questioned as he reached out his hand to shake Riley's.

"I was trailing a herd of hoodwinks this way. I couldn't help overhearing one of them talk about hitting the Fort Macleod courthouse. Only thing is I was never close enough to them to know when. From what I see outside, they've already been here. I hope everyone is okay. Where is Ed?"

"You got time for some whiskey, Riley?"

"By the sound of that question I gather not all is well. What happened?"

"The courthouse was stormed today. Ed was wounded and so was one of our men, plus two families no longer have husbands or fathers. Ed will live, but it is touch and go for our man Tanner. Now you know my need for whiskey. C'mon, Riley lets go have a sit down," Brady said as he made his way into his dad's office, Riley close behind.

"Have a seat, Riley."

Brady directed him to a chair and poured each of them a shot of whiskey.

"Over the hatch," he said as he and Riley tilted their glasses and swallowed.

"Tell me, Riley, what were you doing trailing a gang of outlaws?" Brady questioned as he poured another whiskey.

"Wasn't really trailing them, I just ended up behind them. Let's not worry about that right now. I'm more concerned on what happened here. Go ahead and tell me," Riley responded as he slugged back his second shot of whiskey.

Brady explained what happened and how it all unfolded. By the time he was finished with the explanation the bottle of whiskey was less than full.

"There you have it, Riley. That is what happened here today. Now I have judicial contract that states I need to track those son-of-bitches down," Brady managed to blurt out before he passed out and fell over in his chair.

Riley stood and picked Brady up setting him down on the backroom cot.

"You go ahead and rest Brady. I'll get some coffee going," Riley said as he tossed a woollen blanket over him.

Making his way into the staff room, he fired up the woodstove and set the coffee pot to perk. In a sense he felt as though he was to blame. There really was no reason for Riley to feel that way, but he did, and he knew what he was going to do about it. It was obvious that Brady had every intention on fulfilling the judicial contract and Riley wasn't going to let him do it alone. It was light enough outside that he decided to have a better look at where the ruckus and shootings took place.

His eyes were keen as he sorted out the direction in which Talbot and his riders likely headed, which was northerly, which meant they weren't going north at all. Chances were they would either head west to the Rockies or south to the border. Riley was certain of that. Only by luck did his eyes catch a few places up high on the walls of a building where there was definite blood spatter. It meant one thing to Riley. Some of Talbot's riders had been wounded. The blood spatter was up that high because the wounded were still on horses when they were shot. Satisfied with what he had learned from the scene, he made his way over to the Mounted Police station and introduced himself, although he really didn't need an introduction as the Mounted Police knew who he was.

Through some common questioning, he was informed that eyewitness accounts did claim that some of Talbot's men were definitely wounded before the

The Missing Years – Part II

gang sped off. Next, he asked if anything out of the ordinary had taken place on the day the attacks happened or before. The one constable mentioned that the U.S. Marshals had been snooping around the day before the incident, and in fact had copied down information on Emery Nelson's death and other information that the Mounted Police had on Matt Crawford. This bit of information was a red flag for Riley. He asked who the senior officer on duty that day was. He was surprised to hear that it had been Bob Cannon, the veteran. It wasn't like Bob to fall for a stunt like that which the so-claimed U.S. Marshals pulled on him. Chances were they were Talbot's men in disguise. Riley, though, was the only one who thought that.

"Where is Bob now?" he asked as he continued to lean on the counter.

"He's on guard duty over at the widow Donale's which is where the judge is until his coach arrives. Ed and his man Tanner are there as well. It was the cleanest place for Doctor Dunbar to fix them up."

"Where is the Donale residence?"

"Down the way some. Look for the biggest house southeast of here. You can't miss it. You'll see three or four clotheslines and a constable standing at the front door."

Riley nodded his appreciation and thanked the constable as he exited the building. He wasn't going to search out the Donale residence. There really was no point. He knew Ed's situation and he wasn't likely in a talkative mood. It had only been hours since the incident had taken place. Instead, Riley headed back to the McCoy's office. The bit of information that he was able to glean was enough to track down Talbot and his gang of thugs.

The Missing Years – Part II

Twenty miles west of Candora, Buck and Tyrell were setting up for the evening. They had made good time to be where they were.

"Was a good day today, Buck. How are you faring?"

"A bit hungry and parched. Should I get coffee brewing?"

"I reckon so. I'll gather some wood. There are a few canned goods in my saddlebags. How about grabbing a couple and we'll get dinner going too. Just open them and toss the cans right onto the fire," Tyrell said as he turned and tucked into the bush to gather a few more sticks.

With his arms full of wood, he tossed the stack onto the ground next to the small fire Buck lit.

"That ought to keep the flames going. How is that coffee coming?" Tyrell asked as he removed his saddle and gear from Pony and laid it down.

"It's almost done I reckon. That stew smells good, too. Are we going to eat it right out of the can?" Buck questioned, already knowing the answer.

"That depends. Are you volunteering to wash up some dishes," Tyrell chuckled.

"Hell no. Eating out of can suits me."

Buck poured each of them a coffee and handed Tyrell his.

"Here you go, Travis, Buck brewed coffee," he said with a smile.

Tyrell brought the hot beverage up to his lips and took a drink. It was so strong that he thought he had chewed on a handful of coffee grounds.

"Buck brewed alright. Hope you saved some grounds for tomorrow," Tyrell said with humour.

"Is it a little strong for you?" Buck questioned.

"Ah, it ain't that bad. I reckon it's fine. How about that stew? It ought to be ready by now."

The Missing Years – Part II

Tyrell made his way closer to the fire and sat down on his saddle waiting for his can of stew. A few minutes later, they were wolfing down their evening meal, talking sporadically and slurping coffee. For one reason or another, Black Dog sat up and stared into the undergrowth as though he was seeing something that neither Tyrell nor Buck could see. Then just as quickly, he once more settled and lay at Tyrell's feet.

"Do you suppose the dog saw something?" Buck asked with concern, realising then that he was completely unarmed and the only one holding any firepower was Tyrell.

"I ain't sure. Most times if there is a threat he'd give me a warning of some kind. Could be he caught the scent of a rabbit or something."

Tyrell shrugged his shoulders.

"I reckon we'll sit tight. No use getting all antsy and worried. It is light enough we could see anything approach and I see nothing. How about you, Buck? You see anything?"

"Not from here I don't. I feel kind of naked, sitting without so much as bowie knife," Buck hinted.

Tyrell looked over to him and shook his head.

"Oh oh, I almost forgot you ain't got your side arms. You should have said something earlier, Buck."

Standing, he retrieved one of his rifles and handed it to Buck.

"There, now you're armed."

Tyrell hadn't really paid any attention to the fact that Buck was unarmed. It had slipped his mind completely and, of course, Buck hadn't said two words about the fact.

"I can't believe we came all this way and the whole time I'm the only one that has been armed. I guess I should have surmised that the law would have taken away your guns. Why didn't you say anything until now?"

"To be honest, Travis, it really never dawned on me either, 'til now. And the law don't have my guns. I wasn't carrying any at the time of the event. They are with my gear."

Tyrell looked at him somewhat confused.

"If the law don't have your gear, then where is your gear?"

"At my camp outside of Candora."

"Your camp?" Tyrell asked.

"That's right. I don't spend much time in towns and hotels. I get in and I get out when I have to." Buck replied. "Besides it is summer and who wants to be cooped up in a hotel," he added.

Tyrell snickered.

"Alright, I guess that makes sense. You aren't concerned that someone may have stumbled upon your camp?"

Buck scratched his head as he contemplated the question.

"If they did then they are better off than me. I ain't sure I can even remember the place myself."

"How can you not remember where your camp is?"

"Simple. I set camp up, strode into Candora for a few things and well, that is when everything went haywire. First it was the draft beer, then whiskey and the next thing I can recollect is being accused of cheating at some card game. I ain't even sure I was playing cards. Then came the law. From there to here is the extent of that excursion."

"You never even made it back to your camp since, eh?" Tyrell shook his head. It was somewhat funny but also a little disheartening, especially for Buck. "If you get us close, we'll let Black Dog find the way. I reckon he can do that easily enough. We'll just have to give him one of your smelly socks," Tyrell chuckled.

"Yeah, you go ahead and make jokes. The more I think about the possibility that someone may have stumbled upon my camp, the more it worries me. Everything I own is at that camp, including a tidy sum of cash. I was better off not thinking about that possibility. Thanks, Travis."

"Ah, don't worry about it, Buck. I'm sure it'll all be there. I don't reckon a fellow such as yourself would set up camp right out in the damn open."

"That still doesn't make me feel any better," Buck sighed as he finished the last of his coffee and poured another, offering to freshen up Tyrell's as well.

Tyrell handed him his cup for the refill and they sat down.

"We'll get to Candora tomorrow, Buck and we'll find your camp as well."

"Yeah, I reckon we will. I got a bit of an idea on where it is, but it isn't as clear as it would have been had I simply gathered what I needed and headed back, instead of wetting my whistle with a few shots of whiskey and draft beer. Lesson learned, I guess."

There were a few minutes of silence as the two friends contemplated.

"That aside, Buck, I've been meaning to ask, or rather have been waiting to ask, why it was you didn't want Will to know your real name?" Tyrell was curious to know.

"I don't look at the law the way I used to, not since that little escapade in Willow Gate all those months back. The last thing I wanted was for Will to find out that I was once a bounty hunter and not only that, but a bounty hunter that has a real hate on for one Gabe Roy. I ain't sure which constables are on his payroll and which ones ain't; I know some are. I've been trying to figure that out ever since. To be honest, I aim on putting those crooked bastards in their place, one way or another."

"I don't know, Buck. That sounds a bit vindictive. What all took place between you and Gabe Roy anyway? All I ever heard from Tanner is that Gabe and a couple of his henchmen picked a fight with you and that the law stepped in and took away your credentials."

"It did happen like that, without rhyme or reason. Tanner and I had done our job which was to track you down and approach you to see if you wanted to work for his cowardly ass. For one reason or another, I reckon Gabe wanted to make an example of me. Only thing was, he wasn't expecting what I would bring to the table and his men ended up getting hurt. Once the law got involved and they had me in cells, each of them had a go at me, whilst the others held me down. I ended up with some broken ribs, busted lips, black eyes, a three-week concussion, and a bad taste in my mouth toward the law which is supposed to serve and protect."

"You've decided to clean up the filth and expose the crooked, eh?" Tyrell responded.

"As best as I can, yep."

"I often thought about that, Buck. I don't know much about Gabe Roy," Tyrell lied, "but I know his type," he added as he looked into the flames of the fire and reminisced.

Gabe Roy was at the center of what Buck was feeling and what he alone felt toward the man. Tyrell had disposed of Gabe Roy's son in a fair and even fight. Subsequently, Gabe Roy had bought off the law and sent men out to kill him. It was because of this that Tyrell was running from the law and it was the only reason he had to become Travis Sweet. He felt his own hatred boil up as he thought about what Gabe Roy had also taken away from him.

"The thing is, Buck, folks like Gabe Roy can buy off whomever they want including the law. I ain't sure there is much anyone can do about the likes of him, short of murder. Even if that were to happen, it wouldn't clean up the law that was soiled by him. They'd still be dirty."

"The best way to deal with it, Travis, is from the inside out. I remember the face of every constable that took a swing at me, and one day they'll meet up with me alone," Buck said with sincerity.

"The Mounted Police constables of today are transferred to other jurisdictions on a regular basis. Chances that those constables might still be in Willow Gate are pretty slim, Buck."

Buck chuckled as he spit to the ground.

"That is exactly how I know that one day I'll eventually run into each of them again. I move around pretty regular too, Travis, and my eyes are always looking."

Tyrell nodded his appreciation of Buck for being so honest.

"Promise me one thing, Buck, that you'll keep that rage under control for at least five days."

"No worries, Travis. If there hasn't been an officer change in Candora since I was whisked away, I can safely tell you that none of the constables I hate are there."

The Missing Years – Part II

"Chapter 11"

It was 4:00 a.m. when Brady finally came back to the living. He sat up on the cot and wondered how he'd even got there. Everything seemed like a dream. He wasn't even sure if Riley Scott had shown up. That too, seemed like a dream. Groggy-eyed and head pounding, Brady made his way to the small bathroom and splashed water on his face to wipe the cobwebs from his mind. The scent of coffee wafted up his nostrils as he looked at himself in the small mirror. It made him take a step back. As far as memory served him, he was the only one in the office, other than the dream or what he thought was a dream of Riley Scott showing up. Now, though, he wondered if maybe Riley was there. The smell of the coffee cooking was as real as his pounding head. There was no way it was Ed making coffee and just as unlikely, it couldn't have been Tanner. Cautiously, he stepped out of the doorway of the bathroom and made his way toward the staff room. He was now in view of the staff room and he could see that someone was in there with their feet on the table. That is all he could see.

Stepping into the staff room, he was elated to see that there in the flesh with his hat tilted over his eyes and his feet stretched out on the table sat Riley Scott.

"Well I'll be. I guess I wasn't dreaming after all," Brady announced as he poured himself a coffee and Riley woke up and looked over to him.

"Morning, Brady. You look like hell. Your head hurts a bit, I reckon."

"It does, Riley. I guess you and I finished off that bottle of whiskey?"

"Mostly you drank it. That coffee, by the way, is a few hours old," Riley informed him.

"It don't matter to me much at this point. Anything to scrub my blood clean of whiskey will do."

Brady sat down at the table and brought the hot beverage up to his lips. Taking a swallow, he shook his head.

"Yep, this is pretty old," he said referring to the coffee in his hand.

"I told you it was."

Riley smiled stood up and poured one for himself.

"After you faded into a drunken stupor early evening yesterday, I did a bit of an investigation. I learned from the Mounted Police that on Monday a couple of U.S. Marshals were snooping around here. You know anything about that?"

"Nope. What is the correlation?" Brady asked with interest.

Riley took a long swallow from the cup in his hand.

"U.S. Marshals ain't so inclined to cross their border and come into Canada. I ain't saying they don't, but I can tell you that they don't do that very often."

Riley inhaled deeply and sighed.

"I have reservations that they were who they claimed to be. I'm more inclined to think that they were Talbot's men checking out the security."

"If you learned this from the Mounted Police, what makes you think they weren't U.S. Marshals. Wouldn't the law have figured that out?" Brady asked his head still in a fog.

"Not necessarily. I reckon the Mounted Police were preoccupied with the outlaws that were here. With the right get-up and some sly talking, it probably wouldn't have taken much to pull the wool over their eyes under the circumstances."

Brady took another drink from his coffee.

"I have to be honest with you, Riley. I ain't so sure that they weren't U.S. Marshals, but I will certainly keep that in mind whilst I pursue the escapee."

"Yeah, about that, Brady, I ain't about to let you go off half-cocked alone. I'd like to help you bring Talbot in," Riley replied as a matter-of-fact.

Brady's eyes lit up and he sighed in relief.

"Really? Since we are short some men, I'd appreciate that."

Although Brady wasn't one to ask for help at the worst of times, he knew what he was up against and having Riley Scott in his pocket was a godsend.

"We'll even pay you, Riley."

"I ain't in it for the money, Brady. I want you to be clear on that.

The two men sat in silence as they contemplated what it was they were about to embark on.

Talbot Hunter pulled his horse to a halt.

"We'll rest up here, men," he said as a dozen riders pulled up next to him.

"How many wounded do we have, Skip?" he asked his second-in-command.

"Looks like six men, Tal, three of which ain't likely going to make the distance we need to get," Skip replied as he slid off his horse and helped a couple of the badly wounded off their horses.

"Shoot them then, Skip. We don't need to be slowed down," Talbot commanded as he too slid off his horse.

"No bloody way, Tal, am I gonna shoot men that I have ridden with. No bloody way."

That was all Talbot needed to hear. He walked to the back of the line where his three badly injured men were. Without thought or remorse, he pulled out his own gun and put to rest the three men. Next, he pointed his pistol at Skip.

The Missing Years – Part II

"When I give you an order, Skip, you best follow through with it; and that goes for the rest of you as well."

He pulled the trigger for the fourth time. Skip fell to the ground grasping at the wound as blood seeped through his fingers.

"Is there anyone else that wants to remain here?" he asked with callousness.

Only silence and awe enveloped him.

"Good. I'm glad the rest of you ain't as stupid," he said as he removed the saddles from the horses of the men he had shot and tossed their saddles next to the dead riders. Shooing off their horses, he once more mounted his own horse and he and his remaining eight men headed west in the direction of the Rocky Mountains and their silver canyon hideout.

The nine riders rode hard and steady, only breaking every now and again to let their horses rest. When the Rocky Mountains came into full view, they stopped.

"We've been going at it hard and steady, men. We'll rest up here for now. We'll get to silver canyon in a day or so. Kyle, you're next in line to become second-in-command," Talbot made clear as he sat down on a fallen log and rested.

"Thank you for that, Tal. I won't let you down," Kyle said as he swung off his horse and joined Talbot.

Kyle Rogers had been with the Kingsley Gang longer than Skip Anderson and probably should have been Talbot's second-in-command from the beginning. He wasn't afraid of much and of all the men still alive, he was probably the next quickest draw to Talbot. He wasn't a small man. He was over six feet tall and pushing a healthy one hundred and ninety pounds. He was fit, able, and could be as mean as any rabid 'coon.

Skip Anderson on the other hand had been nothing like Kyle. He was indeed good with a gun and could pick off a squirrel at any distance, but he lacked at most everything else. He was Talbot's second-in-command for one reason only. He was Talbot's nephew. Talbot's sister Hanna and her husband Dirk Anderson had both perished in a house fire years earlier and so Talbot had taken Skip under his wing. That was the gist of the reason why Skip had been Talbot's second-in-command. Talbot Hunter felt no remorse for killing him or the three other wounded men. To him the badly wounded and those who didn't follow his command were burdens, and he had no desire to be burdened by incompetence.

Talbot removed his hat and tossed it to the ground as he ran his hand over his head. His mind drifted as he contemplated what had all taken place in the last day. His gang of outlaws had certainly been thinned out from an army of twenty men to nine in one day. In his opinion, nine were better than none. Rested now, Talbot and his men mounted their horses and continued westerly toward their silver canyon hideout.

It was 9:00 a.m. when Brady and Riley mounted up their own horses. The first thing Brady wanted to do was to swing by the widow Donale's place and check up on Ed and Tanner. The constable at the front door allowed both of them inside and he and Riley made their way to the upstairs bedroom where both Ed and Tanner were. It was a quick visit and Ed gave Brady his blessing to fulfill the judicial contract. Now that Riley Scott was involved, Ed was confident that all would end well. Next Brady walked over to where Tanner lay. There had been no change in his vitals, but he was breathing and that was something.

He looked down at Tanner and smiled.

"Keep fighting, Tanner; keep fighting, my friend," he repeated as he turned heel and he and Riley began to exit.

"Hold up there minute, Brady. Your Ma just left here. She was here all night. She's going to be back soon. Are you going to stick around and see her?" Ed asked in a weak voice.

"Hell no. You know exactly what she'd say and I ain't got no time to listen to her bantering, old man."

Ed chuckled and shook his head.

"Remember we only need Talbot back so don't be going all cockeyed. You and Riley got money?"

"I know exactly what you are trying to do here, old man. Quit stalling me. Of course we got money," Brady responded with aggravated love as he looked at Riley and smiled.

"Any word from Travis yet?" Ed asked, his voice getting weaker from exhaustion.

"Nothing yet. I don't reckon he's near a telegraph," Brady answered.

"Uhuh, okay. Do me a favour, Brady. Swing by the telegraph office here and check would you? And let whoever is there today know that if something from Travis comes in they should bring it to me directly."

"I was going to do that already. I'm also going to have a reply made out that can be sent directly afterward back to him. Now, if there is nothing else, old man, Riley and I need to get."

"What about Tanner? Any change in his situation?" Ed asked.

"All you have to do is look over your shoulder and see for yourself. He is in this same damn room."

Brady shook his head.

"Now, go back to sleep and let me get on with it or I'm going to come over there and put a pillow over your face."

The Missing Years – Part II

"Yeah, yeah. Okay, Brady. You and Riley keep your wits about you," Ed said as he closed his eyes.

"Come on, Riley, let's get," Brady said as they were finally able to leave. "The old man sure can ramble when he wants to."

"Least we know he is going to pull through," Riley stated as he and Brady mounted their horses once more.

"They don't call him lucky Ed for nothing. It's Tanner I am concerned about. He took one close to his heart, but it didn't slow him down. He still managed to put lead into the fellow that shot him. I hope he's going to come out of this okay."

Next stop was the telegraph office. Riley remained sitting on his horse while Brady dealt with that.

Nothing had come in from Travis, no surprise there. Brady informed the telegrapher to let Ed know as soon as one did come in from Travis. Then he wrote out a reply that was to be sent to whatever telegraph office that Travis sent his from when one did arrive. It simply read: *Ed, Tanner wounded. Five good men dead. Seven outlaws dead. Talbot- twelve men- running. Am on trail with Riley Scott. Signed: Brady.*

"There we go."

He slid the telegram wording over to the telegrapher.

"You make sure this is sent to Travis Sweet the moment one comes in from him."

"Will do, Brady," the telegrapher assured as he looked over the wording. "Yes, this will be simple enough. You seem like you are in a bit of a rush. You can pay me later. I'll write the cost down."

"Alright then, I'm off," Brady said as he exited.

Finally, he and Riley were able to get down to business. Picking up the trail of the Talbot riders, they headed north. It was 11:00 a.m. and indeed a late start, but it was a start.

"It has been near twenty-four hours since Talbot and his riders headed this way. How far you reckon they could get?" Brady questioned.

"With the wounded, I don't imagine they'll be running overly hard for too long. It is safe to say that they are at least a half a day ahead, maybe further. We have a good chance, I think, in catching up with them in a couple of days, depending, of course, on what lies ahead."

"Yeah, I figured the same," Brady agreed. "Got any idea on how the two of us are going to take down thirteen men?"

"Each of my pistols holds six slugs," Riley joked. "Of course the only way that is any good is if they ain't shooting back at me or they are asleep," he added with a smile. "One thing I have learned in this business, Brady is that you can't always have a plan. As you know from yesterday's experience, plans don't always pan out. Best way to go about tracking down that many men is to play it all by ear and sight. Never let your guard down and always keep your eyes locked on your opponent. A man's eyes will give away to you what he is going to do next."

"I don't think I could keep my eyes locked onto twenty-six pairs of eyes, Riley," Brady teased.

Riley didn't even respond. Instead he shook his head and smiled as they carried on.

To the northeast on the outskirts of Candora, Tyrell and Buck were scouring through the bush trying to find Buck's long lost camp.

"I can't believe we ain't found it yet. I know it has to be in this general area. This scrub and such looks familiar."

"Look around, Buck. This scrub is the same everywhere, so of course it looks familiar," Tyrell chuckled. "Like I told you last night, pull off one of those dirty socks of yours and let the dog get a snout full. He'll find the damn place," Tyrell said as he inched Pony deeper into the bush.

Not far from where he entered the thick undergrowth, he could see a pile of rubble.

"Hey Buck. Keep your socks on. I think I found it," he hollered as he swung off Pony and walked over to where the gear and shabby lean-to were.

"Yep, this has got to be it, Buck. I found it."

"I knew we were close."

Buck and his horse made their way through the thick bramble to where Tyrell and Pony stood.

"Welcome to Hotel Buck. That'll be seven dollars, please," Buck joked as he looked around. "Sure nice to be home."

He fixed the sticks that kept his lean-to taut, then climbed inside and gathered his side arms, rifle and money satchel, making sure that it was all there.

"All is good, Travis," he said as he strapped his pistol on and leaned his rifle against a block of wood.

"Since we're here, Buck, do you know if Candora has a telegraph office?" Tyrell asked as he pulled up a block of wood and sat down.

"Wasn't there long enough to know either way, Travis. It's a modern town. They might have one, but I ain't going there."

"How far out are we?"

"Two or three miles maybe. Are you planning on heading that way to see if they do have a telegraph?"

"Was thinking about it. I reckon it is a bit late today to head north to Hazelton. We might as well spend the rest of the day here," Tyrell suggested.

The Missing Years – Part II

"I wouldn't argue. We can rest up, have a good meal and head out in the morning."

"Yeah, that is the way I'm looking at it. I do think I'll head into Candora. Are you sure you don't want to tag along, Buck?"

"Hell no. I'll stick around here and make camp a bit more cosy. Might even gather some water and have a bit of a wash up. You go ahead. I ain't got no desire to head into Candora, no sir," Buck replied adamantly.

"That is fine. I don't mind going alone. Is there anything you need while I'm there?"

Buck shook his head.

"Nothing comes to mind."

"Alright then, I'll see you in a couple of hours," Tyrell said as he stood up and hopped onto his saddle. Kicking Pony's flank, he made his way out of the bush and onto the wagon road that led into Candora. Making the distance, he pulled Pony up to a horse rail and tied him up.

"I'll be back in a few minutes, Pony. Just going to look around a bit and hopefully find a telegraph office."

As he made his way along the wooden boardwalk, he came across a bulletin board that had the same wanted poster of himself that he had seen before. He looked around making sure no one was watching him and pulled it down then folded it up and tucked it into his shirt.

Next, he walked across the street to a mercantile and asked if there was a telegraph office in town. The clerk said there was and he pointed Tyrell in that direction. Thanking the clerk, he exited and found his way over to it. He sent a telegram to Fort Macleod stating where he was and that he had requested the expertise of Buck Ainsworth, bounty hunter. With the telegram sent, he paid the small fee and was about to leave when the telegrapher stopped him.

"Sir, there is a reply coming in from Fort Macleod," the telegrapher said as he accepted the reply. "It is from someone named Brady and addressed to you."

He handed the telegram over to him. Taking it, Tyrell thanked the clerk and began to read it.

"Shit," he said beneath his breath.

"What is it?" the clerk asked.

"Nothing. No worries. Thanks again," Tyrell said as he folded the piece of paper and tucked it away in his shirt pocket. He wasted no more time in town and headed out straight away. The information he had wasn't by any means good news. Something terribly wrong had taken place in Fort Macleod and two of his friends had been wounded, how badly he didn't know. Not to mention the fact that Talbot Hunter had escaped, or the fact that now Riley Scott was riding alongside Brady, Tyrell knew that Riley Scott had tracked him into Hells Bottom and was likely still looking for Tyrell Sloan in a roundabout way. *Yep, quite the thing this is now,* he thought to himself as he made his way back to Buck's camp.

"Hey Buck," he began as he swung off Pony's back. "I managed to send a telegram off to the Fort. They've been informed that you're working with me. Got one back in only a few minutes after mine was sent. Tanner and Ed have both been wounded and Talbot has managed an escape. Riley Scott and Brady are tracking him now," Tyrell said in one long-winded breath.

"You got to be kidding," Buck responded with deep concern.

"Nope."

Tyrell handed him the telegram.

Buck read it and shook his head.

"Goddamn, I hope Tanner is okay."

"I don't know. What we do know is he ain't dead. What a crappy day this turned out to be," Tyrell added as he sat down.

"What are your plans, Travis?"

"I ain't sure, Buck. I ain't sure," he repeated in a sombre voice. "I know one thing for certain. Being as we're this close to Hazelton, I don't see much point in turning around even though I feel compelled to. I know that ain't what Ed, Brady, or Tanner would want. I think we'll carry on and hope like hell that Ed and Tanner pull through and that Brady and Riley catch up with Talbot. They're going up against a dozen or so men. The odds ain't good for them and that bothers me some."

Tyrell looked into the small flames of the fire that Buck had lit as he contemplated. He was indeed relieved that Brady wasn't alone. His relief, though, was met with some apprehension. After all, Riley Scott had indeed once trailed him. *What will come, will come,* he thought as he averted his eyes.

Buck removed the coffee pot that was beginning to hiss and pop.

"Can I pour you one of these, Travis?"

"Sure, I could use a coffee," Tyrell responded as he waited for Buck to hand him a cup.

"Chapter 12"

Thursday morning, while the sun remained hidden behind the mountains, Tyrell and Buck loaded up their gear and once more headed northerly.

"It looks like it is going to be another hot day, Buck. We should be able to put on some miles today, I reckon," Tyrell said as they made it to the wagon trail.

"You have any inclination on how far Hazelton is from here?"

"Not offhand, Buck. I do have a map that we can look at once we have some light," Tyrell responded as they continued onward.

"No need for a map, Travis. I know how far it is. Once we get to a place called Vermillion, we'll have two days of riding ahead of us. The terrain gets tough when we're in the vicinity, a lot of bear and such. We might even come across some of the Athabascan in the area. Let me do the talking if that happens."

"Athabascan?" Tyrell questioned. "I thought they were more up in Alaska."

"For a time that is where they stayed and most are up that way still. But, us great white men," Buck stated with sarcasm, "changed things for them over the past thirty or forty years and some have moved down closer to this area. It could be said that they have made their home close to the Kutenai maybe even the Kaska tribes in the area. The Blackfoot are seen around them parts too, but not 'til fall I reckon. The others will be about, making their way to the lakes and west coast to fish and to buy and sell wares. Most times they are friendly, depending, I guess, on how they are feeling. My experience has always been good."

They travelled in silence for a few miles as the sun slowly came to life.

"My question to you, Buck, is how far away is Vermillion from Candora?"

"I'm not so sure. We'll have to use your map for that," Buck replied.

Tyrell shook his head.

"I thought you said we didn't need a map."

"Nope, I said once we get to Vermillion we wouldn't need a map."

Buck began to chuckle.

"No worries, Travis, there are a couple of different ways to go. The way you were going when you came across me and Will is one way. I ain't sure it is shorter, but I've always went the northeastern route and I know once I get to Vermillion, I can ride hard northerly for two days and be in Hazelton."

The sun by now was bright enough that Tyrell could look at the map so the two riders rested as they discussed their route. They could go the way Buck was used to, but according to Tyrell's map that added a few more miles to the trek.

"I think we best stick to the route I was following, Buck. It is shorter by twenty or so miles. Your way brings us right over the Rockies and almost right back into Alberta again. I say we carry on west to this place called Fairmount that looks like it is a day's ride from here. Then, we'll head northeasterly and finally north. Vermillion is, I'd say, about two or three days ride from there. We go this route and we should be getting near Hazelton in four or five days," Tyrell mentioned as he stroked his whiskered chin.

"I ain't got a problem going that way either. Thought maybe by heading northeast from here we'd make better timing, but the map tells me a different story. Westerly it is. Come on, let's get," Buck said as he waited for Tyrell to fold up his map.

That done, the two riders headed west along the wagon road that would eventually lead them into the township of Fairmount.

Meanwhile, Brady and Riley were making good progress in following the trail they were on. The Talbot riders had turned westerly as well and were heading into the Rocky Mountains a hundred miles south of where Tyrell and Buck were.

"I figured they'd head this way. The Rocky Mountains are a good place to hide. We'll find them, though," Riley said as he slowed his horse down.

"Hold up a second there, Brady. Look up ahead."

He pointed toward a couple of stray horses that were munching on some grass.

"What do you make of that?"

"I ain't sure. Likely a couple of wild ponies are all," Brady said as he and Riley looked on.

"I don't think so, Brady. They don't look like wild ponies to me. Let's see if we can get closer," Riley suggested as they slowly walked their horses toward them.

The two horses looked up at the approaching riders and continued eating.

"Nope, they ain't wild."

Riley pulled his horse to a halt and swung off the saddle. Handing his reins to Brady, he slowly approached the two horses on foot. He could tell that it hadn't been long since saddles had been strapped to their backs.

"I think we should keep our eyes peeled for a couple riders that have either been thrown from their horses or worse. These two horses ain't been without saddles long, Brady."

"You don't suppose they'd be some of Talbot's riders do you?"

"Hard to say. It could be that way. Maybe they are a couple of the wounded. We ain't going to know unless we stumble on them. No use worrying about it," Riley responded. "We'll certainly keep a lookout."

He took his horse's reins from Brady and swung back onto his saddle.

"I reckon we'll put a couple more miles behind us and rest up a bit. My old bones don't appreciate these long stints on a horse anymore," Riley mentioned as they continued following the trail they were on.

Five miles into the trek, as they broke through some bramble, they came across the bodies of four dead men. One of the men, however, wasn't quite dead. Brady noticed the man twitch.

"Riley, I think this fellow here has some life left in him," Brady said as he knelt next to the man.

"What happened here, mister?" Brady put his ear close to the man's face, hoping to hear a response from the man, but the man was silent. He was in too much agony and on the verge of death that he couldn't respond to Brady's question. Riley knelt down as he made the distance to where Brady and the dying man were.

"I don't think he's got much life in him," Riley stated as he looked on. "Looks like he took a slug to his stomach. What a painful way to die."

For a moment in time, Brady and Riley could only look on. Then with some effort, the man mumbled a few words.

"What's that you said?" Riley questioned with surprise.

The man once more repeated what he had said. This time Riley and Brady listened closely.

"Silver Canyon... Talbot..." he began then faded once more into a painful realisation that he would soon be dead.

"Silver Canyon. What do you suppose he meant by that, Riley?" Brady questioned.

Again, the man repeated what he said. This time he added that it was Talbot Hunter who shot him and the three other men lying on the ground, dead.

"We have to get this fellow to a doctor, Brady. I ain't sure he has much life left in him, but I reckon he is one of the Talbot riders."

"Not so sure there is much point, Riley. He is pretty much bled out."

"We can't just leave him here, Brady. If he can be saved, then..." but Riley didn't get to finish the sentence before the man pulled one of Riley's pistols from its holster and shot himself in the temple. The sound of Riley's .44 echoed with a loud clap as the man's head exploded.

"Jesus Christ almighty," Riley said as he looked at the mess on the ground.

A slick of blood and brain matter was visible across the moss covered ground.

"God damn it. I don't know how he managed to get my pistol. Jesus Christ, I wasn't expecting that."

Riley inhaled deeply as he took back his pistol from the now dead man's hand.

"Guess he ain't going to be in need of a doctor now, Brady."

Riley stood up as Brady knelt there in shock.

"That should never have happened."

Riley shook his head as he looked down once more at the man and then over to Brady.

"Brady, Brady. Snap out of it. Come on. He's dead," Riley said as he grabbed Brady by his arm and helped him up.

"I ain't ever seen anything like that before, Riley. Holy cow. I can't believe what I just witnessed," Brady said as he turned and vomited.

"Take it easy, Brady. Don't let what happened here affect what it is we need to do. We still need to bring in Talbot. This fellow here obviously chose to do that. It ain't something I've seen often either. Shocked the hell out of me too, but we got to keep our wits."

Brady turned back and faced Riley.

"I know, I know. It would have been less of a shock if he had simply died. Scattering his own brains all over the place like that though... Jesus."

Brady shook his head.

"Should we at least bury the dead, Riley?"

"Nope, they need to be identified by the law. We will have to mark the area so we can remember where they are at. Once we get back to the Fort, we'll lead the law here to clean up," Riley said as he piled a few rocks and cut some branches off a couple of trees.

"There, that ought to do. It shouldn't be hard for us or the law to find this place again. We best saddle up and continue onward. I reckon the silver canyon he spoke of is where Talbot and his riders are heading," Riley said as he swung onto his horse.

"Do we even know where this silver canyon is?" Brady questioned as he followed suit and swung onto his own horse.

"I have a bit of an inclination. There is an old silver mine on this side of the Rocky Mountains. I reckon that might be the place he mentioned. We ain't ever going to know until we get there; another three or four days ride, I suspect. We might get lucky and come across Talbot before then. We ain't too far behind," Riley commented as he kicked his horse's flank and the two riders continued westerly.

They rode in silence for another ten miles before settling for the evening. Pulling their horses to a halt they tethered them to a tree that was close to a small creek that trickled by.

"I reckon this here is as good a place as any to settle for the evening," Riley said as he and Brady prepared their evening camp.

One hundred and twenty five miles north, Tyrell and Buck were making their way into the township of Fairmount.

"There it is, Buck, Fairmount," Tyrell said as they stopped for a minute and looked on. "It certainly ain't that big, is it?"

"It sure ain't. Are we going to see if there is a hotel room available?"

"Nah, I kind of like the outdoors too, Buck. We'll set up a camp north of there a ways."

"Good. I'd rather do that," Buck responded as they rode to the outskirts and found a suitable place to set up.

"Right here looks good," Buck said as he slowed his horse and waited for Tyrell and Pony to pull up.

Tyrell looked around.

"This place suits me fine. If you are happy with it, Buck, then so am I."

Tyrell smiled as they dismounted.

"A couple more days and we'll be in Vermillion. We're making good time, Buck," Tyrell said as he tethered Pony to a few saplings and unloaded his gear.

"I will admit things have gone smoothly. That might change once we get into the Rockies again," Buck responded as he unloaded his own gear. "A lot of bear and such and a few polecats too, I'm sure, are likely waiting for us."

"Are you telling me that a big burly fellow such as yourself is afraid of a couple of bear and polecats?" Tyrell teased as he gathered rocks for their fire.

"Any man with common sense ought to be," Buck retorted with a chuckle. "I'm more inclined to be wary of that horse and dog of yours stirring up trouble. I know neither one likes bear much."

"That is true. If there are any bear that we come across, you can bet one or the other will let us know. But, at least we'll know."

Tyrell shrugged his shoulders as he piled the rocks he had gathered into a circle so they could have a fire.

"Lately, though, the dog and horse ain't been showing much interest in bear, which in itself is a bit odd. Maybe they've grown out of that."

"You keep telling yourself that, Travis. But I reckon they ain't showed much interest simply because we ain't come across any yet."

"That might be and is likely the case. Leastwise, I can hope," Tyrell chuckled as he drew a match across the striker and set flames to the birch bark and twigs that slowly came to life with orange flames and began to snap and crackle.

"Want beans tonight, Buck?"

"Beans, biscuits and coffee sound palatable."

"I never said anything about biscuits, Buck. Nevertheless, I reckon we have the fixings to make some. I'll get on it," Tyrell said as he went about stirring up some flour, water, and stuff to have biscuits.

Buck meandered over to the creek to refill their canteens with water and brought back enough to make coffee as well.

"I'll get coffee going," he said as he went about the task.

An hour later, sitting on their saddles, they filled their gullets with the meal. It was nothing special, but it did hit the spot. Full and fed they drank coffee and reminisced, talking about this, that, and the other thing. Sometimes they just listened to the sounds of night, content to be in the company of one another.

The Missing Years – Part II

"How do you figure your friends are making out in tracking down that Talbot fellow?"

"I ain't sure, Buck. I hope they're doing okay," Tyrell said as he slurped from his coffee. "I am more concerned, to be honest, about Ed and Tanner."

"Yeah, I hear you there. Tanner is a good friend of mine. He and I have done a lot together. I have to admit though, he ain't always the smartest fellow," Buck chuckled. "I remember this one time he got himself into a fix. Had four men waiting to squeeze their triggers on him. He had his pistol drawn and bullshitted his way out of the confrontation. He managed to convince the men to lay down their weapons and then tied them up. Once they were secured, he loaded his side arm right in front of them. The whole time he was bullshitting them, his pistol didn't even have any bullets in it.

Man, did those men get hostile when they learned that. Tanner only chuckled and told them all to shut up. It was quite the sight. There was Tanner with an empty pistol and four men ready to kill him. He has horseshoes up his arse, I think."

Both Buck and Tyrell began to laugh.

"Yep, those were the days," Buck finished as he looked into the flames of fire.

Tyrell too remembered a few stories about Tanner, but he couldn't mention them. He and Tanner rode together years earlier and some of the stories he had to tell about that time would have been a perfect fit for the story Buck told. Tyrell bit his tongue and kept his mouth shut.

"Sounds like Tanner can be pretty cocky."

Buck waved his hand through the air as though he were swatting at a fly.

"Cocky is an understatement. There are a slew of stories I could tell, but they wouldn't be the same without Tanner sitting with us."

The Missing Years – Part II

He took a drink from his coffee and once more averted his eyes to the flickering flames of the fire as he reminisced about those days gone past.

Tyrell also began to reminisce, although he wasn't thinking about the time he and Tanner ran together, but about his home, his grandfather's land in Red Rock. It had almost been a year since he left there. He wondered if Marissa and Grandma Heddy were well. He wondered about old Wesley Wilson and Fry. He wondered if word had reached them about his faked death and he wondered how each felt about it. It was sad in a sense that he had to go that route, but anything was better than swinging from a rope for simply protecting himself and Emma. It was what it was, and it wasn't about to change. Not yet, at least.

He thought back to what Buck had declared; that he was going to see to it that every crooked Mounted Police constable that was on Gabe Roy's payroll was exposed. As he sat there reminiscing, he wanted to be a part of that. With Buck's help it was certainly doable. It would take time, but all he had was time. For now, his efforts would be kept in check as he sorted out the idea. He couldn't think about that while he was looking for Matt Crawford, or Ron Reginal as he was calling himself, and trying to determine the identity of Emery Nelson's killer. However, when it was all over and done with, he might consider helping Buck put a stop to Gabe Roy's influence and expose the crooked law that without a doubt lawlessly ruled Willow Gate. How it would all benefit him in the end he didn't know. In fact, it might not benefit him at all. However, it would certainly benefit the residents of that small town called Willow Gate. Folks like Gabe Roy were a menace and the more they grabbed the more they wanted.

Tyrell inhaled deeply as he swallowed the last of his coffee and poured himself and Buck another.

"You made damn good coffee tonight, Buck. Not nearly as strong as it was the last time."

"I reckoned since I was sitting with a woman, I'd make it weak."

"Are you calling me a woman, Buck?" Tyrell smiled.

"Nah, just funning with you. The last time I did make it a bit strong, even for myself. Figured I wouldn't use as much this time and maybe we'd still have some left. I have to admit it is better than the last pot. Although I do like a strong coffee, I ain't got any complaints about how this turned out."

"So, we're getting low on the grinds?"

"I reckon we have enough to make the distance to Vermillion. We'll have to look over our supplies once we get there. There is a nice mercantile there. Has everything from bullets to boots. A good-looking woman runs the place too," Buck smiled.

"Sounds as though you know her intimately. Do you?"

"Not really. She's a friendly sort and I make sure to stop by there whenever I pass by. Sometimes I don't even need anything, but I still spend a couple bucks. Last time I was there, Tanner was with me. That is where that story I told you about took place. I reckon it's been a year or two."

"Going back to that story, were those men bounties that the two of you were hunting down?"

"Nope, they were just men looking for trouble. Vermillion has those types of fellows wandering around all the time. It is a bit of a hoodwink town. There ain't no law there. The law has to come from Hazelton or beyond. Least that is how it was then. Maybe things have changed by now. I don't know."

"You reckon someone like Crawford would hang out there?"

The Missing Years – Part II

"Hard to say. I don't know much about that fellow except what I have heard second hand. Could be where a petty thief like Ron Reginal might visit. Of course, that is all hearsay. I can't say with confidence if Ron would be near there or not. We'll have to wait and see. It would sure make things simple if he were."

Buck took a swig from his coffee.

It sure would make things simple. But, simplicity ain't something that happens often."

At that moment, Black Dog stood up and began a low muffled growl. Tyrell and Buck looked in the direction the dog was facing.

"You see anything, Buck?" Tyrell asked in a quiet voice.

"Nope, ain't seeing anything."

The two men stood up and waited to see if anything came around the bend or broke through the bush. Minutes passed and still nothing appeared. Black Dog continued his stare and every now and again, he'd take a few steps forward, then stop and continue his low growl.

"There is definitely something coming, Buck." Tyrell said as he grabbed his rifle and loosened his pistols.

If anything pounced, he was ready. Buck did the same and the two stood guard, waiting. Minutes continued to pass without so much as a sound coming from the direction they were looking. Black Dog, though, had certainly seen or sensed something. Then they heard it. The sound of horse hooves as a rider approached. Black Dog was about to dart in the direction, but Tyrell commanded him to stay and pointed into the undergrowth.

"Go there and stay put, Black Dog. Go now," Tyrell said in a low voice as the rider came around the bend and into full view.

"Shit," Buck said in a whispered breath.

"What is it, Buck?" Tyrell asked with concern.

"Looks like that is Crying Wolf from the Athabascan tribe. He isn't a very nice fellow. Let me do the talking, Travis. He and I have a history. Hello there," he said as he waited for a reply.

The rider stopped and looked on toward them. They could only see him in the shadows. Buck repeated his call out. They could see by the light of the moon that the rider crossed his arms across his chest and continued to stare at them. The rider didn't speak for a few minutes. He simply sat on his horse and sized up the situation. Then he finally recognised Buck and the horse and rider came towards them once more.

"It is not often that I would approach two white men. I know the big burly one, though," the rider said as he swung off his horse. "Buck, my friend, how have you fared these last few years?" Crying Wolf asked as he walked over to him and put his hand on Buck's shoulder.

"Crying Wolf, it is good to see you," Buck said as he now put his own hand on the Indian's shoulder. "I have been well; and you old friend, how have you been faring?"

"I am well enough. Who is this white man?" he questioned as he removed his hand from Buck's shoulder and sized up Tyrell. Crying Wolf was not threatened or afraid of Tyrell's presence. He was a warrior, fearless and cunning. His long black hair was tied in a single braid. The scars on his face were from all the hand-to-hand combat he had been in. He had never lost a fight. His buckskin clothing was well-kept, neat, and tidy. His black, piercing eyes were filled with wisdom and showed no fear. Indeed, he was a man who demanded respect.

"This is Travis. He's a bounty hunter like myself," Buck said as he waited for Crying Wolf to respond.

"Yes, I can sense that. He is also running from something."

Crying Wolf reached over and put his hand on Tyrell's shoulder much the way he did to Buck. Tyrell looked over to Buck who was gesturing for him to do the same. Tyrell slowly reached up and put his hand on Crying Wolf's shoulder.

"I am Crying Wolf. You are friends with the big, burly white man, so do not fear me."

"It is with a great honour to meet you," Tyrell said as he looked deep into Crying Wolf's eyes, trying not to show fear or apprehension. He knew if he did, Crying Wolf would not show him respect. It was that way with most of the natives he had met and Crying Wolf was no different.

"Your soul tells me that you are in turmoil. It is a good turmoil. You are looking for answers. Keep looking, Travis. You will find these answers, but you must look beyond what the eye can see."

With that, Crying Wolf removed his hand from Tyrell's shoulder and Tyrell removed his from Crying Wolf. It was as though Crying Wolf had looked deep into his very being and indeed, he had. Tyrell felt a bit overwhelmed and at the same time, a sense of relief. He had no idea what it all meant, but it certainly meant something.

"If I may, I will stay here tonight with the big, burly white man and his friend Travis," Crying Wolf stated as he looked over to Buck and back to Tyrell.

"Of course, you are welcome to share our fire tonight, Crying Wolf. It has been a long time since we have done so," Buck responded, as he gestured for Crying Wolf to sit. "Would you like a coffee?"

The Missing Years – Part II

"Yuk. The last time I drank coffee with you there were not enough leaves in the forest to keep myself clean," Crying Wolf smiled. "That was many seasons ago. Maybe things have changed. Yes, I will have a coffee."

Buck poured their visitor a cup and offered Crying Wolf sugar to go with it.

"I can't remember if you use sugar or not."

"Sugar is fine, thank you."

Crying Wolf put three heaping spoonsful into his cup and stirred it.

"What brings your presence to here?" Crying Wolf questioned as he took a sip from his coffee and added another scoop of sugar. "You are hunting a bad man, I presume?"

"In a roundabout way, yes. I am helping Travis," Buck responded.

Crying Wolf averted his eyes to Tyrell.

"You have good help," he said referring to Buck.

"Indeed I do," Tyrell agreed with sincerity.

"The big, burly white man is a bull. I have seen many men on his back. He bucks them off."

Crying Wolf began to chuckle at the joke and play on Buck's name.

"They were little men, Crying Wolf," Buck said sheepishly.

"Not so true, but I know you are humble. We will say they were little men, not of size, but of heart."

Crying Wolf looked again in Tyrell's direction.

"Your dog, where did he get to?" Crying Wolf asked. He could see the tracks and could even smell the scent of a dog. He wasn't stupid.

"Likely out chasing rabbits; he'll be back."

"I hope no harm comes his way."

"What do you mean?" Tyrell asked with concern.

"There is a grizzly bear not far from here. He crossed my path only a mile away," Crying Wolf replied.

"Well then, chances are he's picked up the scent. He doesn't like any kind of bear."

"This does not concern your kinship you have with this dog, that he would chase a bear?" Crying Wolf asked with curiosity.

"No. He's chased many bear and he doesn't fear them. If he doesn't get to them first, then the horse gets all antsy and does the chasing," Tyrell responded with affection toward Pony.

"There is a legend about a horse that is told around our fires at night, about a horse that chased bear. It is said that this horse once killed a grizzly by breaking the back of the monster. It fended off many bear and always kept its rider safe. It is interesting to hear that your horse does this when I know so well the legend of a horse that does the same. You are blessed, I think."

"Ain't sure it is a blessing and I don't mean any disrespect to your legend, but to be honest Crying Wolf, having a horse that chases after bear is more problematic than a blessing. That is why I prefer the dog to take care of bear. I've been thrown off ol' Pony a few too many times because of nearby bear," Tyrell chuckled. "Grouse have the same effect on him as do bear, and for one reason or another, he often doesn't seem to like it when I cook beans."

"A horse with such spirit and heart should make you smile. You are, as I have said, blessed to have him."

Tyrell shrugged his shoulders.

"Yeah, I reckon so."

He looked over toward Pony and smiled. Crying Wolf was right; blessed he was to have Pony. Black Dog returned to his side.

"Your dog, I can tell, is part wolf. He has double canines. That is the sign of the wolf," Crying Wolf said as he stood up, made his way over to where Black Dog lay and patted him.

"Yes, I have been told that before," Tyrell responded.

He looked on while Crying Wolf continued to admire Black Dog.

"Do not ever think, Travis, that you are not blessed."

That is all he said as he stood up and made his way back to his place near the fire.

"Our friend, Buck, he too is blessed, but in a different way," Crying Wolf added as he sat down again.

Neither Buck nor Tyrell commented. They simply did not know what to say. Instead, the three men once more sat in silence and contemplation. It was Buck who finally broke the silence.

"Where are you heading to, Crying Wolf, if I may ask."

"I have some trading to do with Little Dan of the Kaska tribe. I will make the distance in a few more days. And you, Buck, where are you and your friend Travis going?"

"We are heading to Vermillion and then onward to Hazelton. That is where our business is," Buck responded.

"The outlaw town burned to the ground some months ago. All that is left is a little outpost."

"Burned to the ground?" Buck repeated with curiosity.

"Yes. The lives of many may have been lost, but we do not know this with certainty."

"How did it happen?" Tyrell questioned.

"It is not known by us, how. It was our brothers and sisters to the north that brought the news with them in early spring. The flames by then no longer burned and only charred buildings remained. Perhaps there is no one to blame."

"I don't know about that. Usually towns do not burn to the ground without reason," Buck replied.

The news for him was saddening. There were folks he knew that lived there and it was his hope that those he knew were safe.

"This is true, yes, but the Athabascan do not know how or why. We keep away from outlaw towns. The white man's business is the white man's business. Only a few, like yourself and now your friend Travis, are friends of the Athabascan," Crying Wolf pointed out.

A silence enveloped the three men as Buck and Tyrell contemplated the devastating news.

"I guess we have to head back into Fairmount tomorrow, Buck, if we want to pick up supplies. Vermillion is out of the question now."

Buck removed his hat and ran his fingers through his hair.

"Yep, I reckon. Goddamn! What a bloody shame about Vermillion. I'd still like to make our way there, Travis. I have a few friends that lived in the area. I'd like to make sure they are okay," Buck sighed as he donned his hat again.

"I hear you, Buck. We'll make our way there. Got to go that way anyhow to get to Hazelton."

"I am sorry that this news has upset you, Buck," Crying Wolf stated. "But is it not better to hear it from a friend than to discover it without knowing?"

"It is, Crying Wolf, it is," Buck repeated.

What remained of the evening after that was spent in cheerless conversation.

"Chapter 13"

Friday, June 26, 1891. The sun wasn't even visible that morning when Crying Wolf left the two men and the fire they shared the night before. In fact, the coals from the fire were all that lit his way as he silently packed his belongings. Reaching into his quiver of arrows, he removed the one with the purple feathers and stuck it into a piece of wood. Then, as silent as a gentle breeze, he mounted his horse and continued on his way.

To the south, Brady and Riley were slowly coming to life. They wanted and needed an early start, and had decided the night before to wake early. They knew that the trail they were following was gradually fading; trails always did after forty-eight hours. It was getting close to that time now. There was little time to waste. Even though they had an idea on where Talbot and his riders were heading, they were hopeful that they would catch up to them before they found refuge at the silver canyon hideout. It was always less risky to gather an unexpected bounty than one who was warned or fortified.

Brady rubbed his eyes as he stood up from his bedroll.

"Do you think it is early enough that we could have coffee, Riley?" he asked as he rolled up his bedding.

"Too dark at the moment I reckon to pick up the trail, we might as well," Riley said as he blew on the coals and added a few sticks. "I hope we get a visual on Talbot today. I feel as though we will," Riley stated as he set the coffee pot on the fire.

"What makes you think that?"

"There aren't many horses alive that can run steady. Nor are there many men that could handle it. They have to slow down to a snail's pace eventually and

I reckon after two days of running hard, that is exactly what they are going to be doing today. We might even get lucky, Brady, and find them all snoozing."

"That wouldn't hurt my feelings one bit. Tell me, Riley, do you know why his gang is called the Kingsley Gang if he ain't a Kingsley? I never read anything on him regarding such. I always wondered."

"The story is he shot Brett Kingsley and took over his gang. I guess he had been riding with them and he and Brett had some kind of a confrontation. One thing lead to the other and Talbot shot and killed him. He has a tendency, from what I know and from what we saw with those wounded men of his yesterday, to shoot his own men. I reckon he kept the Kingsley name because of the fear it puts into some folk. There wouldn't have been much point in changing the name, I guess."

Riley shrugged his shoulders as he poured each of them a fresh coffee.

"That is about all I can say as to why his gang still rides under that name."

Brady held his coffee in his hand and gently blew at it.

"It is a lot more than what I knew. Makes sense too, I reckon."

Bringing the cup he held in his hands to his lips, he took a swallow.

"He is about as cold-blooded as a Rocky Mountain rattler, ain't he?"

"And then some," Riley said as he too took a savoury sip from his morning coffee.

"Men like Talbot deserve every strand of hemp rope that makes up a noose, or for that matter, the hot lead from any lucky man that shoots him. Few men would ever stand up against him and that is where the problem with his kind lies."

The Missing Years – Part II

"One man is still only a man, Riley," Brady said as he looked into his cup and sloshed it around.

"Same could be said about an army of men, which at one time the Kingsley Gang was. You and your fellow men knocked them down good. With the four dead fellows back yonder, it means there are nine capable and willing men. That, Brady, is still a small army," Riley made clear.

"It is, I know, but we have the element of surprise on our side," Brady commented as he inhaled deeply. He knew they were close to either Talbot or a simple passerby. He could smell food cooking.

"Talbot ain't no dummy, Brady. He knows there are men on his trail, either us or the law, he knows is following him."

"Smell that, Riley?" Brady asked as he inhaled deeply.

"Smell what?" he asked with authority.

"Salt pork and biscuits. Take a whiff. Someone is cooking and it ain't far from here."

Riley inhaled deeply and by God, he did smell food cooking. It meant only one thing, that someone was near.

"Come on, we best get this fire out. It'll be light soon and the smoke will be seen by anyone near," Riley said as the two of them kicked dirt over the flames and then doused it with their morning coffee and a canteen of water.

"There, that takes care of that. Right now, the best thing for us to do is get up high."

Riley pointed to a ridge not far from where they were. From there, at least they would be able to pinpoint any smoke from a nearby fire and have the advantage of height.

Brady nodded in agreement as they gathered their gear as quietly as possible. Sound always seemed

The Missing Years – Part II

to travel the furthest during the before-dawn twilight and so they knew the quieter they were the better. Even when they spoke, it was in quiet whispers.

Thirty minutes later, from where they stood on the ridge, they could see smoke rising in the distance.

"We sure were close last night, Brady. From here I'd say that fire might be only a mile away," Riley pointed out.

"It couldn't be much further. Figure we should head that way. We know more or less where it is from where we camped last night. It won't take us long to get there. Might even get that distance before the sun rises completely. That would improve our advantage," Brady commented as fact.

"Sure hope it is our man. It is a wild goose chase if it turns out to be someone else."

"We ain't going to know one way or the other until we get close, Riley."

Riley nodded his head in agreement.

"Let's see where all this leads. Come on, Brady, let's get," Riley said as they mounted their horses and headed toward the rising smoke.

It took less than forty minutes for Brady and Riley to get a visual, and sure enough, it was Talbot and his men. Signaling to one another, they headed back to cover.

Sitting on the ground with their back against some boulders, they talked in quiet voices as they developed their plan of attack. It was a simple plan. They were going to go in with their guns blazing.

"We're clear then on how to do this, Brady?" Riley questioned.

"Yeah, I reckon once our guns are blazing it is going to take them by surprise. I noticed a few of the men were still bundled up in their bedrolls. I counted nine men, Riley. At least three were still sleeping. That means six are awake and armed. It can't be that difficult to knock down six unsuspecting men. Are we going to shoot to kill or shoot to wound?" Brady wanted to be clear.

"It doesn't matter to me either way. Wounding them and bringing them in alive only decreases our chances of bringing them all in without incident. Dead men can't fight, wounded men can. If some die, then I guess some die. It's Talbot that we want alive, but I don't reckon the law would care either way. Are you ready?"

Riley and Brady checked over their weapons, making sure they were loaded and ready.

"Am now; rifle is loaded and my side arm is good to go"

"All right then. Let's go knock down some outlaws," Riley said as they headed back toward Talbot's camp.

Once they made the distance to where they could again see the men, they counted to three, stood up, and began shooting. Dust and smoke filled the air, as men ran this way and that. Those bundled up tried to crawl out of their bedrolls only to be wounded with hot lead, incapacitating their attempts to reach their weapons. Talbot dove for cover, his pistol answering every shot fired by Brady and Riley. Bullets slammed into the ground and surrounding trees like a nest of angry hornets buzzing this way and that. Tucking and rolling, two of Talbot's men managed to mount their horses, then were mowed down by Talbot himself. As far as he was concerned, if his men weren't going to stick by him, then they weren't worth the effort to keep alive.

The smell of gun smoke enveloped the camp as the silence of early dawn was broken by the sound of gunfire.

The Missing Years – Part II

The entire event lasted only a few minutes. Finally, Talbot stood up, tossed his guns to the ground and raised his hands. He had been defeated.

By now, Riley was standing next to Talbot, his pistol pointed at him, ready to fire at any moment.

"I reckon you are done, Talbot. Your men, all except that one," Riley pointed at one of the men that was in his bedroll, wounded but alive, "are all dead. You ain't got a leg to stand on."

Talbot said nothing as Riley secured his hands and tossed him to the ground. Brady helped the one wounded man out of his bedroll and secured him. He was likely going to die from his wounds although for now he was breathing.

"You got any holes in you, Brady?" Riley asked as he and Brady looked around making sure all was clear.

"Not a one; you?"

"I'm good. Can't say the same for the dead. This was a slaughter. Kind of leaves a bad taste in my mouth," Riley mentioned as he continued his gaze of the battleground.

"Spit. That ought to take the taste away," Brady said with attempted humour.

"Did you see how Talbot blew those two off their horses? That sure was a surprise. Glad he did, otherwise we still might be shooting and my damn ears are ringing enough. Quite the thing, I'd say. Glad it is ended now," Riley commented as he reloaded his pistols and slapped them back into their holster.

"Thought for sure we were going to have a few holes. Got lucky, I reckon. It ain't often two men can pounce on nine and walk away without losing blood."

At that moment, without rhyme or reason, they heard the whistling sound of a bullet overhead as it made contact with Talbot's chest. A second later, the loud crack of rifle came from a distance. Both men dropped to the ground. Talbot slumped forward, like a limp noodle. The two men looked at each other with shocked looks on their faces.

"Jesus Christ, Riley. Where do you figure that shot came from?"

Brady looked around, trying to decipher where the shooter was, but he saw nothing. He looked over to where Talbot was.

"Talbot ain't moving," he said as he began to stand.

Riley pulled him back to the ground.

"Stay put, Brady. Whoever fired that shot might very well be sighting in on us. Follow me," Riley said as he and Brady crawled to cover behind a few big rocks.

Now hidden somewhat, they began to look around, hoping to see movement or hear another shot, but none came and they saw nothing. For a few minutes they remained hidden. Finally satisfied that they were once more safe, they made their way over to Talbot, and pulled him to the cover of some undergrowth. Out of view now, they looked him over. A hole the size of a thumb in the middle of his chest told them the rest of the story. Talbot was dead.

"He ain't going to hang now, Brady. Man, whoever made that shot knows how to shoot. I heard the loud clap of the rifle after I heard the bullet whistle by. That tells me whoever did this was some distance away. Ain't many folks around could make that shot."

Brady shook his head in disbelief.

"You ain't whistling Dixie. Whoever fired that shot is a damn good shot with a rifle. The only one I know of in these parts that could make a shot like that is Matt Crawford. You don't suppose he is the shooter, do you?"

"I don't know. It doesn't make much sense if it was. Why would Crawford kill Talbot, unless of course they have some kind of history. We ain't ever going to know until your man Travis or someone else brings him in and we get a chance to question him. I imagine, if it was Crawford, he won't say either way."

Riley slowly rose and looked around.

"I reckon we're in the clear, Brady. Come on, we got a mess to clean up."

They rounded up the dead and the one wounded man and loaded them on to the backs of the five horses they were able to catch. That done, they headed back in the direction of the Fort, leading five horses stacked with the bodies of eight dead men and one wounded. The sun, by now, was out and it warmed them as they made their way towards home. With no room left on the horses they led, they marked the trail that would lead the law to the first four dead men they had come across as they tracked down Talbot. That was all they could do for them.

By now, Tyrell and Buck were coming to life. They were getting ready to head back into Fairmount and gather supplies when Tyrell noticed an arrow stuck into a block of wood.

"Hey, Buck, did you see this?" he asked as he pointed at it. "What does it mean?"

Buck made his way over to Tyrell and smiled as he pulled the arrow loose.

"This here is our ticket to get through the Athabascan territory without incident. We run into problems with them, this arrow will grant us safe passage."

"How does an arrow grant us safe passage?" Tyrell was curious to know.

"We show it and they'll know that Crying Wolf has granted us safety. It's a simple gesture given to us by him. Not one of the Athabascan will deny us a safe passage as long as we have it," Buck explained as he slid the arrow into his belt.

"I see. I ain't ever heard of such a thing. If it is what you say it is, then I guess it ain't what I thought it to be," Tyrell responded as he rolled up his bedding.

"And what did you think it meant, Travis?"

"To be honest, I figured it was a warning of some kind."

"Why would you think it was a warning?"

"I ain't sure why I might have thought that, Buck."

"He scared you, did he?" Buck teased.

"Only up until the point where he introduced himself. After that I was comfortable being in his presence. Is he a shaman or something? He seemed to be quite philosophical a lot of the time," Tyrell asked as he continued to gather up his gear.

"Crying Wolf ain't a shaman. He's a warrior that has Christian faith. He can read people and most other living things, too. I reckon his ability is no different from most men who can do the same. Only difference, I guess, would be he uses words like blessed, faith, fate and the rest of them, like most white folk use. Except, because it comes from the mouth of men that we; and I mean white folk in general, consider to be savages, it seems odd to us."

"That is some explanation, Buck. He came across to me as a man that one automatically respects. I imagine those scars he has on his face and arms could tell a hundred stories."

Tyrell cinched up Pony's saddle, turned and looked around.

"It's going to be a great day, Buck. The sky is blue, the sun is yellow, and there is a mild breeze blowing that makes a man feel alive."

The Missing Years – Part II

"I think Crying Wolf's philosophical ideas have worn off on you," Buck teased as he too cinched up his horse's saddle.

"Onward and forward I guess, eh Travis?"

"Yes sir. Onward and forward."

Swinging onto their horses they headed back south. Fairmount was five miles away and it didn't take them long to get there. Pulling their horses up to the horse pole outside the front doors of the Fairmount Mercantile, they dismounted, tethered them, and entered the store. The smell of gun oil, black powder, lantern fuel and leather permeated as they went about their business picking out the few supplies they would need to make the distance to both Vermillion and Hazelton.

Neither man noticed the young woman behind the counter who was looking oddly at Buck. She knew him from somewhere she just couldn't place him now. It wasn't until they approached the counter did she finally recognise him.

"Buck. Buck Ainsworth, you handsome devil, how are you?" she exclaimed as Buck looked at her almost dropping the things he was carrying in his arms.

A smile the size of a dinner plate crossed his face as he finally managed to set the things down without stumbling.

"JoBeth! Am I ever surprised to see you. I heard what happened up in Vermillion. I thought maybe the worst may have happened."

"Let's not talk about that right now. Come over here and give me a hug," JoBeth said as she leaned forward into Buck's arms. "How have you been keeping up and how long has it been?"

"A couple years leastwise. How about yourself, how are you doing?" Buck asked as he hugged tightly, then stepped back and looked at her.

"You ain't changed one bit, Jo."

The Missing Years – Part II

"Thank you, Buck. You haven't changed either. Hey, introduce me to your friend?" she added as she looked at Tyrell.

"Oh, sorry about that, I got caught up by your beauty," Buck said as he smiled and winked at her. "This is Travis Sweet, an old friend of Tanner and I."

JoBeth reached out her hand to shake Tyrell's, but Tyrell instead kissed the top of her hand, teasing Buck.

"Nice to meet you, ma'am."

JoBeth's face turned a little red and she smiled.

"It is a pleasure to meet you too, sir," she responded as she took her hand back.

"What brings the two of you to Fairmount, other than armfuls of supplies?" she asked.

"Actually, were heading over to Hazelton. We have business there," Buck responded. "We were going to get supplies in Vermillion and I was hoping I'd see you there, but I guess Vermillion ain't standing anymore."

"That was a very sad day when it burned to the ground. Some folks died grisly and some are scarred for life physically and emotionally. It was a terrible thing."

She began to add up their purchases as they continued to talk.

"Separate bills, I'm assuming?" she questioned as she looked up to the two men.

"Nope, ring it up on one bill," Tyrell said as he looked around.

"What all happened up there in Vermillion, Jo, if you don't mind me asking?" Buck questioned as she continued adding their purchases.

"It was the Kingsley Gang. That man Talbot and his men came storming in and destroyed the town, all because of a fight he had with Ron..."

Tyrell cut her off there.

"Ron?" he questioned.

"Yes, Ron Reginal. Do you know him?" she questioned when she noted Tyrell's concern.

"Not personally. I am, we are," he corrected himself, "we're looking for a man named Ron Reginal."

"Why are you looking for Ron?" JoBeth wanted to know.

Buck looked at her and sighed.

"He has a five hundred dollar bounty which Travis and I would like to collect."

Buck was at least honest and she appreciated that.

"What could he have ever done? He's a sweet man. Are you sure we're talking about the same Ron?"

"Unless there are a few folks with that name, then maybe we ain't."

Tyrell shrugged his shoulders.

"Until we get a chance to talk to him, we won't know. I understand if you don't want to give much away, but do you know if this Ron survived the attack?"

"Yes, he did. He also saved a lot of people, then he headed out after the Kingsley Gang. It has been months since I or anyone else has seen him."

She looked over to Buck.

"And I am being honest, Buck. Ron saved many who may have perished otherwise and then he took off, hot on the trail of Talbot."

She added the last of their purchases and rung it up.

"Fifteen dollars is the total," she said as she waited for Tyrell to pay the bill.

"I can't believe Ron has a bounty on his head. You guys never did tell me what he did or why he is wanted. Can you share that with me?"

Tyrell handed her twenty dollars.

"We could, but there really ain't much point. It is all petty stuff. The only reason his bounty is five hundred dollars is because it has been years since he skipped his court appearance and as you likely know, the law don't take kindly to that."

She looked over to Buck, unsure that she trusted Tyrell's answer.

"Is that true, Buck?" she asked, as she handed Tyrell back five dollars in ones.

"It is. Ron is a small fish. Not anyone to be afraid of, Jo. You said he went after the Kingsley Gang, right?"

"Yes, I did."

"The Kingsley Gang, or leastwise, Talbot Hunter, was arrested some time ago. He was supposed to face a judge in Fort Macleod this past Tuesday. His gang broke him out and shot a few men, including Tanner."

JoBeth's mouth fell open in shock.

"Is Tanner okay?" she asked with genuine concern.

"All we know for certain is that he is alive. The bounty-hunting outfit that Travis here works for, sent out a couple of men to track Talbot down and bring him in to face the justice he deserves. Perhaps if we could find Ron, he might be of help in finding Talbot. That would go a long way in settling any guilt he may or may not have regarding the simple charges he is facing. Any information you feel you could or would share with us regarding where he hangs out, travels or lives would be greatly appreciated," Buck finished as he looked into her eyes.

"I already told you all that I know, Buck. Ron really stuck to himself, hidden away in that cabin of his. He came and went like the sun and moon. All I can say is that he never hurt anyone that I'm aware of. In fact, most times when trouble was brewing in Vermillion and he was about, he was always the first to put a stop to it. I sure hope Talbot and his gang didn't bury him somewhere."

"Do you know where his cabin is?" Tyrell asked.

"That I don't know, not many people do."

There were a few moments of awkward silence as Buck and Tyrell contemplated what JoBeth had told them. The truth was, they weren't any closer to finding Ron than what they were when they woke up that morning.

The whole thing was going a bit cockeyed, but they had a job to do and a few more leads than they had earlier. Unfortunately, they had no definite answers.

"I hate to rush you and JoBeth away from your reunion, Buck, but we really should try and put some miles on before it gets too late."

Tyrell grabbed the box of supplies and thanked JoBeth for what she did share.

"I'll be waiting, Buck," he said as he walked toward the exit.

"I'll be right there, Travis," Buck said as he watched the door close behind him.

"I guess I better get, JoBeth. I'll be sure to stop back this way sometime soon. We can pick up where we left off, hopefully under different and more pleasant circumstances."

He leaned forward and kissed her cheek.

"I'll be seeing you, Jo. Take care, you hear."

"I will, Buck. You keep your wits about you and be careful."

Buck nodded.

"I'll live long enough to see you again, Jo, I promise."

He winked at her as he turned and followed Tyrell. He was a little saddened and would have liked to visit with her longer, but he knew he also had a job to do.

"There you are," Tyrell said as Buck approached. "I'm sorry to have pulled you away from that beautiful woman, Buck, but we need to put on some miles," Tyrell said apologetically.

"Think nothing of it, Travis. We do need to get on the trail. I'll see her again," Buck responded as he helped Tyrell load their supplies onto their horses.

Ten minutes later they were heading out of town, going north toward Vermillion and Hazelton. Passing their previous evening camp, they continued onward for another twenty miles. It was the quietest twenty-mile ride the two ever experienced while being in the company of one another. Their minds drifted this way and that. They spoke only sporadically as they travelled. Now, though, as they rested and let their horses feed on mountain grass, their words flowed.

"JoBeth is sure a pretty woman, Buck. How does a fellow like you get acquainted with a woman like her?" Tyrell questioned in a teasing manner.

"She was the woman that ran the Vermillion mercantile," Buck responded.

"I already figured that out, but the two of you seemed a bit cosy. I reckon she is more to you than a store clerk."

"Maybe she is, Travis, maybe she is," Buck smiled and winked. "Anyway, that ain't here nor there. What do you think about what she said about Ron?"

Tyrell took that as Buck's way to change the subject, so for now he wouldn't pry.

"I ain't sure what to make of it. Not even sure her Ron Reginal and our Ron Reginal are the same, but I can't see any man other than our Ron having the fortitude to go after a fellow like Talbot and his gang alone. It makes me think that the two are the same," Tyrell said with reluctance and uncertainty.

"If he is, then what happened to him when Talbot was arrested and what way did he go after that, assuming he ain't already dead and buried?"

Tyrell stroked his whiskered chin as he thought about that.

"Hard to say, I reckon. I guess he could be dead. Could be also that the law got to Talbot before he could, in which case we still need to find him to get the answers we're looking for," Buck said as he inhaled deeply and looked around, wondering himself what it all meant.

"That is my thought, too. We ain't going to know either way until that happens. What we do know is that JoBeth claims the last place Ron was seen by anyone was in Vermillion and that was on the day it was torched by none other than the Kingsley Gang headed by Talbot Hunter. Next, we know that a fellow named Ron Reginal, who may or may not be the Ron we are looking for, headed out after Talbot and that was months ago already. We also know there was a confrontation or argument between them that led to the disaster that took place in Vermillion. It is a messed up situation at best, Buck; it really is."

Tyrell took a swig from his canteen as he and Buck, conversed. There really was no clear answer and only time would sort it out.

Rested now, they once more saddled up and continued north. With each mile they drew closer to the Athabascan territory and whatever it was that lay ahead. As dusk approached, they halted for the final time that day and set up their evening camp.

"We're getting into the tundra now, Travis. Keep your eyes peeled for the unwanted," Buck warned as they began to settle.

"Black Dog will let us know about any intrusions. Still, I ain't going to let my guard down either way so no worries there, Buck."

Tyrell struck a match and set their evening fire alight. As the flames began to sway this way and that in the gentle evening breeze, they made coffee and ate beef jerky. Forced on more than one occasion to share the odd piece with Black Dog, they had oats now too for their horses and they fed their faithful companions a few handfuls each as they waited for their coffee to perk.

To the south, Brady, Riley, and the only surviving member of the once infamous Kingsley Gang were also getting ready for the evening. They tied the five horses and removed the dead so the horses could have a rest of their own. Brady helped the wounded man get as comfortable as possible and checked his wound, surprised to see that the flow of blood had slowed to a trickle.

"You might make it after all, mister."

Brady stood up. Satisfied that the man was resting peacefully, he helped Riley set up their own camp. With the fire lit now and the horses tethered, they talked about the day's events, especially the incredible long distance shot that closed Talbot's eyes forever.

"Chapter 14"

Rising at dawn's early light, Tyrell and Buck loaded up their gear. Without having a morning coffee, they continued their trek. They rode in silence for a few miles, Tyrell trailing behind Buck because the trail was too narrow for both horses to be side by side. When the trail finally widened, Tyrell pulled Pony up close to Buck and his horse.

Buck looked over to Tyrell and smiled.

"We should get to Vermillion today, Travis. It can't be more than thirty plus miles away."

"True enough, but we still have to get through Athabascan territory unscathed."

"I ain't worried about that. Did you forget about that arrow Crying Wolf left with us?"

"Nope, but have you seen it lately?" Tyrell asked.

He noticed as he pulled up to Buck that the arrow had been lost. It was no longer sticking out of Buck's bedroll where he knew Buck put it.

"Sure, have it right here..." Buck began as he turned in his saddle to grab it and show Tyrell.

"Damn! Where the hell did that get to? You didn't see it fall, did you, Travis?" Buck asked with hope.

Tyrell shook his head.

"Nope. I noticed it was gone only now as I pulled up beside you."

Buck reined his horse to a stop as he looked again.

"Yep, it is gone. Should we turn back and go look for it?"

"I reckon not, Buck. It would take us a month of Sundays to find."

"Yeah, I suppose you're right. I guess we keep our fingers crossed and hope we don't run into a band of renegade Athabascan."

Only then, since now that they were stopped, did they notice Black Dog meandering towards them. Even from that distance they could see he had something grasped in his teeth.

"Jesus Christ, look at that, Travis. Your damn dog has the arrow."

Buck's face lit up with awe and surprise as he pointed it out.

Black Dog dropped the arrow at the feet of Buck's horse. Buck swung off his saddle and picked it up, tucking it, this time, into his belt where he should have had it in the first place.

"Thank you for that, Black Dog," he said as he scratched the dog behind the ear. "Thought for sure we had lost it. Good thing I reckon that you found it."

"Good boy, Black Dog. Well done," Tyrell said as he reached into his saddlebag and tossed a piece of jerky to him.

"Well, Buck, you got your arrow back, thanks to the dog," Tyrell said with a smile and pride as they continued onward.

"Yep, I sure do and I ain't going to lose it again either. No sir. I'm going to keep it right here in my belt," Buck assured.

To the south, Brady and Riley were making progress with their own trek. The wounded man was still breathing, although he had picked up a fever overnight and didn't look to be in the best of health. Brady was a bit concerned that that the man might die before they could get him to a doctor. He knew it was their responsibility to keep him alive as best they could until then.

"Hope he makes it, Riley. I'd like to see justice served."

They calculated the distance back to the Fort to be fifteen to twenty miles.

"As long as he keeps breathing for the next few hours, Brady, he might make a recovery and face the justice he has coming to him," Riley pointed out.

"I hope so. What do you suppose the law will throw at him?"

"Right off the get go he'll get an aiding and abetting charge, likely murder and a list of others. I'd say he'll get life, might even hang. It depends I guess on what the law decides. He might get a lesser sentence if he cooperates and spills the beans on what the Kingsley Gang have been up to over that last few years if he has any information on that at all. Hard to say at this point, I reckon. He ain't spoke two words to us, so I can't be sure."

They rode in silence for the next few miles until the creek that crossed their trail came in view. There they let the horses drink and rested themselves. Brady gave their wounded man some water and a biscuit as they waited for the horses to have their fill.

The sun, by now, was hot and yellow and because of this, the stink from the eight dead men slowly attracted black flies and a number of other carnivorous flying insects. With every passing minute the numbers increased and the stench became more evident. Riley removed his hat and fanned his face to catch a breath of fresh air and it wasn't long before Brady was doing the same. The horses battled stinging bites from the insects as the insects worked their way to the real reason for their swarm: the dead flesh of Talbot and his men. It wasn't unusual for that many dead to begin to stink, especially when blood, human feces, and urine were involved, not to mention the fact that Talbot and his men were likely not very clean to begin with. The hot sun only amplified the true stench and the breeze that blew increased the stench's perimeter of smell.

Both men knew that more insects would pick up the scent if they didn't get out of the bush soon and back on the trail that led to the Fort. There was a chance that the four-legged type of carnivore would soon be on the prowl as well. The real possibility of getting a mouthful of stench prevented them from speaking to one another to discuss it as they waited for the horses to quench their thirsts. The minutes dragged on and it seemed to be an eternity before the horses gradually pulled their snouts out of the creek and were ready to go. Mounting them finally, they once again headed off in the direction of Fort Macleod. As long as they kept moving, the smell from the dead wasn't as bad. Every now and then they would still get a whiff and it wasn't by any means pleasant. The sound of something heavy falling to the ground made Riley look over his shoulder.

"Damn it, hey, Brady. One of the dead has fallen off a horse," Riley called out as he pulled his horse to a stop. Reining his own horse, Brady turned him around and helped Riley toss the body back on. The body was beginning to show signs of early stage rigor mortis and it took some effort to place the body correctly so that it wouldn't fall again. They had to hold their breath as they accomplished the task.

"If that fellow is as stiff as he is now, the others must be too," Brady said as he stepped back and inhaled a breath of fresh air.

"Let's hope that no more of them fall off. I don't know if I'd want to load up another," Riley pointed out.

Brady grabbed a length of rope.

"Let's tie them to the horses so we won't have to. With them getting stiff as they are, they don't fold over the horses' back like I want them to. We tie them and that'll take care of that."

Cutting the rope into lengths, he handed a few lengths to Riley.

"You get those ones tied and I'll do the same with these here."

Brady pulled the bandanna he had around his neck over his mouth and nose as he went about the task. That was barely enough to keep him from gagging every now and again.

"Jesus, they're really starting to stink, Riley. We don't make the Fort today, these horses are going to have to live with dead tied to them because I don't want to go through this again."

"I hear you, Brady. Tie them tight and they'll keep their form. It'll make it easier to place them again if we have to remove them," Riley commented as he finished tying the last one that he was tasked to tie.

"There, that ought to keep any of them from falling again," he said as he stepped back away from the stench. "They look like sacks of potatoes tied to pack horses."

"Yeah and they stink like a sack of rotten ones," Brady added as the two men swung back onto their saddles and continued in the direction of the Fort.

Ten miles northeast of Vermillion, Tyrell and Buck were getting into the high alpine. The trail they were following once more switched to a single horse trail and since Buck was familiar with the area, he took the lead again while Tyrell took up his position in the back. They stayed close enough to one another that they could talk if they wanted, but they chose to admire the terrain and scenery. It was beautiful up that high. The trees were stunted and not much taller than a man. In the distance on the other side of the draw, they could see fields of mountain grass that rolled on further than the eye could see.

The terrain was steep enough that the trail had a few switchbacks making it less perilous for horse and rider to ascend. It took the better part of an hour to make it to the top and, once there, they stopped and rested. They could make out a small lake in the distance. On the banks of the lake were a dozen or so tepees with smoke rising. Buck pointed in that direction.

"I don't remember that Indian camp the last time I was up this way."

"Likely it is a fishing camp. You don't suppose it might be the Athabascan, do you?"

"Nope. They don't use tepees. Their dwellings are usually somewhat rounded. I reckon they are made the same way, but they don't have the tepee look to them. Those are likely the Blood Plain Indians from the flat lands and I'd rather not run into them. The good thing is, Travis, that lake ain't anywhere near where this trail leads. We head west again, not far from below, and then north. I reckon it is two or three miles away from the lake. I think we'll be okay," Buck said with apprehension and uncertainty.

"I figured a fellow like yourself would have been friends with most of the native population."

"I am with most, but you don't see the Blood around often and when you do it is usually a bit intimidating. They can be an unruly bunch at the best of times. We best do whatever we can to avoid them."

"I have no problem with that. Let's hope we don't come across any of them. I don't reckon that arrow of yours would be much help with the Blood," Tyrell mentioned, already knowing the answer.

"Not likely. I don't know if the Athabascan are friends with that lot or not and I'd rather not find out. On the other hand, the Blackfoot and the Athabascan tolerate each other and it could be that those down there are Blackfoot, but I have my doubts. The Blackfoot don't show up around these parts until fall when the moose and elk start appearing."

"I guess they would have to get their meat from the deer and such in the area since there aren't many bison left. I'm friends with the Blackfoot. I lived with them for a while back when I was working for Mac. He and I helped them track a few renegades. The Blackfoot, I can say, can be ruthless when they need to be. I know. I watched one of them take off the head of one of their own and left a few more tied to trees up in the Rockies. They just left them there to die from the elements and starvation. I often think about that time and often find myself dreaming of it. Oh well, it is their justice, not mine."

Tyrell inhaled deeply as he averted his eyes back to the lake and looked on. His mind drifted back to that time as the sun beat down on his face. For a few minutes as the two of them rested, neither one spoke. Each man was reminiscing about his own past.

Both men were jolted back to the here and now when Black Dog darted forward and Pony reared up snorting and farting. Tyrell knew exactly what was going on and in a desperate attempt to jump off Pony, his foot got stuck in a stirrup. He dangled from his saddle like an apple on a tree as Pony charged forward almost at a full gallop. Tyrell bounced across the ground half sitting and half lying down as he desperately fought to get his foot loose.

Buck's horse reared up too, but it wasn't for the same reason. He reared up simply because Pony had startled it with his sudden outburst of aggression. Luckily, Buck was able to keep his horse from following and under control. Finally, Tyrell's foot came loose and he rolled to a stop, dazed and annoyed. Pony and Black

Dog kept right on going. Rising, Tyrell dusted himself off and cursed.

He was sporting a big bruise that started on his ass cheek and spread up to his lower back. A few scrapes were on his forearms, but the bruise was what hurt the most. Buck, seeing all this, wasn't sure he should laugh although, it was the damnedest thing he had ever seen.

"You okay, Travis?" he asked as he swung off his horse and walked over to him. There was a half smirk on his face.

"I'll live. Goddamn horse and dog anyway."

Tyrell looked at Buck and noted that he was holding back laughter.

"Go ahead, Buck, feel free to laugh. I know if I were on the sidelines, I would be."

Tyrell, too, chuckled a bit as he shook his head.

Buck burst out into a big, old, gut-roaring laugh.

"In all my life I ain't ever seen anything as funny as that. You were bouncing across the moss and grass like a damn rock skipping across water."

Tears were forming at his eyes he was laughing so hard.

"Come on now, Buck, it wasn't that funny," Tyrell said with some annoyance with a mix of humour.

"Damn right it was, Travis, damn right it was," Buck blurted out as he continued laughing.

Tyrell walked back a few paces and picked up his hat. Putting it back on his head, he walked to where Buck stood, still chuckling.

"I tell you, Travis," Buck started as he tried to catch his breath. "I tell you, that was one of the damnedest things I ever did see."

There was a short pause as Buck gathered his composure.

"Are you hurt at all?" Buck questioned in a more serious and concerned way.

"Not really. A bruise and couple of scrapes, maybe my pride," Tyrell chuckled. "I only hope the damn horse and dog don't get hurt or lose my gear. I wasn't quite prepared to get out of the saddle quick enough I suppose. Most times I can get off quickly when this happens. Today is a different story, I reckon."

"How often does this happen? It sounds like it is a regular occurrence."

"Every time there is a grouse or bear close. It ain't happened in a while. The dog usually gets a scent first and takes care of the problem before Pony realises one or the other is close. If that don't happen, well then, this is how it usually turns out."

"How long do they stay away before they wander back?" Buck was curious to know.

"Usually not long, a few minutes. I guess it depends on how far away the bear or grouse get ahead of them. I don't think it takes them long to get bored with the chase then," Tyrell replied as they made their way over to some rocks and sat down to wait.

"Regardless of what happened, Buck, it sure is nice country up here. Peaceful."

"It is indeed. That is why I like the Yukon so much. It is beautiful country up that way and quite peaceful too, especially at night when the timber wolves get going. Evenings ain't as dark either. They are more of a blue color and you can see most things without having to squint. Yep, the Yukon is my type of place," Buck said as he reminisced.

"Were you born and raised up that way?"

"Yep, I was born in a little town called Mistyvale. I never knew why it was called that. There never was much mist. It wasn't a big town back then.

Now, like most established towns, it ain't small like it used to be."

"What did your family do way up there? I always think of that area as a prospector's paradise. From what I know, a lot of gold comes from there."

"It does, but my folks didn't mine. They ran the hotel. My older brother whom I ain't saw in over a decade runs it now. I can't even be sure he is alive anymore as I ain't been back to Mistyvale in twenty years. I left there at eighteen or thereabout. Anyway, my older brother ran the place after my folks grew old and moved away from there. It wasn't long after that they both passed away. It could be that my brother might still be there and I hope he is, but I can't be sure."

Buck looked northerly as he sighed.

"I've returned to the Yukon on a few different occasions, but I have never made my way back to Mistyvale."

"Why is that, if you don't mind me prying?" Tyrell was interested to know.

"Nope, I don't mind, Travis, not at all. My brother is, was, whatever the case may be, a hard-working man, righteous and all. Before he took over the hotel, he did work the mines and it changed him. All his hard work deprived his family of both a husband and a father. I watched what that did to them. Sure, they never went without material things, food and such, but they did go without the other, a husband and father. His work turned him into a hard-nosed prick, as simple as that. As time progressed, he and I had an impasse I reckon. He went his way and I went mine. We stayed in touch for a couple of years, but after that we no longer cared. As I've heard you say a few times, Travis, *'it is what it is'*."

Tyrell was looking at him somewhat saddened by the story.

"Sometimes I guess we fill our own shoes with a life that we choose. I take it your brother expected you to work the mines and live as he did, eh?"

"At best I reckon, the folks probably felt the same way too, or in the least, that I'd make a steady living at one thing or the other. My opinion of that is there are too many things a man can do. Why stick to one? Why not try a few? Free up all that time trying to make a living and instead make a life."

"I couldn't agree with you more. The thing is, not every man or woman can do that. They need their this, that, and other thing. Only those who are like you and me, men and women alike, can live without all those pretty things. I'm quite content with how my life has turned out and what I do."

"Me too, Travis. I like the fact that I am able to see new places if I like or hide as far away from the civilised as I choose. I couldn't do that if I worked at a hotel or a mine."

"You and I are quite a lot alike, I reckon. I like the solitude of getting away as well and would most times prefer to be left alone. It isn't always easy and can get lonely at times, but I tell you there is nothing like it. One day, I'd like to have a homestead and be self-sufficient, raise and sell cattle or something, maybe have a few chickens. Until then, my only complaint is that I have a damn horse that chases bear," Tyrell said.

As he stood up, in the distance they could hear Black Dog barking and the galloping hooves of Pony approaching. Tyrell and Buck thought nothing of it, thinking it was the horse and dog simply returning. It wasn't until Pony broke through the scrub, his nostrils flaring and foam around his mouth, did the two men realise that it was more than their simple return.

"This doesn't look good Buck. You best get mounted and have your rifle handy," Tyrell said in a hurried voice, as Buck darted toward his horse and swung onto the saddle. Pulling out his rifle, he cocked it and pointed it toward the knoll that Pony was now ascending. There was no sign of Black Dog yet. They could hear his aggressive growls a short distance away. Pony now crested the hill and made straight toward Tyrell. Stopping abruptly, he shook his head as the foam around his mouth took to flight like white, fluffy, sticky clouds. Tyrell ignored the frothy splash to the side of his cheek as he quickly mounted him and took control with the reins. Buck a few paces away still had his rifle pointing in the direction from which Pony had come.

"I don't see a damn thing, Travis," Buck blurted out as Tyrell and Pony now pulled up beside him.

"Something is certainly pissing off the dog," Tyrell said as he pulled out his own rifle and cocked it, relieved to see that all his gear was actually still there.

"The horse seems to have calmed down. Maybe Black Dog has the situation under control. He was sure making a ruckus down there."

"Sounds like he's settling down some now. Hope he's okay."

"Most times he makes it back no worse for wear. I guess we're going to have to wait and see. If he doesn't show up in a few minutes, I'll have to have a gander, I reckon. It is best for now that we stay put. Anything coming over that hill that ain't friendly, we have a clear shot."

A few minutes later, around the same time that Pony finally quit huffing and puffing, Black Dog appeared from above them.

"Look at that. He's come from above. Must've chased whatever it was into the high country."

Tyrell swung off Pony and waited for Black Dog to make the distance back. The scrub and grass blocked his view, but he knew Black Dog was coming.

Buck still on his horse had a better view of the dog as it approached. He could see something was wrong. As Black Dog drew closer, Buck could see that the dog had been hit with an arrow. It was sticking out of his right shoulder.

"Ouch," he exclaimed as he swung off his horse. "Travis, your dog has been hit with an arrow," he said as he dashed forward, Tyrell close behind.

"Aw, Jesus, Black Dog. What did you get yourself into."

Tyrell knelt next to him. He could tell the arrow hadn't penetrated his shoulder blade. Still, the dog was in some pain as he whimpered and pawed at Tyrell as though apologising for something. The fresh blood that matted his fur told the story. He had either killed or maimed whoever it was that stabbed him with the arrow. Tyrell knew it was unlikely that the arrow was shot from a bow. If it had been, Black Dog wouldn't be standing there now. The more plausible scenario was that he had likely been stabbed with it, which meant close combat and more than likely death to the dog's assailant.

Taking hold of the arrow with his one hand and using his other to pat Black Dog's head to comfort him, Tyrell slowly loosened the arrow from his dog's shoulder. He did it in a manner that was gentle; then, with one final pull, he yanked it out. Black Dog whimpered loudly and fell to his side into Tyrell's lap. Buck quickly handed him his kerchief and Tyrell tied it around Black Dogs shoulder to slow the blood.

"Think he's going to be okay, Travis?"

"I hope so. Hard to say the same for whoever did this, though. The blood matting his coat ain't his."

Buck picked up the arrow and looked at it.

"It was a Blood Indian," he said as he tossed it to the ground.

"Damn! So that is them down at that lake. I hate to say it, but for our own benefit, I hope the dog made quick work of the brave who did this to him. If he has got away and makes it back to the others, we can count on a fast and furious retaliation."

"What makes you so certain it was a Blood Indian?"

"The arrow shaft is willow or birch and the arrow head is made from the steel strapping from whiskey barrels, plus," he picked the arrow up again and looked at it, "the feathers are black and white, magpie feathers."

The two men averted their eyes to the mountain slope above them and gazed the bush line trying to see if anyone or anything was near, but they saw nothing.

"We could go up yonder and have a look, to see if there is anyone up there dead, maimed, or otherwise," Tyrell said as he continued his gaze.

"I ain't sure I like that idea, Travis. It would be easy for the Blood to ambush us if there is any up there alive. Best thing to do under these circumstances is to get down low off this mountain. Probably best to stay off the trail too until we get further north."

"I don't reckon the dog will be coming around for a while. If you feel that way, Buck, I say we get now. The dog can ride with me on the horse. It wouldn't be the first time," Tyrell pointed out as he picked Black Dog with some effort and help from Buck.

"You got him there, Travis?"

"I'll make it from here, thanks, Buck."

All right," Buck said as he watched Tyrell take a few steps, making sure he was okay. Then he turned, bent over, and picked up the arrow for the second time. He could show it to the friendlier Athabascan if they came across them, as a warning that the Blood were in the area. Friendly warnings like that, Buck knew, went hand in hand with loyalty. He made his way back to the horses only a few steps behind Tyrell and he helped him with the dog.

Once they got him sitting in the saddle, Tyrell commanded him to lie down. At first, Black Dog was reluctant to move his right leg forward so that he could lie down. He did, however, understand the need to do so. Finally, he relented. Now with his front paws on either side of the saddle horn, dangling only a few inches from Pony's neck, Black Dog instinctively put his back legs in position and draped them on each side of the saddle. This way, he knew, he would not lose his equilibrium. His body took up the front and back of the saddle, leaving Tyrell with a foot or two of hard horse hip behind the saddle to sit on. Buck watched in amusement as Black Dog sprawled out on the saddle as though he had done it a thousand times.

"How long did it take you to get him to do that the first time?" Buck asked as he watched Tyrell swing up onto his horse.

"I never showed him. He was sitting up here on the saddle one day after I had stopped off somewhere and was gone for an hour or so. I came back and there he was. He does it on command now or when I invite him up." Tyrell shrugged his shoulder.

"You best mount up, Buck, as you said we need to get down low."

"Yeah, I reckon you are right."

Buck swung up onto his saddle and the two of them headed out of the area. They stayed west of the trail they were following and made their way into the bush that was down at a lower altitude. Somewhat hidden and less likely to be spotted, they coursed their way to a creek that was probably a tributary of the lake where the Blood Indians had congregated. Making sure that it was safe, they followed the creek into the valley that the creek flowed into.

Down low now, they took a moment to rest and looked back in the direction they had come. The mountain pass they had descended was in clear view and they scoured it with their gaze. Making sure they weren't followed, they turned north and headed deeper into the forest. Thirty minutes later, Buck spotted a clearing.

"There is a bit of a clearing up ahead, Travis. We'll rest there."

"Okay, I'm right behind you."

A few minutes later they stopped and dismounted. Tyrell and Buck lifted Black Dog off the saddle and set him down. Tyrell looked over the dog's wound, pleased to see that it wasn't bleeding anymore and that there was a big gooey scab forming. He cinched the kerchief around Black Dog's shoulder again and patted him.

"He ain't bleeding anymore?" Buck asked with elation.

"Nope, a big, old scab is forming. Ain't sure how his walking is going to be. He might have to ride the saddle a while longer," Tyrell mentioned, as he remained kneeling at his dog's side.

"What do you suppose happened back there on that ridge? You figure the dog and horse picked up the scent of a bear or the Indian?"

"I've been trying to figure that out. The only thing I can get to work in my head, is that it was a bear and maybe they ran into the Blood brave. Could be he was tracking the bear and maybe these two disrupted the hunt. One thing lead to another resulting in Pony getting startled and Black Dog in a fight for his life. I've never known Pony to go after a man. The dog is a different story and more so if the man is a threat. I reckon Black

Dog saw the brave as a threat. His instincts are to get in close and to do it fast and that is likely how he ended up with that arrow stuck in his shoulder. There is no way it was fired from a bow, so it had to be up close."

"All that blood matting his fur tells me he obviously came out on top."

Buck crouched down, and scratched Black Dog behind the ear.

"Most times he does. The sad thing is we'll never know if we left behind a wounded and dying man or one that is dead. That doesn't sit well, but there isn't a thing that can be done about it," Tyrell said as he now stood up.

"One thing I can say for sure, Buck, is that if the dog felt as though the brave was a threat, then he likely was."

"I imagine he was, Travis. As I said, the Blood Indian can be an unruly bunch. You fight one you can expect to fight the entire tribe. If whoever your dog fought with ain't dead, there will be consequences. If he didn't survive and is found dead in a couple of days, I reckon the Blood will suspect it to have been a random animal attack."

Rising Buck looked round.

"You figure we should stick it out here for the night? I don't see much point in going any further today, and I'm confident that we weren't spotted up on the ridge or heading this way. The dog would probably appreciate a long rest. It may have been a short day, but a lot happened, and I reckon I'm ready to hunker down."

"We are a lot further west of Vermillion now than when we were on that ridge. Chances are we wouldn't make the distance there today, not now leastwise. This probably is a good place to hold up for the night," Tyrell agreed. He, too, was confident that they hadn't been seen.

The Missing Years – Part II

"Good, then I guess we can get settled."

Although the sun was still high in the sky, they sparked a small fire. They cooked stew and fried bread while they sorted out their gear and prepared what would be their evening camp. It had been a warm and pleasant day for the most part, but after the incident with Black Dog and Pony, both men were worn out.

Now as they sat on their saddles across the flames from each other, they conversed cheerfully as the mid-afternoon sun remained hot. It felt good to be sitting and not in a rush to get somewhere. Black Dog lolled nearby, determined to remove the kerchief Tyrell had tied around his shoulder. Every time that he was caught trying to pull it off, Tyrell or Buck scolded him. Eventually it became a game that he couldn't win and he reluctantly rolled onto his side, choosing to sleep instead. The horses, untethered, happily munched on leaves and grass, staying close as they did so.

Brady and Riley were only a few miles away from the Fort by this time and were quite relieved when it finally came into view.

"There it is, Riley, home sweet home. Can hardly wait to dispose of the dead and turn this fellow over to the law. It has been quite a haul, hasn't it?"

"Yep, it has been. Not as long as it could have been. We were lucky to run into Talbot as soon as we did. I was hoping it would turn out that way. Could have done without all the death, but hunting down folks like Talbot and the number of men he had at his calling, most times this is how it ends, with a lot of bloodshed and hopefully it isn't the good guys bleeding. I'd say things turned out well and the good guys won another."

"I couldn't have said it better myself, Riley," Brady said as they now marched into the Fort. It didn't take long before a few onlookers began to cheer with speculation. For the most part, the two men simply carried on toward the Mounted Police station, but it was difficult not to meet the stares of some. On a few occasions, they found themselves caught up in the excitement and they would tilt their hats, nod and smile. It wasn't until they turned east down the street that lead to the station did the cheers fade.

"I have to tell you, Riley, that was a little annoying, don't you think?"

"Human nature is all that was, Brady. Don't ever let it go to your head. I've seen egos grow and men die because of it. Keep that in mind when you get praise like that," Riley pointed out as they pulled up to the Mounted Police station.

Dismounting, they tethered their horses and helped the wounded man dismount from the one he rode. Making their way to the big front door, they opened it and entered the station. Helping the wounded man to a chair, they got him to sit down. The constable behind the counter looked up from where he was sitting and smiled.

"Brady! I don't think we were expecting you back yet. Things went well I take it?" the constable asked as he stood up and walked over to the counter.

"We have one man alive, eight others including Talbot are dead. It appears as though Talbot himself killed four of his own men and we watched him drop two others with our own eyes when we stormed his encampment," Brady said with little regret. "The thing is, we didn't kill Talbot."

"Hang on there a minute, Brady. I need to get the prisoner secured and check his vitals. He looks feverish. You and Riley go ahead and help yourselves to some coffee, if you like. I'll be back in a minute."

The constable helped the wounded man into a holding cell and laid him down. Ripping the man's shirt so he could view his wounds, he looked at the two gaping holes in the man's shoulder. Swabbing them clean with some water, he patted the man's shoulder dry. Next, he poured iodine onto a piece of cotton batten and placed it on the man's shoulder. Squirming and grimacing in pain, the man sucked in a deep breath as the iodine went to work. That was the best that the constable could do until they could summon the doctor. Cleaning up his mess, he closed the holding cell door and locked it.

"The good news is, gentlemen," he began as he made his way to the front counter "he'll live. He is a bit infected and certainly has a fever, but I think he'll make it. If you are ready, carry on with what you were saying."

Brady sighed and leaned forward resting his elbows on the counter as he once more explained. Meanwhile, Riley made his way over to an empty chair, tilted his hat over his eyes and rested as Brady repeated in every detail what had transpired.

"Who do you suppose shot Talbot?" the constable asked as though Brady should know.

"I ain't got a clue. All we know is the shot came from a distance and it was true."

Brady shrugged as he took a drink from the coffee he held in his hand.

"There you have it. Now if you don't mind, we could use your help with the dead," he said as he put the cup down. He looked over to Riley, but Riley was gently snoring.

"It looks like it'll be you and I dealing with the dead alone," Brady said to the young constable.

He looked again at Riley. Part of him wanted to go over to where he sat and kick him. Instead, he turned and with the constable close behind, they exited. They led the five horses that carried Talbot and his dead over to the undertakers and unloaded them into a cooling cellar.

"Don't forget, there are still four more dead, some thirty or so miles northwest of the wagon road. The trail is marked with rock. You can't miss it," Brady reminded the young constable.

"Yeah, I remember. I got it marked down," he assured as they made their way back to the station in tow with the five horses.

"Do you folks have room for these horses in your corral, Brady?"

"I don't know. They're going to end up as the property of the law anyway in the end. Might as well turn them loose in the Mounted Police corral," Brady replied.

"All right, we can do that. We have a bit of paperwork to fill out. Go head back inside and I'll deal with the horses."

"I'll meet you inside," Brady said as he handed the reins of the three horses he was leading over to the constable.

"Yep, be there in a minute, Brady."

Making his way back inside, Brady poured himself another coffee as he waited. Riley, still sitting in the chair, continued to snore. Finally, the constable returned and the tiresome paperwork began. It took the better part of an hour and two cups of coffee. With the document signed and dated, Brady sighed as he slid it across the counter to the constable.

"Thank God that's done."

He looked over to Riley, then back to the constable who was reading the paperwork and checking it twice.

"I reckon old Riley needs some rest and I have a few more places to stop before I head back to our office.

The Missing Years – Part II

He ain't going ruin the atmosphere is he if I let him be for now?" Brady questioned.

"That's fine, Brady. I'm sure once he wakes up, he'll know where to go. I don't have a problem with it. Go ahead and take care of whatever it is you need to take care of."

Brady rapped his knuckles on the countertop and thanked the constable as he exited. His first stop was the widow Donale's place to check in with his old man and Tanner. He was surprised to learn that the doctor had allowed his old man to go home already, but that was okay. He'd check up on him later. Obviously, he was doing well.

Tanner, however, remained bedridden and struggling some, but he, too, was going to pull through. Brady pulled up a chair next to Tanner's bed. Tanner was able to look at him and he smiled.

"Hey, stranger," Tanner said in a weak voice as he gasped for a gulp of air, a normal reaction for anyone who was recovering from a punctured lung.

"No, need to speak, Tanner. I'm glad to see that in fact you are still breathing," Brady teased as he smiled at him. Tanner returned the smile and nodded his head giving Brady the two thumbs up that indeed he was going to recover. Then his eyes closed and he fell asleep. Brady slid his chair back and got up.

"I'll check in on you in the morning, Tanner. Keep up the good fight," he said as he left the room.

Relieved and feeling good about how well things so far had turned out, Brady swung back to the station and woke Riley.

"Come on, Riley, rise and shine."

Brady kicked the chair and finally Riley acknowledged him.

"Okay, okay. I'm awake. All is good, I assume."

"Yep. By the way, thanks for helping with those stinking corpses and the damn paperwork."

"Sure, glad I could help," Riley replied as he stood and rubbed his eyes. "Off to the office we go I guess, eh?"

"Unless you'd rather swing over to the Snakebite and have a good meal?" Brady responded with hope.

That is what he wanted and that was what he was going to do whether Riley joined him or not.

"What time is it?" Riley asked as he looked to the clock on the wall. "It isn't even dinner time yet. I'd rather head back to the office and sprawl out on the cot for a bit."

"All right."

Brady reached into his pocket and tossed Riley the back door key.

"Let yourself in; I'm heading over to the Snakebite," Brady replied as he exited.

Riley being the first to step into the office since that past Wednesday and the cot being in the back room, he had to pass by the front door and counter to get there. Right off the bat he noticed a few telegrams that had been slid under the door. Picking them up, he found a paperclip, then tossed them on the counter for Brady to see. Making his way to the small cot, he removed his boots and hat. Lying down, it didn't take long before he was once more snoring.

Tyrell and Buck remained where they finally decided to stop that day after the incident with Pony and Black Dog. As they sat there now, waiting for evening to come, Buck once more fiddled with the arrow that had been precariously stabbed into Black Dog's shoulder earlier that day. Adding a few sticks to their fire, they made biscuits and nibbled on beef jerky while their final pot of coffee, the third of the day perked. A few hours later, they rolled out their bedrolls as their small evening fire, gently snapped and crackled.

"Chapter 15"

It was early Sunday morning when the two men rose. Tyrell checked on Black Dog, who overnight had moved from where Tyrell remembered him to have been. Kneeling next to him, Tyrell smiled and scratched him behind the ear.

"Able to walk some, I see. Good progress, Black Dog. How about you show me how well you do get along."

Rising, Tyrell walked away then called for him, trying to coax him to come to where he now stood. Watching this, Buck added sticks to their fire and blew on the one single coal that held an orange glow. As the miniscule flame came to life, he added a few more sticks and so on until the almost exhausted fire once more began to flicker.

Tyrell knelt to be on a lower plane as he continued to coax Black Dog with his gentle plea to get the dog to walk. He knew Black Dog could do it. He wasn't sure on how well he could, not yet at least.

"Come on, Black Dog, get up. You make the distance and I'll make sure you get a big fat piece of jerky," Tyrell pleaded.

Still, Black Dog only looked at him as though he were moping.

"Come on, Black Dog, I know you walked last night. You weren't even close to where I last saw you, so don't moon around. Come on, you can do it."

For a few minutes, Tyrell only knelt there waiting, not saying a word. Black Dog, he knew, was feeling the push to get up and move. Finally, he stood up and with little effort made his way to Tyrell's side.

"Good boy. See, that wasn't so bad. You did that without a problem. A few more walks and you'll be running alongside us in no time. I ain't going to push you to walk for any distance, but you are going to have to walk. When you linger I'll invite you up onto the saddle. No worries there."

Tyrell reached over to his saddlebag that held the jerky and fished around until he found a bigger piece.

"As promised," he said.

As he handed over the piece, Black Dog's tail began to wag. He took the jerky and nonchalantly walked back to where he had been earlier. Both Tyrell and Buck chuckled. It appeared Black Dog got the first laugh of the day.

"Look at that, Travis. He can walk fine. I reckon he was fooling with you that whole time."

Tyrell shook his head in derision.

"Yeah, by God, you may be right, Buck. He tends to do stuff like that every now and again, damn dog," Tyrell chuckled with relief.

"It doesn't mean he's out of the dark yet. I'll have to keep an eye on the wound and watch out for infection. Likely won't push him to walk for too long of periods. We'll have to make more stops as we proceed toward Vermillion."

"Sure, I don't mind. I already saw who I wanted to see of those who used to live there; besides there ain't anything left. I don't mind taking a little extra time to get to where it is we need to get. You won't hear no complaining from me, Travis. If a wounded man can't travel as far as he once was able, then the whole army has to accept that and rest when the wounded need it."

Buck then added, "I consider that dog to be one of us, and if either you or I was wounded, we'd have to rest a little more. The dog deserves the same."

Tyrell nodded in agreement, then sat down on his saddle and aimlessly looked around. It was going to be another warm day. Already the birds were chirping and squirrels chattered back and forth. The scent of morning coffee soon became evident and he poured himself and Buck a cup full. Sitting in the silence of pre-dawn, they waited for the sun to rise and conversed quietly.

Three miles in the opposite direction, a band of six Blood Indians slowly approached. Silent as they were, Black Dog picked up their scent and began to stir anxiously. However, because of the peace and serenity Buck and Tyrell were experiencing as they sat there in the company of each other, Black Dog's anxiety went unnoticed. Nor did they see him dash to some undergrowth instinctively without command. It wasn't until the last bird chirped and the forest surrounding them became still that either one noticed the ominous silence. By then it was too late. Standing before them stood six Blood braves. Taken by surprise, neither man had the opportunity to arm himself, as they were caught without their holsters on. The only weapon of any sort that was within their reach was the Blood Indian arrow which lay on the ground beside Buck. The single arrow, though, was hardly an option.

One of the braves stepped forward with his hand raised.

"Do not fear our intrusion. We do not bring bad medicine with us to your fire this morning. I am Clive, Indian Clive. The six of us have been following you since yesterday's sun. It is you that runs with a dog, yes?" Indian Clive asked.

Tyrell looked around nervously, pleased to see that Black Dog was not in sight.

"We have no dog," Tyrell said as he looked into the eyes of Indian Clive. "Why do you look for a dog?"

Indian Clive looked around suspiciously.

"The dog we look for is good medicine. He may have been hurt in a battle between my son, Running

The Missing Years – Part II

Caribou, and a grizzly bear. The dog we look for led us to where two horses rested. You have two horses."

"That is because there are two of us. We need two horses," Buck volunteered as an answer.

"Yes, but these tracks," Indian Clive knelt down as he looked to the ground, "are not wolf tracks; they are dog."

He looked over to both Buck and Tyrell.

"I understand your apprehension as you are both threatened by our presence. Running Caribou survived the great bear attack with the help and intervention from your dog. He tells how the dog fought with him side by side until the great grizzly was overwhelmed. Running Caribou had but only an arrow in his hand, his bow broken by the powerful blows from the big grizzly as it mauled and tried to kill him.

Many times he stabbed the bear with the only weapon he had. He tells how he grew weaker and the bear more aggressive with each attempt he made to slaughter the bear. Then, with one final push to live, Running Caribou stabbed the dog accidently as the big grizzly relented with its attack and ran to higher country. Running Caribou watched as the black dog continued its chase, even with the arrow stuck into his body. This dog is a great dog and I would be honoured to look into his eyes."

Both men were mesmerized by the tale. With peace established, Tyrell stood up.

"I am Travis and this is Buck. Your tale captivated me, and yes, I do have the dog you seek."

Tyrell whistled for Black Dog who immediately showed himself and sat in the shadows as he looked on.

"That is him," Tyrell pointed.

Indian Clive smiled with admiration.

"May I approach him?"

"By all means, feel free," Tyrell responded with good cheer.

Indian Clive walked the short distance to where Black Dog sat and he knelt down, letting the dog sniff his hand.

"You have a great spirit and from this day you will be praised by the Blood Indian. You have saved the life of a young warrior who one day will be a chief and for this you will live in our hearts."

Indian Clive stood as Black Dog offered his paw. Reaching down, Indian Clive accepted the dog's paw and in his native tongue, he quietly rehearsed an Indian prayer. Turning, he walked back to where the others stood.

"I have blessed your dog with good spirits. His healing will be fast. It has been an honour to meet him. Thank you."

"You are welcome. Thank you for blessing him."

Indian Clive nodded.

"I will not forget your faces either. Do not fear the Blood Indian," he said with sincerity as he signaled to his band of braves that it was time to go.

"Hold on a second," Buck stated as he reached down and picked up the arrow.

"This arrow belongs to Running Caribou, your son. Perhaps he would like it back."

Buck handed it over to Indian Clive.

"Thank you. Running Caribou will be glad to have it."

With that, the band of six slipped back into the forest and vanished from sight.

"Whew, wasn't that something?" Tyrell questioned as he sighed with relief.

"I guess we no longer need to speculate on what took place yesterday."

The Missing Years – Part II

"I reckon not. What happened here is a rarity, Travis. Not often can a man say that he met Indian Clive."

"You know of him?" Tyrell asked as he strapped on his holster, mad at himself that he had neglected to do so that morning when they woke up. It was something he rarely forgot, although today he had.

"I never met him until now. I know his name, though. He is the Blood tribe's chief. Quite ruthless and demanding from what I have heard. He didn't seem that way to me. I was more wary of the braves that stared at us the entire time. Talk about intimidation. They did it well, I reckon."

"I only felt that way because I wasn't armed. I've stared down scarier men I think, but I wasn't unarmed at the time. Today I was and, in fact, so were you," Tyrell mentioned as he sat down.

"Yeah, I guess we better not let that happen again. It was so damn peaceful and quiet, I felt no need to holster up. Caught up in the moment and surrounded by all this made us stupid for a time."

Buck stretched his arm out and grabbed his holster. Standing, he tightened it around his waist. With that done, he meandered over to his bedding and rolled it up.

"The sun is bright; we might as well get. I feel a lot better knowing we ain't got to avoid the trail. It'll make travelling a lot easier and less time-consuming."

"That it will, Buck," Tyrell agreed as he poured what was left of the coffee onto the fire and kicked some dirt into it. Satisfied it was out, he followed suit and rolled up his bedding and gathered his gear. Then, with one final look around, the two men mounted their horses and with Black Dog in tow, they headed east toward the trail that they previously thought they would have to avoid. It didn't take long and as they broke through the last bit of forest and ascended the banks of the trail, they turned their horses north toward Vermillion and Hazelton beyond. By late morning, the charred and empty town of Vermillion finally came into view and they approached.

The only building that remained standing was at the north end of town. All it housed were a few tables, a counter, and a solitary man leaning up against the counter, a cigarette dangling from his lips.

"Welcome to Vermillion. The stagecoach ain't expected for an hour. Would you folks like a coffee?" he asked as they walked over to a table.

"We're not here to catch the coach. Only passing through on our way to Hazelton," Tyrell said as they sat down. "And yes, we'll take coffees."

"All right, I'll get them for you. Want cream and sugar?"

"Yep, cream and sugar too, please," Buck responded.

"What happened here?" he asked as he and Tyrell waited for their coffee.

"From what I've been told, the place burned down a few months ago. You didn't notice that as you made your way here?" the man said half-joking at the obvious.

Both Tyrell and Buck chuckled at the man's attempt at humour.

"We did notice that. Do you know how it happened?"

"Well," the man began as he brought them their coffees and sat down at the table opposite of them, "I heard there was some kind of fight between a couple of brawling types and one of them came back with a bunch of men and threw torches. That is about all I know. The town was already the way it is now when I took the position at this outpost."

The Missing Years – Part II

"Are there any folks that still live around here?" Tyrell asked as he took a drink from his coffee.

"Only those few on the outskirts. I've heard there is one other fellow that lives up on the south mountain near a ridge in an old cabin, three or four miles as the crow flies. I've been here for almost two months and I have never seen or met him. I guess he is a recluse."

The man stood up and pushed in the chair.

"If you folks want anything else, just holler."

He turned and walked back to the counter, stuck a cigarette between his lips and lit it.

"Recluse, south mountain. Ain't been seen in at least two months. What do you make of that, Buck?" Tyrell asked with suspicion.

"I ain't following your train of thought here, Travis. What do mean?"

Buck added more cream to his coffee. It was stronger than even he liked. He waited for Tyrell to respond.

"Your friend JoBeth said that fellow she knows as Ron Reginal lived in a cabin and was here when the place burned and that he took off after Talbot. She said he ain't been heard from since. It's been a couple months since the fire. If this fellow who supposedly lives up in some cabin ain't been seen for as long as our host over there has been working here, seems a bit curious, no? What if it is him that lives up in that old cabin?" Tyrell pointed out making it as clear as he could.

Buck nodded his understanding as he tested his coffee.

"We should try and find that cabin. I get what you're saying. It could be that way, couldn't it?"

"I don't know. Could it be that easy?"

Tyrell brought his cup to his lips and forced down another mouthful of coffee.

"I have to tell you, Buck, compared to this, the coffee you make is way better."

"You can fix it up with cream or sugar."

"Nah, I ain't going to bother. A half a cup of this is good enough for me."

Tyrell slid his cup to the side as they rested and contemplated for a few more minutes. Finally, they stood and headed toward the exit. Stopping at the counter, Tyrell paid for the coffee. Exiting into the fresh air of early afternoon, they mounted their horses and turning south, headed back the way they came.

At one area of the trail, they had a good view of a south mountain with a visible ridge, easily identifiable from the trail. The south mountain, they knew, could likely be any number of mountains south of Vermillion. The *'ridge'* was key, and what they were looking at was certainly a mountain with a ridge.

"What do you think, Travis. Think that might be the area our friend back at the outpost mentioned?"

"Could be. Geographically it is south of town and we can both see a ridge from here."

The two men continued their gaze of the vast forest that led to the mountain some two or three miles away.

"Without asking too many questions of our friend back at the outpost and maybe jeopardising our true intent on why we're snooping around, all we can do, Buck, is head that way and look around."

Tyrell looked down to Black Dog who was sitting near, waiting.

The dog fared well as they travelled to Vermillion that morning and didn't slow down. He was confident that Black Dog could traverse the terrain if they did decide to head southeast into the forest and make their way toward the mountain. The decision, though, remained up in the air. After all, they really didn't need to go on a wild goose chase.

"I reckon it is good territory for an old trapper's cabin, close enough to a town and rugged enough to not warrant many visitors," Tyrell pointed out, "only, I ain't sure it would prove fruitful. What do you figure, Buck?"

"We ain't going to make the distance to Hazelton before Tuesday whether we go have a gander or not. I'm betting we could satisfy our curiosity on whether or not there might be a cabin up on that mountain before the sun sets today. As long as you think your dog can handle some bush stomping, it might be worth the effort to look."

With both men still not certain whether it would be a wild goose chase or not, they made the decision with a coin toss.

"It looks like we're going to be doing some bush stomping as you call it, Buck. I reckon we could cut off the trail here or there."

He pointed to a few places that weren't so thick with scrub.

"Once we get into the bush, I reckon it is going to get thick and unless we come across a pathway or trail, we'll be fighting through thorn bushes and mountain ash. It ain't nothing that we haven't come across a time or two before. Let's get," Tyrell said as he turned Pony off the main trail and over the bank that led into the forest.

Black Dog was ducking and tucking and even got ahead of the two men as they proceeded. Indeed, he was mending well.

Back at the Fort, Brady pulled up to the office and unlocked the front door. It was 11:00 a.m. He hadn't returned to the office the night before. After he ate his dinner at the Snakebite, he headed for home leaving Riley to sleep. He stopped in on his folks to let them know that he and Riley were back and to fill them in on what had transpired over the course of the five days he was gone.

Brady was glad to see that Ed was fine, but under Dr. Dunbar's orders he wasn't supposed to exert himself or return to work for a while longer. Brady would have to run the business on his own for a bit. This didn't surprise Brady. He was used to running the office and had only started getting back into the tracking of bounties since Ed's last incident where he took lead from Nicolai. Perhaps Ed's luck was running thin. In less than two months he had been shot in the leg by Nicolai and had taken two more slugs from Talbot's men. Keeping his old man away from the business for a while wasn't such a bad idea.

Brady made his way to the staff room and lit the wood stove to make coffee. He didn't bother checking on Riley who, indeed, was still sleeping. Next, he made his way to the counter and looked over the telegrams that Riley had obviously found. He was surprised to read the one that Tyrell had sent stating that he had requested help from a fellow named Buck Ainsworth. He wondered who he was, but as long as their man Travis knew the Buck fellow, then Brady was okay with that. He was a bit perturbed that the telegrapher hadn't given the telegram to Ed as he had requested and he wondered then if the telegrapher had followed his other request, to send the one he wrote before he and Riley headed out after Talbot. He would make a point to look into that later that day. Two other telegrams were in the stack and he breezed through them.

The only one that really caught his eye was from Gabe Roy. Brady knew about that fellow and he knew that his old man wanted nothing to do with him. The

The Missing Years – Part II

telegram simply read: *Need hired protection-* signed *Gabe Roy- Willow Gate.* Brady shook his head and sighed.

"We ain't in that type of business, Mr. Roy," he murmured to himself as he ignored the request.

The other telegram came from a woman who lived in the southern town of Weesley, close to the U.S. border. She claimed she had seen the cow rustler extraordinaire, Roger Burton, in the vicinity. His wanted poster was posted on every bulletin board in rancher country from the Fort to the U.S. border and as far away as the coastal towns of British Columbia to the northern ranching towns of Alberta. It was a good tip and he'd keep it in mind. For now, *McCoy's Bounty Hunting Service* was short men and the possibility that Roger Burton may be up to his old tricks again, would have to wait. Besides, his bounty was only $2000 and the McCoy's had bigger fish to fry.

Brady put the telegram in a drawer used for tips such as that. They went through the drawer when times were slow. Lately things had been anything but slow. Indeed the tip drawer was filling up and some were months old already. *Might be an idea to clear that out one day,* Brady thought.

Soon, Riley was awake and the two sat down in the staff room and had morning coffee.

"You didn't make it back here last night, did you?" Riley questioned as he took a drink from his coffee.

"Nope. I figured I'd let you sleep. Besides, I wanted to look in on my old man. The doctor sent him home a couple days ago. He's okay, but can't work for a bit longer. Tanner on the other hand is still bed-ridden, but he's making a comeback slowly. He could barely speak when I stopped in on him yesterday."

"It is good to know he's at least going to be okay. He could have died from that wound."

Pointing that out, Riley took another swallow from his coffee.

"It is Sunday today, isn't it?"

"Yep, all day," Brady responded.

"I guess then, I should take off. It was a pleasure working alongside you, Brady. You have a lot of Ed's traits," Riley mentioned as he stood up.

"Hold on, Riley. What is your rush?"

"There is no need for me to be here. We got Talbot."

"Maybe it is time for you to quit being a lone wolf. As you know, we're short men and could always use fellows like yourself."

"Are you offering me a job, Brady?"

"I am so. We need men as I said. Tanner ain't going to be much help for a while and neither is Ed. With Tanner and Ed down for the count, there really is only me and Travis and a fellow named Buck Ainsworth that Travis hired on. Ain't sure this Buck fellow plans on sticking around and even if he did, having you here increases our manpower and our capabilities."

Riley sat back down.

"I don't know, Brady. I've been working alone for years. Never thought about working from an office. I always took my bounties as I saw them."

Riley looked around as he contemplated the idea. The thought of being tied down to an office wasn't, in his opinion, very appealing. He liked being the only one responsible for his own actions, not having to answer to anyone. The security and the perks that came with working for an outfit such as the McCoy's were indeed not something to take for granted and there was no denying that he was getting up in age. He found himself tired a lot of the time due to all the years he had been on the trails.

He had tracked and turned in over sixty to seventy men over that period of time and took a half a dozen or so bullets. Still, he made a good living at it. He had been younger then and healed quicker, a lot like Ed in a sense. Maybe it was time to slow down some. He had enough money that he could make a move to the Fort. There was some nice land around and buying a piece wouldn't put him in the poorhouse. He looked over to Brady.

"You really got my head spinning, Brady. I'm going to need a few more minutes of thought."

"Take your time, Riley. It is Sunday today. We don't do much on Sunday."

Brady poured each of them another coffee and sat back down. He could tell that Riley was in deep thought and he hoped that Riley would give him the answer he wanted to hear. A man with his reputation and abilities would be a great asset as *McCoy's Bounty Hunting Service* grew. It had always been a small operation, but with the amount of work they seemed to be getting as of late, there was no doubt in Brady's mind that there was definitely room for expansion. He often thought about that. With Travis and Tanner and this new fellow, Buck working for them, Brady knew they were heading down the right road. Adding Riley to the mix improved their professionalism and certainly the services' reach. It took Riley longer than a few minutes to decide, but he finally did. He signed the contract that same day, June 28, 1891. With paperwork out of the way, Brady shook his hand and welcomed him aboard.

"It's a tradition around here, Riley, that I have to take you to lunch now," Brady said with a smile as he stood up.

The Missing Years – Part II

"Sure, I guess I could use a bite. Thank you, Brady," Riley said as they left the office and headed out to lunch.

On their return to the office an hour later, Brady swung by the telegraphers making sure that the reply he wrote before he and Riley headed after Talbot, had indeed been sent to their man Travis. He was assured that it had been and when he mentioned his annoyance that the one Travis sent them didn't find its way to Ed, he was told that the Mounted Police had denied the telegrapher access to the widow Donale's residence. Only family was allowed. Hearing the explanation, Brady apologised for his rudeness, thanked the telegrapher for his time, and met back up with Riley at the office. The remainder of their day was spent in idle chitchat.

Buck and Tyrell finally reached the base of the mountain south of Vermillion. It had been a tough go. Resting now, they looked around for any telltale sign that there may have been human activity in the area at one time or the other that might lead them to a solitary cabin. They found no trail, no path, nothing. There was no sign of anybody having been in the area in years or that is how it looked from where they rested.

"I guess we can carry on a bit further, maybe make our way up to that ridge. It is high enough, I reckon, that we might see something that we can't see now. To be honest, Buck, I would have thought we'd have seen something by now that would tell us that there has at least been activity in and around here in the last few months. I ain't seeing anything except more bush and bramble in all directions," Tyrell pointed out.

Taking a drink from his canteen, Buck glimpsed something shining a short distance away.

"Hang on, I think I see something," he said as he walked toward the object. He was quite surprised at how small the object was and that he was even able to see it.

"Hey, Travis, come here," Buck called out.

"Did you find something, Buck?" Tyrell asked as he made his way through the bramble and over to where Buck was kneeling.

"Sure did. What do you make of this?" he asked as he pulled a Texas Ranger star from the dirt and held it up.

"By God, that there Buck is a five point Texas Ranger star, a silver one too, it looks like. How were you able to even see that from where we were?"

"I saw a gleam. Must have been the way the sun shone on it as I leaned forward," Buck answered as he rubbed it clean on his shirtsleeve.

"Yep, says so right here around the star's border, Texas Ranger, Department of Safety. The star itself says Sergeant. What a find this is," he said as he handed it to Tyrell to have a look.

"Indeed, it is quite a find."

Tyrell looked it over and as he looked on the back of it, he saw the initials M.C. He pointed it out to Buck.

"I reckon this M.C. stands for Matt Crawford, Buck. This also tells us that the Ron Reginal that your friend JoBeth mentioned and the recluse our friend at the outpost said is supposed to live in this area, is more than likely Matt Crawford himself. Damn that is a good piece of evidence, Buck," Tyrell said as he tossed it back to him. "I guess we better spend a bit more time searching this area out. There has to be a cabin around here somewhere."

"I'd bet on it, Travis. We just ain't in the right place. Keep in mind trapper cabins can be dug into the ground, just as easy as being built above. Could be we haven't seen one because we're assuming it would be above ground," Buck pointed out as he tucked the star into his shirt pocket.

"Good point, maybe we ought to be looking for both. "Yep, I'd agree," Buck responded as they made their way back to their horses and once more continued with their search of an old cabin said to be in the area. The tawny star they found proved to them that Matt Crawford had at one time or another been in the area. It was unlikely that the star belonged to anyone else. They were both certain of that. They scouted the area for two more hours before they found what they were looking for. The cabin was so well hidden, it wasn't until they practically stumbled upon it that it became clear on what they found.

Only the moss-covered roof and short stovepipe gave it away. If they had not seen those, there was a real chance that they might have walked past. They remained sitting on their horses as they looked on waiting to see if there were any sounds or movement inside, but it was dead silent. Satisfied that no one was around they quietly dismounted and with slow caution approached the cabin. Buck climbed onto the roof and checked the stovepipe to see if it had been used recently. The squirrel that jumped out at him as he looked on told him that it hadn't been used in a few weeks, months even.

He stood up in full view so Tyrell could see him.

"I don't think anyone has been here in a while, Travis. There is a squirrel nest in the stovepipe."

Tyrell came out from the shadows and met Buck at the cabin's entrance. Both men had to duck down to get in the door. Inside it was quite spacious and standing wasn't a problem.

The Missing Years – Part II

"Not such a bad little place, I reckon," Tyrell said as they looked around.

The place was being lived in; there was no doubt in that regard. There were belongings everywhere and the cupboard and shelf that the cabin housed had canned goods. Wax candles, a small hand mirror and a straight razor lay next to a washbasin. Old socks and a few shirts dangled from a few hooks in the cabin wall. Although these things were dust covered, it was evident that someone was certainly living there.

"I think we have found the home of Ron Reginal and Matt Crawford," Tyrell said as he sat down at the table and bench against the one wall, next to the only window. Small as it was, it let in some light. The roof overhang, however, did hamper the view.

"I feel like an intruder, Travis. I find it odd to be in someone's home without being invited."

"Have you forgotten that we're bounty hunters? We are in our rights to be here, Buck. Sit down. No one has been here in a while and I don't reckon anyone is going to show up anytime soon. Besides, Black Dog is on duty. Sit down and take a load off."

Tyrell used his foot to push the chair opposite where he sat out from under the table so Buck could sit.

"Got a good view here of the forest and the eastern Rockies. Don't see anything else, just the mountain and the forest. The window must have been put here to let whoever built the place know when it was sunrise," Tyrell chuckled with amusement.

"To be honest, Travis, that would make sense," Buck said as he finally sat down. "The bunk is against the west wall. You would most definitely see the sunrise."

He looked out the window.

"And sitting here with your breakfast, you'd be able to tell what time of morning it was by how the sun rose. Makes sense when you think about it."

"Yeah, I reckon so."

Tyrell inhaled deeply as he looked around the inside of the cabin, wondering if they should stick around for a day or two to see if anyone returned. Discussing it with Buck over the next few minutes, they decided to remain there overnight. In the morning, if things hadn't changed they would continue on to Hazelton. After they looked into Emery's death and gathered any evidence they could find on who may have killed him, or find the killer himself, they'd make their way back to the cabin. Maybe by that time Ron Reginal, known to them also as Matt Crawford, would have returned and they could quickly apprehend him and collect the bounty. One thing was for certain, they knew now where to look.

"Chapter 16"

It was early morning when Tyrell and Buck left behind the cabin and headed back the way they had come. Making their way to the trail, they continued north toward Hazelton.

"We're going to be coming into some leftover snow up in those hills," Buck pointed out as they looked on.

"Looks that way. I expected that as it is only the end of June. Snow up that high ain't going to be gone until August and even then there will always be some sign of it at that altitude. I reckon some of it is glacial."

"Yep, some is. Once we start to descend the high country, things will change. I figure we'll be out of the snow-capped peaks by late noon today, so we'll have to deal with snow, cold, and misery for only a couple of hours. After that, it won't be any different than what we're into now. We'll be in Athabascan territory; that'll be the only difference," Buck said as they traipsed onward.

Sitting in his saddle while Pony trudged on in his slow, ambling way, Tyrell was looking over the map that he had, hoping to find a better route than to head up into the blasted cold Rocky Mountain that they were looking at now.

"You know what, Buck. If we wanted to, we could stay down low and avoid the snow easy enough. We could stay westerly. According to this map, heading up and over is shorter, but going west and staying down in the low alpine might make the trip less miserable. We'd still get to Hazelton by tomorrow. What do you say?"

"Staying down low, we risk running into muskeg and swamp and if a man ain't careful in areas like that they might never be seen again. I've gone that way one time only. Any other time I rode up into the high country. Of course, one needs to be cautious. Sometimes avalanches happen."

"I ain't sure I'd like to be in one of those. I'd feel better heading westerly and staying down low, Buck."

"All right, we can do that, I suppose. Just keep in mind also that down low we have a few more risks of running into bands of renegade Indians, and maybe even hoodwinks. Moreover, like I said, swampland and muskeg can cause us grief. But then again, so could avalanches," Buck chuckled. "Either way works for me, Travis."

Tyrell was still looking at the map as he coursed what he thought to be a safe route for them to travel.

"We head this way," he pointed it out on the map as he showed Buck. "We can bypass the tundra, avoid most of the swampy areas and be in some nice country. It mostly looks flat with a few little hillocks only."

They looked at the route together and decided to try it. If nothing else, they certainly wouldn't have to deal with snow, cold and possible avalanches. It was settled. They cut westerly into the forest in the direction of a valley that, according to the map, was about ten miles away. It was that valley which was laden with swamp and muskeg. They would have to be careful.

Through the thick and unrelenting forest they travelled. Black Dog surprisingly was showing no signs of fatigue as they continued on. His wound was healing well and Tyrell often thought if it was due to Indian Clive's blessing.

On a few occasions they had to stop and lead their horses; however, it wasn't as bad as they first thought it could be. Finally, after four hours, the small valley came into view. They stayed near the bush-line to avoid the swampy grasslands as they rested and looked around. Tyrell once more unfolded his map to get his bearings and to study the terrain. It wasn't a big valley and the mountain they'd have to cross to get back on the trail that was on the other side wasn't demoralising. The good thing was they were able to avoid the high Rocky Mountain peaks and the cold, wet snow that remained up high. Where they rested, it was warm and pleasant.

"We would have been almost into the snow and cold by now if we stayed on the trail. The good thing is we can pick up the trail again on the other side of that mountain," Tyrell said as he pointed toward it.

"I think when I came through here, I was further west and had to use my wit to avoid losing my horse in the swamp. I never had a map. I think that would have improved my last experience. I have to admit, Travis, we made a good decision to come this way."

"We can say that now, but we ain't even started to climb that mountain yet. Although it doesn't look as treacherous as the Rocky Mountain that we'd have to cross if we stuck to the main trail, it is still a mountain and any mountain can be a pain. I reckon it is grizzly territory too, but I'd rather be tossed off Pony then swept off some crags by an avalanche. Plus, I ain't so inclined to appreciate the cold," Tyrell pointed out.

"You don't have your warm flannels with you, I reckon."

"I never even thought about bringing them along," Tyrell chuckled.

"I don't even own a pair anymore. The last ones I had ended up needing a lot of stitching and so I burned them. They were probably ten years old. Gonna have to make a note to pick up new ones before fall, I think." Buck averted his eyes toward the mountain they would be crossing.

"I reckon we can get to the summit of that mountain by high noon. If we don't run into any trouble, it shouldn't be that tough to manage."

"I figured that we'd get there at least by high noon or late day. In any case, we should be able to get to the summit before dusk. That is the goal, Buck; that is the goal," he repeated as he folded up the map and tucked it away into his saddlebags.

Grabbing his canteen and a handful of jerky, he offered a few sticks to Buck and, of course, the dog. Sitting on the grass-covered slope, they looked out across the swampy valley enjoying the view and the short rest as they nibbled on the jerky. Soon they mounted up and headed along the bush-line. As they grew closer to the base of the mountain, they halted near a creek that fed the swamp. The water was crystal clear and cold. It was obviously glacial water.

They filled their canteens and let the horses drink. The creek was swift and, in some parts, quite deep. Slowly, they coursed their way to the other side. Their boots and pants were soaking wet by the time they crossed, their legs and feet numbed by the cold water. Black Dog was swept away and ended up downstream, but on the same side. Buck and Tyrell dumped out their boots and wrung out their socks as they waited for him. Finally, he came traipsing up to them, wagging his tail as though the little swim he had was nothing at all.

"You didn't find that damn water cold, Black Dog? My legs and toes turned blue," Tyrell knelt next to him and scratched him behind the ear.

He noticed that the swift water had washed away the scab where Black Dog had been stabbed and he was bleeding some, but it wasn't going to slow him down. He was raring to go, almost antsy.

"Settle down, Black Dog. Let Buck and I get on a dry pair of socks. I don't know what has got into him, Buck, but he sure seems titillated by something."

Tyrell pulled on a pair of dry socks and slipped back into his boots, wet as they were. He knew the sun would dry them in no time.

Buck, on the other hand, tied his boots to his horse.

"You ain't going to put on your boots, Buck?" Tyrell asked with curiosity.

"Nope, going to let my boots dry and air out. Every time my feet get wet, they always seem to have an odoriferous odour. I'll ride with my socks for now."

"Jesus, I ain't ever seen a man riding a horse with only his damn socks. I think you are half crazy, Buck."

Buck chuckled as he pulled up next to Tyrell and grabbed one of his boots. Tyrell almost gagged as he waved the boot in front of his face.

"Stink don't they?"

He began to laugh as Tyrell spit to the ground trying get the taste out of his mouth.

"God damn, Buck. Was that even necessary?" Tyrell asked as he inhaled a gulp of fresh air.

"Nope, but now you know why."

Buck sped up his horse and took the lead laughing as he went. Tyrell could still smell the boots since Buck was ahead of him and he shook his head.

"Yep, I reckon he's gone mad, Pony," Tyrell said as he rubbed Pony's neck, heeled his flank, and caught up with Buck a short distance away.

"The horse almost fell over, Buck. You took off ahead on purpose, I'm sure. That damn stink trailing behind you probably killed some plant life down in that swamp," Tyrell teased.

"The boots will dry soon enough. The sun is getting hot and it won't be long before they smell like roses again," Buck chuckled as they carried on.

The Missing Years – Part II

"I think once we get to Hazelton, Buck, you should pick up yourself a pair of new ones. Those ones are rotten."

"Maybe, but they sure are comfortable."

For the next few miles, they rode in silence, talking sporadically and making jokes. Before they knew it, they were close to the summit and it wasn't even high noon yet.

They had indeed made good progress and things had gone well. Now as they ascended the last stretch to the summit, the rocky outcrops and steep incline slowed their pace. Although the horses struggled with the climb, slipping and sliding on the moss-covered, rocky surface, they kept their balance and maintained a steady progress. When they finally arrived at the summit, Buck's horse began to limp. One of the horse's back feet had a jagged rock stuck in his hoof. Even after Buck pulled it out, it was hard for his horse to carry him.

"God damn it," Buck said with disappointment. "We're going to have to stop here for a bit, Travis."

"Yeah, I reckon so. No point in putting that horse of yours through anymore trauma. Likely take a few hours for him to feel up to snuff. We made it to the summit and we did it in less time than either one of us thought. Resting here for a few hours doesn't hurt my feelings any, nor will it hurt the horses. That was quite the climb, frightening almost in some parts."

Tyrell looked down toward the valley where they last rested and out across the draw they traversed as they made their way to the valley.

"That is some nice country down there. I didn't realise how vast it was."

"It does go on for quite the stretch, doesn't it?"

"Yep, it does. What do you figure, Buck? Since we're going to be held up here for a few hours, maybe we should prepare for the unexpected, gather some wood and stuff. One never knows what might come."

"Probably not such a bad idea. Might as well take the saddles off the horses, too. It's going to get hot over the next couple hours and being here on a south hill, we're going to feel the heat. If we can feel it so can they."

"Alright, let's do it," Tyrell said as he and Buck went about the tasks.

They led their horses to a patch of grass and removed their saddles. Setting them down, they went about gathering wood and rock so they could make a small fire if need be or if they decided to cook something while they rested. Black Dog lay in the shade close to the horses. That way he could keep his eye on them. He, too, wanted a rest. The last push to get to the summit caused him a bit of pain and his instincts told him he needed a rest. Where they were now was the perfect place, warm and peaceful.

A few minutes later, the two men sat on their saddles shaded by an overgrowth of mountain ash. The sun was warm. Even the mountain breeze as they sat there in the shade seemed to be warmed by the sun and its intense heat. Tyrell took a drink from his canteen as he looked around and took it all in.

"I don't reckon there are many places that I've been to where the best memory of that journey wasn't times like this. It is always the best part when you find that place where you can simply sigh in awe."

"You'd like the Yukon, I reckon. Right now at this time of year you can be on a ridge like this and it wouldn't matter the time of day, the sun would be shining."

"I always wondered how that would be, twenty four hours a day of light, every day. I imagine a man

The Missing Years – Part II

could get a lot done. Winter, though, likely a different story."

"Yeah, winters ain't always pleasant, but I'd say they are more times than not. You just got to get your business done early on, then fire up the wood stove. The days are shorter and nights longer and colder, but you learn to live with it."

Buck looked out across the horizon, to the tops of the trees across the draw.

"I like this area too, a good balance between night and day and the seasons."

Tyrell nodded in agreement as the two men continued their gaze of the area, both in deep thought. They had been lucky in all actuality on how things had been going. Other than a few unexpected mishaps along the way, things could have been a lot worse. The big pay-off would be rounding up Ron Reginal. This trip to Hazelton was a side job. There was no payoff in it other than learning a bit more about Emery Nelson's murder and maybe coming up with a possible motive and name of the killer. They were a lot closer to finding Ron than they were in discovering the motive behind Emery's death. It was more of a favour to the McCoy's, especially now with what they had learned about Ron Reginal. It didn't matter anymore if Emery had tracked him to Hazelton or not. The information was moot.

The good thing was that once they arrived in Hazelton they could concentrate their efforts on one problem and not be side-tracked by following leads on where Ron Reginal or Matt Crawford may or may not be. They had already answered that question and it was only a matter of time and luck that stood between them and his capture. If it went as Ed planned, then Matt Crawford would be exonerated from all his past and present crimes, even more so now that he had been witnessed saving people and risking his own life as the

The Missing Years – Part II

town of Vermillion burned to the ground. The McCoy's and each of them, Tyrell knew, would walk away with a nice tidy sum and Matt would walk free. That was the plan, but plans didn't always ring true. Tyrell knew anything could happen between Matt's apprehension and the return to the Fort. If it went as well as their trip so far, then things might go as planned.

The minutes turned to hours as they conversed and enjoyed the warm summer day. Finally, Buck's horse seemed to be walking without a limp and Buck mounted him without his saddle to see how well he could handle the weight of a rider. The horse walked fine.

"I think we can carry on, Travis. My horse seems okay now."

"Good. I figured it would take a couple hours. You might find him limping as we continue on. We'll keep our eye on him. If he starts limping, we'll rest again," Travis said as they saddled up their rides and loaded up their gear.

Whistling for Black Dog, the two men continued with the descent, their goal being to ride until dusk. Hopefully by then, they would be within a stone's throw from the trail that lay on the other side of the mountain. It all depended on how well Buck's horse could maintain the pace.

Back at McCoy's office, Brady was at his desk with some paperwork and Riley was thumbing through a few wanted posters when police lieutenant Bob Cannon showed up. In his usual manner, he walked up to the counter and leaned against it. There was a yellow envelope in his hand and he set it on the counter. Brady wasn't too enthused about the visit as he slowly stood and made his way to where Riley was standing. Riley on the other hand was. He had a few questions for Cannon and had every right to ask them. Although he would wait until their visitor was finished talking, he would certainly be asking.

"Afternoon, Brady, Mr. Scott. I went through the information I have on how things developed when the two of you apprehended Talbot. Although I would have liked him alive to face justice and hang, you fellows did good work. I understand neither of you pulled the trigger that killed him and I have a few questions regarding that. First, the wounded man back at our cells goes by the name of Kyle Rogers. He's almost as notorious as Talbot; has been running with the Kingsley Gang for nearly as long as Talbot himself."

The lieutenant paused for a moment as he looked around. What he was about to tell them put his own reputation on the line, but he needed to tell them.

"Any chance we can sit down and discuss this a bit further over a coffee?"

"I suppose, lieutenant. We've got coffee on in the staff room. Follow me," Brady said noting the seriousness in Cannon's voice. Whatever Cannon wanted to say was obviously of some importance.

"Thank you, Brady. Mr. Scott, you might as well join us too," Cannon mentioned as he waited for Riley.

"Alright," Riley said as he turned and followed behind Brady, Cannon following him.

Brady poured each of them a coffee then joined them at the table.

"What is this all about, Bob?" Brady asked as he added cream and sugar to his coffee.

"On the 22nd of June, the day before Talbot's court hearing, the Mounted Police were visited by a fellow who claimed he was a U.S. Marshal. He went by the name of Arthur B. Talmore."

Cannon took a drink from his coffee.

"The thing is we did a quick search through our records two days after Talbot managed an escape, so last

The Missing Years – Part II

Thursday. We did that because it all seemed to be coincidental. We even sent a telegram to the Department of Safety down south. Their reply back was that there was no one with that name working for the U.S. Marshals."

"You got fooled, did you?" Riley commented as he looked over to Brady and then back to Bob Cannon. "I already came up with that assumption, Bob. I spoke with one of the younger constables early Tuesday evening after Brady passed out from whiskey. He mentioned the visit. It didn't take me long to see the correlation. In fact I was quite surprised to hear something like that. U.S. Marshals don't often take much interest in their criminals that come up this way and most times my experience has been, they'd rather not. That is why there are bounty hunters."

Riley took a swig from his coffee before he continued.

"I reckon this fellow Talmore was here to look over the security that the town had. Seeing what it was and what it may not have been, he managed to pull off a sudden and deadly attack on the town. The worst thing, Bob, is the fact that the Marshal talked to you. Now, how does a fellow with your experience get fooled by someone like that?" Riley was curious. His intent wasn't meant to sound rude. It was a simple question which needed to be asked.

"Your analysis, Mr. Scott, isn't totally correct. He did fool me that is true. I certainly should have been more analytical and paid more heed to that entire charade, so I don't have an answer on how except that he did. The information he was seeking was the information you folks handed over to us regarding Matt Crawford and Emery Nelson's death. This part of the ruse doesn't have much to do with Talbot's escape at all, but it might have something to do with his death."

"How exactly is that?" Brady questioned next. He and Riley were both now perplexed. Maybe there was a different motive and they waited for Cannon to carry on.

"What we did find out is that Arthur B. Talmore is a fellow named B. Atalmore," Cannon began as he now opened the envelope and removed a few documents. "B. Atalmore is a U.S. Ranger, no different than Crawford. Both are specialists. Both are wanted by the U.S. Safety Department and U.S. Marshals. Atalmore is running with three other men who have not been identified. I have had our sketch artist draw a likeness of the man that finally came back to our station and wrote down the information regarding Crawford under the pretext that he was a Deputy Marshal."

Cannon slid the picture over to Brady who looked at it and set it down for Riley. Next, he showed them a picture of Atalmore.

"That man there," Cannon began referring to the last picture, "is the man that claimed to be U.S. Marshal Arthur B. Talmore. We can assume they are an elite group and it is possible they are in the area to meet up with Crawford for one reason or another."

He took a drink of his coffee as he waited for Brady and Riley to look at the pictures again and any response they might have.

"Are you saying that Atalmore or one of his men may have shot Talbot, or are you saying these men are in the area to meet up with Crawford?"

"You're talking in circles," Riley pointed out. He hated the way the law always lollygagged and he wanted Cannon to get to the point.

"To be honest, I believe both. What we don't know is why."

Cannon pulled another document out of the envelope.

The Missing Years – Part II

"This here, Brady, is another contract that the Mounted Police herewith give the McCoy's full control over. It is a private investigation contract usually appointed to law enforcement agencies. The judge in this case, however, Judge William Frank, the presiding judge during last week's excitement, has requested that you folks be offered it before he appoints it to upper law enforcement. It is quite an honour."

"I have never heard of such a contract. What exactly is it?" Brady questioned as Bob Cannon handed it to him.

Brady read it briefly.

"You want us to track down both Crawford and this Atalmore fellow when only a couple of weeks ago, we were told we can't pursue Crawford because the law believed him to be the murderer of our man Emery. Something about conflict of interest or some lame crap like that. I don't know, Bob. We are short men. Travis is up north somewhere, Tanner is bed-ridden and Ed ain't able to work right now. There is only me and Riley holding down the office," Brady mentioned as he continued to scroll the document. "What does it mean 'full control of the investigation'?"

"You would have full access to all and any Mounted Police resources you may need. No other law enforcement agency in Canada, including other agencies such as McCoy's, can encroach on the investigation or receive any bounties without firstly notifying you or your men. This type of thing isn't usually practised here in Canada. The judge, however, believes it is you folks that can bring these men in alive so they can be arraigned on charges of impersonating U.S. Marshals to obtain information. There will be other charges laid by the U.S. Safety Department as well, but that has nothing to do with Canadian law. That is the gist of it, Brady."

"What if we can't bring them in alive? Men like these ain't likely going to let anyone take them in without a fight and maybe bloodshed," Riley pointed out.

"Good point, Riley. What happens then, Bob?"

"There is nothing in that contract, Brady, that says they have to be brought in alive. I am sure extreme force would be tolerated. The fact of the matter is that dead men can't be arraigned so it is with hope that is how they are brought in, not how they have to be. The bounty for both Crawford and Atalmore together is well above twenty thousand dollars and we won't even know what the bounty on the three men running with Atalmore is until we know who they are. You would still be entitled to that whether they are breathing or not. In addition, McCoy's will get full honours for their capture."

"Who pays for our time? We are bounty hunters that work on a type of commission. For something like this, I think we might be entitled to some kind of fee, not just the bounty."

"Read further, Brady. All inherent expenses will be paid including an undetermined fee that will be decided by the Provincial government to be no less than five thousand dollars and no more than twenty thousand dollars."

Brady scrolled down the page further.

"Okay, yeah. I see that now. We could be looking at a maximum of forty thousand and all our expenses plus whatever those other three are worth."

Brady was showing interest now. Even twenty five thousand dollars and all their expenses, plus whatever the bounty was on Atalmore's men was appealing.

"I assume the expenses would be included for every man we had working on this, wouldn't it, Bob?"

"That is the only way it could be, Brady. It doesn't only entitle one or two men. We know the more you have working on it, the quicker the results."

"Can you leave this with me for a day. I'd like to discuss it with Ed and Riley."

"I see nothing wrong with that, but I will need an answer tomorrow. Does that give you enough time, Brady?"

"I reckon. Swing by tomorrow, Bob. I'll have an answer for you then," Brady said as he stood up and Bob followed suit. "I'll walk you out."

Brady followed him to the front door and thanked him.

"I'll see you tomorrow."

"You bet, Brady; see you then."

Bob nodded and exited the office. Brady turned and made his way back to the staff room where Riley waited.

"What do you think of that, Riley?" he asked as he sat down again and looked at the contract.

"It is quite the thing, I think. A lot of money could be made, at what cost we don't know. These are U.S. Rangers after all and as you may or may not know, I've been tracking Crawford on and off for a long time. He is a ghost. I am interested, though."

Riley slid his chair out from the table and poured himself another coffee.

"You want another, Brady?"

"I suppose, yeah, fill me up. Thanks, Riley. I should let you know one thing that maybe you don't know. Matt Crawford has an alias. He also goes by the name Ron Reginal. Our man Travis is looking into some information regarding both Matt Crawford's last appearance in Hazelton, which is where Emery was able to track him before he was shot, and the possible whereabouts of Ron Reginal. The last known location of both men was up that way."

Riley freshened their cups and sat back down.

"That is something I didn't know about Crawford. Interesting, but whether or not Crawford is using an alias or not it doesn't change who he is nor does it make him easier to corner. I understand now that comment you made to Cannon regarding 'conflict of interest'. Your man Emery was tracking Crawford when he was gunned down, wasn't he?"

"Yep, and the law believes Crawford did the killing. Since they rank us, they pulled the heavy and made it clear we couldn't track him anymore until Emery's murder was investigated further. What they didn't make clear, and may have simply neglected to say so on purpose, is that we couldn't track his alias, Ron Reginal. You get the picture, Riley?"

"I sure do and that is exactly what I would expect from any bounty hunting agency under the same circumstances. It ain't anything different than I'd do myself. No need to say more on the subject, Brady, I'm clear. What I'm not clear on is why would a U.S. Ranger want to gun down Talbot?"

"I ain't got a clue. I reckon that is one of the reasons the law would rather see them taken alive, so they can ask all their questions and interrogate them. We take this contract on, it wouldn't be our job to find out. The law only wants these men brought in. That is all we have been asked to do. We'll leave the 'why' up to the law to decide."

As they continued with their discussion they heard the front door open again and Brady stood up to meet whoever it was. He was surprised to see that it was Ed.

The Missing Years – Part II

"What is going on, old man? You ain't supposed to be coming around work yet," Brady smiled. "Got tired of sitting on your derriere, eh?"

"I ain't here to work, Brady. I did get tired of sitting on the porch. I thought I'd pop in on Tanner and see how he is doing as he's coming around. I also wanted to swing by here and see if Riley was around still; wanted to thank him for his help."

"He's here. I guess Ma never gave you the news I asked her to relay last night when I headed home. Riley works for us now. I hired him yesterday," Brady said with apprehension, thinking for sure that Ed was going to scold him for going above his head. Instead, Ed's face lit up with instant approval.

"You got that old bastard to sign a contract? You're a better negotiator than I, Brady. Where is he? Slurping coffee, I reckon," Ed exclaimed with jubilation, as he walked past Brady and to the staff room.

"Brady only now tells me that you signed on with us. Welcome aboard, Riley. You and I have talked about this before and you always said 'no'. What the hell did the boy offer you that I didn't?" Ed teased as he reached out his hand and shook Riley's. "I can't tell you how much I appreciate this, Riley. I mean that."

"Truth is, Ed, I ain't sure how much longer I can keep up with it and when Brady offered me a job, I thought it was a good opportunity to slowly step away from the business altogether. I ain't going to quit on you folks tomorrow by any means. I reckon I have a couple years left before I get too old and slow. Until then or I die, whichever comes first, I'll stick with you."

"That there is more than any man can ask, Riley. You are welcome to stay on board for as long as you like."

Ed poured himself a coffee and sat down.

"That aside, any other news here? Have you heard from Travis?"

"Again, last night while you were snoring, I told Ma that we did get a telegram from Travis. He was in Candora some distance west of Fairmount. He seemed to have stumbled onto an old friend of his who goes by the name of Buck Ainsworth, another bounty hunter. I think I've heard Tanner speak about him a time or two. Anyway, Travis requested Buck's assistance and I guess has contracted Buck's services for now. Haven't heard anything else," Brady said as he sat down. "Why wouldn't Ma have told you any of this? It isn't like her to so forgetful."

"Ah, she's stressed out. Thinks I've taken a few too many slugs lately and that my luck is running thin. Dunbar has her on some kind of medication. She'll snap out of it, Brady; she always does."

Ed slurped at his coffee.

"I guess a lot has taken place since last week. Interesting that Travis ran into that Buck fellow. I haven't heard Tanner mention the name, but Travis did. Said Buck and Tanner actually worked together. I reckon if Travis vouches for him, then all is good. Strange how he hasn't telegraphed us since; that concerns me some," Ed said as he finished his coffee. "Oh well, I guess I better get back to the house."

"Hold on a second, old man. Now that you are here, Bob Cannon came by not long before you. He left us with this. I was going to swing it by tonight. You might as well have a gander now."

Brady handed Ed the contract.

"What do you make of that? Figure we should consider?"

"We've never had one of these before. It's quite an extensive contract," Ed mentioned as he continued to read it. "Forty thousand is a good payout; says here expenses will be covered too. There is a lot of risk involved, Brady. These folk are U.S. Rangers. Short as we are on men, I ain't sure we have the capability."

"We have Travis and that friend of his up north. They are already on the lookout for Crawford. Plus we have Riley now. Add me to the mix, I'd say we have four willing and capable men and their numbers only equal five. The odds seem fair to me," Brady pointed out.

Ed nodded in reluctance knowing Brady was right. The odds were favourable considering they would also have the resources of the Mounted Police at their disposal. Ed looked over to Riley and asked him what his opinion was. It wasn't any different than Brady's and he also pointed out the same thought Ed had regarding the fact that they would also have police resources. Ed sat in silence for a few minutes as he contemplated the contract. Fulfilling it would certainly increase business. The amount of money offered was a tidy sum and getting honours from a Federal Judge such as Judge Frank would secure the business' future and advancement. There really was no reason to say 'no'.

Inhaling deeply, Ed averted his eyes to Brady.

"If you think this is something that you can pull off, Brady, then I'll let you decide, but you have to understand my reluctance. Once your Ma finds out, she'll probably spank me," Ed responded.

"I understand the reluctance. I also know we are capable of this undertaking. It is true these five men are former U.S. Rangers, but I don't reckon they know any more than the four of us. Their only advantage is their ability to shoot from a distance, but before they can do that they need targets and if we don't give them any targets, then they are only men," Brady said as a matter-of-fact.

"I can't argue that, Brady. I can hold down the office and take care of logistics and communications. Hard to say how long something like this can carry on for."

"We know the location where Talbot was shot. It has already been established that he was shot from a distance and that Atalmore had been in and around town the day before Talbot's escape. Obviously, this ain't by coincidence. Either Atalmore took that shot or Crawford did. We only have to pick up the trail. There has to be some kind of evidence left behind. If nothing else, we have a good chance in learning the direction the shooter is heading. We come across four sets of horse tracks then it might be safe to say it was Atalmore; one set means Crawford. Either or, we'll know in what direction the shooter is traveling. That goes a long way in bringing the undertaking to an end quickly," Brady pointed out.

"That is all theory. No one can say how long it may or may not take, Brady. There are too many variables to consider. You are right; the tracking is half the battle," Riley wanted to make clear as he voiced his opinion.

"I know there are variables; there always are. Assuming we can pick up the trail in a couple of days, how far ahead would that put the shooter? Not far I reckon. He or they can only be four days ahead.

"That is still a big area to cover," Ed remarked.

"As long as we don't lose the trail, we might be looking at a minimum of ten days. Lose the trail and that is I guess where one of those variables comes into play. We just won't lose the trail," Brady said with confidence. "I say we go ahead with the contract."

"Alright. If that is your decision, Brady, I won't try to stop you."

Ed stood up and began to walk away.

"Let me know the plan tomorrow, Brady."

"You got it. Not sure it would be a good idea to say anything to Ma yet."

"She won't hear a thing from me until I know for sure what it is you have decided."

Ed exited into the late afternoon, inhaled deeply, mounted his horse, and headed for home, his mind racing with all possible outcomes. How he prayed the outcome would be good.

The Missing Years – Part II

"Chapter 17"

Tyrell and Buck hadn't made the distance they hoped they would have made as they ascended the mountain the day before. Buck's horse started limping again due to the wound and rock bruise he suffered, forcing them to stop earlier than they wanted. Now as they rose to life in the early dawn, Buck's horse looked as though he was up to the task of travelling.

"I reckon he's going to be able to put on some miles today, Travis. He seems to be okay," Buck said as he looked the horse's foot over.

"He ain't showing any tenderness, Buck?" Tyrell asked.

"Not enough to slow him down, I don't think. We'll know more once we start putting on miles. Is the morning coffee ready, Travis?"

"A couple more minutes and it will be."

"Good. We'll have a cup and by then it should be light enough to descend further. Might make Hazelton by late afternoon. How far away does that map of yours tell us Hazelton is, Travis?"

Tyrell unfolded the map and using the light from their early morning fire, he studied it.

"The damn print is so small it's hard to see without proper light."

He leaned a bit closer to the fire and the map took on a flame.

"I guess I didn't think that through," Tyrell said as he put the flame out. "I almost lost the entire map from that fiasco. Glad to have at least saved some of it. We still got Hazelton and a few other places we can see on it. Some of the map is gone. Stupid thing I did there, Buck."

Buck was shaking his head.

"You must be asleep, Travis. You definitely need coffee to take those cobwebs away," Buck chuckled. "So after all that, we don't know how far away Hazelton is."

"Nope, it is best to wait for some light, I reckon."

Tyrell poured coffees and handed one to Buck.

"Here you go, Buck. Travis made."

"Thank you, Travis," Buck said as he gently blew on it to cool it down before he took a slurp. "Damn, that there is good coffee."

He took another drink as he sat down near the fire.

"Warm again today. June has certainly been a warm one."

"Yep, and July I reckon is going to be sweltering," Tyrell said as he took a drink from his own coffee.

"You figure we'll make Hazelton by late noon, eh?"

"I imagine so. We can't be that far away from the main trail. Once we descend this side of the mountain, it will be easy going."

"Yeah. From here on, I guess we really have to keep our eyes open for the Athabascan. I'm quite surprised that we ain't saw one yet, except for that friend of yours, Crying Wolf. That was some distance back. Ain't we already in their territory?"

"We are. I ain't sure myself why we haven't come across a few more from his tribe."

Buck shrugged his shoulders.

"Could be they know about the Blood being in the area and are more concerned about them than about passersby. To be honest, it doesn't hurt my feelings much. I only hope we don't come across a tribal war. That always seems to ruin a man's day. I think we have been lucky up to this point, other than the few bumps along the way."

"Yeah, I suppose. Got real lucky actually in finding that tawny star near Ron's cabin. You figure anyone has returned there by now?"

"Your guess is as good as mine. I think it is safe to say someone will return there. When, well, that is anybody's guess, I reckon."

Buck reached into his shirt pocket and pulled out the five-point silver star.

"You have any inclination on why a U.S. Ranger would run from the U.S. Department of Safety, Travis?" Buck asked, as he looked his find over and in a sense admired it.

"I know a little bit on why. Matt Crawford was set up by the U.S. Government and was expected to meet the firing squad. From what I know, he was discharged without honours for not obeying a direct order to assassinate a left wing Government appointive, a woman by the name of Anne Greenwhich. When they took away all Matt's medals and pension and tossed him in jail, he turned rogue is my understanding. He escaped prison and shot a bunch of folks that were all involved in the conspiracy to take out Anne. Then he came up this way to Canada. He has been here most of the time since. There is more to the story, but only Ed can tell it. I can tell you this much. We bring Matt in alive, he'll be exonerated and will get all that was took from him back again."

"Damn, that is a shame that a Government can do that to one of its elite law enforcers. The U.S., in my opinion, is mostly backwards. I don't have much use for them. Their mind is a little bit off kilter, I think."

Buck slurped again from his coffee.

"That ain't so true, Buck. We have our problems up here as much as the south has down their way. Think

The Missing Years – Part II

about that. You and Tanner were asked to track me down and convince me to work for that fellow Gabe Roy. When you weren't able to convince me, what happened? Because he's rich, he had the law take away your credentials and beat you up some. Folks like that aren't a dying breed here in Canada any more than they are in the U.S. The rich hold the power and use civilian folk like puppets. They take their land or run them off, whichever they feel is convenient at the time. Look at what our Government did to the Indian. They wiped out their source of food for sport, raped their women for sport and rounded them all up forcing them on to reserves and such. Nope, the world ain't what it used to be and it isn't ever going to be. It is only going to get worse and more corrupt as men find ways to do so," Tyrell sighed as he looked around and reminisced.

"Keep in mind, Travis, the Indian returned the favour. They raped our women too. Ransacked farms, stagecoaches, killed men and they, too, did it all for sport. I hear what you are saying and the good book says 'an eye for an eye'. I'm just glad that the wars against the white man and the Indian of the area ain't happening anymore. We did see it in our time and I'm certain our world is going to see a lot more war. 'Cause, like you say, the world ain't what it used to be and the rich and those in power ain't all nice folk."

"It all boils down to greed in my opinion. Who are we to march into Indian territory and chase them off. We did that to them before they revolted against us. The reason we did that, Buck, was because we wanted the resources. When we learned we couldn't simply take them, the Canadian Government had men trained to come in with their long rifles and U.S. designed Gatling guns and what have you. It was because we wanted to make the point that we were intelligent and that we could simply take what we wanted. It cost the loss of tens of thousands of men. That to me doesn't seem intelligent; sounds like greed and the overuse of power."

"You make some good points, Travis, and I get it, but if none of that took place we wouldn't be where we are now."

Tyrell smiled.

"My exact point; and how did the white man get here, Buck? It wasn't through a peaceful solution. It was through death, cruelty and war. We took advantage of the less fortunate who fought with crude weapons, whilst we knocked them down from greater distances than their arrows could fly. White men can never hold grudges against the Indian. I think the Indian has every right to hold grudges against the white man. I believe they do and always will. And guess what? The white man brought that on himself."

"All true," Buck said as he looked into the fire. The silence of dawn enveloped the two men as they finished their coffees in muteness. A few minutes later, Buck stood up.

"It's light enough now. I reckon that we can have a quick gander at that map of yours to see what the distance to Hazelton might be. I don't think it is much further."

Tyrell unfolded the map and looked at it now that he could.

"Yep, you'd be right, Buck. I reckon we're on this ridge here."

He pointed it out.

"The trail is about five miles away and Hazelton looks to be close to double that, give or take. I think it is safe to say we have no more than fifteen miles to go once we get to the trail. Not much further at all."

Tyrell kicked dirt into the coals and poured out what was left of the pot of coffee.

"If you're ready to get, Buck, so am I."

The Missing Years – Part II

"Let's gather up and get then," Buck said as they went about gathering their gear and saddling their horses.

The descent from the ridge went smoothly enough and Buck's horse was holding its own. It took only a short while to make the distance to the trail. It was a welcome sight as they broke through the bush and onto the flat dirt surface.

"It'll be easy going now, Travis. We can take our time and enjoy the trek. Ten or fifteen miles ain't that far," Buck said as they rode on side by side.

The tall trees on either side of the trail cast out the sun, and it was shaded and cool.

"It sure is nice through here, eh Travis?' Buck questioned to break the silence.

They had travelled for at least five miles not speaking and he was getting bored with the monotony.

"Indeed, it is. Surprised actually at how peaceful it has been, that is, until you started talking," Tyrell chuckled. "I'm only teasing you, Buck. I was getting tired of the silence too. Was caught up in reminiscing and enjoying the ride."

"Yeah, me too. I guess we'll have to get a telegram off to your friends back at the Fort once we get to Hazelton. Make sure you ask how Tanner is doing. Have been thinking about him today. Hope he is well."

"I do too, Buck. I hope the same for Ed and I am certainly curious to know how things may be going for Brady and that Riley fellow. Brady ain't that old. It'd be a shame if something bad happens. I ain't been at this business long, Buck. I don't know much about the circle of folk that walk as we do. This Riley Scott seems to have quite the reputation."

"I think what makes Riley a known name in the bounty hunters' circle is that he has been doing it for so long. I ain't sure about the numbers of men that he has singlehandedly brought in, but I've heard it is more than the number of fingers and toes you and I have together. He is quick with his side-arms, knows how to fight, and tracks like no other bounty hunter. I reckon he's getting old by now, but back when I first got into the business, he had already been at it for years. It is the only thing he has ever done from my understanding. That is about all I know."

"I reckon if you do only one thing in life, you can only get better at whatever it is you've chosen to do. That is what makes men professionals," Tyrell responded with thought, as they continued onward.

It wasn't long after that Hazelton came into view.

"There it is, Buck, Hazelton. Looks like a busy place even from here."

"For a mountain community, it is. Many folks, however, come from afar. I don't reckon it is much different than any pioneering town this side of the Rockies. There are a couple of stores, a post office, hotel saloon, a barber, and of course, there is a gold commission office. The law has an outpost southeast of town," Buck described as they made their way. "I think I might actually grab a room and clean up a bit, Travis, whilst you send off a telegram. You want me to grab you a room as well?"

"Sounds like a good plan. I could use a bed and hot shave myself. I'll get the telegram sent and maybe look around some. If this hotel is the only one, it has to be the hotel where Emery was gunned down. It's a good place to start asking questions."

"It is the only one here. I'm a bit superstitious, Travis. What room did that take place in, do you know?" Buck asked with apprehension.

"You mean to tell me a fellow your size believes in that mumbo jumbo?"

The Missing Years – Part II

"I really don't care to be sleeping in a room where someone has died, if that is what you mean."

"Likely there ain't a room in that hotel where someone hasn't died, Buck."

Buck lowered his head and shook it.

"I know that, but I only know about one man being killed in there and that is Emery. The rest don't matter 'cause I don't know, but thanks for pointing it out, Travis. Now you know why I like staying in a damn lean-to."

Tyrell chuckled.

"Emery was killed in room three, Buck, so stay away from it."

"Thanks, I will," Buck said as they pulled up to the horse pole. "I'll check us in, Travis," he said as he swung off his horse and tied him.

"The telegrapher can be found in the post office," Buck began. "Head down to that barber shop and hang a right. You can't miss it. See you when you get back."

"Thanks for the directions, Buck. I'll see you in a bit."

Tyrell reined Pony in the direction. The post office was only a few minutes from closing. They also doubled as a stagecoach outpost and when the stage was due, the post office closed and locked everything up. Tyrell had made it just in time.

"Afternoon," he said as he approached the counter. "I'd like to send a telegram to Fort Macleod."

"Sure," the man behind the counter responded. "I hope it won't be a long one. The stagecoach from Edmonton way will be here soon. The law says we have to lock up before then."

The man walked over to the telegraph machine.

"There is paper there. Go ahead and write it out. Let me know when you are ready."

The man sat down and waited as Tyrell scribbled it out. It took a minute or so for Tyrell to finish.

"Alright, all done."

He reached over and handed it the man. The man took it and with a few taps with his fingers, sent it off. Standing he stood and went behind the counter again.

"Was a short message, fifteen words, seven dashes and one numerical. The fee is two dollars," the man said as he waited impatiently to be paid.

Reaching into his pocket, Tyrell fetched out a few coins and counted out two dollars.

"Here you go," he said as he set it on the counter.

The man scooped it up and put it into the cash register, then slid the heavy screen shield over the counter to protect what was behind that part of the outpost.

"I'll be at the hotel if anything comes back from the Fort that is addressed to Travis Sweet. I'd be obliged if you'd track me down."

"I will," the man assured as he went about his business waiting on the arrival of the stagecoach.

"All right, then. Thank you very much," Tyrell said as he turned and exited.

The message he sent to the Fort was brief. It simply read: *Hazelton- today- staying at hotel-any news on Ed or Tanner- signed- Travis- June- 30*. Tyrell looked down both sides of the street as he made his way to Pony and mounted up. With the telegram out of the way now and as early as it was, he wanted nothing more than to head for his room, clean up and maybe have a nap. Meeting up with Buck back at the hotel and finding his way to his room, he did exactly that. Buck managed to avoid room three. His and Tyrell's rooms were five and six. The rooms were small, but the beds were comfortable. Tyrell threw off his boots and stretched out. He slid his hat over his eyes and, making sure that his pistols were within reach and accessible, he closed his eyes. Buck, however, paid for a bath and had a hot shave before he did the same. They had agreed to meet up later at the eatery across the street.

Riley and Brady had been back on the trail, heading in the direction of where Talbot was shot and killed since 7:00 a.m. that morning. It would take them at least one more day before they were close. It was their hope to pick up the trail of the shooter and track him or them down as quickly as possible, but the rider or riders had a four-day advantage and it wasn't going to be easy. Ed agreed to take care of the office and communications, and would relay the events to Travis once he finally felt the get up and go to do so. It wouldn't be that day. His wife, Beth Ann, had scolded him and made him stick near to the house. He spent most of Tuesday sitting on the porch avoiding his wife's wrath for letting Brady take on such a contract. She was not at all happy and she made it a point to let him know it. There would be only a cold supper for him that night.

Tyrell rolled out of his nap at 5:00 p.m. Meeting up with Buck at the eatery, he was shocked to see him. Buck looked like a new man. Tyrell walked up to him at the table where he was sitting.

"I'm looking for Buck Ainsworth. He kind of looked like you, but ain't as clean."

"Had a nice hot bath, a shave and dug through my gear to find cleaner clothes. I wasn't sure you were going to show up, Travis. Glad you did."

"Yeah, I figured since I woke up, I'd see if you were around. Sure smells good in here. Have you eaten yet, Buck?" Tyrell asked as he sat down.

"Nope, splashed some coffee down my throat. I am hungry and now that you are here, let's order."

Buck put his hand up to signal to the server that they were ready to order.

"Been here for about thirty minutes give or take. It is a busy little place. I hope the food is as good as it smells. What are you going to order, Travis?"

Tyrell looked through the one page menu.

"I think I'll have the beef stew, biscuit and a coffee. Yourself, Buck?" Tyrell asked as the server showed up.

"I reckon the beef stew and biscuits sounds good."

He looked up to the server.

"We'll take two orders of the beef stew and some coffee too, please."

"Sure, I'll get the order to you right away," the server said as she traipsed away. A few moments later, she showed up with their meal and coffee and set them down.

"Enjoy your dinner," she said with a smile as she turned to walk away.

"Thank you, we will," Tyrell responded with a return smile. "This stew sure looks good," Tyrell stated as he took a drink from his coffee. "The coffee is good too. Bon appetite, Buck," Tyrell said, as he scooped up a spoonful.

The beef stew was as good as it looked. It took only a few minutes for the two men to finish their bowls and mop them clean with their biscuits. Tyrell inhaled deeply as he finished the last bite.

"Yep, that was some nice stew, Buck. I wouldn't have expected it to have been that damn good; almost as good as out of the can," Tyrell joked.

Buck took a drink of coffee. As he looked around, he took notice of four men as they pulled up to a table on the other side of the eatery. The first thing he noticed was that neither man wore a pistol that he could see, but leaning against their table were four rifles, nice rifles at that, shiny and clean .45-70's Buck assumed them to be. He noticed the barrel lengths right off the bat. They were longer than most .45-70's of the era. He lightly kicked Tyrell under the table and gestured for him to have a look.

"What do you make of that?" he asked quietly as he took another drink of his coffee and waited for Tyrell's response.

Looking in the direction that Buck motioned to him, Tyrell casually turned his head and did a quick study of the men.

"Ain't that something? They certainly stick out. They look like shooters to me. The length of their rifles tells me that," Tyrell said as he looked over to Buck.

"Yeah, that was my thought too. What do you suppose men like that are doing up in this area? It seems kind of suspicious to me."

"Why?" Tyrell asked as he brought his coffee up to his lips and took a swig.

It was somewhat odd to see four nicely dressed men in such a place. Tyrell didn't really care either way. They could have been on the stagecoach for all they knew.

"Firstly, those rifles they're displaying ain't ones I'm used to seeing. Long as they are means they're likely used for long distance shooting, kind of like our friend Matt Crawford does. Seems odd."

Buck waved his hand through the air.

"Ah, could be they're up this way hunting bear, I guess. They caught my eye is all."

"You bring up a good point. You are right that their rifles ain't ones you'd expect around here and hunting bear from a distance is a pastime for some. Could be they're American businessmen going on a Canadian grizzly hunt. Could be also, they're looking for someone, maybe even Matt. It does seem suspicious, but there are a hundred different reasons that may have brought them here and we have no way of knowing which."

"I reckon you're right. What do you say we head over to the hotel saloon and have a draft beer?"

"I don't think so, not myself at least. I'm going to head back to my room, order a bath and clean up. I'll likely pick up newsprint, catch up on some reading and stay in my room. Don't feel much like drinking, Buck. We got stuff to do tomorrow and a good night's sleep will put our minds into perspective. You go ahead if you feel the need."

"I suppose you are right. I ain't really much in the mood to drink either. I always seem to find trouble when I do," Buck chuckled as they stood up and made their way to the counter to pay for their food.

"I got this, Buck," Tyrell said as Buck began to pull out his money satchel.

"All right, thank you, Travis. I'll meet you outside."

Buck turned and made his way to the exit, glimpsing the four men one last time before he stepped out onto the street. There was something about them that didn't sit right with him. He didn't know exactly what it was, but there was something and he remained suspicious as he looked up and down the street waiting for Tyrell.

It was a warm evening. Folks were heading home and folks were going out to dinner. Some headed to the saloon for a cold whiskey, their day, as well as his and Tyrell's, were slowly coming to an end. He looked across the street to their hotel and saloon, wondering if maybe he did want a cold draft. *Nah, trouble always follows,* he thought as Tyrell met up with him. The two men made their way back to their hotel. Buck volunteered to get their horses stabled for the evening and Tyrell ordered a bath at the front desk.

"I'll meet up with you later, Buck."

"Yep, I'll be around," Buck responded as he exited and took care of the horses.

Tyrell gathered up some clean clothes and made his way to his hot bath. The hot water felt good against his skin as he soaped up and washed away more than a week's worth of sweat and campfire smoke. The water once clean and steaming didn't take long to dirty up with his filth. The long whiskers he shaved away from his itching face and neck floated around like a million logs on an open lake. He kept pushing the water towards his feet to keep the whiskers at bay as he finished up. Finally, he rose and dried himself off. He felt like a new man. Slipping into cleaner clothes, he pulled the plug and watched as his filth went down the drain. Cleaned, shaved, and feeling good, Tyrell returned to his room.

Sitting at the writing desk, he stretched out his legs and put his hands behind his head as he contemplated. The next thing he heard was someone knocking on his door. Rubbing his eyes he realised it was dark outside. Swinging his legs off the desk, he stood up, went to the door and opened it.

"Hey, Buck, come on in."

Tyrell motioned Buck inside.

"I think I dozed off there for a bit."

"I figured as much. I had a quick nap too after I read some newsprint and got the horses stabled. Feels good to be clean, don't it?"

"Yes sir, it sure does. My damn neck has been itchy for a few days. Sure glad I was able to shave. I can put up with my own stench for a time; going unshaved though, that is a different story," Tyrell said as Buck walked passed him and sat down on one of the chairs near the desk.

Tyrell followed suit and sat down as well. Buck visited for a couple of hours before finally heading off to his own room for some shuteye. They made plans to meet at the eatery in the morning to discuss their business plans for the day. There was still a need for them to get information on Emery's stay and whoever he may or may not have met while he stayed in Hazelton. After that, they could decide to stay another night or to head directly back to Vermillion and the cabin where they believed Ron Reginal or Matt Crawford had been living. Tyrell walked Buck to the door and bid him good night.

"I'll see you in the morning, Buck."

"Yep. See you then, Travis."

Tyrell closed the door and headed to bed. It had been a tiresome couple of days and although he had slept most of that day, he still longed for some solid sleep. It didn't take long before his eyes closed and sleep found him.

The Missing Years – Part II

"Chapter 18"

Ed slipped out of the house early next morning. It was Wednesday, July 1. Brady and Riley had been on the trail for a day already and he knew he needed to make contact with Travis. The only way he could do that was to be in town when a telegram came in from him. After all, he was expecting one, and as far as he knew, one could already be there. It didn't take Ed long to make the distance to the office. As soon as he opened the door he saw that indeed a telegram had been delivered. Bud or one of the other telegraphers had simply slid it under the door. He bent down and picked it up. It was from Travis, sent the day before. It read that he was in Hazelton and would be spending the night.

  Ed smiled with relief as he set it on the counter and fired up the woodstove to get coffee going. He was in a rush that morning to get out of the house before his wife awoke and didn't bother with coffee before heading out, but right now he wanted one. It would be another hour before he would be able to send a response to Travis in Hazelton as the telegraph office didn't open before 7:00 a.m.

  Ed sat down as the coffee pot slowly began to perk. He decided to write out the response now as he waited for his first coffee of the day. It was a lengthier response as there was a lot that needed to be relayed to Travis. This is what it read: *I'm fine-Tanner-recovering-contract work-looking for four men- discharged U.S. Rangers- known name of one B. Atalmore- three riders unknown-Talbot dead-long distance shot-Only one surviving member of Kingsley Gang in custody-Judge Frank gives us authority to bring in Matt Crawford-Brady- Riley- on the trail looking for Talbot's shooter- heading North- Possibly mentioned four riders involved-*

or Matt Crawford- will stay in touch-Respond. Signed Ed- July 1.

    Standing, Ed poured himself a coffee now that it was ready, turning the damper down so the woodstove would burn low and slow. He sat back down and read over his telegraph response to Travis. Bringing the fresh cup of coffee to his lips, he inhaled the aroma as he gently blew on it before taking a long swallow. He was satisfied with the response. It relayed everything that needed to be said. He knew that if Travis found anything unclear, he would ask for clarity when he responded; otherwise all was good and understood. Finishing the last of his coffee, Ed stood up and made his way outside. The Fort was slowly coming alive with patrons as shop owners opened up for the day. Ed greeted those he knew and tilted his hat in friendly gestures to those he didn't as he walked toward the telegraph office. He arrived only minutes after it opened.

    "Good morning, Bud?" he said as he leaned up against the counter, glad to see it was Bud running the office that day.

    "Morning, Ed. Nice to see you up and about. How are you?" Bud questioned as he met Ed at the counter.

    "I'm doing okay. I got an urgent lengthy telegram I need sent to Hazelton to the name of Travis."

    Ed slid the message across the counter to Bud.

    Bud picked it up and looked it over.

    "Sure, we can send this right away. It is quite an extensive one, isn't it?" Bud responded as he counted out the words and dashes.

    "It is, but there isn't any shorter way to relay the message," Ed responded as he waited for the cost and for it to be sent.

"Eighty five words and eighteen dashes," Bud said as he calculated the cost. "How does three dollars even sound, Ed?"

"Sounds fine by me," Ed responded as he pulled out some coinage and counted out three dollars.

"Here you go, Bud, three bucks even."

"Thank you, Ed. Now let's get this thing off."

Bud turned and made his way over to the telegraph and tapped away. It didn't take long.

"There we go, sent," he said as he stood up and walked back to the counter.

"Is there anything else, Ed?'

"Nope, not at the moment. I'm going to be at the office all day. Will you chase me down if any telegrams come in?"

"We certainly will, Ed. We always do."

"That is true. Thanks again," Ed said as he turned and made his way to the exit.

Back at the office, he poured himself another coffee, sat down and waited to see what the day might bring. Soon bored, he went into his office and thumbed through some overdue paperwork. That didn't help his boredom and he soon became bored with that. He hated being tied down to the office. Not being able to take part in the hunting and tracking of bounties was a pet peeve of his, but someone had to be there to relay communications and handle logistics. He only wished it wasn't him.

At 7:35 a.m., the knocking on his door woke him up. Tyrell looked toward the window surprised to see that the sun was shining. It seemed as though he had only closed his eyes for a few minutes, but had actually slept through the night. Yawning, he swung out of bed, dressed and answered the knock as he strapped on his holster.

The Missing Years – Part II

"Who is it?" he asked as he made his way to the door.

"Telegraph office," came the reply.

Tyrell opened the door and met the voice.

"This came in for you only a few moments ago," the man said as he handed the paper to Tyrell.

"Thank you. I appreciate you bringing this to me," Tyrell responded as he took it from him.

"I told you I'd drop anything off for you, if something happened to come in and something did, so there you go. I'll be at the office if you need to send a reply," the man said as he turned and walked away.

"Yes, thank you. Thank you very much," Tyrell slowly trailed off as he read the telegram.

Interesting, he thought as he closed the door and continued to read it as he sat down.

As he understood it, Ed was doing fine. Tanner was still on the mend and Talbot had been killed by someone other than Brady or Riley. They had a contract to track down four other discharged U.S. Rangers. Only the name of B. Atalmore was known; the three other men were unknown. It was possible that one of the four or Matt Crawford himself, had shot Talbot. There was only one surviving member of the Kingsley Gang and he was in custody. Judge Frank had given them full authority to track down Matt Crawford.

Tyrell scratched the side of his face as he read it a couple more times to be sure he understood. Satisfied he wrote out a response on the backside of the paper. *Received-understood-Four men seen here-suspicious-long rifles-possible coincidence-will look at this-nothing yet discovered regarding Emery-likely heading back to Vermillion soon- last known location of Ron Reginal. Will send again from Fairmount- a few days-please send responses there. Signed, Travis, July 1.*

Tyrell read the message again making sure there was nothing he needed to add.

"I reckon that'll do," he said in a quiet voice to himself as he yawned once more.

Gathering up his gear, he exited the room and knocked on Buck's as he passed by.

"I'll meet you over at the eatery, Buck," Tyrell sounded from behind the closed door, half expecting Buck to be sleeping.

Instead, Buck opened the door, his gear already packed.

"Morning, Travis. I thought I was going to have to be the one knocking on your door," Buck smiled.

"It might have been that way, hadn't I been woken by the telegrapher."

"You got one back from the Fort then."

"Yep, he handed the piece of paper over to Buck."

It took Buck a few short minutes to read it.

"Some things have certainly changed, I see. Interesting to know that Talbot is dead. Even more interesting to know it wasn't Brady or Riley that did the shooting. I wonder if the four men we saw yesterday are them four spoke of in the telegram."

"I wonder myself, Buck. I've responded back to Ed that we saw four suspicious fellows yesterday. The reply is on the back. Have a look through that and let me know if I've missed something."

Buck turned the page over and read Tyrell's reply.

"No, I reckon that about sums it up."

He handed the paper back to Tyrell.

"You thinking maybe we should find out if anyone registered here under that B. Atalmore name. That would give us the answer real quick."

The Missing Years – Part II

"Before we do that, I need a coffee and want to get the horses saddled. It is definitely something we can look into after we eat," Tyrell responded as he opened the door and the two of them stepped out onto the street.

"Which way is the stable, Buck?" Tyrell asked not knowing since Buck had taken care of that the night before.

"Not far, follow me."

They walked to the end of the block and then turned left. The stables were visible by now and Buck pointed.

"Yeah, I see them," Tyrell responded as they made the distance.

A few minutes later, they made their way back to the hotel, tied their horses once again, and headed over to the eatery for coffee and a hot plate of eggs. The eatery wasn't busy and they were served rather quickly. It took only a few minutes to get their breakfast and only a few more to finish. Sitting now with their coffee, they discussed that day's plan of attack.

Tyrell would send off the telegram to Ed back at the Fort whilst Buck snooped around the hotel to find out if anyone by the name of B. Atalmore had spent the night. From there they would visit the Mounted Police and request information regarding Emery Nelson's death. If all went as planned, they could be on their way back to Vermillion by day's end with information on Emery's death and the possibility that a B. Atalmore had or had not spent the night or was a registered guest at the hotel. If it turned out that he had, then they could be certain that the four men they saw the day before were likely these men. In that case, they would have to decide in what direction the men travelled after leaving the Hazelton hotel or if in fact they remained in the area. It was all basic and they were ready for whatever the information might tell them in both regards.

Finishing their coffee, they stood up, paid at the counter, and went their separate ways, Buck to the hotel and Tyrell to the telegraph office.

"I'll meet back with you in a few minutes, Buck. It shouldn't take long to send this off to Ed. I'll meet you in front of the hotel, say."

"Yep, that works, Travis."

Tyrell made his way to the post office where the telegraph was. Entering the building, he walked up to the counter. It took a few minutes before the telegrapher served him.

"Good morning," he said as he handed the telegrapher the piece of paper. "I need what is on the back of this telegram sent to Ed in Fort Macleod."

"Yes, sir. We'll get it off right away."

The man added the fees up as he counted the words and characters.

"Thirty nine words and ten dashes, that'll be one dollar and seventy five cents."

The man turned and sat down at his desk while Tyrell fished through a pocket full of change and counted out the fee. The man tapped a few times on the keys, stood and met Tyrell once more at the counter.

"All done," he said as Tyrell handed him the exact amount. "Thank you. Is there anything else?"

"Not at the moment. If you get a response in a few minutes, will you let me know? I'll be in town for a few more hours."

"Are you at the hotel?"

"Nope, we've checked out of there. I'll tell you what, I'll check back before I head out. That will probably make things easier."

"Yes, it would."

"Alright, I'll come by later," Tyrell said as he turned and began to exit.

"I'll be here," the man said as he went about his business.

Back at the hotel, Buck was questioning the clerk if four men had registered as guests.

"One name would be, B. Atalmore. Has anyone with that name registered here?" Buck questioned as he leaned on the counter waiting for the clerk to skim through a list of names.

"I don't see that name. Four fellows did register here last night. They left before the sun rose. The one that paid and booked the rooms was an A. B. Talmore, but that ain't the same name. It's close, eh?"

"Yeah, that is quite a coincidence. May I have a look at the name."

"Sure."

The clerk handed Buck the hotel registry and he pointed the name out.

He figured that it was likely the B. Altamore that he was indeed looking for. Chances were B. Atalmore had simply disguised his name.

"Would you have noticed which way the men headed?" Buck asked as he slid the registry back across the counter.

"I do believe I overheard one say they would get to Vermillion in a day or two, so I guess they headed southwest to Vermillion."

The man shrugged his shoulders.

"That is all I know."

"Thanks again for answering my questions."

"No problem, I don't mind."

The clerk put the registry back under the counter as Buck turned heel and began to walk away.

"Have a good day," the clerk said as Buck made his way to the exit.

"You, too."

Buck tilted his hat and exited into the street. *I reckon those four men are the ones mentioned it that telegram. Interesting to know they may be heading to Vermillion,* Buck thought as he waited for Tyrell.

"How did it go, Buck?" Tyrell asked as he approached.

"Four men were here last night. They took off before sunrise. The man that paid signed his name A. B. Talmore. A play on words, I think."

"I'd agree. Any idea where they may have headed?" Tyrell questioned as he looked around.

"The clerk seems to think he heard one of the men mention Vermillion."

"Uhuh, I see. Well then, that makes sense. That is the last known place where Crawford under the name of Ron Reginal was seen. I think we have something now. It couldn't have been anyone of those four that shot Talbot. Whoever did that was likely Matt Crawford. What these four want in Vermillion is anyone's guess, considering the town doesn't exist anymore. My guess is they are either meeting up with Crawford or are here to kill him. That is the only thing that doesn't make sense. What we need to do now, I figure, is find out what we can about Emery's stay. After we learn a few things, then we'll head back to Vermillion ourselves. If the four of them left before daybreak, they'll be a good day's ride ahead of us."

"Yep. We won't catch up to them today, might get close tomorrow," Buck said as the two men walked over to their horses and mounted up.

"Off to the station, I reckon."

"Indeed, Buck. Let's get."

They turned their horses in the direction and set off. Ten minutes later, after Tyrell showed his credentials to the constable on duty, they discussed a few different scenarios, but ultimately received no new

The Missing Years – Part II

information on Emery's stay or his death. The only different information that hadn't been mentioned in the report that Ed received was that apparently Emery Nelson had made a couple of enemies. One was the husband of a woman who Emery had been seen with; another was a fellow who Emery had fought with over a card game.

The constable told Tyrell and Buck that both of the men had been investigated and were cleared on any wrongdoing. This left the only suspect, according to the Mounted Police, to be the man that Emery had tracked to Hazelton, Matt Crawford. It made no sense to Tyrell. There had to be more, but he and Buck it seemed, were beating a dead horse. Every possible scenario that they came up with was dismissed by the constable. It almost seemed as though the constable himself knew more than what he was telling.

Deciding to leave it at that, Tyrell thanked the constable for his time, and he and Buck left. Once they made it back to the Fort, Tyrell would certainly fill Ed in on what his opinion of the constable was. There was something the constable wasn't telling them, Tyrell was certain of that. Their time in Hazelton was coming to an end. They didn't have the time to investigate further, not with the possibility that they were close to finding Crawford, or for that matter, discovering what the four riders were doing. Emery's murder would have to be put on the back burner for now.

"That was a waste of otherwise valuable time, wasn't it, Buck?" Tyrell stated as he swung onto Pony's back.

"It seems as though it was, yep. Off to Vermillion we go, I guess."

"I want to check back at the telegrapher's to see if Ed or somebody has responded to my telegram. If no one has, then like you say, off to Vermillion we go."

"Are you going to send another regarding what we learned about those four riders?"

"I thought about it. Probably makes good sense to do so. At least, then Ed and the others will know what has transpired here. Yeah, I reckon I will," Tyrell mentioned as they pulled up to the horse pole outside and tethered their horses.

It took another few minutes to send a second telegram. It simply read: *A.B Talmore-registered guest at hotel-left before dawn- heading southerly to Vermillion- nothing new in regards to Emery's death- will discuss in greater detail upon return to the Fort- leaving Hazelton now-please send responses to Fairmount- will eventually make distance there. Signed- Travis- July 1.* Paying the small fee again, Tyrell and Buck exited and headed southwest to Vermillion.

Brady and Riley finally made the distance to where they had tracked Talbot and his men before the slaughter took place. It took them the better part of the day to find the lost trail, but they did.

"Looks like it was only one rider," Riley said as he knelt next to the old almost faded tracks. "It would have been around here somewhere that the shot was fired. You see anything, Brady, like a casing over there?" Riley questioned referring to the area that Brady was searching.

"I don't see anything that catches my attention, other than the horse tracks. One rider though, I'll agree with that. Means it wasn't that Atalmore fellow and his men. I'd say it was Matt Crawford; that'd be my guess."

"Hard to say with certainty, but I reckon you are right. We know it wasn't Atalmore; there is only one set of tracks. The shooter headed northeast, looks like."

"Towards Vermillion or Fairmount maybe. Those places are close enough to make a run for. From either place, one could certainly head south or even further north. If I was running, that is where I'd head. We ain't going to know either way until we follow the trail some," Brady pointed out.

"You're right in that respect. I figure we have a few more hours of daylight. We might as well follow the trail until we can't see it anymore. Could be the rider may have headed west down the trail some. Let's get," Riley said as they mounted their horses.

They followed the trail for an hour or so. The rider certainly knew what he was doing. He crisscrossed his own trail a few times making it difficult to follow and to slow down anyone wanting to do so.

"He's a smart bastard, the way he went this way, then that way and so on. He certainly doesn't want to be followed. That proves guilt to me."

"Remember, we are dealing with a U.S. Ranger. He knows his business, that is for sure. I'm surprised we've been able to follow his trail this far already. Looks like he continues north from here. There is a creek and lake not far from here I used to fish it when I was a kid. The trail kind of heads in that direction. Could be he knew about the lake too. May have spent time there. I figure if his trail leads us closer to the lake, it would be worth our effort to check it out."

Riley nodded his head.

"Could be you are right, Brady. A lake out here in the mountains would be a good place for someone running to hold up for a day or two. It is only speculation at this point."

"Speculation or not, let's see where the trail leads. That is all we can do for now," Brady responded as they heeled their horses' flanks and continued following the faded trail.

That evening before the mosquitoes got bad, Brady and Riley decided it was time to set up for the night. Reining their horses to a stop in a grassy glade, they dismounted.

"What do you make of this, Riley?" Brady questioned as he stumbled onto the remains of an old fire.

They weren't surprised to discover that the area had at one time also been used by another traveller.

Riley bent down and reached into the charcoal remains, sifting through it to see if he could decipher how long it had been. Dry as the charcoal was, it crumbled in his hand.

"It hasn't been too long since this was last used, a few days maybe. I would bet this is where the shooter spent that first night after killing Talbot. We should maybe take a look around. Could be something around here that might give us a few clues."

Riley stood up and glanced around.

"You mean something like this?" Brady picked up a couple of empty cans of sardines.

The oily cans were still fragrant with the smell of the canned fish.

"Whew, they still stink. I don't reckon they've been here long. They would have been licked clean by some kind of vermin by now if they had been."

"That is a good find, Brady. If the cans are oily and stink, the rider that was here can't be more than a couple of day's ride ahead. He might have left here the day before yesterday."

Riley walked over to where Brady stood. Brady handed him one of the cans.

"I'd say these are pretty fresh. You'd think that if they had been here for two days, they'd be licked clean and these ain't. I'd argue that whoever was here might have left as early as yesterday, no later."

"That is a good observation, Brady. The damn oil in the can is still liquid."

Riley tossed the can over to the fire pit.

"It makes me wonder why would the shooter, if indeed whoever stayed here is that man, why would he spend so much time in the area after plugging Talbot? That doesn't make much sense at all."

"Like they say, the criminal element sticks close to the crime or returns to the scene. I ain't certain that has any play here, though, under these circumstances. It is a bit off."

Brady shrugged his shoulders.

"It is going to be dark soon and there ain't no point in trying track the rider any more today. We're getting close to him, I think."

"Yeah, we are."

Riley looked into the darkening forest that surrounded them.

"Forest as thick as that is will help our tracking. Might not see tracks, but there will be broken branches and plenty of them," Riley pointed out.

He could recall many bounties that he had tracked who had decided to go bush. They were always easier to find than those that stuck to trails and used small growing townships to their advantage. There was only one reason, too. A man could only go so far in a day when trailblazing. True to the fact also, was the fact that if they lost the trail, all could be lost. Riley, however, was confident that they would not lose the trail.

"We might as well gather up some wood. I could use some food."

"You and me both. I'm a bit hungry too," Brady responded as the two men went about the task.

It took only a few minutes and a fire gently glowed in the darkening evening. Brady opened a couple cans of beans, and set them on the low burning flames.

"Beans again tonight, Riley. We maybe should have picked up a few different items. Got lots of beans."

"Nothing wrong with beans, Brady. They go good with campfire coffee. Do you have any of that cooking?"

"Grab one of the canteens and we'll make a splash. I reckon coffee would be good."

Riley walked over to his saddle and grabbed his canteen.

"Yeah, there should be enough in this one to make coffee."

He handed it to Brady.

"Why can't you make the coffee? I'm cooking the beans," Brady responded as he took the canteen.

"If you cook, you make coffee too," Riley chuckled. "I'll bring our saddles over so we have a place to sit."

"All right. Tomorrow you cook and make the coffee."

While Brady said that, he noticed the shiny glint of a brass casing. It was turning red fast.

"Jesus Christ, get behind something, Riley. A damn bullet is about to explode," Brady exclaimed as he dove for cover. Riley dropped his saddle and fell to the ground. A few seconds later, the bullet popped and then another. The fire was put out by the force. Their cans of beans shot into the air, landing a few feet short of the fire.

"What the hell do you think of that, Riley?" Brady called out still in cover.

"God damn. I ran my fingers through that pit and didn't see those. How many fired off, Brady. Were you able to count?" Riley hollered back.

"Two at least; might have been more."

Brady peeked from behind the tree he had hid behind.

"The fire is out. Reckon it's safe?"

"Stay put for a minute. Could be there are more. It'll take a bit for them to cool down if there is."

Riley slowly picked himself up off the ground and looked over to where their fire once was. The few coals that survived the blast continued to smoke, but he could tell they were losing their heat.

"Okay, Brady. I figure the danger has passed. That was one of the oldest tricks in the book. I don't know why I didn't pay more attention. I must be getting older than I'd like to admit."

Brady walked over to where Riley stood.

"You ain't the only one to blame. I should have thought about that as well. That was close. We could both be lying here with shrapnel freckling us."

He picked up the canteen.

"This ain't of any use anymore. Looks like it took the brunt of at least one bullet."

"I'd rather it be the canteen than one of us. Too bad about the beans. I'll tell you it sure snaps a man back to the seriousness of this business. From now on, we make our own damn fire pit," Riley said with conviction.

"Should we get one built then? I'd still like a coffee."

"Might have to open up another couple cans of beans too. What do you say?"

"I figure my appetite is ruined. Help yourself, Riley. I'll settle for coffee," Brady said as he took the rocks from the one fire pit and used them for their own.

He was a bit shocked at how close the booby trap had come to injuring him or Riley, or both of them for that matter. It could have been a deadly situation. He was angry with himself, but furious at the man who put them there.

"All I have to say about that incident, Riley, is that I hope the man we are tracking comes in peacefully, because I won't hesitate to put an ounce of lead into his heart," Brady said as a matter-of-fact.

"I feel the same way, Brady. We're going to have to be more careful, keeping in mind this is a trained man we are tracking."

"As I've said before, he is still only one man, trained or not. He is a crafty bastard; I'll give him that."

Brady knelt down and striking a match, he lit the fire. The flames flickered and danced in the warm mountain breeze as he set the coffee pot once more on the flames.

"Are you going to cook beans, Riley?"

"Nah, we only have so many cans and I rationed them out over a period of a few days. I'll go without. Coffee is good enough tonight."

The two men looked into the fire, their minds adrift, as the sounds of crickets at night began their chorus and their coffee slowly perked.

Tyrell and Buck travelled twenty miles west that day along the trail that lead back to Vermillion. The town itself was another day's ride ahead.

"I'm getting eaten alive with all these damn mosquitoes, Buck. We should find a place to hole up for the night and smoke the bastards to death. Besides, I'm getting saddle tired."

"Yeah, the mosquitoes are becoming a damn nuisance. I ain't sure how many I've already swallowed."

"So no stew for you tonight, or did the nasty critters make you hungry?" Tyrell snickered.

"I'll need vegetables to go with all the bugs I've eaten and stew has that. Stew sounds good to me, that and biscuits topped off with a nice strong coffee."

Buck pointed up ahead.

"There is a place around the bend that we can set up for the night. It has a little creek near it. Hopefully, it ain't dried up yet," Buck said as they carried onward. "How far ahead do you suppose them four riders are? I've been paying attention to their tracks and they certainly did travel this way."

"I've been watching too, Buck, and I figure they're closer to Vermillion than we are," Tyrell chuckled at his own obvious remark. "That is, of course, if that is where they are heading. They're certainly heading west, but that has always been our assumption. As long as their trail doesn't cut off into the bramble, we ain't going to be too far behind when they get there," he added in a more serious tone.

By now, they had found the place where they would spend the night. Buck slowed his horse to a stop.

"Yep, can hear the creek. Good to know it hasn't dried up yet. We're getting low on water and without water, we got no coffee; and without coffee, journeys like this ain't the same," he said as they dismounted.

"This is a well-used place it looks like," Tyrell said as he walked over to an old fire pit.

"We have some wood already stacked, a creek nearby. Definitely a good place to spend the night, I reckon. We certainly would have stopped here when we were heading to Hazelton if we hadn't cut through the damn bush."

Tyrell inhaled deeply as he looked around.

"We had good reason for that. It was shorter by ten or so miles.

Buck removed his horse's saddle and tethered him to a sapling.

"I'll get flames going, Travis. If you want to gather some water, we can put some coffee on."

"You bet," Tyrell said as he removed Pony's saddle and set it near the fire. Black Dog had already been to the creek. He came panting up the bank, sopping wet. Shaking himself dry, he walked over to where Pony was and lay under a nearby tree. Tyrell grabbed their canteens and coffee pot and made his way over the bank and to the creek.

It wasn't quite dark yet and it wasn't quite light, but he could see the silvery color of the creek's rapids as the water gently rolled by. He looked up to the sky. It was clear and speckled with a million stars. He lost himself in the moment as he continued his gaze, but that isn't all that he lost. He also lost his equilibrium from staring into the heavens. He was lucky enough to catch himself before falling into the water completely, but he certainly got wet.

"God damn it!" he exclaimed as he found his footing and stepped back onto the bank.

Buck, hearing this, hollered to him.

"Is everything okay down there, Travis?"

"I'm fine. I slipped and fell into the creek is all."

Tyrell shook his head as he heard Buck chuckling.

"How'd you manage that?"

"It doesn't matter, Buck," Tyrell said with annoyance as he filled the canteens and coffee pot. Making his way up and over the bank, he handed Buck the coffee pot.

"Leastwise you didn't fall in over your head," Buck teased as he set the pot down and added the coffee grounds. "Sit by the fire and you'll be dry in no time. Was the water cold?" Buck asked.

"I wouldn't say so. It was kind of warm, actually. It was the tumble that startled me more than the wet."

"You have to admit that it was a hot and long ride today. The water probably wasn't so bad."

Buck now put the coffee pot near the flames as he opened the two cans of stew. They conversed back and forth while their meal cooked. It took a little longer for the coffee to perk than for the stew to cook simply because the flames were so low, but with their last mouthful of stew and the smack of their lips the coffee was done. In all honesty, it was the coffee each one craved more than the meal. It had been one of those hot days where heat takes away appetite and loss of appetite increases thirst. Water probably would have also sufficed, but they had drunk enough of that as they coursed their way to where they were now. The coffee was a well-deserved, treat.

"You know what, Buck? As I sit here drinking this horribly strong coffee you made, I've been thinking, trying to piece together those few things that constable mentioned in Hazelton today. You have any thought on why the Mounted Police are so sure that Crawford killed Emery?"

Buck took a drink from his coffee as he contemplated.

"I can't say for certain, but I reckon Crawford is an easy scapegoat for the law. The little you have told me about him, I can't make sense either on why he'd be blamed for it. I understand Emery was tracking him, but I bet Crawford lost him long before he made his way to Hazelton. Could be it ain't related to Crawford in any way except that it was known McCoy's man Emery was hot on his trail, supposedly. Like, I have said before, Travis, the law ain't as clean as most might think. I reckon there is something that ain't being spoke. I couldn't tell you what it is."

"I feel the same about that. It is curious, ain't it?"

Tyrell looked into the orange glow of the small fire.

"It is curious, but until we find Crawford and question him in regard to that accusation, we ain't going to know a thing. I'd put money on it that he ain't involved."

"I wouldn't bet against you."

Tyrell brought his cup to his lips and took another swig of coffee. He thought about the four riders they were also pursuing and what part, if any, they were playing in the grand scheme of things. The information they had wasn't a lot. They could be certain of only two things: the four were wanted by the American and Canadian law and B. Atalmore was their leader. The conclusion was based on a lot of speculation. What Buck had said about Crawford, the same could be said about the four men. Until they were apprehended, there was nothing more Tyrell and Buck could learn about them.

Speculation and assumption would lead a man to believe that the four men and Crawford had something in common. Even the killing of Talbot had something to do with something and somehow it seemed that it was all related one way or another. The calm, silent evening made his mind drift further than that. He wondered how was he going to deal with Riley Scott when their introductions took place.

It was Buck's persistent voice that brought him back to the here and now.

"Travis, hey Travis, anyone home?" Buck repeated.

Tyrell shook his head and looked over to him.

"Yeah, I'm here. I got carried away in deep thought there for a moment. What's up?"

"Nothing, except you ain't spoken in a while. I thought you had dozed off with your peepers open. What the heck were you daydreaming about?"

The Missing Years – Part II

"Everything I reckon. Trying to make sense of a few things, if's, so's, and whatnot's."

"If's, so's and whatnot's?" Buck asked with curiosity.

"Yeah, you know. Things like, what do these four men have in common with our current objective? and why the hell would Crawford presumably shoot Talbot? and what the hell happened to Emery?"

Buck softly chuckled.

"Sometimes, Travis these things are best left alone. You start thinking about this, that, and the other thing, and soon you ain't thinking straight at all and everything becomes a big pile of crap. Best thing to do under these circumstances is to think of the events that are taking place as totally different events that aren't related at all, because it is only assumption at this stage that they are. The only things we are clear on are that the four men are wanted, Crawford is wanted, and Talbot and Emery were both shot under two different circumstances."

Inhaling deeply, Buck shook his head.

"I will admit it is a lot to think about."

Tyrell's mind was not the only one that drifted now as they sat in silence. As time slipped away and the red sky to the west faded into dark, they rolled out their bedrolls. Tomorrow they would be that much closer to finding the answers to so many questions.

The Missing Years – Part II

"Chapter 19"

Major B. Atalmore of the U.S. Rangers special forces elite blew gently on the orange coals from their past evening fire. His men, U.S. Ranger special forces Captain Allan Webber, Lieutenant Junior Spence Hamilton and Ensign Colby Christian continued to sleep. All three men were well versed in survival, firearms, and hand-to-hand combat. They belonged to a special elite group named the U.S. Rebel Rangers, all discharged from the U.S. Department of Safety for one thing or another. Rebellious as they were, they all worked well together and in most cases for the better good. Major B. Atalmore was older than his men, in some cases by twenty years; his silver grey hair proved this. His deep brown eyes had seen a lot of death. Fearless and most times quite serious, he also had a fun side. When it came down to business, he demanded respect and his men gave it to him.

    Captain A. Webber had been with him since the conception of U.S. R.R. He was in his mid-forties. Fit and intelligent, his forte was close combat. His shoulder length hair was jet black and his blue eyes were piercing. He was a one-man force to reckon with.

    Lieutenant Junior S. Hamilton was probably the most serious person of the four. He liked to do things by the book and followed its example even now. Although he no longer belonged to the U.S. Department of Safety, he continued to follow their ethics. He had been running with the U.S. R.R. for over five years. At thirty years of age, he would have made it to Commander by now if he hadn't been discharged from the U.S. Rangers. For now, he was happy with his rank in the U.S. R.R., and knew one day that he would take Webber's place as Captain. Lieutenant Hamilton excelled at logistics and ballistics.

The Missing Years – Part II

He could speak many different native tongues, from the northern tribes to the southern tribes.

The kid, Ensign Colby Christian, was quick on his feet, fearless and not much different than what Atalmore had been in his younger days. He had never belonged to the U.S. Rangers, but he knew how to shoot and was probably the best long distance shooter, next to Matt Crawford, that Major Atalmore had ever seen. What he lacked in experience, he made up for with that ability. Able to shoot with either arm, he may have even been better than Crawford. A couple of years younger than Spence Hamilton, Colby's youthful looks, blonde hair and blue eyes were the crew's envy. He too was a force to reckon with. If he sighted his beloved .44-40 Marlin rifle in on any man, that man always died. He had an uncanny ability to understand ballistics which he could never explain. Major Atalmore discovered Colby by accident. He had seen him shoot a man clear off his horse at a distance he estimated to be seven hundred feet. He never did learn why Colby killed the man, nor did he bother to ask. One day a few years back, he ran into Colby again and acquisitioned him, giving him the rank of Ensign, a guaranteed wage, and promised advancement. Colby cared little about rank. He had never been taught that discipline.

Batalmore, as his men called him, sat down on his saddle as he waited for the flames to reach the three thin lines of gunpowder that he had laid out toward each of his sleeping men. It wasn't meant to hurt them. He wasn't that cruel. It would, he knew, scare the sleep out of their bodies. He leaned back and waited for the fireworks to start, a half smirk across his face.

"Ten, nine, eight," he began in a low, quiet voice as he counted down the seconds.

He didn't make it to 'one' before the flames finally ignited the three little trails. The gunpowder spit and hissed as it travelled within inches of his men's snoring mouths. The brightness of the glow and the everlasting smell and taste of gunpowder caused quite the ruckus and Atalmore burst out into a lighthearted laugh.

"Rise and shine, men. It is 04:00 and we have places to be. The coffee is almost done, so take care of your bladders or change your shorts, whichever it is you need to do."

"Jesus Christ, Batalmore. Couldn't you have simply banged some pots together?" Captain A. Webber said as he pushed himself up from the ground, his bedroll wrapped around his ankles.

"Nope, a man gets used that tripe quick enough. This here, you never expected. Are you complaining, Webber?" Atalmore asked with a chuckle.

"I ought to be. You could've lit my damn bedroll on fire."

Webber shook his head. He never knew what to expect from Batalmore.

"I have to butt in here for a moment. I thought it was funny as hell. Scared the cobwebs right out of me. Once I figured out what had taken place, I almost pissed myself with laughter, never mind the fright especially when you fell, face first into the ground, that bedroll of yours wrapped around you like a skirt," Colby said as he stepped into some bushes and took care of business.

"I ain't sure it was so funny. I'm with you on this one, Webber," Spence said as he too gathered himself. "You can't be wasting powder like that, Batalmore. We only have so much."

"Out of the three of you, the kid is the only one with a sense of humour," Atalmore commented as he poured himself a coffee. "You two could do well if you followed his example."

"This isn't kid games, Batalmore. If the bounty hunters or law get to Matt before we do, we could be in for a lot of fecal matter. Now, I ain't so opposed to a few laughs, but what you did just now is a plain waste of gunpowder," Webber commented as he began to chuckle, the more he thought about it the funnier it did seem.

"I don't see the humour in it."

"I wouldn't expect you to, Spence," Atalmore responded. "You've always had a stick up your arse. You have to learn to laugh a little, Lieutenant. Life can end in the blink of an eye. Let's forget about the jokes for now and get some coffee down before we head out."

"Yeah, I suppose you're right, Major," Spence responded as he poured himself a coffee. "Anyone else," he offered with the coffee pot in his hand.

"I'll take a splash."

"Make that two," Colby said as he made his way to the group. "It is going to be bitching hot today. What are we into here month-wise? We into July yet?"

Colby took a drink from his coffee as he waited for someone to respond. It was clear by the silence that neither man knew.

"I reckon we are. I'd say July."

Spence nodded in agreement.

"A quick calculation of the days we've travelled since Fort Macleod, you wouldn't be wrong, Colby. I'd say July 2nd."

"I can't even remember when we were there, late June wasn't it, Spence?" Atalmore questioned as he scratched his whiskered face.

"Would have been June 22nd, Batalmore," Colby was quick to say. "Isn't that right, Spence?" he second-guessed himself as he thought about it for a moment.

The Missing Years – Part II

"Yep, dead on, Colby, it was June 22nd. I think it was even a Monday."

"Sure feels longer than ten or so days of being on the trail," Webber pointed out. "Haven't even had any fun yet. This unit is getting damn boring," he teased.

"It has only been boring for you because you ain't scratched those itchy knuckles of yours in a while."

Captain Webber shrugged his shoulders.

"That, and I ain't used my itchy trigger finger either. There used to be a time, Batalmore, when you and I never went two days without some kind of satisfaction. These long treks of ours that we seem to go on to right some wrongs ain't like the old days."

"Nope, but we all know what kind of liability Crawford can be. He has run rampant for almost three years and now that we know of his whereabouts, we better damn well stop him or the U.S. R.R. could face exposure, and we can't have that," Atalmore expressed with authority.

They were close to overturning a Federal election that went to the wrong party a few years earlier. It was the election that Anne Greenwhich ran in. They had the names of all those who were involved in the conspiracy to assassinate her and disrupt any political attempts by her to advance her left-wing party.

The problem was, Crawford was killing the conspirators one by one and they knew he wasn't going to stop. Anne was Crawford's sister and those that jousted her out of government and set him up to take the fall for deaths he had nothing to do with, would reap his wrath. Anne and Matt were raised in a close-knit family. They had always looked out for one another. When Anne left for the big city and an education in politics, Matt joined up with the U.S. Department of Safety and eventually became a Sergeant of the U.S. Rangers, a rank he well deserved. The careers the brother and sister chose went hand in hand. Once Anne began her campaign to run for government office and her popularity exploded into the political scene, Matt was approached by the late Governor General William Hunter, Talbot Hunter's older brother, and ordered to assassinate Anne. Not knowing that Anne was Crawford's sister was a bad mistake on the Governor's part.

Matt defied the order and a few days later, with the help from his younger brother and the Kingsley Gang, Governor General William Hunter had Talbot kill eight men who were all part of his very own cabinet. The two of them framed Matt with the murders. William Hunter immediately had Matt arrested and revoked all his credentials that identified him as a proud Sergeant of the U.S. Ranger Corps. With that revocation, Matt lost all rights to any benefits and pensions he otherwise would have been entitled to. From there, it became the war that Matt was in now, a three-year battle to put to rest the bastardly people who had attempted the assassination of his sister and stripped him of all the humanity he ever had.

When Matt managed to escape the prison cell that was to keep him behind bars until he died, it was Governor William Hunter who reaped his reward first. Matt picked him off with one shot through the heart, with a nice follow up shot that took off most of the good Governor's scalp. That was the first and only time that Matt wasted more than one bullet to kill a man. Although he did it in spite, he felt the rush and satisfaction both times that he squeezed the trigger. Shortly thereafter, he joined up with the newly formed U.S. R.R. and for a time he remained loyal to them and embraced their political views. They stood for *'A Just and Fair Government for all U.S. Citizens.'*

The Missing Years – Part II

Their work behind the political scenes of the U.S. Government had exposed countless frauds and land scandals that were neither ethical nor legal, however they did not solely focus on these upsets. They exposed corruption at all levels of Government, right down to the U.S. Department of Safety and lesser law enforcing agencies. They weren't all bad nor were they all good. Then one day, for reasons only Matt knew, he headed into Canada leaving behind a trail of dead, highly important, U.S. government officials who had one way or the other conspired against him and his sister Anne.

Atalmore dumped out the last of his coffee. It was 04:30. It was time to clean up their camp and continue west to the town of Vermillion and a peaceful encounter, he hoped, with Matt Crawford.

"Let's get saddled up, men. Next stop Vermillion," Atalmore said, as he mounted his horse and started toward the town. "We'll likely be in the vicinity of Vermillion by mid-day," he commented as his men pulled alongside. "On another note, keep alert, men. We're going to be in Indian territory soon. The Athabascan, I've heard about, that run around these parts, ain't always the friendly sort. So keep that in mind as we proceed."

Fifteen miles north and heading west were Tyrell and Buck. They rose at the crack of dawn, shortly after Atalmore and his men saddled up and left behind their past evening camp. Buck looked to the east, the yellow sun now visible.

"It's going to be hot again today, Travis."

"I reckon it will be. I'd rather travel in the warmth of a summer day than on a cold, blustering day of winter. Days like this always make for good travelling. I reckon we're twenty to thirty miles northeast of Vermillion. Might make the entire distance today."

"That will depend, I guess, on what lies ahead. We've been graced thus far with good travelling conditions and very few setbacks. Our luck might be running thin by now," Buck snickered.

It was true. Between where they were now and the town of Vermillion, anything could happen. There was still the high alpine of the Rocky Mountains that they would have to descend.

"True as that might be, I feel good about today for one reason or another," Tyrell responded as they carried onward.

"What might those reasons be?" Buck asked wholeheartedly.

"For one, we're alive; and for two, we're getting close to some unanswered questions."

"I suppose, but we could also be getting close to an all-out gunfight."

Tyrell looked over to Buck and smiled.

"Tell me. Is the sun halfway up or halfway down?"

"I reckon you are referring that I'm a pessimist."

"I would never think that about you, Buck."

"Yeah, and bear don't crap in the woods, either."

"I think you are wrong about that. Bear crap wherever they want. A fellow of your stature that likes the outdoors so much ought to know that," Tyrell teased.

Buck saw no need to respond and instead chuckled.

"It is good to see that above all your pessimistic views, Buck, that you still have a sense of humour."

"Without a sense of humour, Travis, what are we but savages?"

They rode in silence now. The only sound heard was that of their horses clip-clopping and the pitter-patter of Black Dog as he trotted alongside them.

The Missing Years – Part II

Further west than the town of Vermillion and travelling northeast, were Brady and Riley. They picked up the trail they were following which lead them through some of the thickest and unrelenting bush they so far had encountered. Their arms, legs, and faces bore the welts and scratches they received from the never-ending assault of mountain ash, tree branches and thorn bushes. Even when they were forced to lead their horses, they could not escape the hazards. Finally, a reprieve came into view and they stopped to catch their breaths.

"We haven't travelled more than a couple of miles, due to all this damn bramble and whatnot," Brady pointed out as he swung off his horse.

"The good thing is, we can assume our friend ain't having any more luck then us. He'll have been slowed down by all this too, Brady."

"I suppose. Still, what a damn pain in the backside it is trying to make any distance. We've been at it for an hour already and I'm betting we haven't even put two bloody miles behind us."

"Probably not, but every mile we gain, brings us that much closer to our adversary. We haven't lost this battle yet. The day is young and eventually we will make better progress. It can't all be thorn bushes," Riley said with optimism.

"I sure hope not. I got more scratches and welts then I have fingers and toes."

It wasn't until they both stopped talking that they were alerted to how silent the forest had become. Not even the early morning of chirping birds they had been hearing sounded. It seemed odd and they looked around with cautious intent. Something had caused the disruption of sound there was no doubt about it. Whatever it was remained hidden and they saw nothing.

Riley shook his head as he continued his gaze of the silent wood.

"I don't know what caused the abrupt silence. My experience tells me we aren't alone. We best not let our guard down. Keep alert, Brady."

"No worries. You won't need to tell me twice. It is kind of eerie, in a sense, ain't it?"

"It always is when you feel like you are being watched, but can't see the damn reason why you feel that way."

Riley was about to add something else when they heard in the not so far distance, the sound of breaking branches and the sound of something big running away from them. Both Riley and Brady drew their side arms and looked in the direction from which the ruckus came. The forest being as thick as it was only gave up a glimpse of a horse and rider, but they lost any visual as the rider disappeared into the shadows of early morn.

"I'd say we're a lot closer to finding our foe than we might have assumed," Riley commented as he quickly holstered his pistol and swung back onto his horse.

"I'd say the same," Brady agreed, as he too, saddled up and they made a mad dash to where they saw the rider last.

"It would have been around here somewhere, Riley, that we lost visual."

Brady looked to the ground and pointed at the fresh tracks left behind as the horse and rider bolted.

"The rider headed westerly from here. He can't be too far ahead. Come on, we have to keep moving or we're sitting ducks."

"Right behind you, Brady. Keep low and use your surroundings to your advantage. That will make it a lot more difficult for anyone to squeeze off a possible death round."

No sooner had Riley said that when the first shot rang out. It echoed with a loud clap as the whistling

The Missing Years – Part II

bullet hit a tree directly behind Riley. The two men swung off their horses and dove for cover. A second shot sounded. This time the bullet drove into the ground only a few paces from Brady, spitting up dirt as it did so.

"I can't see where the hell he's firing from. Were you able to get a visual, Riley?"

"I'm as blind as mole as to where it came from. It sounded like it may have come from our flank. Stay down. There is no way he has a clean shot at us. Otherwise, we'd be dead."

A third and fourth shot came in succession and their horses fell to the ground.

"Damn it, he's picked off our horses," Riley blurted out as he watched his horse try to stand, only to fall one last time.

Brady's horse didn't move. It was stone cold dead from the bullet that ripped into its chest. The next thing they heard was the sound of a galloping horse as the shooter once more headed into the unknown. The two men waited with anxious anticipation for what seemed like an eternity. Finally, Brady stood up and dashed to where his horse lay.

"The son-of-a-bitch blew out my horse's lungs. God damn it. I'm going to put six ounces of lead into that prick's head," Brady exclaimed, as he knelt next to his dead horse.

A rage greater than he had ever felt consumed him as he stared into his horse's dead eyes. On that day, Matt Crawford made a big mistake. Any innocence he may have had, died like the horses he shot. By now, Riley, too, was feeling the rage as he looked down at his own dying horse. Pulling out his pistol, he pointed it at his horse's head. Turning away, he squeezed the trigger.

"This day has just got a hell of a lot worse for us and for Crawford," Riley said as he looked over to Brady.

"Without rides, Riley, we ain't got a hope in tracking him any further. We're going to have to walk out of here."

"Yep, and we are at least five walking days away from the Fort. Let's get the horses' saddles off, gather what gear we can carry and head back," Riley said with trepidation. "This day hasn't played in our favour."

The two men solemnly went about the task of gathering the gear they could comfortably carry, a couple cans of beans each, their bedrolls, canteens, rifles and saddlebags. The saddles, along with all other gear, they reluctantly left behind until the day they could return for them. With their saddlebags over their shoulders and rifles in hand, they began their trek back to the Fort. An estimated five-day journey lay ahead.

Matt Crawford steadied his rifle on the big rock as he adjusted his Winchester rifle scope. The man he sighted on had been tailing him for almost three days. He had no idea yet who the man was, but he watched from a distance as the single man killed the two horses ridden by two other riders. He did not know who those men were either. The cowardly act of killing another man's horse didn't sit well with him, nor did the fact that he knew the single rider had been trailing him. He estimated the rider to be approximately five hundred feet away. It was an easy shot for him. Pulling back the hammer of his long barrel .45-70 Winchester, he inhaled a deep breath as the man came into view of the telescopic scope and ever so slowly, he squeezed the trigger and expelled the long breath of air that had filled his lungs. The loud clap of his Winchester rifle reverberated with deadly accuracy as the man below slumped forward on his horse then fell to the ground, as the heavy .45-70 trajectory found its mark and pierced the man's heart.

The Missing Years – Part II

Riley and Brady had been walking for only a few minutes; dropping their gear, they dove for cover.

"Is he shooting at us again?" Riley asked with exasperation as he looked around.

"I don't know, but if I see the son-of-a-bitch and have a clear view, I'm going to send one right between his eyes," Brady said as a matter-of-fact.

They were hostages to the thick forest and the maniac they had been following. They saw nothing. They heard nothing. The forest once more became deathly silent as they prepared for what was to come.

Crawford, by now, had made the distance to where the dead man lay. He rolled him over to get a better look at him and snickered when he recognised him. He was the same man who had framed him in the callous murder of the bounty hunter known as Emery up in Hazelton. The dead man was the true culprit involved in that death. He had plugged the bounty hunter with six .45 slugs while he slept. The man was a coward, plain and simple. Crawford shuffled through the man's pockets hoping he would find some kind of identification that could put a name to the dead man's face. Finding what he was looking for, he was surprised to learn that the man was an agent for the Pinkerton's National Detective Agency.

"Well, detective Miles Ranthorp, I reckon you have defied the Pinkerton Code of Conduct. You know *'accept no bribes', 'never compromise with criminals',* and *'refuse cases that initiate scandals'*. I reckon there are a few others too, but the few I mentioned sum up your last days on earth. What a pity," Crawford said as though the man could hear him. "I'll be gathering up your horse. There are a couple of riders I'm sure could use it."

It took only a few moments to round up Detective Ranthorp's horse. Crawford threw the detective's body onto the horse and, leading him, he made his way in the direction of where he had last seen the two riders. He had no idea who Brady and Riley were and he didn't care. He would give them the horse and request that they turn the detective's body over to the nearest law. He spotted the two men hunkered down behind some rocks. It was then he recognized them to be the two who took out Talbot's men. They were bounty hunters, obviously.

Stopping his horse, he pulled out his rifle and held it in one hand as he approached the two men. He wouldn't let them know what he knew about them. He circled around so that the rays of the sun would be behind him, that is, what little bit there was that found its way through the tall cluster of trees.

Riley heard the snap of a twig and he turned to face the shadow on the horse, his pistol cocked. He couldn't see much of the rider due to the bright sun, but he certainly saw the long barrel of the .45-70. Brady now looked in the direction as well and his view of the rider wasn't any better than Riley's. He too, could see the glint of the rifle.

"I ain't here to hurt either one of you, but please toss them pea shooters to the ground out of your reach."

Crawford pulled the hammer back on his rifle. The audible click told Brady and Riley that whoever the man was, he wasn't playing games.

"There are two of us and one of you," Brady said as he tried to call the rider's bluff.

"True as that may be, that bright sun shining in your eyes will only foul any attempt you might wish to try. I, on the other hand, have a clear view of each of you. I'll ask again. Toss those pistols to the ground."

Riley looked at Brady and nodded.

"I reckon we best abide."

"I don't know, Riley. That rifle won't fire quicker than our pistols. He can't kill both of us."

"Nope, but one of you will die. I will guarantee that. Like I said, I ain't here to cause either of you two grief. Not long ago, I watched a man kill both your horses. That man is now dead and I have his horse and his body. I'm here to give you both."

"What do we want with a dead man?" Riley asked.

"You can't have one without the other. Do you want the horse or not?"

"I reckon you probably already know that answer."

"All right then. Toss them pistols to the ground. I won't ask again. I'll simply back my horse up and be gone."

"Okay," Brady said as he and Riley tossed their pistols out of their reach.

"Good."

He pointed at Riley.

"I think you are the reasonable one; step forward."

Riley slowly stood and stepped in the direction of the man on the horse. Crawford watched him as he approached.

"That's far enough. Here," Crawford said as he handed the reins of the dead man's horse over to Riley.

"That dead coward on the horse is Detective Miles Ranthorp, a Pinkerton Agent. He shot your horses and murdered a fellow up in Hazelton that went by the name of Emery. Have his guns looked at by the law and have him identified. I think there is a Mounted Police station in Fort Macleod that would oblige."

As Crawford spoke, he slowly backed his horse up, his eyes locked on the two men. Before either Brady or Riley could respond, the shadowy figure simply vanished into the undergrowth. They didn't even hear his horse as the man disappeared.

"What the hell just happened, Brady?" Riley questioned as he walked back to where Brady stood.

"Damnedest thing I ever did see, Riley. One minute he was there, the next he was gone. I reckon we have had our first encounter with Matt Crawford. I have to admit I do appreciate him bringing us a horse leastwise, and if that dead fellow is the man that shot our horses and killed Emery, well then, I appreciate the fact that he no longer breathes."

Riley was looking at the dead man's identification as Brady spoke.

"He didn't lie to us. This man is a Pinkerton on the wrong side of the law, I would assume."

Riley handed Brady the ID.

"Yep, Detective Miles Ranthorp is what it says. Ain't that a thing?" Brady commented as he continued his stare of the card he held in his hand.

"Damn right it is. We have enough time to toss together a skid of sorts to drag the body back to the Fort. You and I can double. One horse is better than no horse. Come on, Brady lets strap together a couple of poles," Riley said as he grabbed the axe that was tied to the horse.

Walking a few paces into the wood, Riley chopped down four lengths of poles.

Using the lariat wound up around the horse's saddle horn, they strapped the poles together leaving enough length to tie the skid to the saddle. They used woollen blankets to finish the skid. It took the better part of an hour to accomplish the task. Next, they struggled with the body and secured it to the skid.

"There we go, all done," Riley said as he sat on a fallen log and wiped his brow. The sun beat down on

The Missing Years – Part II

them hot and heavy as they rested and contemplated what had all taken place.

"You know what, Riley? I reckon there is enough room on that skid for both our saddles and the rest of the gear. What do you think?"

Riley looked over to the skid. He wasn't sure it could hold the weight of the body and all their gear.

"I don't know, Brady. Two saddles and a body. Not sure the skid would hold."

"It is easy enough to reinforce it, make it a bit stronger. A couple more poles in the middle, horizontal or vertical, would do."

"That might work," Riley nodded as he thought about it. "Yeah, okay. I'll start with that. To save some time, do you figure you can wrestle with the two saddles and that bit of gear we did leave behind?"

"I wouldn't mind making a couple of trips if I had to. I care for my saddle enough to do something like that, rather than leave it here."

"All right, let's get at it."

Riley stood up and with Brady's help they removed the body so that Riley could reinforce the skid to accommodate the extra weight. That done, Brady walked back to where they left their extra gear. It took two trips to gather it all, but it was well worth his effort. Now, once more in motion, Brady, Riley and the body of Miles Ranthorp headed southeast in the direction of the Fort, a two-day ride with a horse.

By now, Buck and Tyrell had stumbled upon the past evening camp where Atalmore and his riders stayed. Buck looked closely at the tracks.

"They left here, I'd guess eight, maybe nine hours ago. What time do you figure it is now, Travis?"

"My watch ain't worked in a while, but by the height of the sun, Buck, we could argue that it ain't morning anymore," Tyrell chuckled. "I reckon we're into mid-day. That means Atalmore and his men left here somewhere between 4:00 a.m. and 5:00 a.m. They are a good distance ahead, that is for sure."

"Ah, eight hours ain't that bad. They'd have been ahead of us no matter what. I reckon we might as well have a rest here for a bit and sit in some shade. Damn hot out."

Buck swung off his horse and led him to a patch of grass. Finding a shade tree, he sat down, took off his hat and unbuttoned his shirt; damn he was hot.

"We're going to be in for a hot summer, I think," he commented as he wiped his brow.

Tyrell sat next to him and inhaled deeply.

"I think you are right. I haven't seen Pony sweat like that in a long time, only after he has been ridden hard, which he ain't been today, leastwise; so it must be hot."

"About five miles from here, maybe further, is that lake we saw when we travelled to Hazelton, the one that had the Indian camp. It's been a few days since then. If they ain't there, we should let the horses have a swim. The dog, too, probably wouldn't mind. We could stay there this evening and head out again before dawn rises. I reckon Atalmore likes to get moving whilst it ain't yet light out. We could do the same and make contact with them sometime tomorrow evening or early next day," Buck commented as he looked around.

"It isn't going to take us all day to get five miles, Buck. We'd be quitting early if we did that."

"There ain't any other place I know of between here and Vermillion that has water and grass for the horses. I will admit this heat is breaking my balls."

"Yeah, it is damn hot, I'll give you that."

Tyrell fanned his face with his hat as he ran his fingers through his hair. He should have taken a haircut in Hazelton. The top of his head was hot and sweaty.

An hour later, the two men saddled up and headed down the trail toward Vermillion and the glacial lake some five miles away. It was a nice ride. That part of the trail was blocked by the sun because of the high peaks of the Rocky Mountains that were now on either side of the trail, making for a cooler, shaded journey. The lake came into view less than an hour later after some bush stomping and about a two-mile ride off the trail. There were no signs that Indian Clive and his band were or even had been there.

"They sure clean up their camps nicely, don't they?" Tyrell mentioned as he dismounted and led Pony to the edge of the lake for a drink.

"Most of them do. This land is their dinner plate and they respect the fact that they can eat from it. White folks would do the same if they cared. Most don't," Buck added.

Buck followed Tyrell to the lakeshore so his horse could have cool drink as well. Black Dog had already been in and out a few times. He was soaking wet and now lay on the shore panting in the shade.

"Nice place this lake is, quite pristine. I reckon it is probably a fishing camp for Indian Clive and his fellow tribesmen. There has to be some nice Rocky Mountain lake trout in the depths."

"A few other tribes fish here too. I've seen mostly the Athabasca. It was odd seeing Indian Clive this far northeast. He could have only been here for the fish, maybe the bear. Deer types ain't going be around here for a bit. Soon, though. You figure we should spend the night, Travis, or do you want to carry on? I care either way. Only problem is, we wouldn't make it over the pass before night fall. Could be cold up high."

Tyrell looked up to the mountain that seemed to be looking down at them and sighed.

"I think I could stay here. It's near pre-evening and you are right about the pass. We would never make it down the other side before dark. Chances are that Atalmore and crew have already crested the mountain and could be close to Vermillion. But, this place here, I'd say, is a fine place to spend the night."

"Good. Let's get settled then."

As the shadows of early evening began to fan out toward the lake, they lit a small fire and cooked some food. Black Dog, surprisingly, managed to snap up a few small trout he found in a shallow pool. He gnawed on those for his dinner and was quite content with that. The horses continued grazing on the patch of shore grass that was near.

"The loons will be sounding soon and I reckon the dang burping of frogs, too. Might even hear a wolf or coyote pack. They seem to like the far side of the lake, closer to the mountain, I guess. Every time I've been here, I've heard one or the other howling. Hope it won't entice your dog," Buck pointed out.

"Nah, Black Dog won't care. He might howl back and give them a run for their money on which can howl the longest."

Tyrell looked over to his dog.

"Ain't that right, Black Dog? You ain't going to worry about no wolf or coyote are you?"

Tyrell and Buck chuckled as the dog looked over to them and wagged his tail, then rolled over and continued to snooze.

"Do we have enough canteen water to make coffee, Buck?"

"Likely do. We could use the lake water too. It'll be boiled so anything living in it won't be living once it is done. Probably best, in fact, to use it. There ain't much water between here and Vermillion, a slew or two, maybe a bit of runoff. Best keep the safe water for that."

"Good point."

Tyrell shuffled through their gear and found the coffee pot. Walking to the lake, he knelt down and filled it, then looked out across the water to the rock mountain face on the far east side and admired the shadows that the mountain created as the sun to the west slowly began to fade. His mind drifted to a faraway place called Red Rock and he reminisced about the time he spent there. It actually startled him that he even thought about that place since it hadn't crossed his mind as of late. That night, it did. He stood up and made his way back to the fire. Conversing with Buck, he knew, would take his mind off Red Rock. He handed Buck the pot and sat down on his saddle.

"Once that sun heads west, it sure doesn't take long to grow dark, eh?"

"Not up here. The mountains are high enough that they block off the early evening sun. It probably ain't any later than 6:00 p.m. or 7:00 p.m."

Buck added coffee grounds to the pot and set it on the flames.

"Should have some Buck brewed coffee shortly."

"You know what I find quite surprising is the lack of folks we've actually ran into on this trek. Don't folks visit the mountains anymore? This place here is a dream."

"Since most know that Vermillion has burned down, there ain't much traffic or reasons to be on this trail. I figure Fairmount and Hazelton are the main places folks go to now. Vermillion has always been one of those towns that was off kilter from the beginning, a lot of riffraff and such. With it not being inhabitable for the time being, not even the riffraff have a reason to be there. I figure because of its location, the outpost will remain. It is central to both Fairmount and Hazelton. Eventually I think it'll turn out to be a ghost town like all the others that lie between here and the Fort, which, in a sense, makes it safer in these parts."

Tyrell nodded in agreement.

"Yeah, I guess not as many bad guys flooding the place."

"Yep, they'll flood the other places now."

Buck reached over and grabbed the coffee pot. It had perked for a while and was now ready. He poured each of them a cup and handed one to Tyrell.

"Thanks, Buck," Tyrell said as he took it from him.

The coffee as usual was as thick as tar. To be honest, he was getting used to it.

To the southwest and one day closer to the Fort, Brady and Riley were also settling for the evening. They were now in the area where their shoot out with Talbot and his men had taken place. Their fire also burned gently as the sounds of evening became more audible with each minute that passed.

"I figure we did all right today, considering things, one horse and all," Riley mentioned as they sat there, looking into the flames.

"Certainly managed more miles then we could have on foot. My mind has been drifting all damn day on why Crawford would give us a horse. In a sense, he's made it a little bit easier and a lot faster for us to get to the Fort, gather a couple more horses and head after him again."

"I ain't got the answer for that either. There is no way that he didn't know what it was we were doing in the area. He had to have seen us when he popped Talbot. It certainly puts into perspective the kind of man he actually is, doesn't it?" Riley pointed out as he took a swig of coffee.

"It does. Makes it harder for me to swallow bringing him in. I know we have to. That is our job. I only hope we can bring him in peacefully. Any other way now don't seem right."

"I know. That is my thought too," Riley commented.

They sat in silence for a few more minutes.

"I figure I'm going lay out my bedding, Riley. See you in the morning."

"Yep, see you then, Brady."

Riley remained sitting near the fire and continued his gaze as he contemplated. He finished off another cup of coffee as he reminisced. Yawning, he stood and rolled out his own bedding. Night had fallen.

"Chapter 20"

Buck and Tyrell were up before the first bird chirped that Friday morning. They would be over the pass by noon if they didn't run into problems and after that only a few hours north of Vermillion. If it all went as planned, chances were good that by early evening they could be in close proximity of the cabin where Matt Crawford had been living under the name of Ron Reginal and where they believed Atalmore and his men were likely heading.

"It is hard to see the trail we used to get to the lake in the blackness of early morn, eh Travis? Good thing the horses got eyes."

"It is dark. The tall trees and high mountains on either side don't help. The sun will be lighting our way soon enough I reckon. It has to be near 4:00 or 5:00 a.m., I'd think."

Tyrell sighed and there was a short pause.

"I have to get my watch looked at soon I reckon. Hard to keep track of time without one, other than looking at the sun that is."

"Ah, all anyone needs to know is night and day," Buck mentioned as he and his horse climbed the bank and reached the main trail.

"I suppose. I ain't really missed the time piece," Tyrell shrugged.

Four hours later they were at the summit. They halted their horses and looked back the way they came.

"Well, we've made the summit. It wasn't far from here that we cut through the bush after that incident with your horse and dog when we headed this way."

"I recognise the area. I think it was up over that hillock," Tyrell pointed.

"Yep, that is the spot. We might as well dismount for a few and have a rest. We've done good so far. Although that great big yellow sun is going to get hot, it feels cool up at this altitude. Good thing we didn't spend the night up here. It might have been a bit cold."

Tyrell swung off Pony and let him roam. "I can't remember how far from here Vermillion is, but I don't suppose it is far, another four hours maybe. That would put us in town, say near 1:00 p.m., if I'm reading the sun right."

"That is probably close, give or take an hour. Going down may be a bit tricky. It is quite the incline. A lot steeper than what we came up. We'll take our time and be careful. That is all we can do," Buck responded as they rested and drank from their canteens.

"You want some jerky whilst we rest? I'm getting myself a couple sticks," Tyrell asked as he walked over to Pony and his saddlebags.

"Sure, that'd be good. Thanks."

Buck continued his gaze of the valleys below and the vastness of the area. It reminded him of the Yukon, cool and beautiful. Tyrell grabbed a few sticks of jerky and tossed one to Black Dog. Catching the piece in mid-flight, he dashed to some shade and gingerly went about gnawing it. He was content.

"Here you go, Buck," Tyrell said as he handed him a few sticks.

"Thank you."

Sitting in silence, the two men chewed at the jerky as they admired the area. Tyrell pointed to some Rocky Mountain sheep he could scarcely make out on the high hills of the mountain.

"Incredible how those sheep can bounce around on those cliffs, eh? You ever hunt sheep?" Tyrell questioned as he looked on.

"Nope. I've eaten it. It can be a little tough, but it is tasty."

"That is what I've heard."

"You've never eaten mutton then?" Buck was a bit surprised.

"That I have not. I've eaten most everything else, even bear, but I didn't like it one bit. It is so oily and greasy it sits on your tongue and you practically have to scrape it off."

Tyrell took a bite from his jerky.

"Beef, that's the best."

"Some wild meat ain't bad, venison and such. Bear meat, I tend to agree that 'Yuk' is all that needs to be said."

Buck yawned and stretched.

"I guess we should saddle up, get this mountain out of our way and get back down on the better trail."

"I'll be right behind you."

Tyrell stood up and gathered Pony. Swinging onto their horses, they set off and made their way down the steep trail. They took their time to prevent injury to the horses and themselves as they cautiously proceeded. The sun was hot by then and it baked their skin and clouded their eyes with sweat. Their shirts were unbuttoned and their heads tilted so the brim from their hats could provide them with at least a bit of shade. It was hot especially since they were on the south side of the mountain. They longed for the shade that the trail would provide once they got to lower altitudes where the tall trees grew and skirted the trail on either side.

The four men they had been trailing were now approaching Vermillion. They had gone a different route when they made their way to the town and had used an outdated map that had led them northerly to Hazelton and from there they made their way to Vermillion. They were expecting more than a simple outpost.

"Looks like the town has been gutted. Wonder what happened?" Atalmore commented as he swung off his steed and tethered him to the horse rail outside the outpost. His men followed suit.

"Looks like it burned down," Colby said as he looked around.

"That is obvious, Colby. We'll go inside and ask a few questions. A place like this might have coffee, most stagecoach outposts do. Besides, I think we could all use a rest. We might get lucky and they might serve what resembles food, if any of you are hungry."

The four men entered the small station and were greeted by the man who had greeted Tyrell and Buck a few days earlier.

"Afternoon, gentlemen," the man said as he stood up and met them at the counter.

"Does this place have coffee?" Atalmore questioned as his men sat down at a table.

"Yep, sure does."

"All right, we'll take four coffees. What about food?"

"We have a bit of a menu, nothing spectacular. Would you like menus, too?"

"Yeah, I suppose one is good enough."

"I'll bring it along when I get your coffees. What about cream and sugar; you want some of that?"

"Cream and sugar, yes," Atalmore nodded as he sat down at the table with his men.

"How long ago did the fire take out this town?" Atalmore asked as the man brought them their coffees.

"Months ago already. What brings fellows like yourselves to these parts?" the man questioned with friendly enthusiasm.

"Just passing through. Did anyone survive the fire? It looks like it was quite a nasty one."

"From what I know, most did. They moved on; and yes, it was a nasty one."

"How did it happen?" Captain A. Webber asked as he blew on his coffee.

"To be honest, I didn't live here when it happened. The story goes that a feud or fight between two fellows erupted and one came back with a few men and torched the town."

"So, everyone packed up and moved out?" Colby questioned as though he cared.

"I don't reckon there'd have been much point in anyone staying. There ain't much left."

The man walked back behind the counter and set the coffee pot back on the stove.

"A few folks on the outskirts of town stuck around. I see them most every day. Another fellow lives in cabin from what I've been told. I ain't so sure he stuck around because I ain't ever met him. He's a recluse or trapper or something. I don't know. I've been here for a few months and ain't ever seen him. I was conversing with another fellow that lives on the outskirts just yesterday. He said that fellow was named Ron Reginal or something like that. He said he ain't saw Ron in a long time. Seemed a bit concerned. I believe the man exists, but I have yet to meet him. You folks ready to order some food yet?"

"Not yet. Give us few more minutes. I'll holler for you once we decide," Atalmore responded.

"All right, I'll go back to my business."

The man walked a short distance to where he was seated when they first came in behind the counter.

"What do you think of that?"

"Think of what?" Webber asked as he looked at the menu.

"Use your head, Webber. Ron Reginal, R.R. are the initials for Rebel Rangers. Matt always used those damn things."

"Could be there is a real person named that. How do we know it is Matt?" Spence asked.

"We don't, but we'll find out. You are right. Could be there is a real person named that. Under these circumstances, I'd put money on it that it is Matt."

Atalmore took a drink from his coffee.

"Yeah, I do recall Matt doing that on occasion, when I think about it."

Webber handed the menu over to Colby, now that he had decided he'd have the beans.

Colby looked at the menu.

"There really ain't much in way of food on this menu. I think I'll stick with the coffee."

Colby handed the menu to Spence.

"If I'm making sense of this, Batalmore, you're thinking that this trapper fellow who lives in a cabin and goes by the name of Ron Reginal is our man Matt?"

"That is what I'm saying. Matt Crawford always used short forms for one thing or another."

"Even if that is so, we don't know where the damn cabin is."

"Quit being a pain in my ass, Spence. We'll find out. Watch and learn."

Atalmore called over to the man.

"We're ready now to make our order."

"Sure, what will it be?" the man asked as he came closer.

"I reckon we'll all go for the beans and another round of coffee. Where did you say that fellow Ron lived?"

"I didn't say. Why?"

"I thought you mentioned he lived on the edge of town?"

"No, no, some folks do. That Ron fellow lives in a cabin on the south mountain, near copper creek. I think five or so miles from town."

"Oh, well, my mistake," Atalmore responded.

"Beans all around?" the man asked not caring about the previous conversation.

"Yep, and bread, too."

"All right, I'll get it to you folks shortly."

The man turned and walked away.

"Did you see that Spence? Did you see how I found out where Ron lives?"

Spence chuckled and rolled his eyes.

"Yeah, real class act there, Batalmore."

"A roundabout question, which gave us results. Simple. If I had asked for directions, chances are he'd get suspicious. In cases like this, off the wall questions gives a fellow a basic idea without bringing attention to himself. Common sense is all that is."

Atalmore winked and smiled as he finished the last of his coffee.

"And where is copper creek?" Colby questioned with a smirk. "You didn't find that out."

"Come on, Colby, he said south mountain five miles away. Obviously that'd be south of town, five miles away. We'll find it. There has to be a trail of some sort to follow. It might turn out to be nothing at all, but worth the effort, I reckon. Especially since we know Matt is around these parts. That information that Webber wrote out at the Fort tells us that. When I heard the name Ron Reginal and the fact that Matt is prone to use initials like some kind of code; well, the rest of the story tells itself."

The man returned with a pot of beans and four plates with bread on each. He set the plates down and the pot.

"Here you folks go. Thought, since there are four of you, you might as well finish the pot of beans up."

"Thank you," Atalmore said as he scooped himself out a plate full. It didn't take long for the men to finish their meal and a few minutes afterward they were outside saddling up.

"We'll head south from here toward Fairmount. Keep your eyes peeled for any sign of a trail that cuts in toward the south mountain as we traverse," Atalmore commented as the four men left behind the burned out town of Vermillion. They travelled for a few minutes when Captain Webber noticed a set of old horse tracks that cut off the trail and headed toward a distant mountain.

"Hold up, fellows. What do you make of these?" He swung off his horse and knelt next to the tracks. "Two riders headed down this bank. The tracks ain't fresh, a couple days old I reckon. Odd how they'd simply cut off the trail here and head toward that mountain over yonder. What do you think, Batalmore? Think we should follow these tracks? Could be Matt and a friend. They do head southeasterly."

Webber stood on the edge of the bank and looked out over the vast forest.

"Damn thick down there; easy to hide."

By now, Spence and Colby were standing next to him and they all looked on.

"Could be that is where we need to head. I can see how it'd be easy to hide in all that thick bramble. I say we follow these tracks for a bit; might turn out to be something. Might not too," Atalmore said as they mounted their horses.

The four men cut off the trail and followed it as best as they could. The trail was lost to them a few minutes later, but they could hear the whispering sound of a creek and they followed the sound. The creek wasn't big when they finally came upon it.

"Could be this here is Copper creek. Look at all the green rock and such."

Atalmore looked around.

"I think we are in the right area, men. There has to be a cabin around here somewhere."

"Are you serious, Batalmore? This creek don't mean anything. There are probably a hundred creeks that look as this one does. Just because it has some green rock, don't mean this is Copper creek," Spence spoke out.

"Always the naysayer ain't you, Spence?" Colby questioned as he looked around. "I'd say we're five miles or less from Vermillion. There are four of us. We should split up and look around. If one or the other of us comes across a cabin, fire a couple shots into the air to let the others know. That is what I think we ought to do."

Colby spit to the ground. "But don't put me with Spence."

"I reckon that is a good idea, Colby, and yes, I'm putting you and Spence together. The two of you have issues to work out," Atalmore chuckled.

"I don't want to be riding through all this bramble with a cry baby such as Spence. Send me and Webber together or Spence and Webber and I'll look around with you, Batalmore."

"Nope. You get Spence or Spence gets you, whichever. Webber and I will follow this creek downstream some. You and Spence head southerly toward that mountain range up yonder. You come across anything that resembles a cabin, fire off a couple rounds. We'll hear you. Come on Webber, let's get," Atalmore ordered as he and Webber continued following the creek.

"Okay, Colby, looks like you and I get to ride alongside one another. Come on."

Spence turned his horse south and Colby followed. It took them only a few minutes before they picked up the trail they had been following. Colby reined his horse to a stop and looked down at the tracks.

"Hey, Spence, I think I found them two sets of tracks again. Looks like they headed a bit west here."

Spence pulled up next to Colby and looked down at the tracks.

"Good eye, Colby. Let's follow them as best we can."

They didn't lose the trail again after that and less than an hour later they found the cabin.

"Look at that, Colby, a cabin," Spence said as he looked on.

Colby was unable to see what Spence was looking at until he was right beside him. He smiled.

"Well I'll be. Ain't that something. It doesn't look like anyone has been here in a long while."

"Nope except them two riders. Can't be sure it was Matt or not, but two riders did come this way."

Spence pulled his rifle from his scabbard and fired three shots into the air.

Webber and Atalmore, hearing the shots, turned their horses in the direction of the sound.

"Sounds like someone found something. Come on, Webber. The shots came from this way."

Atalmore heeled his horses flank as Webber caught up to him.

"They ain't that far away. Just over yonder, I reckon," Atalmore said as he pointed.

"Yep, right behind you, Batalmore."

Webber, now tailing close behind, followed Atalmore. Finally, they could see through all the bramble and thick bush to where Spence and Colby's horses were. Pulling their horses up next to the empty saddles of Spence and Colby's horses, Atalmore called out. He couldn't see a damn thing.

"Over here," Colby called as he came close.

"There you are. All right."

Webber and Atalmore dismounted.

"You found the cabin, did you?"

"Sure did. Hard as hell to see. It is built into the ground."

"Lead the way," Atalmore said as he and Webber followed.

"It doesn't look like anyone has been here in quite a stint, but someone has been living here," Colby said as the cabin now came into full view.

"There it is."

The four men entered and looked around.

"Looks like a nice place to hide."

Colby sat down at the small table as Atalmore and the others started snooping, looking for anything that would identify the person living there. They found only a bunch of old clothing and few knick-knacks and patty whacks.

"There ain't nothing here that says this is where Matt has been living."

Spence sat down across from Colby as Webber and Atalmore continued with their snooping.

"I reckon that is where you are wrong, Spence," Webber began as he found a few spent shell casings from a 45.70. "These here shell casings are Government issued. You can't just buy these in a store. These are a special order. Matt uses a 45.70. He also reloads his ammo."

The Missing Years – Part II

Webber tossed the empty shell casings on the table for Spence and Colby to look at.

Spence picked one of the casings up and looked at it.

"Anyone can order these, Webber."

"True enough, but who except someone who wants not to be seen ever would. These casings are made for long distant shooting, well over nine hundred or more feet. There aren't any hunters would want something like that, I don't reckon."

Atalmore picked up the other casing and looked at it closely. Webber was right. The casings were Government issued.

"I tend to agree with Webber on this. These shells were made with one thing in mind, long distant shooting which is Matt's specialty. Put two and two together, Spence, and I'd say we've found Matt's place."

"It is all assumption, Batalmore, and you know it."

"Sometimes, Spence we have to follow our assumptions. Trust me on this. These are shell casings for a 45.70 Winchester, likely the same damn rifle that the U.S. Rangers use, that you have used, that I have used as well as Webber has used. Don't be blind to this, Spence."

"I do get your point, Batalmore, but without more convincing I'll remain sceptical."

Atalmore shook his head.

"Be sceptical all you want, but I'm in charge here and I'm telling you this is more than coincidental that we'd find this cabin and find these casings. What we need to figure out now is where the hell Matt is."

"Maybe he'll come back this way," Colby interjected.

"By the look of the dust on everything in here, I'd say there ain't been anybody here in a few months.

There isn't even any tracks outside other than the tracks we followed here. I ain't found which way they went after being here. They lead here but I don't know where they head," Spence said as he stood up and did some snooping of his own. "There has to be something else here amongst all this junk that'll tell us one way or the other. I ain't convinced just because we found some Government issued shell casings that this is Matt's hideout."

Spence stepped closer to the woodstove and he noticed one of the floorboards seemed loose.

"What have we here?"

Kneeling down, he gently lifted up on the floorboard. Underneath was a small wooden box. Pulling it out, he opened it. Inside was a black and white photo of Matt Crawford standing outside the U.S. Department of Safety building in Washington. Spence smiled as he looked at it.

"I'm convinced now."

He handed the picture over to Atalmore.

"Ain't that something? Ain't sceptical anymore are you, Spence?"

"Not with proof like that. A few shell casings on the other hand, I still would be," Spence responded as he continued looking through a few of the papers and whatnot that were in the box.

There was nothing substantial other than the photo and a piece of paper with the name Talbot Hunter. That is when things became clear to all.

"Hey, Batalmore, I got a name here on a piece of paper of one Talbot Hunter."

"What?" Atalmore questioned as he reached for it.

Spence handed him the piece of paper.

"Can you guess why Matt would have the name of Talbot?" Spence questioned as he looked at Webber and Atalmore. The three of them knew who Talbot was. The only one who didn't know was Colby.

Atalmore sat down as he read the name a few more times.

"In case you are wondering, Colby, what this name is all about, I'll tell you. It was Governor General William Hunter who had Matt arrested. He pinned a few murders on him that his brother Talbot committed. The Governor was one of the first men Matt put to rest. Then he rifled his way up here into Canada, killing everyone who was associated with the Governor. Talbot Hunter, the last I heard, was running with the Kingsley Gang. I haven't heard a thing about them in a few years."

"Whatever you just spewed out doesn't mean a thing to me. Can you give me a bit more history than that?" Colby asked.

"Sure can," Atalmore said as he went about explaining to Colby the exact correlation between Matt and Talbot. It took a few minutes to give Colby the rundown, but he was clear now.

"That is an interesting story, I'll give you that. I get it now. Essentially, our friend Matt has been taking care of those who tried to mess with his sister and those who messed with him. Sounds reasonable to me. I would do the same thing," Colby said as he now looked at the picture. "So, that is Matt Crawford."

"Yep."

"Answer me this, Batalmore. If Matt ain't doing anything other than taking care of the bad taste in his mouth left by the U.S. Government, why are the Rebel Ranger's so desperate to find him? Is it because there are bounty hunters and the like looking for him? You want to warn him, or what?"

"Basically. I ain't got any gripe with Matt, Colby, but he is a liability to the R.R. We need to find him before the law and others do. If he gets taken in, he can be linked to us and that could cause our downfall. We can't have that."

"That there is damn funny, Batalmore. Come on, do you really think a fellow like Matt is going to give up the names of the R.R.?" Colby asked as a matter-of-fact. "I'd say not very likely. I don't think any one of us here would. What makes you think Matt might?"

"To be honest, I have my doubts that he would, Colby. Still, there is that slight possibility that he might say something whether inadvertently or not. Our job is to find him and make certain that he doesn't."

"And how exactly are we going to do that? The only thing I see as a viable alternative is to kill him. Is that what we're supposed to do, Batalmore?"

"You knew from the beginning, Colby, that we were tracking Matt Crawford and that our intent was exactly that," Atalmore conceded.

"I didn't know any background story. I do now; and I don't see it as Matt doing anything different then what we do. Sounds like bullshit to me, now that I know what I know," Colby shrugged. "It matters little to me either way."

"Good then, we'll leave it at that."

Atalmore was authoritative as he said that. He didn't want to kill Matt. It was the furthest thing from his mind. Matt, he knew, had always been a one-man show. The fact that he was now being sought by the law and bounty hunters, Atalmore knew it would be best to approach him, warn him, and hopefully convince him to once more ride with the R.R. If not, then maybe he would have to kill him in order to protect the R.R and the good that they did.

By now, Tyrell and Buck had finally made it to the trail that was shaded by the trees. It was cool and warm all at the same time, but it was a lot better than being fried alive. The sun that day was terribly hot.

The Missing Years – Part II

"The shade feels good, doesn't it?" Buck questioned as he took a drink from his canteen.

"Shade or no shade, I still got sunburned. I don't remember the sun ever being this hot at the beginning of July."

"I'd agree with you, Travis. Today is only the 3rd of July I think. Seems more like the 30th with heat this hot. Can't imagine what August is going to be like. It's good for crops, I suppose. Ain't so good for travellers."

"Yeah, we're going to have to rest the horses in a bit. Pony is sweating. The last thing I want for him is to get saddle sore."

Tyrell pointed up ahead to a big tree.

"Right up there is a good place to let the horses cool down."

A few minutes later the two men dismounted and let their horses rest while they drank from their canteens and conversed.

"Got to be getting close to Vermillion by now, eh Buck?"

"I reckon another hour's ride, maybe less."

Buck took a long swig from his canteen and then shook it.

"Almost dry. I've been drinking a lot of water today. We'll have to refresh our canteens once we get to town."

"You got that right. Hopefully we can find some water for the animals, too. Pony seems to be thirsty."

Tyrell poured some water in his hand and let the horse drink it.

"I know it ain't much, Pony, enough to wet your snout, though. Here, have another drink," Tyrell said as he poured more water into his hand.

Next, he did the same thing for Black Dog, giving him a few swigs too, enough to keep the dog happy.

"There you go, Black Dog. That is all I can offer you for now. We'll get more water soon enough."

Tyrell patted him on the head.

"Surprised at how well you've healed up, ol' boy. That wound you had ain't nothing more than a scab and it has only been a few days."

Tyrell walked over to where Buck was sitting on a big rock and sat down himself.

"Well, Travis, do you figure we've sat long enough or do you want to sit a while longer?"

"A couple more minutes of rest, Buck. I was calculating how long I've been on this trail for. It's been going on a couple weeks. Getting tired of it. Can't wait until it is all over. We'll have to head to Fairmount sometime and see if there are any telegrams for us from Ed or the others. Makes me wonder how things are going for Tanner. Hope he's going to be okay."

"I've ridden with Tanner for a few years. He'll bounce back if ain't died. We ain't going to know until we either get back to the Fort or, as you say, there is a telegram waiting for us."

Buck looked down the trail and back again.

"If we have a run in with those four men, you got any plan on what we should do?"

"The last telegram said they are wanted for one thing or another. They catch up with Crawford before us, we'll have to deal with it, I reckon. Hopefully, Brady and Riley are making progress in tracking him. Taking in four men is a bit of a challenge, but as long as we have surprise on our side, we might be okay. If not, well, I guess it will be whatever it will be. I ain't going to worry so much about it until the time comes. I'd like at least a couple more hours of peace," Tyrell smiled with assurance.

"That is about all that we're going to get, unless, of course, they ain't headed to Crawford's cabin."

"I'd put money on it that they are. They're here for one thing or the other. I still ain't figured out which. Could they be here to kill Crawford or are they here to join up with him? To be honest, none of it makes any sense to me yet. I just don't get it."

Tyrell took another swig from his canteen.

"I know one thing for certain. Someone shot Talbot and since these men weren't around then, that leaves one other person that we know about who could make that shot. That is Matt Crawford. The *why* is what I don't get."

"Yeah, that is what has my head spinning too. The closer we get, the more I think about it, and the more I think about it, the less sense it makes."

"We need more information, I guess, but we ain't going to get anymore until we have him caged. Same as with those other four. Not until it is all said and done, do we even know what the hell is going on."

There was a short pause as Tyrell thought about it all.

"This here is a strange business, Buck."

"That it is," Buck responded as he stood up.

"I say we get into Vermillion, get these horses watered and head back to that cabin. Maybe we'll get some answers, maybe we won't. One thing is for certain. By day's end we'll either be ending it with a smile or we'll never smile again."

It was clear what Buck meant by that. Either they would survive it or they wouldn't.

"I have every intent on smiling, Buck," Tyrell said as he too now stood.

Mounting their horses, they headed into Vermillion.

It was early evening when they found themselves hiding in some bushes and looking at the cabin that now had four horses tethered outside.

"There is our answer, Buck. Looks like they've been here most of the day. They have to be waiting for someone or something," Tyrell said in a hushed voice as the two men looked on.

"How do you suppose we proceed, Travis?"

"It is going to be dark soon. I think we're better off waiting until then to make any moves. They ain't got a clue that we are here, but we know they are. We wait until it is dark, maybe we can get the drop on them then. I reckon all four are inside. We can't just storm in, although that is an alternative. I'd rather strike in the dark. What say you?"

"Yeah, I reckon that be best."

The two men mounted their horses once more and headed toward the ridge that overlooked the cabin. From there they had a clear view of anyone coming or going. It was going to be a long four or five hour wait before it would be completely dark.

The Missing Years – Part II

"Chapter 21"

Riley and Brady were only a few miles outside of the Fort. They had made good time in making the distance and had managed to do it in less time than they had first anticipated.

"Only a few more miles, Riley and we'll be home long enough to gather a couple more horses and head out again. Might as well spend the night at the office and get a good start again in the morning."

"I agree. No point in heading out in the dark," Riley responded as they continued onward.

Finally, the Fort came into view and a few minutes later they were at the Mounted Police station talking with one of the constables. They turned the body of Miles Ranthorp over to the constable and explained to him who and what he was and why he was dead.

"You're saying Matt Crawford punched this fellow's heart out because he shot your two horses?" the constable asked with some confusion.

"There is a little more to it than simply that, but yeah, he shot our horses and someone we suspect to be Matt Crawford shot him. The guy is a Pinkerton from down south. Must've been tracking Crawford or something. Crawford also claimed that Miles here shot and killed our man Emery Nelson up in Hazelton," Brady pointed out.

"Jesus, Brady, the more you try and explain it the more confusing it gets."

The constable paused for a few minutes as he wrapped his head around what Brady was telling him.

"In a nutshell, this fellow shot Emery Nelson, tracked down Crawford, killed your two horses and then was shot by Crawford. Is that the gist of it?"

"It is," Brady responded.

"Alright. We'll get this squared away in the morning. Are you going to be around in the morning, Brady?"

"Nope, Riley and I will be heading out again. We have a man to track down. Have this fellow's name looked into and I'm sure you'll discover one thing or the other and will find out he ain't a nice man. Now, I haven't got the time to explain this to you repeatedly, but this fellow shot our horses. A witness claims he also shot Emery. There ain't nothing more that I know than that. The rest is up to the law to figure out."

"All right. We'll do our best to make sense out of this. Maybe if you find the time once you get back again, you could swing by and maybe we'll have some news to share with you."

"I ain't interested in any news about this fellow other than the fact that he might very well be Emery's killer. If the law can prove that, then that'd be the only thing I'd have an interest in knowing. Christ's sake, he shot my horse. I care little about him. Anyway, we're going to head back to the office and rest up. Come on, Riley, let's go."

"I'm right behind you, Brady. Goodnight, constable," Riley said as he stood up from the chair he was sitting on.

"Yeah, goodnight to you folks too," the constable said as he grabbed some paperwork and returned to his desk.

Brady and Riley left the dead man's horse tethered outside the station and walked the distance back to the office carrying their gear.

"I don't know, Riley. The law always seems to be a bit confused on what they get told. There was no simpler way to explain to that constable who Miles is than what we explained and he still seemed confused."

"Might be the way you tend to explain stuff, Brady. You leave out a lot of detail."

"The hell I do. I told him exactly what we know. The only thing I didn't do was draw him a damn picture," Brady said as he set down his gear outside and pulled out his keys to unlock the back door to the office.

The smell of fresh paint wafted up their nostrils as they stepped inside.

"I guess Innis has been hard at it. His paint must've showed up early," Brady mentioned as he looked around at the freshly painted walls while they walked to the back staff room.

"Looks pretty good, I'd say. Not so dull in here anymore," Riley said as he sat down at the table.

"I agree it does look a lot better in here."

Brady walked over to the woodstove and touched it to see if it was still hot or in the least still had coals burning inside.

"The stove is still warm. Should I add a couple of sticks and make coffee, Riley?" Brady asked as he opened the door and looked inside at the orange, glowing coals.

"I wouldn't say no. Sure, I could use a coffee."

"Yeah, me too."

Brady added a few pieces of wood and grabbing the coffee pot, he dumped out what was in it and added fresh water and coffee grounds. Sitting opposite Riley, the two of them conversed about the past few days as the coffee slowly perked. They were on their first cup when they heard the back door open.

"Who could that be?" Brady questioned as he stood up to meet whoever it was.

Stepping out of the staff room he saw Tanner.

"Tanner! Hey, sure glad to see you up and about. How are you doing?"

"Hey Brady, wasn't sure I was hearing things or not. Thought I'd check. I'm doing okay. A little sore, but I am alive."

"Come on in to the staff room. We have fresh coffee. Can I get you one?"

"Sure, I'd have a coffee," Tanner replied as he followed Brady.

Sitting at the table, he looked over to Riley and nodded.

"Hello, Mr. Scott. Ed told me you signed up with the McCoy's. How are you liking it so far?" Tanner asked with interest.

"Truth be told, I ain't finding it any different than when I didn't work for Ed. Nice to meet you, Tanner."

Riley reached his hand across the table and the two men shook.

"Quite the pleasure to meet you as well, Riley," Tanner responded with respect.

"How long have you been up and about?" Brady asked as he poured Tanner a coffee and handed it to him.

"Just found my footing today. The doc gave me a clean bill of health. A few more days of laying down and I'd have ended up with damn bedsores. Was out for a time, I reckon."

"Indeed you were."

Brady sat down and took a swig from his coffee.

"Does Ed know you are up and about?"

"Yeah, he was here today. We weren't expecting you two for at least a few more days. I take it things went well?"

Tanner brought his coffee to his lips and took a drink.

"Nope. Things didn't go well. We managed to track Crawford, but got side-winded by a fellow that shot our horses," Riley pointed out.

"Really, how did that happen?" Tanner asked with curiosity.

It took a few minutes for Riley to explain.

"I'm sorry to hear about your horses. I reckon that fellow deserved the lead that Crawford put in him. You say that Miles fellow also shot Emery?"

"That is speculation at this time. It is what Crawford told us, so hard to say. The law will sort it out, I'm sure," Brady added.

"Let's hope. Ed also mentioned that Buck Ainsworth is helping Ty...Travis out?" Tanner questioned almost saying Tyrell's name. How he hoped that neither man heard the mistake he almost made.

"Yep, that is right. I still don't know how that came about. Have to wait for when Travis and Buck get back to learn more about that. It is good to know he has help. I ain't so sure he knows exactly what has been going on around here. Everything has happened so damn quickly," Brady responded.

"I know Ed sent off a couple of telegrams. That is what he's told me. I ain't sure how up to date they were, but I'm sure Travis will get the picture once he gathers them. Things have changed again, haven't they?"

"I'd say so. I'm having a bit of an issue in wanting to bring Crawford in now. If it wasn't for him, we would still be walking."

"Yep, that is true. We have to remember that Crawford is a wanted man and we've been selected as the folks to take him in. We can't stop now, Brady. The contract that the judge signed has been signed by us and we accepted the task," Riley pointed out as he looked over to Brady.

"I know, but things do change, Riley. I haven't got the same hate I had for him now that he helped us out. He could have easily left us there and could have likely put us both into the ground, but he didn't."

"True as that might be, we have a job to do."

"If it'll make you feel any better, Brady, I'll go with Riley," Tanner suggested.

"I don't know, Tanner. You only started walking today. Riley and I will finish up what we started. Might not be such a bad idea for you to tag along if you feel you can."

"Sure, I'd like to get back in the field. I wouldn't think twice about it."

"All right. The three of us will head out again in the morning. We'll leave a note here for Ed so that he can pass that information onto Travis and that Buck fellow."

Tanner nodded his agreement and, finishing his coffee, he stood up.

"I'll meet up with you two in the early morning then."

"Yeah, say 5:00 a.m. would give us a nice early start," Brady said as Tanner began to leave.

"5:00 a.m. it'll be. I'll see the both of you then," Tanner said as he left for his room above the office.

"Good to see he is back with the living. A wound like he took could have put a lesser man into the cold earth. He got lucky, I think," Riley said as he finished his coffee.

"I reckon so. The bullet punctured one of his lungs and came damn close to his heart. He seems to be in good spirits and has recovered well enough to want to join us."

"We might have a bit of an advantage now that there will be three of us. I hope Tanner can keep up the pace."

The Missing Years – Part II

"I wouldn't have asked him to tag along if I didn't think he could, Riley. He's a good bounty hunter. He'll keep up."

Brady was certain of that. After he and Riley drank another coffee together and conversed a while longer they flipped a coin to see who would get the backroom cot and who would sleep in one of the holding cells. Brady lost.

Tyrell and Buck had been watching the cabin now for a few hours and it was starting to grow dark.

"Not much longer and we'll be able to make our move," Tyrell said as he gazed up to the darkening sky. "How do you want to approach them, Buck?"

"With my pistol in my hand, of course," Buck chuckled. "The first thing I reckon is that we need to hide their horses so they ain't got a chance to mount up and take off or, for that matter, grab their rifles. Once that is out of the way, we'll have a couple of different options, I suppose."

"No matter how many options there might be, I reckon there will be lead flying no matter what. These are trained U.S. Rangers on the wrong side of the law don't forget and they ain't going to be so inclined to surrender without some kind of fight."

"Yeah, I know," Buck said solemnly as he looked down to the cabin. "What about burning them out, Travis? A cabin like that wouldn't take much to set on fire."

"The problem I see with that is it might light the damn mountain on fire dry as it has been. We might want to think on that a bit longer. One thing is for certain, they'd be disoriented and confused."

"If that is the advantage we want, maybe we can confuse them another way. Eventually they're going to need to sleep and there is only one bed in that cabin, so men are either going to have to sleep on the floor or outside. If we wait until then, we aren't going to be able to hide their horses because I'm sure they'd miss them, which doesn't work in our favour. But we could get in position closer to their horses and when they come out to gather their gear, we get the drop on them then. That'd be just as confusing to them, not expecting us to be there."

"There might be a hole in that plan too. What if they only send out one fellow to gather the bedrolls?" Tyrell pointed out.

"Good point. Well, I'm out of ideas. Your turn."

Buck looked again toward the cabin as he pondered and waited for Tyrell to respond.

"You've been in this business longer than I, Buck. What would you do under normal circumstances?" Tyrell questioned. He wasn't sure exactly how to proceed. They were up against professionally trained men, U.S. Rangers for God's sake.

"What does your gut instinct tell you, Travis?"

"It tells me that we should ditch their horses and storm the cabin with guns blazing if need be, although I know a dead man ain't worth a live one... that might be our only solution."

Buck was about to reply when they heard the cabin door open. Averting their eyes, they watched with intent as one of the men came out and walked behind the cabin.

"He must be needing to take a piss," Buck said beneath his breath.

"I reckon, keep your eye on him, Buck. I'm going to see if I can get the drop on him," Tyrell said as he signalled for Black Dog to follow.

Buck turned quickly to watch Tyrell slip into the undergrowth and then he turned back and kept his eye on the backside of the cabin. He could faintly see that

The Missing Years – Part II

the man was still standing there. A few moments later, he saw Tyrell. A bit of ruckus followed next and the man and Tyrell both faded into the shadows.

Tyrell had his arm around the man's neck as he pulled him back into the bush.

"Don't speak a word or that dog is going to make a snack out of your dangly parts," he warned as he threw the man onto the ground face down and rammed his knee into his back. The man tried desperately to get away until Tyrell pulled out his pistol and cocked it.

"You can stop with that fighting now or I'll put an ounce of lead into your skull."

It took a few minutes before the man finally relented. Tyrell rolled him over onto his back and stood up, his pistol pointing at him.

"If you want to live another day, stand up as quietly as possible. Don't speak a word and walk in that direction."

Tyrell gestured with his pistol.

The man slowly stood up, turned and began to walk in the direction he had been told with the barrel of Tyrell's .45 jabbed into his back. Making the distance back to Buck, Tyrell pushed the man forward.

"One down, Buck, three to go."

"Who the hell are you guys?" the man asked as he looked at both Buck and Tyrell.

"We'll get to that soon enough. Who are you is the question."

"You expect me to answer that?"

"Actually, I don't care either way. I have a fair idea on who you are. I know you aren't B. Atalmore. That means you are one of his men and that is all I need. I work for McCoy's Bounty Hunting Service and you are hereby apprehended. That is all that matters," Tyrell said as he tied the man's hands and pushed him to the ground.

Doing a thorough search of the man's pockets and removing his small calibre pistol that was in an underarm holster, Tyrell found a piece of identification and looked at it.

"Buck, I'd like to introduce you to Spence Hamilton. Spence, this here is Buck. He's a bounty hunter as well," Tyrell commented as he read the man's name.

"I guess that means we now know the name of two of the four, Travis. Spence, here and B. Atalmore. Can't wait to be introduced to the others," Buck chortled.

"I reckon it won't take long. Spence's friends are bound to miss him sooner or later."

"You guys go ahead and make all the jokes you want. Neither one of you know what you are getting yourselves into."

"No, probably not, but we do have a job to do and we intend on doing it," Tyrell said as a matter-of-fact. "You know, Spence, you don't have to say anything to us at all. In fact, I think it be best that you don't."

"Anything I say won't make a difference to how this is going to end," Spence retorted. "There are three men down in that cabin, two of which are discharged U.S. Rangers, and you think two aimless bounty hunters are going to take them down. You are fools to think that," he added.

"It is what we get paid for, Spence. To us, you folks are four wanted men, nothing less and nothing more. You were easy enough to take down and ain't you also an ex-U.S. Ranger?" Tyrell questioned with animosity.

Spence didn't say a word after that. He only glared at Tyrell and shook his head. It was true. He had been out-classed by a measly bounty hunter. Buck was tired of Spence's lip anyway and even though Spence clammed up after that, Buck still tied a kerchief over his mouth to keep him from speaking at all.

"That ought to keep him silent for now. What do you figure we do next, Travis? There are still three men down there."

Buck looked over the ridge down to the cabin.

"Soon it is going be too damn dark to see anything from up here. We're going to have to get closer."

"Yep. You got that right. It won't be long, I reckon, before someone goes looking for Spence."

Tyrell signalled to Black Dog to sit and guard the U.S. Ranger they had tied up.

"I'll tell you one time, Spence. Black Dog here won't play any games with you. If you so much as try to move, you won't like what happens next."

Tyrell knelt next to Black Dog and smiled at him.

"You watch this fellow. He moves, do whatever it takes to subdue him."

Standing now, he and Buck headed on foot down the ridge toward the cabin. They tried to be stealthy, but a few obstacles got in their way, and before they could even make the distance, all three men came outside to see what all the noise was about. Tyrell and Buck slid behind a couple of large boulders and waited to see what would happen next.

One of the men called out Spence's name and when there was no response they immediately drew their weapons and looked around suspiciously. The jig was up. Tyrell and Buck were now faced with the fact that the three remaining men were armed and alert.

"Where the hell do you think Spence got to?" Webber asked as he ducked behind the cabin alongside Colby and Atalmore.

"I ain't got a clue, but something ain't right. You see him anywhere, Colby?" Atalmore asked with concern.

"Nope. I don't see him anywhere. Hey, Spence, can you hear me? Where the hell are you?" Colby called out again as he peeked around the corner of the cabin.

"I don't like this one damn bit, Atalmore. Something has happened to him. You don't suppose Crawford took him out, do you?"

"I can't say for sure. I'd like to think that ain't the case."

"Hang on a second," Webber began. "I think I see someone up on that ridge and it ain't Spence."

Atalmore slid along the wall to where Webber was.

"What are you seeing there, Webber?"

Webber pointed to a big rock.

"I could have swore I saw someone up behind that rock. I'm going to try and get closer. Keep me covered."

Webber darted into the bush and circled around to get a better view, almost stumbling into Buck.

"Good evening," Buck said as he cocked his pistol and pointed it at Webber.

Webber wasn't about to give up that easily and he took a swing at Buck who ducked out of the way and, with pistol in hand, drove his fist into Webber's face knocking him out cold. Colby, seeing this from the corner of his eye, fired his pistol in Buck's direction missing him by only a few inches. Buck dove into the bush and fired back. By now, Tyrell was on the opposite side of the cabin his back up against the wall as he slowly made his way around to the other side where Colby and Atalmore were. They were obviously distracted by Buck and weren't paying much attention to what was behind them.

Tyrell knew he had only a few seconds to make his move. Hell, if he had a long stick he could have swatted both men in the back of the head, he was that close. Standing up, he stepped away from the wall. Both of his .45's were drawn and ready.

"I reckon that'd be enough," he said as he made himself visible. "Drop your weapons and step away from that wall. There are ten men surrounding this place. You folks ain't got a chance," Tyrell lied as he stepped forward.

"Who the hell are you?" Atalmore questioned as he pointed his little .38 pistol at Tyrell. Seeing both bores of the big .45's pointing at him, he knew he didn't stand a chance and so he tossed his pistol to the ground. Colby on the other hand hesitated, for a moment.

"Don't be stupid. Throw that pistol you have in your hand to the ground or reap what will follow," Tyrell said as he kept his eyes on the young man who seemed to have balls of steel.

"Do as he says, Colby," Atalmore spoke up. He knew Colby didn't stand any better chance than he did.

"You best listen to that friend of yours. You are one man against ten."

"I only want to shoot you and I bet I can do it," Colby replied with a crackle in his voice.

"I don't bet with dead men, so I'll ask you one more time. Toss down your weapon and step away from the wall," Tyrell demanded.

"Jesus Christ, Colby. Toss that damn pistol to the ground now. That is an order," Atalmore blurted.

A few minutes of dead silence followed and finally, Colby relented and tossed his pistol to the ground.

"That's better. Now get over there with that friend of yours," Tyrell gestured with his pistols.

Colby sauntered over to where Atalmore stood.

"All right, Buck, we got things under control. Come on out," Tyrell called as he gathered the two pistols that were lying on the ground and tucked them into his waistband.

"I'd like to help you out there, Travis, but I got my hands full with a big lug of a fellow over here who keeps waking up and wanting to fight. I got him unarmed now, but he's still being a bit of a brute."

"I'll leave you to it then. In the meantime, I'll get these two squared away," Tyrell responded nonchalantly, knowing full well that Buck had things under control with whomever it was he had pinned down.

Forcing the two men into the scantily lit cabin, he tied them up.

"There, I reckon that ought to keep you for a few minutes. I'll be back," Tyrell said as he exited and walked over in the direction where he knew Buck to be.

"What do we have here, Buck?"

"Some crazy son of a bitch that won't stay down," Buck responded as Webber once more came to and began swinging his arms. It didn't take long for Buck to knock him down again.

"See what I mean, Travis."

"I do, indeed. Ain't that something," Tyrell smiled.

"Don't just stand there. Give me a hand."

"Alright."

Tyrell moved closer and struggled along with Buck to get control of the man.

"There, you got him now, Buck?"

Buck's big burly arm was around Webber's neck and his other hand was holding onto Webber's right arm and pressed tightly against Webber's back.

The Missing Years – Part II

"I reckon I got control now," Buck replied as Webber continued to struggle.

"You go ahead and keep right on fighting. I ain't letting go and the more you struggle the harder I'm going to squeeze this neck of yours," Buck said as he squeezed the man's throat a bit harder. It took a few minutes of struggling, but finally they made it to the cabin. Tyrell opened the door and followed in behind Buck. Buck threw the man to the bed and stepped back expecting another go. Likely, that would have been the case if Tyrell wasn't standing there with his .45 pointing at the man's head.

"You seem a little winded, Buck. I got him covered."

Buck turned and stepped away from the bed.

"God damn. I ain't struggled like that before with one man," he inhaled deeply to catch his breath. "It didn't turn out so bad. We got all four."

"We did so, Buck."

Tyrell kept standing there his pistol still pointing at Webber's head.

"Got your wind back yet?"

"Give me a minute, Travis."

Buck leaned up against the cabin wall to regain his composure as he looked at the three men. He was glad things had turned out as they had, surprised at the fact how it all came together by accident. It was quite the thing.

"Time is ticking there, Buck. We need to get some rope and tie this fellow up."

"Yeah, yeah. I'm back with the living," Buck responded as he gathered up some rope and tied the man while Tyrell held his pistol on him.

"There we go, tied up like a steer in a rodeo," Buck commented as he stepped back.

"Good," Tyrell said as he slapped his pistol back into its holster.

He looked at the three men and smiled.

"Let me guess, you are B. Atalmore, a onetime U.S. Ranger dropped from the service because of bad behaviour. Mr. Atalmore, I work for McCoy's Bounty Hunting Service and you are hereby apprehended. The same goes for your man Spence Hamilton and these two as well."

He looked at Colby and shook his head.

"How did you ever get involved with this crew? You are too young to have ever been a Ranger."

"I ain't going to say two words about anything," Colby responded.

Tyrell shrugged his shoulders.

"You are in the same boat as your friends here, wanted for one thing or the other. The judge will sort it all out. Buck you want to go on up and bring us Spence."

"Hell no, I've had enough strenuous activity for a day. I'll stay here. You go get him."

Tyrell chuckled and shook his head.

"All right, I guess that is fair enough. I'll be back in a couple of minutes."

"Hold on a second," Atalmore began as he looked at his men and then back to Tyrell.

"There is only the two of you?"

"I'll tell you what, Mr. Atalmore. I'll give you that answer when I get back with your man Spence."

"Damn, there is only the two of them, Atalmore. I knew it. I knew there weren't ten men out there. We could've plugged them both," Colby interjected with exasperation. "I blame Spence for this. He should have been more aware of things, stupid son-of-a-bitch."

"There ain't no one to blame but ourselves, Colby. Leave it at that."

"Bullshit to that."

Colby looked away and shook his head.

"None of my men will be saying anything more until we get counsel."

"Thank you. I'm glad to hear that. I'd get tired, I'm sure, of listening to you," Tyrell said as he exited.

It took a couple of minutes to claw his way back up to where Spence and Black Dog were.

"Good boy, Black Dog."

Black Dog stood up and wagged his tail as Tyrell drew close.

"I hope Spence here didn't cause you any grief," Tyrell said as he pulled Spence to his feet.

"I'm here to invite you to a party, Spence. Your friends are waiting. Come on."

Tyrell gestured for him to take the lead and they carefully descended the slope and made their way back down to the cabin, Black Dog trailing close behind. With all four men now neatly apprehended and sitting on the bed, Buck and Tyrell sat down at the table, the four men in full view in front of them. On the table were four pieces of identification. Tyrell read the names out loud and after reading each name, he added, 'you are hereby apprehended'. With the legalities now out of the way, they had to plan how they would transport the four men back to the Fort which, from where they were now, seemed like a million miles away.

"We do have some clout, the backing of a federal judge. I'm wondering if we couldn't have the Mounted Police escort these fine gentlemen back to the Fort with one of their prison coaches."

"That would make our efforts a lot easier," Buck responded. "Only thing is, I know from experience there aren't any prison coaches nearby. The law transports their prisoners in these parts on horseback."

"It will take us near ten days to make it back to the Fort on horseback. There has to be an easier and more efficient way, Buck."

"Might find that with the backing from that judge you mentioned we could rent a stagecoach, put all four inside, cuffed and shackled, hire a driver and request a police escort. It won't make the trip any quicker, but it would be a lot more secure. That is my thought."

"It is a good one, too. I'll head into Vermillion in the morning. Maybe that fellow who works at the outpost can help with securing a stagecoach. There is that small Mounted Police station on the outskirts of town. I ain't sure there would be any extra constables that could tag along with us. We get a stagecoach and we could do the transporting ourselves. It would make things a lot simpler that is for sure. I think it might be quite the task to keep the four of them from trying to escape if we're on horses alone. With a coach we could keep them contained."

"There is no way a stagecoach could make it to this cabin. There ain't no damn trail."

"That is true, but we do have a wagon trail that'll get us into the Fort. We'd obviously have to march them to the trail on horseback, once we get them to the trail we could load them up, tie their horses to the back and off we go. As for a driver, you or I could do that, whilst the other does the scouting on horseback."

"We'll need a two or three horse coach to make the trip," Buck mentioned.

"Yeah, I know. Four would even be better. You know what, Buck? We already have four horses. I reckon Pony could pull an empty coach to a meeting place on the trail. Then, we use their four horses to pull it to the Fort."

The Missing Years – Part II

"Goddamn, that is a brilliant thought, Travis. I reckon that would work fine. All we need now is a damn coach."

"All we can do, Buck, is see if we can't get one from around here somewhere. We might get lucky. Maybe the outpost in Vermillion does have an old one out back or something. As long as it has wheels and yokes, we might do all right. I ain't caring much about seating, except for the driver's port. Inside will make no never mind. The four of them could sit on the damn floor for all I care."

"All right, I guess that is settled. We still have to get through the night and this cabin ain't very big. I care less about the four of them. They can sleep sitting up. I, on the other hand, need to stretch out. I say we take four hour shifts. You want to toss a coin to see who gets the first shift?"

"I'll take the first shift, Buck. You can find yourself a nice cosy place to stretch out on the floor or outside somewhere. I don't have a problem sitting up for a while. I might even make some coffee," Tyrell said as he walked over to the woodstove and looked it over. "I'd say this stove looks good enough to use."

"If you are going to make coffee, I'll sit up with you for a bit and have one with you."

"All right Let's get the stuff we need and get at her."

A few minutes later, a small fire glowed inside the woodstove and on top of it, a pot of slow brewing coffee began to perk. True to his word, not one of Atalmore's men spoke as Tyrell and Buck slurped coffee and conversed. Two hours later, Buck finally retreated outside and made up his bedding. He found a flat grassy area near the west side of the cabin and, within minutes, he was fast asleep.

Tyrell sat at the table inside the cabin, his feet stretched out to the seat on the other side. Every now and again he had to catch himself from dozing. His four hour shift turned into six and at 2:00 a.m. he ventured outside and kicked Buck awake.

"Time to wake up, Buck. Your turn to watch over our herd of sheep."

It took a few minutes for Buck to wake up and wipe the cobwebs from his head.

"All right, I'm awake," he said as he sat up, yawned and stretched.

"You got your bedding, Travis?"

"Yep. I ain't so sure I want to roll it out here, though. I think I'll lay my bedroll out near Pony. I like to be close to my horse."

He helped Buck stand and they went back to the cabin. Tyrell rolled out his bedding near Pony.

"Wake me up in four hours, Buck. I'll head into Vermillion then."

"You bet, Travis. I'll see you then," Buck replied as he went inside and sat at the table. Still groggy, he dozed off for a few minutes and then snapped out of it. He sat at the table his head in his hands and he reminisced, about days gone by. The four hours that he sat there went quick it seemed and at 5:30 a.m., he plugged some wood into the stove and perked coffee. By 6:00 a.m., he and Tyrell were both sitting together at the table having a morning coffee. It was Saturday, July 4th.

The Missing Years – Part II

"Chapter 22"

Tyrell made the distance to the Vermillion outpost by 8:00 a.m. and was talking with the man behind the counter.

"We do have an old stagecoach out back as a matter of fact. It is missing a wheel. I'm sure we can find one that might match. We have enough old ones kicking around."

"Can we go have a look?" Tyrell asked.

"Sure can, follow me."

The man led Tyrell out back to where a graveyard of old beat up and run down stagecoaches had found their final resting spot.

"This one here is the best out of the four or five we have. We use them mostly for parts and pieces. I'd sell this one to you. We only need to find a wheel."

The man looked around and walked over to a pile of old wagon wheels that had grass growing through the spokes. Tyrell helped him pick through the pile and after some time of digging through the pile, they finally found one that was best suited for the coach. It was only a smidge smaller, but it would work.

"This one here will do the job, I reckon."

"If you say it'll work, I can't argue with you."

Tyrell helped with rolling it over to the old coach and using a bit of muscle and leveraging, they managed to slip the wheel onto its axle.

"That don't look bad at all."

"Actually, fits better than I expected. I got some grease we could use for the axels."

The man traipsed away as Tyrell looked inside and out, making sure it was at least somewhat driveable. He was surprised to see that the seats inside remained intact and the driver seat and yokes were still in decent shape. It would do. By now, the man had made it back with a tub of grease and the two of them lathered up the wheels and axles. They even greased up the pins that went through the yokes and couplers. Anything that needed grease, got some.

"There, I'd say she's good to go. That big horse of yours won't have any trouble pulling this rig. You might as well get him and we'll hitch him up."

"What is this going to cost me?"

"The damn thing has been sitting here I imagine for a couple years. I'd sell her to you for two hundred dollars cash. You have that kind of change?"

"I do and I ain't got a problem paying that amount for it. One thing I would ask for, though, is a cash sale receipt."

"Of course I can do that for you. You also said you were transporting an army of four wanted men. It wouldn't take much to rig it up with some lag bolts that you could use to lock the door from the outside. Hell, it wouldn't take much to add a few cattle rings too. You could use those to tie the men to so that they don't cause you any grief. The Fort is a good distance away. Might be a good idea. I won't charge you any extra to do those few things. Could have her done in a couple of hours."

"I wouldn't turn that down. I'll give you hand in fact."

"Sure. Let's get that horse of yours hitched up and we can get the old coach into the shop."

"All right. I'll be back in a minute," Tyrell said as he walked around front and led Pony to the back.

It didn't take much to hitch him up and a few minutes later the old stagecoach creaked into the shop. The wheels were a bit stiff, but that was to be expected since the damn thing hadn't moved in a few years.

The Missing Years – Part II

"It'll take a bit for that grease to do its job, but I'd say within a few miles she won't creak no more," the man said as he went about gathering a few tools and bolts.

Tyrell helped as best as he could. When all the lag bolts and cattle rings were installed and it was finished, they cleaned it up a bit. The old stagecoach looked almost new.

"I may have undercharged you," the man joked. "She looks good, don't she?"

Tyrell nodded in agreement.

"Sure does, I'm quite pleased by how it all turned out, actually. There ain't no way anyone can escape her once they're locked up inside. Your idea about putting a few bars on the windows was good thinking."

"It's been a while since I've done any monkey wrenching. It felt good to do something for a change rather than handing out coffee and beans and selling tickets."

"I appreciate all your efforts and I thank you for all of it."

"No problem, I had fun doing it. I guess we best get the paperwork of the sale over with. I'll open the big front door so you and your horse can get on with your day."

The man walked to the front of the shop and pulled open the door. Tyrell climbed up onto the seat and snapped the reins to get Pony going. The old stagecoach creaked out of the shop. Reining Pony to halt just outside the door, Tyrell jumped down and entered the outpost. The man was already behind the counter writing out a sales slip. Tyrell reached into his money satchel and counted out two hundred dollars.

"We agreed on two hundred dollars, right?" Tyrell wanted to be clear.

"Yes sir, two hundred big ones. Who should I make this sales slip out to? You or a business name?"

"I'd like something to hold over my boss' head," Tyrell chuckled. "Make it out to Travis Sweet."

The man looked up with surprise, unsure he should ask what it was he wanted to ask, but he did anyway.

"Travis Sweet? Are you the Travis Sweet that took down Earl Brubaker?" the man asked with some uncertainty.

Tyrell shook his head.

"I might be; might not be too."

"That's okay. You don't need to answer. Hell, I'm sorry I even asked."

The man continued writing out the slip of paper.

"I was only curious. That fellow Brubaker is the man that shot and killed someone close to me a few years back. Anyway, it matters little. The bastard is dead. Here you go," he finished as he handed Tyrell the sales slip. Tyrell handed the man the money and waited for him to count it.

"Yep, two hundred dollars. Thank you, Travis."

"And thank you. I'm sorry, I didn't catch your name."

"Sorry about that. I'm Arch Masters."

"Alright. Thank you, Arch for helping me out with fixing up that old coach. As I said earlier, I appreciate all you have done."

Tyrell tilted his hat in respect, then turned and began to walk away.

Arch called after him as he was about to exit.

"You are him, aren't you? You're Travis Sweet, the man that took down Brubaker."

Tyrell simply looked back, smiled, and stepped outside. Climbing onto the coach, he snapped the reins and left behind the town of Vermillion and a new friend

The Missing Years – Part II

named Arch Masters. Five miles later, he pulled Pony to a halt, unhitched him, saddled him up, then cut back through the bush toward the cabin. He had been gone for nearly half the day and although he knew Buck could easily take care of himself, he didn't like the fact that he had been gone as long as he had. He honestly didn't expect to find a coach as quickly as he had, and although it needed work, the work was done and it was ready to transport Atalmore and his men. Finally, the cabin came into view and with a quick turn-around, they'd be heading back to the coach in only few minutes.

Tyrell dismounted and entered the cabin.

"All ready to go. Got a coach," he said as he entered.

"Good, glad to hear that. Where the hell did you have to go to get it? Vermillion is less than an hour ride. You've been gone a lot longer than that."

"Picked it up in Vermillion and with Arch's help we fixed her up. Got bars on the windows and everything," Tyrell smiled. "It is quite the rig, Buck. I think you'll like it."

"We'll see. Now let's get these men out of here and tied to their horses so we can get moving. They're starting to stink," Buck said as he and Tyrell jostled with the four men and secured them to their horses.

Satisfied, they saddled up themselves and with Tyrell in the lead and Buck trailing behind, they traversed their way to the trail and the awaiting coach. By the time they got the men contained and their horses hitched up, it was late afternoon.

"I'd say we're all set to get. You want to drive the horse team or be the outrider?" Buck asked.

"I already drove it once. You go ahead. I'll outride today. Might even join you at the helm later."

Buck tied his horse to the back of the coach and then climbed onboard.

"You sure do get a nice view up here," he looked down to Tyrell. "I'm ready if you're ready."

"Let's get," Tyrell said as he turned Pony in the direction of the Fort and taking the lead again, they headed for home. A few miles later as the grease finally fed the axels, the annoying creaking from the dry and rusted wheels dissipated. The sound of six horses and their clip-clopping hooves were louder now than the coach itself.

"How you doing up there, Buck?" Tyrell asked as the coach drew close and he waited.

"I ain't sure how far along we are, but I ain't got one complaint about sitting up here driving this team. It ain't nothing like a wagon, I can tell you that."

"That it ain't. Sounds like the grease is finally working. The horses are making more noise now, it seems."

"Yeah. That would have been my only complaint, the damn squealing and creaking of the wheels. Good thing she's greased up and glad it finally stopped. How about yourself? How you doing? You've been running ahead quite a bit."

"Making sure the trail is still good and such. I've been thinking, Buck. We should head into Fairmount and check to see if Ed or someone has sent us any telegrams. Plus, I reckon I need to send them an update as well."

"We won't make the distance today, I don't think."

"I don't know, Buck. We carry straight on through, we could be close by late evening."

"Nope, best not do it that way, Travis. We're better off travelling until dusk and then let each of our prisoners out one at a time, to stretch, piss, whatever it is they'll need to do. We have to also feed them, and make sure they are comfortable for the night. We are transporting prisoners and we are allotted by law four-hour intervals between piss breaks and such. And as our good book says, we have to transport prisoners with humanity and dignity."

"Good point, Buck. You're right. It is a bit different when we're transporting outlaws, ain't it?"

"It has to be that way. They got rights too, and you know how I feel about that."

"I know. We'll go by the book," Tyrell agreed as they continued onward.

He did understand Buck's reasoning. After what he had been through in both Willow Gate and Candora, it was understandable on why he wanted to go by the book. As far as Tyrell was concerned, that was the best policy.

It was 6:00 p.m. when they stopped for the night. They had travelled nearly twenty miles with thirty left to go before they'd make the distance to Fairmount. They let each of Atalmore's men out, one at a time, for a fifteen minute stretch and anything else a man could do in that amount of time. While Tyrell took care of that, Buck threw together some food. It wasn't much, but it would feed all six of them and that was all that mattered. It was up to the men if they wanted to eat it or not. They were short a couple plates and bowls, so he and Tyrell ate out of the empty cans. With everyone fed and somewhat comfortable, Buck brewed some coffee and rinsed the cans out. If their prisoners wanted coffee or water, they could drink out of those.

All in all, the trip and apprehension of Atalmore and his men had not seen any setbacks whatsoever. It was quite daunting for Atalmore and he never spoke much about anything. His men, too, were tight-lipped. This didn't bother either Buck or Tyrell. In fact, they both appreciated this code of silence.

"I'll tell you, Travis; that coach sure makes transporting that many men a lot less dangerous. I couldn't imagine the fiasco if we had to do this by horse alone."

"I reckon it is the only way to do it when transporting more than one man. It ain't too difficult to keep one man contained on a horse. Four, however, yeah, forget about it. It would be quite the task trying to keep all four under control. This way, they're all contained with no hope for a silent escape."

"My thought exactly."

Buck poured himself another coffee and offered their prisoners a second if they wanted, but none did.

"What about you, Travis? You want another?"

"Yep, I'm getting used to this damn tar-like substance you keep making."

Tyrell chuckled as he held his cup out for Buck to fill.

"It kind of grows on you, don't it?"

"I ain't sure it could grow on anything, but one does get used to it."

Tyrell brought the cup to his lips and blew on it. Taking a swallow, he inhaled deeply as he looked around. It wasn't quite dark yet and the evening was warm. The trail they were on hadn't seen any traffic in a few weeks. The old wagon ruts he remembered were like canyons in the ground that had been baked by the sun. Nor were there any recently fresh horse tracks. It was as though the wagon trail they were on existed only for them. It made sense with Vermillion being the only gathering spot between Fairmount and Hazelton. Since the fire wiped it out, there really was no need for any passerby to use the trail. There were other routes to Hazelton and Fairmount. A road less traveled, like the one they were on, wasn't always a safe place to be. Each

The Missing Years – Part II

of them would keep that in mind as they took their turn on guard duty that night.

By mid-afternoon the following day, they had reached Fairmount and had retrieved the two telegrams that awaited them. Not much had changed in the plan of attack from Ed's side of the equation. The only thing different was that Tanner was up and walking and, in fact, headed out with Brady and Riley on one final attempt to track down Crawford. Tyrell sent a reply back stating he had received the telegrams and was on his way back with Atalmore and his three men.

It was late Tuesday, July 7 when they finally returned to the Fort with their prisoners. With all four now locked up in holding cells, Buck and Tyrell sat in the staff room talking with Ed.

"Do you want to work for McCoy's, Buck?" Ed asked as he slurped from his cup.

"I ain't sure if you are aware, but the Willow Gate law took my credentials."

"I'm aware of that. It is nothing for us to get it reinstated."

"I'll need to think on it a bit. I do have plans to stick around long enough to talk with Tanner. Then I was thinking I'd head up to the Yukon, look in on what is left of my family. I ain't been there in a while."

"Come on, Buck, we could use you around here. Hell, we have Tanner and Riley Scott. We add you to the list, I'd say there ain't no one McCoy's couldn't track," Tyrell mentioned as he poured another coffee.

"I appreciate your confidence, Travis, but I ain't sure this is where I want to be."

"I understand, Buck, I truly do, and I'll be okay with whatever you decide. You were a great help in bringing in Atalmore and his men and I reckon you have some pay coming to you for that. Which reminds me, Ed, what is going to happen with the four of them?"

"They'll face a judge for impersonating U.S. Marshals. Probably face a few months in prison and then sent on their way to face what the U.S. has in store for them."

"The four of them ain't spoke but a couple of times. Atalmore did request counsel, so I guess we have to find a defense lawyer for them, no?"

"I'll let the judge decide on that, but in most circumstances they'll be given counsel. I ain't sure how the U.S. law handles such a thing. I know we apprehended them and their bounty is rightfully ours, but because they are U.S. citizens, I don't reckon it'll be as quick. As for Buck's share of the bounty, if he decides he doesn't want to stick around, I'm sure we can afford to pay him out of company funds. The bounty we'll receive in time will replace any amount we pay him."

"To be honest, Ed, I care little about being paid. I'm just glad to know I was able to help and that my old running partner Tanner is alive."

"In spite of that, it is our policy that we pay you something for your time and effort. What would you say is fair, in that case?"

"I'd be happy with five hundred dollars, if you insists on paying me something. Five hundred will see me through to the Yukon."

Ed stood up and walked into his office. Returning with a banker's check, he scribbled out a payment twice of which Buck agreed to be fair.

"Here you go, Buck. You can cash this anytime. I've made it out for a thousand dollars."

Buck reached over and took the bank note.

"Thank you, Ed. I'll accept it."

"Good. I'm glad that you would. It is late now, so I'm going to head off home. We'll get Atalmore and his men arraigned tomorrow morning. What comes of that we'll have to wait and see."

The Missing Years – Part II

Ed dumped out the last of his coffee.

"By the way, Travis, you and Buck did a good job in bringing Atalmore in alive. Let's hope Brady and his crew can do the same with Crawford."

"I'm sure things will turn out that way. From what we've discussed here tonight, it sounds like Crawford ain't such a bad apple after all, once one knows why he's been running."

"Yeah, that is quite the reason ain't it. And to think he was kind enough to look out for Brady and Riley by giving them Ranthorp's horse."

"That is what I mean. I can't see a cold blooded killer being so cordial. Are we sure we know everything about him?" Tyrell questioned.

"We know all we need to know to bring him in. Everything else has to be up to the law to decide. The judge will be informed of his good deeds, including the fact that he saved a lot of folks up in Vermillion as you mentioned. He may get lucky and simply be sent back to the U.S. with no charges laid here in Canada. Depends, I guess, on the judge's mood."

"I hope the judge does take that into consideration," Travis said as he took a drink from his coffee.

"Wasn't he supposed to have killed a few folks around here?" Buck wanted to know.

"Some say he has, but the more I think about it, I think it is all hearsay. We aren't even completely sure that he took out Talbot, but when you add it all up, it does add up that he did. Even though he obviously had his reasons and men like Talbot are never missed, it is still murder."

Ed shrugged his shoulders.

"Again, it is going to be up to the law courts to decide."

"I guess we leave it at that."

"That is all we can do, Travis."

Ed turned and bid them good night then headed for home.

"It is getting late, Buck. You are welcome to lay out your bedroll upstairs in my room. Come on," Tyrell said as he checked on Atalmore and his men before heading upstairs, Buck trailing behind. It was 11:00 p.m. when the two men finally closed their eyes and were swept away by sleep.

"Chapter 23"

By Wednesday July 8, 1891, having been on the trail for three days, Tanner McBride was feeling the effect it was having on his healing process. They were getting close to where Brady and Riley had last seen Matt Crawford, so Tanner didn't complain just yet. He could live with the pain for a while longer.

"We're getting close now, Brady. Was just up yonder I think where we tossed together that skid to haul back Ranthorp's limp carcass," Riley stated as he slowed his horse down.

The smell of decay from their two horses which Miles Ranthorp had killed days earlier became more noticeable when they finally found the spot they were looking for.

"Whoa," Brady said as he pulled his horse to a halt. "Here it is, fellows. It was right here that we built that skid."

Brady swung off his horse as Tanner and Riley came close.

"Yep, this is it. I knew we were close once we started smelling the rot from our horses."

Riley pulled his horse up next to Brady's and he dismounted while Tanner remained saddled.

"It was right here where he got the drop on us. Came from that way, so let's go have a look to see if we can't come across his trail. It's going to be tough trying to find in all this bramble. You coming, Tanner?" Riley asked.

"To be honest, Riley, I think I'll stay saddled for now. I ain't feeling so good. I'll keep the horses in check."

"What do you mean Tanner? You all right?" Brady asked as he turned and looked at him.

"Up until about an hour ago I was fine. Starting to feel some pain in my lungs. Could be from that damn horse rot smell. I don't know. It ain't going to kill me, Brady, so you two go ahead and see if we can't pick up Crawford's trail."

"You sure you are going to be okay?"

"Hell, yeah. No worries."

"All right. We won't be but a couple of minutes anyway," Brady said as he followed Riley into the undergrowth.

The two of them walked a few paces into the dark forest, keeping their eyes on the ground hoping to see a horse track or two that would give them a fighting chance to find a couple more and so on. The forest floor was so deep with pine needles and shrub bushes that it was near impossible to find any sign of a track, wild or tamed. Not even their footprints left much to see on the forest floor.

"You'd think a damn horse would leave a track or two. I ain't seeing any. What about you, Riley?"

Riley shook his head.

"Nope, but I can see up ahead a few broken branches."

Walking the distance he looked around and saw a few more.

"Got a few more broken branches over here, Brady. I'd say Crawford headed easterly, I ain't found any tracks, but an educated guess tells me he headed east. The branches are broke leastwise in that direction."

"No tracks, eh?" Brady responded.

"None that I can see."

It was then he noticed what looked like an old track. He walked the short distance and squatted.

"Correction. We do have tracks, horse tracks too. I'd say they are Crawford's and he is indeed heading east."

The Missing Years – Part II

"What do you think he is planning, to head right over the Rockies?" Riley responded as he met up with Brady.

"There are a few wagon trails in that direction. Damn, he could be anywhere, even back in the U.S. by now. We'll have to get the horses and see how far we can follow the trail. Hopefully, we'll be able to decipher which way he finally headed once we get into the thinner bush. This here stuff is damn thick."

"We best wait for full daylight. We'll rest a couple hours. I think your friend Tanner needs it."

"Yeah, you're probably right. He wasn't looking so good, was he?"

"We've been riding hard these past couple of days and especially hard since early morn because we knew we were close. A rest is well-deserved. We have a place to start now," Riley said as he and Brady walked out of the bush and made their way to Tanner and the horses. Tanner was sitting on a log waiting.

"I heard you holler a few times. You found some tracks, did you?" Tanner asked as he squinted.

"Yep, he's heading east. We're going to rest up here for a bit and wait for the sun to come out full."

"Don't let me be the reason for that," Tanner said as he was about to stand up and instead fell over unconscious.

"He's burning up, Brady," Riley said as he helped Tanner up. "Hand me that canteen. He needs some water."

Brady handed the canteen over.

"What do you think is wrong, Riley?" he asked with concern.

"I don't reckon he was quite yet ready to travel, let alone track anybody. Damn, his fever is high. Give me a hand, Brady and we'll get him situated under that shade tree," Riley pointed.

The Missing Years – Part II

A few minutes later Tanner was propped up against the tree trunk.

"There, we'll let him rest for a bit. He'll come around soon. He ain't going to be much use to us, Brady. He needs rest and a lot of it. We ran him a bit too hard I think."

"What are we going to do? This Crawford thing has been cursed from the get go," Brady said with sincerity.

"It sure seems that way, doesn't it? The only thing I can come up with, Brady, is that we wait and see how Tanner feels in a couple of hours. If things ain't good, one of us is going to have to head back with him."

Brady nodded in agreement.

"Yeah, I reckon that'll be our only recourse. In the meantime it might be an idea to throw some food on a fire. Maybe that'll give him back some strength. We should have ate some biscuits or something this morning before we saddled up. We never had a thing to eat."

"It might have helped, I suppose. You going to make coffee, too?"

"I will if you want some."

Brady made his way over to his horse and fumbled through his gear, looking for the utensils and whatnot he'd need.

"Well, we had none this morning. We got too damn excited about getting close. You might as well perk some. We're going to here for a couple more hours."

"It turns out one of us needs to take Tanner back to the Fort, which one of us is it going to be?" Brady questioned as he got a small fire going and began making food and coffee.

"We could flip a coin, but to be honest I think it would be you that takes him back."

"Why me, Riley?"

"Simplest explanation is he's your friend. Plus he works for you."

"True enough."

Brady didn't mind, actually. He was, in a sense, kind of tired from their two previous attempts to find Crawford.

"You know what, Riley? If it wasn't for that contract, I'd call this off. We've seen a lot of death over this past while, from horses, to men."

Riley knelt there nodding his head.

"True as that might be it is the nature of this business, Brady, you know that."

"Even so, I ain't so humble to say it ain't affected me. I feel drained."

"That will pass Brady. Things are already looking up, we have an idea in what direction Crawford has headed. Tanner is alive and Ed, well, he's already back to his old self practically."

"I guess you're right. I shouldn't mourn the death of a bunch of bad guys. Especially since it is because of them, that Tanner and the old man were knocked down for a bit," Brady said as Tanner came back to the living.

"Still feeling a little weak, Tanner?" Brady asked.

"I ain't sure I feel weak, but I certainly feel pain in my lungs with each breath I take."

"It won't be much longer and the salt pork and biscuits will be ready. You want a coffee, Tanner?"

"I guess, it couldn't hurt. I suppose."

Brady poured him a cup and handed it to him.

Tanner took the coffee and had a swallow.

"Damn, even hurts to swallow. I'm sorry about this fellows. I thought for sure I could keep up, but I ain't so sure anymore."

"Brady and I talked about this while you were passed out. He'll ride back to the Fort with you."

"I don't think I'll need an escort, Riley. I can find my way back."

"It ain't going to happen like that, Tanner. It is my responsibility to see to it that you make it back safely," Brady made clear. "We'll eat some salt pork and a couple of biscuits and then you and I are heading back to the Fort."

"You figure an old timer like Riley there can handle Crawford on his own?" Tanner said with humour.

Riley shook his head and smiled. Finishing up their late breakfast and cleaning up their gear, Riley headed east, while Brady and Tanner headed south back to the Fort.

"I have to tell you, Brady, I feel damn bad about messing up this expedition."

"No need to feel bad, Tanner. You did well. You rode alongside of us for three days of hard riding. It ain't your fault that you're having a relapse. You took a bullet to your lungs not long ago and haven't healed up yet. It is no big deal. To be honest, I'm kind of glad to be heading back. We've had a few attempts in trying to track Crawford. All have failed up to this point. Maybe Riley will have better luck on his own."

"He might end up dead too, Brady. You do realise that?"

"I do, but Riley knows what he is doing and I have faith in that."

"Yeah, I suppose you are right. If he wasn't good at what he does, he'd have been dead by now."

"Yep," Brady responded as the two men continued on their way.

At 10:00 a.m. on that day, Atalmore and his men stood in front of circuit Judge Henry Theodore who

The Missing Years – Part II

arraigned them on charges of impersonating officers of the law and remanded them into the custody of the Mounted Police until August 27, 1891, giving them enough time to seek counsel. The prosecution would rest until that date, but were going to push for a maximum sentence for all four men. It would be at most a simple six month sentence in Canada, and would likely be less. The charges they had coming to them in the U.S. would have to wait until their charges in Canada were dealt with, although minor as they were for now. The prosecution, of course, would be looking into more viable charges to present the judge on that date. The four men were whisked away under guard of the Mounted Police and McCoy's Bounty Hunting Service was relieved of any further responsibility for Atalmore and his men.

"That didn't turn out too bad," Ed said as he, Tyrell and Buck sat down in the staff room of McCoy's.

"I can't believe they were arraigned on simple impersonation of law officers," Buck said as he tried to wrap his head around the minor charge.

"That isn't all they'll be charged with, Buck. The prosecution and Mounted Police will be looking into other charges as well. Judge Theo only arraigned them with that for now. He needed to charge them with something to keep them here in Canada," Ed added. "Either way, I'm just glad you fellows were able to bring them in. The U.S. now owes us a tidy bounty on them, which we will collect eventually. What is even better is that they are not our responsibility anymore. Our job is done with that lot. Now, all we need is Crawford. Then we can finally get back to the regular rat race of this job."

"I will admit, Ed, these past weeks have certainly been busy," Tyrell said as looked into his empty coffee cup. "I'm going pour another coffee. Any takers?"

The Missing Years – Part II

"Yeah, sure. Pour us all another round, Travis," Ed said as he handed his cup over and Buck followed suit. "Regarding Matt Crawford, we've had a couple of chances to get him, but he somehow always seems to slip from our fingers. You'd think the four men you two brought in would have been a lot harder to apprehend than one man alone."

"We had them surrounded with ten men," Buck chuckled. "Or at least that is what convinced them to throw down their guns. It could have turned out a lot different if Travis wasn't quick on his feet in convincing them of that lie."

"True as that might be, they still managed to fire a few shots at us. We certainly had luck on our side. Got lucky coming back this way too. The good luck outweighed the bad in that case. Hope the others have the same luck. I'd have to say one man is certainly a lot harder to track than four; we had a few pluses on our side when we came across Atalmore and his men. They weren't prepared to see us. If they had been, I'm certain, like Buck says, things would have turned out different."

Tyrell poured coffee into each of their cups and handed them off as he sat back down.

"With Atalmore now out of the big picture and resting comfortably in a cell along with his men, what else does McCoy's have on the table?"

"No much at the moment. The other day we got that wanted poster for that fellow Tyrell that popped Heath Roy back in Willow Gate last year. There isn't much we can do with that bounty since we haven't even got his last name or a half decent mug shot photo, just some drawing. To be honest, I'm not sure McCoy's would even look for him. After all, he did everyone a favour. Also got another thing from Heath's old man, Gabe Roy, requesting private protection, which, even if we were in that business I wouldn't send any of my men to do. I have had a dislike for Gabe Roy for a long time. He isn't one of my favorite folks."

Ed took a sip from his coffee.

"Yeah, I once did some work for him, Tanner and I both, actually. He hired us to look for Travis last fall. Figured he could hire him to help locate Heath's killer. When we made our way back and told him Travis had no interest, everything went sideways for me. The son of a bitch Gabe and a couple of his henchmen, along with the corrupt law of Willow Gate, figured it would be worth their effort to have a go at me. It didn't help their cause any. That is when the law revoked my credentials. I think Riley had a run in with him as well. From what I heard, he also told Gabe to take a hike. Anyway, he ain't one of my favorite people either."

"I have nothing to add to that. I never met the man or knew his son, Heath," Tyrell lied. "When Buck here and Tanner located me and ran past me what Gabe wanted, I knew then that I didn't want anything to do with him. I've heard other stuff about Gabe since and I have to say, he ain't on my list of the good and righteous either. He sounds to me like a man with a lot of money who thinks he can buy anything he wants. Men like that are nothing more than brutes."

Days came and days went. Brady and Tanner returned to the Fort and Tanner finally recuperated after a few more days of rest. Riley Scott also returned some days later without Matt Crawford, who it seemed had vanished off the face of the earth. Their search for him, though, wouldn't end. Once Riley was introduced to Tyrell, he knew exactly who he was, but said nothing. As far as he was concerned, Tyrell Sloan would always be known to him as Travis Sweet, bounty hunter.

Buck headed to the Yukon after Tanner recuperated and as he made his way there, he stopped off in Fairmount and swooned JoBeth. Together they made their way North into the Yukon where they married and settled down.

McCoy's Bounty Hunting Service continued to operate on a day-to-day basis and retained Travis, Riley and Tanner as their top three bounty hunters. Brady took over the daily grind of working in the office alongside his old man and McCoy's Bounty Hunting Service began a new chapter in their everlasting desire to make the west a safer place for all.

Forthcoming: The Missing Years- Part III

"The hunt for Matt Crawford"

Author: Brian T. Seifrit
Fan Email: tbseifrit@gmail.com
Website: www.booksbybriant.com

Other Books by Brian T. Seifrit

A Bloodstained Hammer (with Alison Townsend MacNicol)
The Coalition of Purgatory
Voracity
Red Rock Canyon
Return to Red Rock
The Missing Years Part I

The Missing Years – Part II

A Biography of Brian T. Seifrit

Brian is a seven-time published author. In September 1988-December-1989, he attended Columbia Academy of Radio, Television & Recording Arts, in Calgary, AB, where he majored in Broadcast Journalism. Following that, and ten years later, he attended Selkirk College in Castlegar BC, from September 1999-April 2001 where he was Enrolled in UT Courses – English History, Philosophy, Creative Writing, and Canadian Literature and majored in Print Journalism.

He has been happily married for 27 years and counting. He has four children, two from previous relationships, and two with his current wife. He grew up on a small hobby farm outside of Fruitvale BC.

In 2000, he wrote for the Source a community newspaper in Fruitvale BC, and since then has done freelance writing of human interest for the Trail Daily Times.

When he writes for himself, he tries not to stay in only one genre, He finds that one genre gets stale after a while. Instead he chooses to write in as many genres as he can. Imagination and creativity are wonderful tools, and he uses them both. From the list of the titles and brief descriptions above, you will undoubtedly agree that Brian is a multi-faceted writer with a vivid imagination.

Brian lives in the Kootenays in the British Columbia interior in a wild part of Canada.

Any communications with Brian can be emailed to:

tbseifrit@gmail.com

William Jenkins, Publisher

This publishing activity was established in 2014 for the purpose of self-publishing stories that he had written. These stories are supplementary reading for elementary school students (about Grade 5). They are mystery-adventure stories with intriguing titles as follows:
- The Case of the Ancient American
- The Case of the Brainy Birds
- The Case of the Cannabis Cat
- The Case of the Diligent Detectives
- The Case of the Electrified Envoy
- The Case of the Forgotten Fort
- The Case of the Greedy Goat
- The Case of the Hidden Hound

He also edits and publishes stories submitted to him for free. See http://williamjenkins.ca for details.

Mr. Jenkins can be contacted at:

williamhenryjenkins@gmail.com

Previously, Mr. Jenkins published under the corporation Your ESL Story Publishers Ltd. That corporation was dissolved on December 31, 2014.

For more information, see williamjenkins.ca.

The Missing Years – Part II

Made in the USA
Charleston, SC
07 February 2016